ALSO BY ALAN RUSSELL

Multiple Wounds

No Sign of Murder

The Forest Prime Evil

The Hotel Detective

The Fat Innkeeper

SHAME

A NOVEL

ALAN RUSSELL

SIMON & SCHUSTER

SIMON & SCHUSTER
Rockefeller Center
1230 Avenue of the Americas
New York, NY 10020

This book is a work of fiction. Names, characters, places, and incidents either are products of the author's imagination or are used fictitiously. Any resemblance to actual events or locales or persons, living or dead, is entirely coincidental.

Designed by Ruth Lee

Manufactured in the United States of America

10 9 8 7 6 5 4 3 2 1

Library of Congress Cataloging-in-Publication Data

Russell, Alan, date.
Shame : a novel / Alan Russell.
I. Title.
PS3568.U7654S48 1998
813'.54—dc21 97-50508
CIP

ISBN 0-684-81527-3
0-684-85189-X (signed edition)

ACKNOWLEDGMENTS

I am grateful that there were so many individuals willing to assist in the writing of this novel. My heartfelt thanks go out to Norman R. Brown, Don "Cookie" DeWolf, Erica, Sherry Gerrish, Lori Gore, Master Chief Doug Gorham, Eric Hart, Lieutenant Gerry Lipscomb of the San Diego Sheriff's Department, Eugene Morris of the Florida Department of Corrections, Chip Owen, Abigail Padgett, Mary Jane Tatum, and Kathy Wilson.

Any mistakes made in the research of this book are mine and shouldn't reflect on any of those acknowledged.

To good friends:
Penny Travis,
whose big heart and good soul
have always been there for me;

Terry and Norman Glenn,
with whom I have had the pleasure of
sharing wonderful food
and even more wonderful food for thought; and

Wadestein,
who on a weekly basis lectures me on
his theories of plausible deniability.

Love takes off masks that we fear we cannot live without, and know we cannot live within.

—JAMES BALDWIN,
THE FIRE NEXT TIME

INTRODUCTION

November 3, 1970

To the casual observer, the 225 square miles of New Mexico's White Sands National Monument are a wasteland. Few places on earth are as dry as the Tularosa Basin. It is that very dryness that allows the gypsum to dominate the landscape. In a wetter climate the gypsum would dissolve, but in the Tularosa Basin the crystal granules come together to form nature's ever changing monuments.

From a moving car, White Sands appears to be almost devoid of life. Trees are small and infrequent, mostly Rio Grande cottonwoods, and plants have a difficult time scrabbling out a foothold amid the shifting dunes. And those few plants that do raise their heads in the sheltered low areas between the dunes are often buried as the ephemeral dunes give way.

The dunes have swallowed more than plants. Hernando de Luna was a follower of Francisco Coronado, engaged in his expedition to find the Seven Cities of Cíbola and Gran Quivira. Struck down by the Apaches in 1540, de Luna fell among the shifting white sands.

Manuela de Luna was a newlywed in the first blush of love who could not accept the news of her husband's death. The lovely bride left her home in Mexico City in search of her beloved conquistador. It is said she was also lost among the white sands, and over the centuries many have claimed to have seen a beautiful Spanish woman walking among the dunes, the long train of her white wedding dress trailing behind her. The native people all know the Legend of Pavla Blanca and believe she looks for her husband still. Manuela appears, they say, just after sunset, gliding along the whipping eddies of sands.

Almost as ghostlike as Manuela are the predators that stalk among the White Sands, their passage usually detected only in the powdery gypsum; the serpentine markings of the three species of rattlesnake; the footpads of fox and coyote. These ghosts also leave behind remains of the vanquished, cast-off fur and bones and scat easily seen atop the spectral white dunes.

Park Ranger Nolan Campbell spotted the body of Alicia Gleason while driving on rounds. At first he doubted what he saw.

"Sometimes you see things out here," Campbell said, "and you rub your eyes, and they usually disappear, but she didn't. She wasn't Pavla Blanca, or any mirage."

Alicia hadn't just been dropped in the desert, but had been put on display. Two miles from the entrance to the park her naked body had been propped at the base of a fifty-foot sand dune. She was naked, her legs spread, a message written on her flesh. Everyone wondered at the word: *SHAME*. The just concluded decade of the sixties was supposed to be a time for people to lose their shame. There wasn't a place for shame in the Age of Aquarius. That was an emotion that belonged to the Puritans, and Cotton Mather.

But everyone who saw Alicia's naked and dead body felt shame. They also felt fear. A terrible predator, hitherto unknown, had announced his presence.

When Alicia was discovered in the morning, the gypsum hadn't settled on her, but around her. After her body was removed, a picture was taken of the outline it had left. Nature had silhouetted her body better than any coroner's chalk. One detective was moved to tears, saying it looked as if a snow angel had been left behind.

—Excerpt from the book *Shame*
by Maryelizabeth Line

1

May 4, 1998

The front door was slightly ajar, opened just a little more than a crack. Caleb Parker raised his finger to the doorbell yet another time. He had already walked around the manicured pathway to the back, had checked for Mrs. Sanders at the swimming pool, the tennis courts, the gardens, and the stables. Out in the corral he had found three horses, the same three he remembered from his visit two months earlier. It didn't look as if Mrs. Sanders was out riding.

If it hadn't been for the open front door, he would have been sure she wasn't home.

The Sanderses had a beautiful house, even by Rancho Santa Fe standards. There was no moat protecting the palatial estate, but there were signs all around the property warning of alarm systems and armed response. A rose showing its thorns, Caleb thought. A fortune had been spent on security.

Which again made him wonder why the front door wasn't shut tight.

Earlier that morning Caleb had talked with Mr. Sanders on the phone. Sanders had persuaded him to make the time to come right over to cut down an acacia tree. It was playing havoc with his wife's allergies, Sanders had told him. "My wife will be waiting for you with bated—if not wheezing—breath," Sanders had promised.

Caleb pushed the doorbell again. He could hear the chimes sounding throughout the house. A minute passed but still there was no sound of footsteps, nothing to indicate that anyone was home.

Except for the opened front door.

Caleb reached out with his right hand, rapped with his knuckles. As expected, the knocking caused the door to open several inches, enough for Caleb to get a look inside.

"Hello," he called. "Anyone home?"

Caleb wondered if he might have set off one of those silent alarms, wondered if at that very moment guards were being dispatched to the house. But he wasn't afraid of burglar alarms so much as the alarms going off in his mind. Caleb sensed that something was very wrong. He could feel it. Standing at the threshold, he was afraid to go forward, and afraid to retreat. Scents from inside reached out to him, the beguiling aroma of freshly cut flowers and potpourri, but he still didn't feel reassured.

"Hello," he shouted again, willing his voice to be loud and strong.

Again, nothing.

Caleb couldn't bring himself to just push open the door; that wouldn't be quite right. Once again he knocked on it to achieve that same purpose. The front door was oversized, and made of heavy wood, but it was well balanced. The door swung completely open, allowing him to see in. Windows and skylights made the interior light and cheery. He contemplated the tiled hallway. It led forward, first to the living room, and beyond that to the stairwell.

"Anybody here?"

Even to Caleb's ears, his voice sounded strained. Almost desperate. Turn around, he tried to tell himself, and walk away. But he couldn't. Caleb took a deep breath. No one would be able to fault him for going a little ways forward, maybe as far as the stairwell, where he could shout upstairs. The circumstances all but dictated that. It was possible Mrs. Sanders had succumbed to her allergies. But he still found himself balking at the doorway, his foot hovering over the entryway as if he were girding himself to jump into cold water.

The foot dropped. He was inside. He took a second step forward, then a third. Caleb saw that the Sanderses had white, plush carpeting in their living room, a color that bespoke no children, or the ability to afford very frequent carpet cleaning, or both.

Then he saw the bare leg.

"Hello," Caleb said, the word coming out as not much more than a whisper.

The leg didn't move.

Caleb stepped into the living room and found Mrs. Sanders. She was naked, her back propped up against a love seat. Her legs were spread apart. On the inside of her upper right thigh the red letters *S* and *H* had been written. An arch wound its way along the outskirts of her golden pubic patch, with a letter barely visible through the hair. An *A*. The *M* and the *E* were scripted on the inside of her left thigh.

SHAME.

Caleb wanted to be shocked. He wanted to feel outraged. But he couldn't. It was almost as if he had expected just such an encounter.

I tried to believe I could escape, he thought, but it's always been there, always been a part of me.

Caleb turned and ran.

As fast as Caleb was driving, the terror was still catching up to him. He sneaked another glance in his rearview mirror. Nothing pursuing him, at least not yet. The mirror showed only his white face and his scared eyes. He didn't find his reflection in any way reassuring.

He's dead, Caleb told himself. He's been dead for more than twenty years.

Caleb took a deep breath. Maybe I should go back, he thought, and call the police. But facing up to the situation frightened him. It went against a lifetime of habits. His urge to deny everything was strong, too strong. Given a choice, he didn't want to be connected in any way with Mrs. Sanders, but as fervently as Caleb wanted to believe that his stumbling upon her was an accident, the word—the curse—belied that.

Someone knew his secret. Caleb had been found out. He had always dreaded the thought of this moment, but the death of Mrs. Sanders made it even more horrific than he had ever imagined, and he had always imagined the worst.

Thinking about her made him feel sick, and also guilty. He hadn't even made sure she was dead. He'd been too afraid, too panicked, to check. He had to do something.

Neither of the pay phones at the supermarket was being used. Caleb punched 911.

"Emergency nine-one-one," the dispatcher answered.

Disguising his voice, making it atonal and low, Caleb said,"Go to thirty-four seventy-two Via Monterrey in Rancho Santa Fe.There's a woman there who has been seriously injured."

"Thirty-four seventy-two Via Monterrey in Rancho Santa Fe," the dispatcher repeated."Is that correct?"

"Yes."

"And can you tell me the severity and type of injury?"

"Get there quickly," Caleb said.

"What's your name, sir?"

Caleb hung up.

That afternoon a call was made from a different pay phone. A woman answered, but didn't offer any other greeting than "Answering service."

The caller knew his voice wasn't known to the operator, but he disguised it anyway:"I'd like to leave a message for Maryelizabeth Line."

"I'll connect with her voice mail."

Maryelizabeth Line had told him that in an emergency he could have her service page her, but the man didn't want to talk to her directly. It was easier just leaving a message.

I feel like a fucking spy, he thought. Making this kind of cloak-and-dagger call wasn't for him. He was a cop, a San Diego County deputy sheriff who'd never even had the ambition to hide his badge in his wallet.

A computer-generated voice interrupted his thoughts: "Leave your message now."

The artificial voice didn't sound very different from the operator who had answered. The deputy sheriff knew Maryelizabeth Line needed to protect herself. It came with her turf. But he wondered if her friends got tired of this routine.

"There's been another one," he said."It happened this morning in Rancho Santa Fe.That's where a whole lot of rich people live. It's in the north of San Diego County. The victim's name is Teresa Sanders. Same MO as the other one. This one's a bit older, she's thirty-two, but I'm told she was pretty and could have passed for twenty."

The officer looked all around. There was no one within hearing distance, and no one who appeared to be looking his way.

"They're putting a big clamp down on the investigation. I was lucky to hear as much as I did. Prepare to be stonewalled. Prepare to be counterquestioned. I guess I don't need to be telling you that. It's not like you don't know the routine. If you need to talk to me, call from a pay phone and leave a message on my machine. Identify yourself as Aunt Millie, and leave a safe number where I can get back to you."

The deputy sheriff scanned the area a second time, and decided he could say a few more hurried words.

"I heard he used her lipstick to write the word, but that's probably third- or fourth-hand information. A male made a nine-one-one call and said a woman had been seriously injured. The call came from a pay phone in Encinitas, about six miles from where she was murdered. There are a lot of theories going along with that call. Did a Good Samaritan see something, but was too scared to get involved, or was Shame playing some kind of game? That's what they're already calling him: Shame."

He lowered his voice to a whisper: "Course that's not supposed to get out to the public on threat of severe reprisal. It's not only the secrecy thing. People are worried about a panic around here."

If this Line woman hadn't helped out his brother Larry, he'd never have dropped a dime. Larry was also a cop, and Line had saved his brother's ass a few years back, had validated his police work in print when the entire city of Seattle was ready to ride him out of town. The family owed her. This was her marker.

"Bet you never thought you'd be writing about Shame again," he said. "He's all yours, lady. Shame on you."

2

The news break allowed Maryelizabeth Line a five-minute respite from the phone calls. She left her headphones on, and listened to the newscast, a junkie indulging in her habit.

The door to the broadcasting booth opened, and the talk jock waved to her. He went by the name of Kip, or, as he seemed to prefer, "the Kipper." As he donned his headset he winked at Maryelizabeth, did a sound check with the engineer, then signaled to her that they were about to go on air. His signal came by hand instead of eye, and for that Maryelizabeth was grateful. The Kipper moved slightly forward to his microphone. He was round and his puffy face had an almost neon-pink hue, but he was porcine without the squeal. The Kipper had a mellifluous and powerful voice, and had the power to make the inane sound important.

"You've got the right-right station," he said, "because this is the Knight-Nights show coming to you live from our nation's capital in Washington, D.C."

No more late-night book promotions on radio, vowed Maryelizabeth.

"This is the Kipper," he said, "and we'll be continuing for the next hour with our special guest, true-crime author Maryelizabeth Line.

"For those of you who were with us during the last hour, you know we've been talking murder, folks. Maryelizabeth's latest is *A Magnolia Hanging.*

"We've got Dave from Springfield, Missouri, on the line, and I do mean line as in our guest Maryelizabeth Line. How ya doing, Dave?"

"Doing fine, Kip. But after listening in tonight I went around and made sure all my doors and windows were locked, and I just now put a loaded gun under my pillow. I can't say you've got a very reassuring guest."

As if, Maryelizabeth refrained from saying, Dave and the loaded gun under his pillow were cause for comfort.

"She does have some mean stories, doesn't she, Dave? But you'd never know it to look at Maryelizabeth. You'd think she was some model, not some milk carton chronicler."

Maryelizabeth supposed that was a compliment. "Thank you, Kip," she said.

"Well," Dave said, "I wanted to ask her a few questions about Shame."

What a surprise, Maryelizabeth thought. In her first hour on the show most of the questions had been about Gray Parker. They always were.

"I'm listening, Dave," Maryelizabeth said.

Usually she was able to get out of coming to the studio. She preferred being a call-in guest, doing the so-called "phoners." Radio booths made her feel claustrophobic. But her publicist thought it was good PR to make occasional personal appearances, especially on shows with a national audience. In a weak moment she had agreed to do the spot.

"Yeah," Dave said. "I've heard that after Shame died they cut him up and sold his body parts. Supposedly some college got his brain to study. But I also heard some woman paid twenty-five thousand dollars for his, um, johnson. I was told it's floating around in this ten-gallon bottle. Word is that it's, uh, about as big as Einstein's brain, you know, real oversized, and that it's available for private showings."

"You mean *privates* showing," Kipper said.

The two men laughed.

"Well, how about it, Miss Line?" Kip asked. "We got a killer's genitalia on the loose?"

The Kipper offered his question while stroking the large microphone in front of him. There was a good reason, Maryelizabeth thought, why many radio personalities did much better as voices than as people. Kip thought he was God's gift to women. During the break he'd suggested that Maryelizabeth hang around until he was off at 1 A.M., at which time they "could catch a bite, or whatever."

That's why very long bubble baths had been invented, Maryelizabeth thought. To wash away certain days.

"I'm afraid the reports of Gray Parker's body parts," Maryelizabeth said, "have been greatly exaggerated."

Even Shakespeare, Maryelizabeth comforted herself, had often resorted to ribaldry to amuse the groundlings. Over Kipper's laughter, she continued. "I'm not referring to the size of his organ. Of that, I have no knowledge to offer. But the rumors of his bodily remains have persisted for years.

"The basis for the talk, I'm fairly certain, stems from his attempts to have his organs donated. Parker wanted his death to have some meaning, or at least that's what he publicly stated, but his method of execution didn't allow that. To be usable, organs have to be removed while the donor's blood is still circulating, and his being electrocuted eliminated that possibility."

"You don't think there's any chance, then," Dave asked, "that someone collected a souvenir?"

"No," Maryelizabeth said. "He was cremated just a short time after his execution."

"Then how's come I keep hearing there's a big market out there trafficking in everything from his fingers to his ears to his, well, you know."

"Guess we'd call that a *Gray* market," Kip said.

Maryelizabeth let their laughter die down before answering. "No part or parts of Gray Parker survived his execution," she said, "but that's not to say there hasn't been a morbid history of the collecting of such souvenirs. There was a hanging in Kentucky in the thirties where people fought over the disposition of the death mask, and worse, hacked off pieces of the body as keepsakes."

"You got *whut* in your freezer?" said Kip.

"And it wasn't that long ago when sideshow exhibits displayed the bodies of executed criminals. But luckily, those days have passed.

"Incidentally, Dave, the rumor about Parker and his supposedly gargantuan organ isn't anything new. The same stories were told about John Dillinger. It seems that every generation wants its villain to be some sort of superman. Why that is, I don't know."

"Thank you," Dave said.

He sounded sort of breathless, Maryelizabeth thought. She hated to think what might be exciting him.

"In the pursuit of science," Kip said, "I think I should take this opportunity to offer a twenty-five-dollar reward to anyone who can produce Gray Parker's penis in a bottle. It'd make a hell of a centerpiece at a *cock*tail party I'm having next week."

Kip gave Maryelizabeth his best "ain't I a bad boy?" look. She mentally added another five minutes to her long-awaited bath.

"And now," Kip said, "I'm afraid we're going to have to kill a little time with a commercial. Stay tuned for more of Maryelizabeth Line and true crime."

Kip patted Maryelizabeth on her knee, took off his headphones, and stood up. The removal of his headphones caused his toupee to tilt. "Got to powwow for a minute with Chief Engineer," he said.

Maryelizabeth didn't tell him it looked as if he had already been scalped. He patted her shoulder before leaving the room, and she began to reconsider her stand on the death penalty.

The broadcast room was in semidarkness. Maryelizabeth didn't know whether the Kipper liked to do his show in a dimly lit studio, or whether the lights were low for her benefit. She rolled her head, but couldn't get a crick out of her neck. With a sharp movement of her head she was able to produce a resounding crack. It was a good thing the sound hadn't been broadcast, Maryelizabeth thought. Chiropractors would have been flooding the lines. She closed her eyes and felt the tiredness in her body. It was her job, she reminded herself, to remain upbeat, to sound as if every question was new to her. She was supposed to be a professional cheerleader. Give me an *M,* give me a *U,* give me an *R* . . .

"Miss me?" asked Kip.

D,E,R, she thought.

He didn't wait for an answer, merely settled into his broadcast paraphernalia, signaled the engineer with a gesture, then started talking.

"We have the pleasure of hosting the Queen of True Crime tonight, Miss Maryelizabeth Line. She's here to talk about her latest book, *A Magnolia Hanging.* It's the story of a young Kentucky woman found hanging in a small town's showcase magnolia tree. The circumstances of this woman's death are, to say the least, mysterious. No one's quite sure whether she hung herself, or whether she went unwillingly to the noose. But there she was found one June morning, swaying in the midst of all those resplendent magnolia blossoms.

"You stayed for a time in the town of Little River, Kentucky, where all this happened, didn't you, Maryelizabeth?"

"I was there for six months," she said. "Whenever I write a book I always include a lot of background and history of the area."

"The local color," said Kip.

"That," she said, "and more. Sometimes there are histories and patterns to certain locales that seem to repeat themselves. It's almost as if people get caught up in webs they're not even aware of."

Kip's eyes glazed over. There was no way *he* was going to be drawn into some metaphysical discussion. He changed the subject, offering a safer question.

"What did people think of you, an outsider, coming in and nosing around?"

"Most of them realized I was there to do a job. On the whole the citizens of Little River were very accommodating to me."

"Well, we have a lot of listeners waiting for you to accommodate them, Maryelizabeth. Here's Ken calling from the city of angels, Los Angeles, California."

"Hello, Ken."

"You're attracted to the rough stuff," he said, "aren't you?"

Ken's voice was gravelly, making his question sound all the more harsh. His words were slightly slurred.

Another caller emboldened by alcohol, Maryelizabeth thought. "Violence is unfortunately a fact of life in this country," she said. "There are over twenty thousand homicides in America every year, and at any given moment the FBI estimates there are more than thirty-five serial killers out there trolling for victims. That's my beat, so to speak, and yes, it is a rough one."

"Ever stop to think a lot of bitches out there need killing?"

Maryelizabeth took a long breath. She and Kip exchanged glances. His hand signal deferred to her.

"Is that your opinion, Ken?"

The caller laughed—harsh, barking, mirthless. "It's more than my opinion," he said, his voice mocking.

"Do you know anything about such killings, Ken?" she asked.

"Oh, I've got a couple notches on my belt. Plan to get a few more, too."

"Have you murdered any women?"

"I've done me a few bitches," he said.

Maryelizabeth suddenly heard the engineer's voice in her right headphone: "We just bleeped that out, Kip, and we'll be going from the jingle to commercial break. But if Ms. Line can keep him talking, we'll put a trace on the line."

She turned to the engineer, and signaled to show that she understood. She was glad that half a million listeners weren't going to be privy to this particular conversation.

"Can you tell me about what you did?" she asked.

"Why should I?"

"Because I'm curious as to what those women did to anger you."

"Curiosity killed the cat," he said, then laughed. "Here kitty, kitty."

"You didn't really kill anyone, did you, Ken?"

"I got two ex-wives, and I do mean ex, who'd beg to differ, lady."

"You're saying you killed your wives?"

"Yeah. And a couple whirly-girlies aren't trading anymore because I put them out of business in a permanent way."

"Whirly-girlies?"

"Whores. Hookers."

"Have you been convicted for any of those crimes?"

He laughed. "Haven't you heard? Wives run away all the time. That's what the cops told me, and I believed them, oh, yes, I did. And who cares about hookers?"

"What's prompted you to act as you have?"

"Like my daddy always said, 'If bitches didn't have a pussy, there'd be a bounty on them.' I never run short of no reasons to do away with them."

Maryelizabeth could see the engineer working feverishly, doing his best, she was sure, to land her fish.

"What reasons?"

"They're nosy, like you."

"And for that you killed them?"

"And sometimes they acted high and mighty, like you're acting now."

"How did you murder them?"

"That's a trade secret. But I'm always willing to learn new tricks. I like the way Shame took care of business. You was real good about describing that in your book. Made me feel like I was right there."

She had wanted readers to be sickened by those passages. His reaction, his exultation over the violence, made her feel ill. She didn't want to continue talking, but Kip kept gesturing to her, his hands coming together and apart, imploring her to stretch the conversation just a little longer.

"So you admire Gray Parker?" she asked.

"He had the right idea, that's for sure. The only mistake he made was not doing you when he had the chance."

"You'll forgive me if I don't agree with you."

"I'm not sure if I will. I'm not sure if I don't owe you one for Shame. The way I see it, you're just unfinished business."

"Are you threatening me?"

"I don't make threats. I just do what I do."

"And if we're to believe you, what you do is murder."

"If you get rid of vermin, you're an exterminator, not a murderer."

Somehow Maryelizabeth was keeping her voice steady. Unflappable. Behind the calm voice, though, were shaking knees and a face gone pale. The caller was scary. She half believed him.

"Is that so?"

"Yeah, poetry lady, that's so. Think you're so goddamn superior, don't you? Well, reciting poetry in the middle of the night isn't always gonna save your ass. Fact is, I've been working on a poem for you, seeing's how you like poetry so much. I'm thinking of carving it somewhere. Maybe on your ass."

"I hope it's a short poem then," Maryelizabeth said. "I'd hate to think that part of my anatomy could support a really long poem."

"You're a smart-mouthed cunt."

"Do you really have a poem, Kenny? Or is that just another one of your lies?"

"You're afraid of my truth, lady. And you should be."

"You're wrong there. That's my job. I look into dark corners. I open doors that most people would leave shut."

"If I were you, I'd be shitting in my pants, bitch."

"I'm sure you would, Kenny."

He started cursing, didn't stop until he needed a long breath.

"Did that make you feel better?" she asked.

"Cutting off your head will make me feel better."

"I think only one of us has lost our head in this conversation."

"Talk is cheap. Bitch like you thinks you're so smart, spouting off words. I've got a few words for you."

"I thought you had a poem."

"I do."

"I'm listening."

Ken didn't say anything for several seconds. Maryelizabeth didn't offer him an out, just waited in silence. Then he started his reciting:

"I hear your heart beating,
Awaiting our meeting,
I wonder at your greeting,
When my knife meets your flesh.

Will you scream out in pain,
Will your tears run like rain,
Will your blood gush from a vein,
When my knife meets your flesh."

He wanted her to react. Maryelizabeth knew that with certainty. He wanted her to be afraid, to plead with him that he shouldn't be thinking those thoughts. He hoped she would scream, or shout that he was a sick bastard, or hang up in fear.

Instead, she asked, "You know what, Kenny?"

Suspiciously: "What?"

"I think you should take your knife to the poem before you direct it my way. We're talking major league awful."

"Fuck you."

"But you know what I like best about that poem, Kenny?"

He hesitated before asking, but he had to know: "What?"

"That it's over."

Sounds of raw anger came over the phone, inarticulate guttural hatred, and then another sound—a dial tone.

The phone trace proved successful, but only to the extent that they learned where the call had been made.

"Pay phone in Anaheim, California," the engineer announced. "Near Disneyland, I'm told."

"Must have been Mickey Mouse calling," Maryelizabeth said.

They continued with the show, making no on-air references to the call. There was no reason to encourage other kooks. At the show's conclusion, Maryelizabeth declined Kipper's offer to escort her personally up to her hotel room "just to make sure everything is okay." Everything would be okay once she got her bubble bath.

As the bath was running, Maryelizabeth called her service for messages. The deputy's call finally caught up with her at 2:32 A.M. She found it much more upsetting than Ken's call.

"Shit," she said, punching in her code to replay the message, and listening to the deputy sheriff's information a second time. "Shit," she said again, then called the airport to get the first flight out to San Diego.

She never did get her bubble bath.

The jet shook yet again. More turbulence. The pilot came on over the intercom.

"Sorry about those bumps, folks, but we're going to be experiencing some Rocky Mountain love taps for a while yet. Please remain seated with your seat belts fastened."

Maryelizabeth thought that the turbulence suited her frame of mind. She remembered how Gray Parker—Shame—had turned her life upside down. Parker had been the impetus for Maryelizabeth's becoming the Queen of True Crime (a label her publisher insisted upon putting on every one of her books—all twelve of them).

Shame had been her first book. Even with all her books since, Maryelizabeth's name was still linked with Parker's nickname, so much so that she was convinced there was some unwritten rule that emcees and announcers and interviewers were obligated to say their names in the same breath.

The jet dipped again. Stomachs lurched, and anxious voices called out. The man sitting next to her reached for his air sickness bag. But Maryelizabeth didn't feel the topsy-turvy motion in her stomach so much as in her head. Thinking about Gray Parker did that to her. With the new developments there was this sense of things past, even if that wasn't appropriate. Any mirror could tell her that. She was twenty when he came into her life, and now she was forty-seven. Besides, this wasn't Parker. He was dead. This was just a copycat murderer.

Maryelizabeth had first heard from the officer the week before when he'd called to tell her about the young woman's body that had been left in the desert, her back to an ocotillo, the word *SHAME* written on her naked flesh. At the time, she had hoped it wasn't the beginning of a pattern, had thought it possible that someone had just written the word to mislead the authorities, to divert attention.

So much for her wishful thinking.

The timing was bad, she told herself. She was halfway through another book. She didn't like the idea of stopping and starting, of literary coitus interruptus. But that wasn't really it. She had closed a lot of personal doors on the original Shame murders, and had no desire to open them. At the same time she had a proprietary attitude about anything having to do with Gray Parker. It was her beat, and she wanted to stake her claim.

She wondered at the timing of the new murders. Parker had been executed over twenty years earlier, and copycat killers usually strike while the headlines are large, while they can be part of the notoriety. Old murders were yesterday's news, forgotten by everyone save those close to the victims.

Maryelizabeth closed her eyes, remembering the night Gray Parker had come into her life. She had awakened to him saying, "Don't scream."

Her first thought was that her boyfriend Dan had come over to apologize. They'd had a fight the week before and in that time neither of them had offered an olive branch to the other. But Dan wouldn't have sneaked into the sorority so late at night. The room was dark, but there was enough light for Maryelizabeth to make out the shape of the man's head. It definitely wasn't Dan sitting on the bed next to her, but she was suddenly sure who it was.

"I won't scream," she said.

I won't give you that satisfaction, Barry Gilbert, she had thought. But you're never going to come into my room uninvited again. Whenever Barry came over to see Tracy his eyes always lingered on her, and though Maryelizabeth had tried to ignore his attentions, he had always made a point of seeking her out. Tracy seemed oblivious to his flirting, and Maryelizabeth hadn't wanted to make an issue of it, so nothing had ever been said.

"I'm tired," he said. "I've never been so tired before."

Everyone was tired, Maryelizabeth thought. She had little sympathy for him. It was finals week, and she had allocated herself only four hours of sleep. "What are you doing in my room?" she asked.

He didn't answer her question. "All the other times were so exhilarating. They made me feel so—connected. The power went from my fingertips to my spine and then up and down my body."

Maryelizabeth had to will herself to continue breathing. Her chest felt frozen. It wasn't Barry who was sitting on her bed. Barry was from New Jersey, and sounded like it. This man had a Southern accent. Did she know him? Should she scream? She wanted to believe he was a drunken student just blowing off steam from the pressures of finals, a friend of Tracy's or Paula's.

"I keep looking for bridges," he said. "Something to get me over to the other land."

"What other land?"

She saw his hand reach out, not to her, but into the darkness. "The land of the living."

Silence draped the room like a shroud. Maryelizabeth was sure she didn't know this man, had never known him, and was afraid of knowing him. He turned to her and sensed her unease.

"What are you thinking?" he asked.

There was something invasive about his words, and something angry. She didn't tell him what she was really thinking, or how she really felt. The only time Maryelizabeth could recall being this scared was the time she had gone camping and awakened to a big bear sniffing outside her tent. But this was even more frightening. The bear had only been rooting around for food. She wasn't sure if this man even knew what he wanted.

"I was considering what you said," she said, her voice deceptively calm, as if to soothe a beast. "You're right. All of us need bridges."

He appeared to relax slightly. He rubbed his chin and kept looking around the room. "You have a lot of books in here," he said.

The Kappa Omega sorority house had several wings. Maryelizabeth lived in the so-called nook section along with Tracy and Paula. They all had their own rooms. Instead of the usual posters, Maryelizabeth had lined her bedroom walls with cinder-block bookcases filled with books. They cocooned her, keeping the noise of her sorority sisters, and the world, away from her. She had always loved being in the isolated nook—until now.

"I'm a literature major," she said, as if apologizing for the books.

"Have you read all of them?" he asked.

"Yes."

"And have they made you smarter?" he asked.

Through the sheets she could feel the heat of his body. Maryelizabeth found herself trembling. She didn't know what to say, but was afraid not to say something.

"Not smarter," she said, "but they helped me to understand things better."

"Understand what?"

"People," she said.

"People," he repeated, and with his echo was a sound that was part laugh and part sob. "Tell me about these people. Explain them to me."

He was leaning close to her, and that frightened her. She could sense his agitation, his anger.

"I can't explain people, but there was a poem that Whitman wrote," she said, her tone shrill despite her best efforts to sound calm, "that taught me how to try to understand a person. He said:

'Agonies are one of my changes of garments;
I do not ask the wounded person how he feels . . . I myself become the wounded person.'"

It was several moments before the intruder responded. "Oh," he said, as if hurt, as if wounded. "Oh."

He edged off the bed, and started pacing around her room. Maryelizabeth saw him as a shadow, something darker than the dark, making his way back and forth. His hand kept moving to his brow and rubbing, as if wiping away sweat, as if a fever had broken.

"No one understands," he said.

"I'll try to," she promised.

He retreated from her, as if now he was the one who was afraid. She heard him feeling through the darkness, moving toward the front of the room. When he opened the door, there was enough light from the hallway for her to catch a glimpse of his face. Maryelizabeth was surprised at his appearance. He was a very handsome man, with dark good looks and sensuous lips. The lips moved for her.

"Don't scream," he said, and then was gone.

Several minutes passed before Maryelizabeth raised herself from her bed. She had been afraid he was still out there, still waiting. She finally nerved herself to turn on a light. With two hands she grasped a letter opener, and slowly made her way out to the hallway. There was no one in sight, and all was quiet. Tracy's room was the nearest to hers. The door was slightly ajar.

Maryelizabeth pushed it open. There was no sign of the intruder. Tracy was in her bed, all tucked in. She called to her, but Tracy was a heavy sleeper. She usually set two alarm clocks to get up, and sometimes that wasn't enough.

"Tracy. There was a man in here."

Tracy continued to snooze. Maryelizabeth pulled back the bedcovers. Tracy wasn't wearing any clothes, but there was a length of panty hose trailing down her back.

"Tracy, wake up."

As Maryelizabeth was shaking Tracy by the shoulder, she noticed that the panty hose was twisted around her neck. She turned Tracy over, and confronted the horror.

The panty hose had dug so deeply into Tracy's neck that it looked like a balloon tied into sections. Her face was even worse, her eyes distended and bulging, her tongue huge.

Maryelizabeth had promised she wouldn't scream, but she did.

She opened her eyes, and let the memories recede. Even after all these years, she sometimes awakened screaming. Parker had murdered both Tracy and Paula, but for whatever reason, he had let her live. When he was finally captured, after he had murdered seventeen women, her testimony helped convict him. She was the only eyewitness, and the only woman who had survived his calling upon her.

The captain came on the intercom. He promised a smooth flight the rest of the way to San Diego.

Liar, Maryelizabeth thought.

4

October 10, 1971

Twenty-four-year-old Kathy Franklin had gone on a Sunday outing with her friend Suzanne Epstein to watch the clustering of hot-air balloons. At mid-afternoon Kathy left Suzanne to go back to her car for more film. Parker intercepted her on the way there.

"I hate to bother you," he said, his voice reflecting a shy, Southern upbringing, "but I'm kind of in a fix."

The "fix" was obvious—his left leg was in a cast. The handsome stranger looked as if he wasn't used to asking for favors. Even without the cast most women would have gladly helped him, but the cast was magic. His helplessness gave women who might have been intimidated by his good looks an easy bridge to cross.

"My car has this big trunk," he said, "and I can't reach inside far enough to get this compressor we need. I wouldn't bother you except that my crew is ready to take off."

"Your crew?" Kathy asked.

"I'm a pilot," he said, then tapped his cast with his crutches, "or I was until I broke this."

His plaintive voice was played to perfection, his need apparent. Kathy immediately offered to help the "wounded pilot." No combat ace ever assumed such a manly pose. They talked all the way to his car. He apologized that it was so far away, explained its distant location by saying that he had arrived late and hadn't been able to park in the main parking lot. Kathy said she liked to exercise anyway. She was a tall woman, with long, straight blond hair that went almost all the way down her back. Parker commented on her hair, said it was long like that woman in the fairy tale, Rapunzel, who was always having to let her hair down for her prince to climb up. Kathy laughed at that. She was a pretty woman, had broken up with her last boyfriend a year earlier, and she enjoyed the handsome stranger's attention.

When they arrived at Parker's car they were off by themselves, though not in a completely deserted location. The balloons, in all their shapes and rainbow colors, were just taking off and had seduced all eyes but Parker's.

Parker opened the trunk of his Ford Galaxie 500 and said the compressor was in the "very back." Kathy bent over, and started tapping with her hand, futilely looking. "I don't think . . ." she started to say, but never had the chance to finish her sentence. From behind, Parker grabbed her, applied a choke hold, then strangled her to death.

Overhead the balloons, in all their splendor, floated by in the azure Albuquerque sky. Some of those in the gondolas waved down to the earth.

The balloons raised themselves higher and higher into the sky, but Kathy's friends and family believe she preceded them into the firmament. Unlike the balloons, though, Kathy never returned to this earth.

—Excerpt from *Shame*
by Maryelizabeth Line

The door hadn't opened easily.

Maryelizabeth had been stonewalled by the sheriff's secretary, and referred over to Sergeant Hardy, who headed up the sheriff's Public Affairs office. She repeated to Sergeant Hardy that she needed to see the sheriff, and to make her point she handed the sergeant one of her books and referred him to a particular section.

Hardy had kept a poker face while reading the passage, and then had asked to be excused for a minute. When he returned, Hardy offered Maryelizabeth a personal escort over to the Sheriff's Office. Her book had evidently preceded them.

Sheriff Bill Campbell held up the copy of *Shame*. "Unique calling card, Ms. Line," he said.

He thumbed through the book, examined her picture on the back cover, then gave her a pointed glance. Maryelizabeth felt her neck get hot. She'd wanted to update the author photo, but the publisher had preferred her Dorian Gray image. Though she looked young for her age, she was no longer the girl in that picture.

She pushed a piece of paper across the sheriff's desk. "I also asked your secretary to give you this. My references. I've had a lot of dealings with law enforcement, and the people listed there will vouch for me. I've earned their trust, and I'd like to earn yours."

The sheriff looked at the sheet for considerably less time than he had her book picture, then passed it on to Sergeant Hardy. He turned his eyes back to her, volunteering nothing, waiting for what she had to say.

"I referred the sergeant to a section in the book that deals with the death of Kathy Franklin," said Maryelizabeth. "She was Gray Parker's second victim."

"Is that supposed to mean something?" the sheriff asked.

Maryelizabeth knew that in San Diego County the sheriff was an elective position, and that there were those that thought Sheriff Bill Campbell was more politician than lawman. He wasn't a large man, but he acted large in the way he talked, and the way he moved his hands. His face was oversized, with big eyes, and nose, and ears. He had Hollywood hair, thick, curly, and dark. And not one of those hairs was out of place.

"If it didn't, you wouldn't be seeing me now," she said.

The sheriff didn't move, didn't blink. Hardy adopted the same expression.

"I want to be involved in your investigation," Maryelizabeth said. "You've had two recent homicides. I understand they are being called the New Shame Murders. Your murderer is using Gray Parker's MO."

Campbell's face showed nothing. "Where did you get your information?"

She shook her head. "The issue here isn't sources."

"Well, I'm just curious as to where you heard this rather fantastic story."

"This isn't a fishing expedition," said Maryelizabeth. "Lita Jennings was the first victim. She died three weeks ago. She was strangled in Del Mar, but was transported out to the desert, where she was left propped up. Teresa Sanders was yesterday's victim. She was found posed in her Rancho Santa Fe home."

Campbell looked at his fingers as if he were looking at cards. But his bluff had been called, and he was holding a bust hand.

"I really can't comment on ongoing investigations, Ms. Line."

Maryelizabeth stood up. "Thank you, then."

The sheriff gave Hardy a quick, surprised look. He had expected her to wheedle and cajole, and then accept whatever bone he chose to throw her. He couldn't afford to have her leave without knowing what she intended to do. His look prompted the subordinate to speak.

"What are your plans?" the sergeant asked.

"This is a breaking story," she said. "I have a lot of history invested in the original Shame murders, which is why I consider this *my* story. Since you're not prepared to help me at this time, I'll have to proceed on my own."

There was another moment of brief eye contact between the two men. They're wondering how to handle me, Maryelizabeth thought. They're not sure whether to use soft words, or a club. Or both.

Sergeant Hardy straightened his tie. He looked and acted more Madison Avenue than cop, had nicely styled salt-and-pepper hair and a mellifluous voice. "You must realize that any premature releasing of information could ruin our investigation. And the potential for panic might be catastrophic."

"Let me in, then," Maryelizabeth said. "You'll get my silence in return for giving me that inside track."

Her threat was implicit. If they didn't involve her in the case, they had no hold on her silence. The men exchanged glances again.

"It won't be a one-way street," she said. "I can help you."

"How?" This time the sheriff did his own talking.

"If this is a copycat killer," she said, "no one knows more about the original homicides than I do."

Maryelizabeth could feel them wavering, but she also knew how very conservative law enforcement was. They protected their closed doors, and resisted letting strangers into their inner circle. Especially women.

"I'd like to hear about the death of Teresa Sanders," she said.

The men reacted uncomfortably, moving in their seats, saying nothing.

"In particular, I'm interested in knowing about the crime scene."

Maryelizabeth could see she had pushed too hard. The men folded their arms, held them tight to their chests. The doors were closing on her.

She had to say something, and took a chance: "Were there any balloons at the crime scene?"

Both men tried not to react. Both men did.

"Balloons?" the sheriff asked.

"Yes."

"That's an odd question," he said.

"Yes."

It was her turn to stonewall. She had considered all the different possibilities, and then thrown out the most likely.

The sheriff tried to draw her out. "If you have any information about this homicide . . ."

"Am I in?" she asked.

After a long moment's hesitation, the sheriff said, "We'll cooperate with you."

His remark was open to interpretation, but Maryelizabeth decided to take him at his word.

"Kathy Franklin was strangled while a flotilla of hot-air balloons sailed over her head. At her outdoor memorial service, balloons were released. Your copycat would have known that."

The sheriff and the sergeant looked at each other for the briefest moment. There was something furtive about their glance, something guilty.

"Mrs. Sanders's autopsy will be performed in the morning," the sheriff said, "but there was a preliminary examination of her body this afternoon."

His unsaid "and" hung in the air. The sheriff sighed, shook his head, then met Maryelizabeth's eyes.

"There were balloons found in her vagina. Seventeen of them. All different colors."

5

Once more unto the breach, thought Maryelizabeth. She felt like Daniel going into the lions' den, but without his faith. As the detectives entered the room she reminded herself to smile, though she figured that tactic worked about as well on cops as it did on lions.

The Sheriff's Department homicide detail was located in a building several blocks away from the administrators in Ridgehaven. Everyone seemed to like that arrangement.

Maryelizabeth's participation in the new Shame murders had been shoved down the throat of Lieutenant Jacob Borman. The Shame murders were considered so hot that all three homicide teams, each with four sheriff's homicide investigators and one sheriff's homicide sergeant, were working them.

Lieutenant Borman and Maryelizabeth sat at opposite ends of the Central Intelligence Division conference room. As the sixteen homicide detectives trickled inside, the first thing they noticed was the stranger in their presence. What Maryelizabeth noticed was the dark circles under their eyes and their dark moods. Most had been working all night; none was in a mood to hear a lecture.

"Let's get to it," said Borman, calling to a few men standing at the doorway.

Most of the men took seats in the mismatched chairs at the long, rectangular table. One investigator showed his disinterest by lying down on the sofa and offering Maryelizabeth only one open eye. Maryelizabeth noticed that there was only one other woman in the room. She smiled at her, hoping to engage at least one sympathetic face, but the detective pointedly turned away.

From across the table, Lieutenant Borman nodded in her direction. "Maryelizabeth Line is our guest this morning," he said. "You're going to be seeing her around."

Borman's announcement sounded more like a warning than an endorsement. His tone made it clear that he wasn't thrilled to have her among them. He patted the crown of his head, found a slight cowlick, and worked on smoothing it down. With his brown, bloodshot eyes, curly brown hair, drooping face, and perpetual lip curl, Borman looked like a basset hound with an attitude.

"*Ms.* Line," he said, "is a writer. In front of each of you is her book *Shame.* That's what she's here to talk about."

Maryelizabeth debated whether to stand up, and decided the room was too small. She understood their collective tiredness, and their distrust of her. She was the outsider let in on their ugly secrets.

"I appreciate how extremely busy all of you are," she said, "so I will try to keep my comments very brief. As you probably gathered from the title of my book, I wrote about the original Shame murders. As to what relevance ancient history has to the homicides you're working on, my best answer is that your murderer has apparently read my book very carefully. He also seems to know quite a bit about the life of Gray Parker.

"I have not yet had the chance to get up to speed on your investigations, but it's my understanding that in many ways your two homicides parallel Parker's first two murders. Rather than compare notes, I thought I'd tell you what I know about those earlier deaths, and let you draw your own comparisons."

The eyes weren't so hostile now. Encouraged by that, Maryelizabeth told them about Alicia Gleason and Kathy Franklin. She didn't need to refer to notes; the memories surfaced readily. Whether that was a blessing or a curse, she wasn't sure. She had visited where the women had lived and died, had in fact done that for all of Parker's victims. His trail of death had taken her from New Mexico to Florida. In many ways, Parker had been her guide. Before leaving on her trips she had asked him questions, and he had answered them matter-of-factly. She always tried to come away from her pilgrimages with three sets of impressions: her own, the victim's, and Parker's.

"I hope your murderer isn't as naturally elusive as Gray Parker," she said. "There was one detective who called him the man of a thousand faces. He was wrong. Parker didn't disguise himself; he knew how to be invisible. Most of the time he passed himself off as a college student. That gave him license to keep odd hours. It also gave him a certain anonymity, with people seeing him as a student more than as an individual."

She didn't want to overload her audience with too many details, and yet there were so many things she wanted to say.

"What distinguished Parker's first three homicides from those that followed is that there was significantly more posing involved. By this I don't only mean his signature—his postmortem ritualized writing of *Shame* on their flesh—but his purposely situating the victims in specific spots.

"The first placement was in White Sands. Parker was a regular visitor there, and knew the area well. He was fixated on how ephemeral life was, and how White Sands showcased that. 'Until the next dune buries them,' was a favorite expression of his, words he had lifted from one of the White Sands exhibits. In a convoluted leap of logic, Gray decided he was that next dune, and that his calling was to take life. The very act of placing Alicia Gleason's body inside the monument revealed the extent of his compulsion. The road into White Sands is closed at night, and to get her body to the preselected spot, he had to carry her for two miles.

"Parker was similarly obsessed with the posing of his second victim, situating her at the Three Rivers Petroglyph Site. He was fascinated by the rock drawings. I suspect he saw them as tablets with messages as clear as the Ten Commandments. His fascination with Indian drawings wasn't anything new; whenever he was at his wife's home in Eden, Texas, he always visited the neighboring community of Paint Rock to look at its renowned Indian pictograph site. It's a pretty spot, a half-mile bluff that overlooks the Conchos River, a place where a number of Indian tribes have left artifacts for over a thousand years. Some have even offered up their stories in relatively modern times. In eighteen sixty-five Apache warriors kidnapped a fourteen-year-old girl named Alice Todd. They were fleeing pursuit, but took the time to paint symbols of what they'd done on the rocks. They drew two crossed lances, which is the warpath symbol, and next to that they painted two long-haired scalps, which depicted the killings of Alice's mother and a black slave girl. A third drawing showed a girl posed horizontally, a typical depiction of a captive. What ultimately happened to Alice is not known. Her body was never discovered, and she was never seen by the white community again. The last evidence of her existence is that drawing."

Maryelizabeth paused in her telling. They didn't need to hear about Parker's fascination with Alice Todd. It would be more helpful to them to hear about Kathy Franklin. Maryelizabeth had extensively toured the Three Rivers Petroglyph Site, had spent two full days walking up and down the ridge and studying the area where the Franklin girl's body had been posed. Anthropologists had documented more than 21,000 rock carvings at Three Rivers, drawings more than a thousand years old. Many of the petroglyphs told stories; the bighorn sheep pierced with three arrows; the representations of mountain lions, bears, and game birds; the staring faces and masks; the mysterious crosses, circles, and patterns—all believed to have religious significance.

She had never felt exactly alone at Three Rivers. It was an easy place to be spooked. The weather always seemed to be changing, and the wind constantly tugged and talked. Even immutable objects never looked the same. From one moment to the next the Godfrey Hills to the north, the Sacramento Mountains and Sierra Blanca to the east, and the San Andres and Oscura Mountains to the west seemed to alter in stature and color. And below, looking northwest to the Chupadera Mesa, Maryelizabeth always thought she was on the verge of seeing visions.

She had hinted to a BLM ranger how she felt, how the spot seemed to her to be alternately holy and eerie, and he told her he often felt the same way. He took her down the trail and showed her what he called the Little Man, but what he said others called the God of the Petroglyph.

"He's the watcher," the ranger said. "He's the holy man looking out for this site. I've come up here some nights, and I've seen these weird lights in the area, sort of bluish and green. The Little Man puts on quite the light show."

Something else the detectives didn't need to hear about. "Parker didn't leave a drawing at Three Rivers," said Maryelizabeth, "no picture of Alice Todd. He left Kathy Franklin's body."

There had only been a dirt road out to the petroglyph site back then. Gray had brought Kathy at night, had laid her down beneath a petroglyph of one of the goggle-eyed beings. The figure looked alert, even afraid, its hands raised in alarm, and its eyes wide open. Maryelizabeth wondered if that was how Kathy had reacted as Parker had put his hands around her neck. She coughed, not sure if it was out of reflex or sympathy, and remembered her audience.

"It's clear the recent homicides have somewhat paralleled the original murders. I don't have an opinion as to whether the San Diego homicides are copycat killings, ritualized murders based on the Shame MO, or whether the killer is staging these homicides for as yet unknown reasons. At this juncture, though, I think it's important that Parker's third murder be examined. Looking back might give you the opportunity to plan ahead."

Maryelizabeth stopped talking, ostensibly to take a sip of water, but in reality to gather her thoughts about Heidi Ehrlich, another name from her personal memorial wall.

"Heidi Ehrlich was a woman who liked to help others. She was a college student who chose to be a Good Samaritan to the wrong person. She met Gray Parker in an Albuquerque park late one afternoon. She heard him calling out, 'Anubis, Anubis.' Then he approached her and asked if she'd seen his dog. Heidi helped him look. When she ventured into some brush, he strangled her with a leash.

"For those who know their Egyptian mythology, Anubis was the jackal-headed god who escorted the dead to judgment. Perhaps that had some bearing on where Parker transported the body. He took Heidi to the Santuario de Chimayo, a famous shrine, sort of the Lourdes of New Mexico. For almost two hundred years people have been taking pinches of clay from a small well there, believing the clay to have healing properties. And during Easter weekend a few tons of local dirt are brought in and blessed by the priest. Miracle dirt, people call it. They take it home in plastic bags."

Maryelizabeth remembered the room at the church that was overflowing with crutches and braces and medical equipment, items left behind by all those who thought that God and the clay had cured them. She had visited on a warm summer day, had gone inside and marveled that there were so many lit candles in such a small shrine. Then, as now, there was no shortage of people looking for a miracle. Inside and outside were signs of heartfelt offerings: beads, makeshift crucifixes, photos of loved ones, cut-out pictures of the Baby Jesus, and drawings of the Virgin Mary.

"Breaking into the church would have been easy, Parker told me. He had considered laying Heidi beneath one of three large reredos, antique paintings that look much like orthodox icons, but instead he placed her upon a cement altar in the amphitheater behind the church. It's a beautiful spot, with a canopy of oak trees, and a stream running behind it.

"I've often wondered if Gray was asking God for the ultimate in miracles, bringing Heidi back to life. He found holy places for all of his New Mexico victims, shrines of nature and man. It was as if he were giving his victims a chance to recover. All they had to do was get up, or better yet, tap into the holiness around them and overcome their circumstances."

But the women disappointed him, Maryelizabeth thought, as women always had. They deserted him, or so Gray thought, and then compounded that treachery by not coming back to life.

She lifted up a copy of her book, covering her youthful picture with her hand. "I hope there might be something in this book that can help you in your current cases. For those who prefer to skip the reading and go right to the source, I'd be glad to answer any questions."

The bodies in the room shifted. Maryelizabeth looked around the table. The silence seemed condemning. I didn't reach them, she thought. I should have dug deeper, and said more. Then, to her relief, a hand was raised. She acknowledged the questioner with a nod.

"I was wondering, ma'am, if you had any theories on why Mrs. Sanders's body wasn't moved like the Franklin woman's."

The speaker, in his mid- to late twenties, was younger than everyone else in the room. Maryelizabeth decided she could forgive him for calling her "ma'am."

"I haven't had a chance to read the case files, Detective. Given that disclaimer, I'll still hazard a guess or two. There was a nine-one-

one call, I understand. It's possible the murderer was disturbed by the caller. It's also possible there wasn't an appropriate petroglyph site in San Diego. From what I know, the murderer appears to be picking and choosing how he emulates the original Shame homicides. It's possible he didn't feel compelled to move Mrs. Sanders's body, and also possible he didn't want to assume the risk of such a move."

Another sheriff's detective, the one lying on the sofa, spoke. Both his words and bearing were contentious: "Jennings and Sanders don't match up physically with Gleason and Franklin."

"No, they don't." Maryelizabeth's response was firm. "And I'm sure there are any number of other differences in the two sets of murders. But those might be clues in themselves."

The woman detective spoke, not to Maryelizabeth, but to the group: "If this guy's out to get college students, he's not going to have any shortage of targets. The county has over a dozen major colleges. Last figure I heard there were more than fifty thousand women enrolled in college courses in the San Diego area."

The number hung in the air, daunting them.

"We could run some decoys at popular college hangouts," said Lieutenant Borman, thinking aloud.

Nothing was said, but faces were openly skeptical. Borman read the expressions around him. "Lottery odds, I know," he said, "but we can't be passive in this. We also can't be unrealistic. Let's stake out the local shrines."

It was the next logical grisly step, but Borman looked none too pleased at having to concede another murder.

"We got any local shrines?" one detective asked.

"My wife would tell you Nordstrom's," said another.

Much-needed laughter swept through the room.

6

Sergeant Dean Eick was the case agent for the Lita Jennings homicide. Because the same murderer appeared to have killed Teresa Sanders, Eick had also been made the lead investigator for that homicide. As the case agent, he had responsibility for assembling what all the investigators referred to as "the Book."

Eick was short and stocky, and had the figure of a fire hydrant. When he was instructed by Lieutenant Borman to allow Maryelizabeth access to the Book, his suddenly red face made him look that much more like a fire hydrant. Allowing outsiders access to the Book just wasn't done. Sometimes consultants were brought in on cases, but they were only given access to that part of the investigation they might shed some light on.

"I'd also like the crime scene photos," said Maryelizabeth.

Just short of breathing fire, Eick said, "You would, would you?"

Maryelizabeth nodded.

Eick's foot pawed the ground, reminiscent of a bull wanting to charge. His complexion turned even more red, if that was possible.

"Follow me," he finally said.

The two of them walked over to a nearby office. A woman looked up from her computer keyboard. "Louise Coleman," Eick said as way of introduction, "Maryelizabeth Line."

The women nodded at one another.

"Ms. Line is going to be confined to your office, Louise. She will have access to the Book. She may take notes, but there is to be no photocopying and no photographing of material. The Book is to stay in your office the entire time, and when Ms. Line is finished with it I want it secured in Evidence. While in possession of the Book, Ms. Line is not allowed to leave the confines of this office unaccompanied. Is that understood?"

Louise didn't look intimidated. She gave the sergeant a wink and said, "You can count on me, Dean."

Eick pointed to a vacant chair and desk, then reluctantly relinquished the Book. With a disgusted shake of his head he left the office.

Louise craned her neck, and made sure the sergeant was out of hearing range, before saying, "Confined to my office. That's a first. Old Dino spent too many years in the marines. Word is that he even starches his boxers."

Short, stout, and gap-toothed, Louise was on the long side of middle age, but still quite certain she was irresistible to all the sheriff's deputies. In that she might have been right.

"Can I get you a cup of coffee?" asked Louise.

"No, thank you."

"So you're the one who writes about all this murder stuff?" she asked.

"Yes."

"Why?"

Maryelizabeth had to laugh. It was a question she had asked herself many times, but not one she could remember anyone else ever asking her.

"You want the short answer," Maryelizabeth asked, "or the long answer?"

"I'm a civil servant," Louise said. "Let's go with the long."

"I write because it helps me to understand. I write because it fills my own needs, as well as the needs of my readers."

Maryelizabeth paused for a moment, "I believe I write the books to try to bring a certain justice to the dead, to show that their lives were much more than the brutal act that ended them."

A bad cause requires many words, Maryelizabeth thought. Noble sentiments or not, her explanation had been windy. Louise apparently thought the same thing. She gave Maryelizabeth a sideways glance.

"What's the short answer?"

"I'm nosy," said Maryelizabeth.

"Thought so," Louise said.

Maryelizabeth repositioned the Book on her desk. It was at least three inches thick. Heavy reading, literally.

"If you need anything just ask," said Louise.

"Thank you."

Louise went back to her typing, while Maryelizabeth immersed herself in the Book. Lita Jennings had been a junior at the University of California at San Diego, the daughter of well-to-do parents, her father a surgeon, her mother an interior designer. The twenty-year-old had been strangled outside her Del Mar apartment, but her body had been driven to the Anza-Borrego Desert, some two hours away. Maryelizabeth traced the distance on a map. San Diego County was larger than some states. Del Mar was in the north county on the beach, while Borrego was inland. What the two areas had in common was no witnesses, and that forensics had come up empty at both locations.

In the beginning, Gray Parker had taken the same pains to remain invisible, Maryelizabeth remembered. She had been the first big break in the case. The eyewitness. When he was finally captured a year after their encounter, Maryelizabeth was still the only person who could definitively place Parker at a murder scene.

Water under the bridge, Maryelizabeth tried to tell herself. She needed to direct all her attention to the current cases instead of getting mired in the past. All indications were that Lita Jennings had been taken from behind, surprised on the doorstep of her apartment after coming home from a study group. She had been subdued with a sleeper hold.

Maryelizabeth knew the same hold had been used on Teresa Sanders, though she hadn't been surprised in the same way. Apparently she had opened her front door to the murderer. The house had an elaborate alarm system, one she had deactivated at 8:37 A.M. According to her husband, Teresa would have looked through the peephole before opening the door. Investigators wondered if she had been expecting someone, or if the murderer was someone she knew. It was also possible the murderer had been wearing a costume or disguise.

Maryelizabeth knew that manual strangulation was usually a personal crime. It wasn't the way in which a stranger usually killed, but the copycat aspects of the crimes didn't rule out these women being unknown to the killer.

No, Maryelizabeth decided. ***These women weren't random victims.***

She was certain of that, even without the evidence to back up her theory. You work with pitch, she thought, and it rubs off. She had studied the criminal mind until it had become second nature for her. Or maybe even first nature. Gray had warned her about that, yet had been all too willing to show her the way.

He had surprised Maryelizabeth by agreeing to be interviewed, especially as he'd allowed the media very little access to him. Maryelizabeth had written him to say she was writing a book, and would like to do a series of interviews with him, and he had replied,

> *"Come with your questions. I do not give lectures or a little charity. When I give I give myself."*
>
> *She hadn't known it at the time, but he'd been quoting from Whitman's* Song of Myself.
>
> *He was on Death Row at Union Correctional Institution in Raiford, Florida. Going there the first time frightened her; that was something that never changed. What Maryelizabeth remembered most about her first meeting with him was how she felt like a little girl wearing grown-up clothes.*
>
> *The guard closed the door of what everyone called "the lawyers' room" behind her. She hadn't thought she would be alone with him ever again. The officer had tried to reassure her that he'd be just outside, had pointed out where he would be watching. The interview room had glass on three sides to allow ample observation by both the security staff and personnel of the assistant superintendent of operations. The booth was soundproof so as to provide for lawyer-client confidentiality. She wondered if the prison officials, sitting at their nearby desks, would be able to hear her screams.*
>
> *Maryelizabeth felt claustrophobic. The room was small, too*

small. She could barely breathe, and was afraid to meet Shame's eyes. That was how the world knew him: Shame. He sat there calmly observing her. He was wearing the orange T-shirt that marked him as a Death Row inmate. Around his wrists were handcuffs. They seemed more of an inconvenience than something that could truly deter him from putting his hands around her neck.

"I have no desire to hurt you," he told her.

His words didn't reassure her. He didn't say, "I am not going to hurt you." She sat down anyway.

She felt around in her bag. All fingers. The prison administration had refused to let her bring in a tape recorder, citing security concerns. What she had was a pad and a pen, a felt pen. Her ballpoint pen had also been deemed a security risk.

If they were so worried about security, why hadn't they stationed a guard in the room? No, two guards.

Maryelizabeth looked at her watch. She was supposed to have an hour's session with him. She wasn't yet sure whether that was too much time, or not enough.

"'The clock indicates the moment—but what does eternity indicate?'" he asked.

"Excuse me?"

"Whitman," he said. "You started me reading him. I'm afraid that I now quote him to excess. I am not sure if that means I've run out of things to say myself, or whether he just says them better."

She sneaked a quick glance his way. He was pale, the result of being hidden away from the light of day. Death Row inmates, she knew, were allowed out in the exercise yard only twice a week for two hours at a time. She looked down at her sheet of questions. When she'd been preparing them, she had kept wondering, What do you ask the devil?

"Is that why you spared me? Because I quoted Whitman?"

He didn't answer. Instead he looked at her, and made her look at him. "Why are you here, Miss Line?"

"To interview you," she said.

"Then it seems only fair that I have the opportunity to interview the interviewer."

Maryelizabeth nodded.

"Do you really have any idea what you're doing?" he asked.

"I was a literature major. I wrote—"

"I'm not inquiring about your writing skills. I assume you can join a noun and a verb together and make a passable sentence. But I wonder if you know exactly what you're pursuing. You say you want to talk to me. What if the things I have to tell you change you forever? Are you prepared for that?"

She allowed herself a moment's hesitation, a moment's thought, before replying, "I'm prepared to listen to what you have to say."

"Is money your incentive for writing this book?"

"No. I've been offered money, yes, but I'd write the book for free. I've always wanted to be a writer."

"But is this the book you always wanted to write?"

"I suppose I won't know that until I finish it. What I do know is that I wouldn't have chosen to be one of its main characters."

He nodded, as if to say "fair enough," then asked, "What do you hope to get out of this?"

"Some understanding. Some coming to terms with what happened."

"'But now, ah now, to learn from crises of anguish, advancing, grappling with direst fate and recoiling not.'"

"More Whitman?"

"More reality, Miss Line. Are you willing to look into the abyss? To crawl to that edge and stare down? You thought you lost your innocence that first night we met, but that was just the initiation, the cakewalk."

They were seated five feet apart. His right hand was on the table. He moved it forward, just past the line that people always establish for each other: this is my territory, that's yours. It made her want to turn her head to the hack's window, want to make sure the guard was standing there watching, but she was afraid of finding him absent and having Shame make that same discovery.

"Right now your heart's pounding," he said, "and it feels as if there are these hands squeezing your chest and your face. You want to walk away, and go back to your old world. If I were you, I'd do that. Let someone else write your book. You can be one of those "as told to" authors. That's the safe way. In a couple of years you'll even be able to forget I came into your life. I'll just be a big, bad dream."

His hand had moved imperceptibly closer to her body, another inch over the line. She was afraid, but she also felt herself growing angry. He had made her feel powerless once, something she often reflected upon. She didn't want that to happen a second time.

"I'm going to write my own book."

"Stubborn," he said. "But then you've always been stubborn."

She wondered how he knew that about her, but was too stubborn to ask. He must have known that as well.

"Your name announces how stubborn you are. Most people would have shortened it. They'd be Mary, or Liz, or Beth, or even Elizabeth. Your whole life you've been facing up to people with axes who have tried to chop at your name, but you haven't let them. Would you like to tell me why?"

"Would you?"

Her reply seemed to amuse him, but only for a moment. He took up her challenge, his words coming fast and hard: "Because you've always been afraid you were common, and having a long name was your one defense against that. When you were a girl you used to imagine that the blood royal ran through your veins, that some mistake had been made, and that your real residence was a palace, not your mean little shanty-Irish Catholic home, and your lower-middle-class neighborhood."

Maryelizabeth's face was red, but she wasn't going to cry, no matter how hurting—and accurate—his words.

"You grew older, and you tried to fit in, but you never really did. As an adolescent, you rubbed your face a lot, hoping to erase your freckles. The habit remains, even though most of the freckles don't. You still rub at them, and you don't even know it."

She drew her incriminating hand away from her face, and tried to find a place to bury it.

"All good little literature majors read Heart of Darkness, *Miss Line. 'The horror, the horror,' Mistah Kurtz said. If you're going to write about me, you're going to have to face up to what Kurtz saw, and what ultimately killed him. Do you really want that for yourself?"*

Her jaw didn't want to move, nor her mouth open, but somehow the words came out. "I do," she said.

Even to her own ears, it sounded as if she were taking wedding vows.

* * *

Maryelizabeth found herself shaking. Maybe I should hire a goddamn priest, she thought, and have him do an exorcism. Her past kept popping out at her like some demonic jack-in-the-box. She turned her head quickly, and saw that Louise hadn't noticed her shakes. The computer screen had her full attention. Maryelizabeth returned to examining the Book, did her best to study it with single-minded purpose. Every report done by everyone and anyone was in the Book, from the first sheriff's deputy on the scene to the medical examiner's report.

Immersed in her scrutiny, she didn't expect a packet to fall on her desk. She jumped. That seemed to give Sergeant Eick some satisfaction.

"The photos are not to leave this room. Is that understood?"

"Yes."

"When she's done with them, Louise, I'll need you to take possession of them and walk them back to Evidence."

"Aye, aye, Sergeant," said Louise.

As Eick walked out of the room the two women's eyes met—they could barely refrain from laughing.

Maryelizabeth put the photos aside and returned to the Book. She saved the body for last. She didn't like her impressions of the investigation sullied.

She reviewed the transcriptions, and sketches, and the breakdown of who had been responsible for what in the investigation. There were aerial photographs to examine, and field reports she had to work her way through. Most of what was in the Book was a study in futility. The investigation had been methodical and thorough, but for all that, they had very little to go on.

When she finally finished with the paperwork, all that remained was for her to look at the photos. Maryelizabeth hated to look at such pictures, and yet needed to see them for what they had to say. "Scene of the scream" was how one homicide detective had referred to crime scene photos.

That phrase had stayed with her over the years. She could never pick up the photos without thinking about that, and how true it was. Over the years she'd seen so many pictures. She wished she could forget them, but couldn't. They even surfaced in her sleep. She had this recurring nightmare where she'd find herself staring at crime scene photos only to realize that she herself was the victim.

Though she often woke up screaming, she still could not stop herself from going on to the next case.

Maryelizabeth turned over the first photo and looked at the picture. It was a close-up of Lita Jennings's face. Though she was dead, her green eyes were still open. Doll eyes. There had been a time when murderers hadn't wanted their victims to look upon them as they died, believing that what a dying person last saw became imprinted on the eyeball.

In essence, Maryelizabeth wanted to fulfill that superstition, to become that eyeball and see beyond death.

She turned more pictures over, moved them around like a tarot reader. There were close-ups of the bruised neck, of Lita's discolored skin. Of her bluish tongue. Of her propped legs. Of the red *A*, almost indistinguishable in her brown pubic patch. Of her twisted mouth.

Still screaming.

He had taught her to how to contemplate such scenes without looking away, without even blinking. Gray Parker, mentor.

Not passionate.

The impression, no, the certainty, overwhelmed her.

More purpose than compulsion.

First the impressions came, then she tried to apply the logic. A choke hold had killed Lita. The murder appeared to be methodical, without rage.

Scripted. Rehearsed.

The evil hadn't been random. This wasn't a chance death. And it wasn't the work of a serial killer, or even a copycat killer. The revelation surprised Maryelizabeth.

But he still enjoyed it.

The murderer had taken his pleasure in the planning, in Lita's execution. He was sure, prideful. She sensed that in the way he had posed her.

Maryelizabeth suddenly gasped, but not for air. Sometimes she looked at pictures, or visited crime scenes, and felt the evil as if it was still there. But this was different. This time wasn't like the others. She wasn't looking at the evil; it was as if it was looking at her.

Staring right at her.

Maryelizabeth put the pictures back into the folder. She'd seen more than enough. And tomorrow she'd probably get the chance to study Teresa Sanders's pictures. And there would be others, of that she was certain.

Maryelizabeth looked at her watch. A little after six. What it was on the eternity scale she couldn't be sure.

The FBI might describe her scrutiny as a primitive form of profiling, but when Gray Parker had taught her to look at evil, and let it tell her its story, the science of profiling hadn't existed. Maybe on some level she was doing the same job as one of the Feeb's Investigative Support Unit shrinks, but she resisted the comparison. The FBI was famous for checking off boxes and taking in data. She just felt. The bureau had learned its profiling trade from conducting hundreds of interviews with serial killers and rapists. Maryelizabeth hadn't interviewed nearly as many killers, but believed she had the dubious distinction of having learned from the best.

Maryelizabeth stood up and stretched. "I guess I'm finished for the day."

"Wish I could say the same." Louise leaned back in her chair. The women had said remarkably little to one another for having shared an office for so many hours.

"Pull up a chair," said Louise. "Take mine if you want, especially if you're a good typist."

Maryelizabeth made a cross of her index fingers as if warding off a vampire, and both of them laughed. "So what are you working on?"

"A Lieutenant Borman project. Bore-man. The man does live up to his name."

Louise gestured disparagingly at the paperwork. Maryelizabeth reached for the nearest pile, and came away with a stack of bills and invoices.

"The lieutenant wants me to make a list of service people that might have been at the Sanderses' during the last two months. It's not going to be easy. Their house was entertainment central. They always had florists, caterers, wait staff, and party rental people going in and out. And talk about upkeep. They had a regular army working there, what with gardeners, painters, pool service, and contractors."

People with uniforms, Maryelizabeth thought. Mrs. Sanders

might have easily opened her door to someone with a uniform.

"Thought we might have had something earlier," Louise said. "One of the Sanderses' neighbors, Ruby Davidson, thought she saw a gardener's truck parked in their driveway yesterday morning. Problem is, Ruby's eighty-two years old, and she's the first to tell you that she doesn't remember like she used to. Turns out the landscaping service didn't come yesterday, but the *day before yesterday.*"

Maryelizabeth made sympathetic clucking noises while continuing to flip through the bills. Louise was right, it did seem as if an army had been employed by the Sanderses. And it would take an army of detectives ultimately to interview everyone. In the pile she had grabbed were bills for tack and feed, cable, tree service, security . . .

The thought suddenly came to her: what if Ruby Davidson wasn't wrong? What if a vehicle had been parked in the driveway that looked like a gardener's truck? Perhaps a tree service vehicle. That might even explain the 911 call. Some tree trimmer could have seen something, but been too panicked to become involved.

Maryelizabeth pulled the invoice. Mister Tree had removed two eucalyptus trees on March 16, less than two months earlier. Teresa Sanders had paid by check, and a receipt had been given to her. Maryelizabeth examined that receipt. If the signature hadn't been so textbook neat she wouldn't have noticed the name.

Caleb Parker.

The name jumped out at her. Before she had always thought that expression a sorry cliché, but that's how it felt, a name standing out amid everything around it. Impossible, she thought. She was jumping to conclusions. Parker was a common surname.

But she knew Gray Parker had fathered a son. The boy had been named after him. Maryelizabeth had seen him only a few times. She remembered the boy's pinched, sad face.

And she remembered something else. To differentiate between the two Grays, the mother had sometimes called her boy by his middle name.

She'd called him Cal, or Callie. And sometimes, especially when she was upset, or she wanted to get his attention, she'd called him Caleb.

Maryelizabeth rang the doorbell.

She knew this was crazy, but she had to see for herself, had to know whether this man was Gray Parker's son.

Wild-goose chase, Maryelizabeth told herself. Waste of time. Caleb had to be in his middle thirties. Someone that age didn't suddenly become a serial murderer. They almost always started killing at a much younger age.

But still, palmed in her right hand, was a pepper-spray canister. And in her purse she had her gun.

The door opened. Involuntarily she whispered, "My God." There was no question. Caleb Parker had his father's dark hair, and blue eyes, and too handsome features. This man was the picture of Gray Parker. Looking at him brought on a feeling of vertigo.

"Are you all right?" Caleb asked.

Without taking her eyes off his face, she managed to nod. Caleb was sure he had never seen this woman before, but she stared at him as if he was familiar to her, as if she knew him.

"May I help you?" Caleb asked.

The woman didn't answer immediately. She was well dressed, her tailored clothing fitting her tall, thin frame nicely. She had highlighted red hair, wide blue eyes, and skin translucent enough to reveal blue veins. Her age was difficult to gauge. She was blessed with the sort of timeless good looks that left him wondering whether she was closer to thirty-five or fifty.

"I came to ask a question," she said, "but I don't need to ask it now."

Her scrutiny unnerved Caleb. This was the start of it, he knew. She wasn't the police, but he had this feeling she was something just as bad. He wanted to slam the door on her, but didn't dare. The dining room was just off the kitchen, within sight of the front door, and though his children were paying no attention to the visitor, Caleb saw Anna throw him a questioning glance. He stepped out onto the porch and closed the door behind him. Though they stood in the semi-darkness, Caleb kept his eyes averted from the visitor's, knowing that she was still staring at him. He didn't ask her what she wanted. She would tell him in her own time, tell him things he didn't want to hear.

"Is that your family?" she asked.

Still looking away from her, he nodded.

"My name is Maryelizabeth Line," she said.

It was almost enough to make him look at her. He knew who she was. It gave him a momentary surge of anger. This woman had done enough damage to his life. How dare she just appear on his doorstep?

"I have nothing to say to you," he said.

"I take it by your refusal that you're familiar with my writing."

He finally looked at her. "I'm aware of your *reputation,*" he said, "not your writing. I've never read *any* of your books."

"You sound pleased about that."

"It's just the way things are."

"Your father always used that phrase."

Caleb's face tightened up, and his hands clenched together in fists. Maryelizabeth took an involuntary step backward, and brought her right hand up, ready to spray him. But he wasn't advancing on her, and he didn't notice her defensive posture.

His head was lowered, his arms held stiffly at his sides. He looked like an embarrassed little boy. "I am not my father," Caleb whispered.

The door opened, and light penetrated to the front porch. "Cal?" asked Anna.

"It's all right," he said. "Ms. Line came over to discuss a business matter."

Anna was a handsome woman, tall with dark brown hair and large hazel eyes, but there was a severity to her. She offered a rigid beauty with her pursed lips and narrowed eyes and set chin. She looked from Caleb to the stranger, and then back to her husband again. Something was wrong, Anna knew; something had been bothering Caleb. But as usual, he hadn't been willing to talk about it.

"Your dinner's getting cold," she said.

"I'll be right in," he said.

The two women regarded each other. Anna's glance asked, Are you the reason my husband's been so upset? What she read in Maryelizabeth's face didn't reassure her. Anna pointedly turned on the porch light before closing the door behind her.

"Are you—" started Maryelizabeth.

Caleb interrupted her. "Don't ask me any questions," he said. "Not here. Not now."

"Where and when, then?"

"I walk the dog after dinner. You can meet me down the street."

It was getting darker by the minute. There were rural spots in the neighborhood, canyons good for dog walking, but places Maryelizabeth didn't want to be with this man. There would be nothing to stop him from taking the leash off the dog and turning it on her. She had seen firsthand what his father could do with a pair of panty hose.

Maryelizabeth suppressed her shudder. "Alternate plan," she said. "Let's meet at a coffee house."

"I remember now," he said, finally looking at her.

"Remember what?"

"People looking at me like that—that look."

"I don't know what you're talking about."

"Your scared look. But at least you're better than some people."

"Which people?"

"The ones with the freak show stare. The kind who looked at me like something at the zoo."

Maryelizabeth stood silently until he said, "Heavenly Café. It's a few miles west of here on the beach. There will be enough people around for you to feel safe. I'll be there in half an hour or so."

Her second cup of coffee was long cold, and the crowd at Heavenly Café had thinned. The help was pointedly putting up umbrellas and tidying the patio, unmistakable signs that the welcome mat was being pulled. It was after nine o'clock, a time when most people weren't looking for a caffeine fix. Only one other outdoor table was still occupied, and the couple sitting there looked ready to depart. Two hours had passed since Caleb Parker had promised to meet her in "half an hour or so."

I probably shouldn't have confronted him, Maryelizabeth thought. Maybe I spooked him, sent him running. Or maybe he decided to talk with a lawyer instead of me. She hoped that she hadn't jeopardized the investigation. As she waited, Maryelizabeth wondered if Caleb knew how much he resembled his father. Seeing him had shocked her, had been like seeing a ghost. She also wondered if the resemblance was only skin deep.

That lingering thought made her look around. She tried to make her head movements appear casual and unconcerned, but she took notice of every dark corner. Gray Parker had often scouted out his victims, had sometimes watched them for days before attacking them. He had described his spying as a form of "intimacy." She was relieved when her surveillance revealed no lurking figures.

Next door to the café was a Mexican restaurant with enough people still dining to make Maryelizabeth feel as if she wasn't alone. Their laughter kept reaching out to her. She watched as diners happily sipped on their colorful margaritas. Her vantage point offered her a good spot to take in the southern California ambience. The Pacific Ocean was close enough to be seen and heard, and the night was balmy, with a gentle ocean breeze.

A voice interrupted her reverie, startled her: "Last chance for java."

The last call for caffeine was made by what she guessed was a full-time surfer and part-time help. The young man's long, brown hair had sun-streaked strands of gold running through it. The way he walked and talked and breathed was an endorsement of insouciance. Probably his only worry in the world was whether the waves would be breaking in the morning.

"I'll pass."

The young man appeared happy with her choice, and Maryelizabeth relinquished her cup to him. She reached for her purse and pulled out her car keys. Out of habit, she positioned her longest key between her index and middle finger and made a fist. She stood up, and then her reactions took over. Shame was there. She'd had too many nightmares not to react to him, too many evenings of awakening in a soaked nightgown thinking about him. Her hand shot up toward his face, the key brandished like a knife.

"Don't," he said.

Don't scream, she remembered.

Maryelizabeth was slow to lower her arm. To let go of her memories. "You're late," she said.

He nodded.

No explanation, she noticed. She wondered if he had purposely waited for the café to close before showing up.

"If you still want to talk," he said, "there's a bar nearby."

Probably a dark bar, she thought. And people who were drinking would be unreliable witnesses.

"I don't like bars," she said. "And I'd prefer talking where it's well lit and there's lots of foot traffic."

Caleb didn't answer immediately. It wasn't clear whether he was unhappy with her alternative, or just trying to think of the right spot. "D.G.'s," he finally said, his hand pointing the direction. "It's a doughnut shop just down the street."

She nodded, her eyes never leaving him. "Wait here," she said, "until I get in my car."

Maryelizabeth walked past him, went down the steps, then paused at the street. She looked both ways, then looked behind her to make sure Caleb was still standing there, before hurrying across the street to her car.

She drove over to a small strip mall and slowly circled the parking lot. The doughnut shop met her requirements. It had ample lighting and a glassed expanse that allowed good visibility for looking both in and out. On one side of the doughnut shop was a restaurant, and on the other side a bar. Across the street was an upscale pool hall. She watched young bodies bending over the tables and lining up their shots.

The aroma coming out of D.G.'s reminded Maryelizabeth how hungry she was. The array of sweets displayed behind the counter didn't do anything to abate her hunger. A young woman, vivacious even with a hairnet, smock, and smudge of flour on one of her red cheeks, helped Maryelizabeth decide between a buttermilk bar and a raised glaze with chocolate frosting.

"When in doubt," she said, "get both!"

A young man was also working behind the counter. "Brandy knows from experience," he said, "that one doughnut just isn't enough."

"Guilty as charged," Brandy said with a laugh.

"And here I always heard that people who worked with sweets got sick of eating them," Maryelizabeth said.

"I wish," said Brandy, laughing.

Caleb entered the shop as Maryelizabeth was paying. He walked by her, and chose to sit at the table farthest from the counter. It wouldn't have been Maryelizabeth's choice, but it still appeared safe enough. She joined him at the table, offered him one of her doughnuts, but he declined. Maryelizabeth looked at him, saw the image of his father, and had to turn away. She looked at him a second time, but couldn't hold her glance. Caleb reacted to her chagrin, kept having to confront his own embarrassment about who he was, and found himself looking away as well.

With averted glance, he said, "I almost didn't come tonight."

Maryelizabeth stared at the bridge of his nose, an old trick that made it seem as if she was maintaining eye contact. "I'm glad you did."

Head lowered, Caleb massaged his temples with his thumbs. "How'd you find me?"

Maryelizabeth carefully considered what to tell him. "I was going through the Sanderses' receipts and saw your name."

"That's it?"

"That's it."

"Have the police connected me with—him—yet?"

Why did he act as if he was more concerned about the police linking him with his father, than with the murder of Teresa Sanders? Maryelizabeth wasn't sure how to answer his question. An honest response had its potential dangers, but to lie might stop him from talking.

"No."

"You haven't told them?"

"No."

"Why?"

"Because I wasn't sure until I saw you."

"But you plan to tell them?"

"Yes."

He shook his head and moved his hands. Several times he opened his mouth to speak, and each time bit back words until he finally said, "I didn't do it."

"What?"

"Murder Mrs. Sanders. I mean my doing that wouldn't make any sense, would it?"

"How do you mean it wouldn't make any sense?"

He again struggled for words, before giving up and saying, "I'm not comfortable talking about any of this."

"It's not something you can remain silent about."

"I suppose you have a recorder going."

"No."

"But you're making your mental notes for another book, aren't you?"

"That remains to be seen."

"I'm just supposed to trust you, is that it? What I say remains between you, and me, and a million of your readers."

"You're presuming much," she said.

"And so are you. Because of my father, you've condemned me."

"No. That's not so. But I certainly have questions."

"You've come to the wrong person, then."

"What do you mean?"

"I've never had any answers."

"Tell me about Mrs. Sanders."

"I wouldn't have murdered her, especially not that way. I run from trouble. That's why I don't want to talk to you, or anyone, about my father. I've spent my life trying to forget my past."

Especially not that way. The words echoed in Maryelizabeth's head. With her left hand she raised one of the doughnuts to her mouth, while her hidden right hand delved into her designer purse. Her handbag was special not because it had some French name on it, but because it had a secret compartment for a gun. She pulled out her Lady Smith & Wesson, but kept it out of sight under the table.

"I hope forgetting your past doesn't include forgetting yesterday morning," she said.

"No. But I wish it did."

Maryelizabeth's eyes were centered on him. So was her gun, even though he didn't know it. *Especially not that way.* How did he know about the Shame MO?

"Tell me about it."

"I got this call a little after eight. A man identified himself as Mr. Sanders. He said that his wife was suffering terribly, that an acacia tree was wreaking havoc on her allergies. He was very persuasive about getting me to come over to cut down that tree. I promised to make it out there within the hour. He told me Mrs. Sanders would be waiting for me, waiting, he said, with *bated breath.*

"Cisco and Bart—that's my crew—weren't expecting me that morning anyway. I was supposed to be doing bids on half a dozen jobs. I figured I could cut down the acacia tree quickly, and then get to the bids. I arrived at the Sanderses' house at about nine-fifteen. When I walked up to the front door I noticed it was slightly open. I rang the doorbell, but no one answered. Then I walked around to the back. I assumed Mrs. Sanders might be there. When I didn't see her, I went back to the front door and rang the bell again. Then I knocked at the door, which pushed it open some. I went inside to yell that I was there, and that's when I saw her."

Maryelizabeth continued to stare at Caleb. She kept trying to read something in his expression. Anything.

"Will Mr. Sanders be able to confirm that he called you yesterday morning?"

Caleb shook his head. "No."

"I thought you said . . ."

His hand made a cutting motion, a movement that caused Maryelizabeth's trigger finger to involuntarily tighten. "I heard Mr. Sanders interviewed last night on the eleven o'clock news," Caleb said. "He definitely wasn't the man who called me."

"How can you be so sure?"

"I'm good with voices. Once I hear a voice it stays in my head."

"You think the murderer called you up?"

"I don't know what else to think."

Another SODDI defense, Maryelizabeth thought. Some Other Dude Did It. The Bogeyman again. "Do you have any enemies?" she asked.

"No," Caleb said, a tinge of regret in his voice. "No one's ever had strong enough feelings about me to hate me."

"Who knows your history?"

"No one."

"Your wife—"

He interrupted: "She doesn't know."

"Old friends?"

"I don't have any."

"What about relatives?"

"They stopped knowing me when my father was arrested. They don't even know I'm alive."

"And you've never stumbled upon someone from your past?"

"No. I buried my past."

"You didn't change your name."

"I thought I did. I lost my first name, his first name, and went by my middle name." He met her eyes for a moment, suddenly angry. "Besides, to the world my father was never Gray Parker. He was, and is, Shame. You, and others like you, gave him that name. It was like he was a rock star or something. No one remembers what he was called before."

Maryelizabeth didn't respond to his bitterness. "If, as you say, you have no enemies, and no one knows about your past, how do you explain someone setting you up for Teresa Sanders's murder?"

She made a point of not mentioning Lita Jennings.

"I keep hoping it's an incredible coincidence," Caleb said, "keep hoping that it will just go away."

"The longer you indulge in your wishful thinking the more guilty you look."

He nodded. Caleb knew what she said was true, but that didn't make him any more ready to act on it.

"You know what it's like to have a terrible secret?" he asked. "A secret you're not even comfortable thinking about? A secret that's as bad as a cancer?"

Yes, she did. She knew exactly. But she wasn't about to tell him that. "Maybe it's that bad because you've kept it secret."

"There's a simple reason for that," he said. "Living a lie is far preferable to living the truth."

"You don't know that."

"Yes, I do."

"You need to think about clearing your name."

"Clearing my name? My real name is Gray Parker, Ms. Line."

"You should get a lawyer. I can recommend several excellent ones."

"Tomorrow," he said.

Maryelizabeth nodded. She had the feeling Caleb had overused that word his entire life. Now tomorrow was finally about to come.

8

As Maryelizabeth stood to leave, Caleb didn't raise his head to meet her eyes, but instead spoke to the table: "Don't worry, I'll stay put for a few minutes." She didn't, Caleb noticed, tell him that wasn't necessary.

During the hour they had sat together Caleb had repeatedly told the writer that most of his early life was "just a blank." That was a lie, and he was sure Maryelizabeth knew it, but she never called him on it. Only once did he almost open up to her. She had forced him to make eye contact, had stared at him intently and asked if he remembered the night they had met. Caleb told her he didn't, but he did. They had been introduced in a holding cell at Florida State Prison just a few hours before his father was to be executed. He had been coming, and she'd been going, and his goddamn father had been holding court. His father had been transferred to the Starke prison the week before when the governor had signed his death watch. That's where the electric chair was. The chair was antique, a three-legged oak model built by inmates in 1923. It waited for him.

The lights in D.G.'s flickered. The coastal breeze had picked up. Two of the fluorescent lights faded out, and then began the laborious process of coming back to life, making sounds like insects being fried by bug lights. The flickering lights took Caleb back to his last meeting with his father. There were so many things to hate his father for, but in the end, he had tainted even that pleasure. Damn you for that, Caleb thought. Damn you for everything.

* * *

"Your father wants to see you," his mother told him. She was already packing his bags.

"I don't want to see him."

"Shut your mouth. This might be the last time you'll ever talk with him."

"Good."

His mama slapped him across the face. Then she started crying. That made Caleb feel worse than the slap.

The bus trip from Texas to Florida seemed to go on forever. His mama was used to it by then. She'd been to Florida for both of the trials, had left Caleb to look after himself for up to a week at a time. None of their kin was willing to take him in. He'd never told her how their own home had become a prison to him, how packs of boys had come around yelling taunts and throwing things. He hadn't told her lots of things.

It had been almost two years since he'd last seen his father. They brought Caleb to a holding room where a man stood up that he didn't even know.

"Hello, son," he said.

His father looked so different. He'd always been so handsome and cool, but now his head was shaven and his eyes were wide and agitated. He kept looking up at the fluorescent lights, kept flinching whenever they flickered and cracked. He stared at them as if he was following the flow of electricity. Then, he finally remembered his son was in the room with him waiting. They were both waiting.

"They're juicing up Old Sparky again," his father announced. "They've been playing with Sparky all week. Getting him ready for the big show. If you listen real close you can even hear him humming."

Caleb hadn't known what he was supposed to be listening for, but he tried his best to hear something. He tilted his head to the right, and then to the left, but he couldn't make out any humming.

"Hear it?" his father asked. "Hear it?"

To please him, Caleb nodded.

Caleb kept sneaking glances at this stranger, at his father. What struck Caleb most was the lack of barriers between them. Even before his father's imprisonment there had always been a distance between them that seemed unbreachable. But not now. In the holding room there wasn't anything separating them. Their being so close scared Caleb, even though his father was shackled in manacles and chains, and there were two guards in the room. It wasn't that Caleb was afraid physically, but more that he wasn't comfortable with their unexpected intimacy.

The condemned man noticed his son staring at his shackles. He shook the chains. "Like my bracelets?" he asked with one of his old smiles.

Prison hadn't changed his father's large, snow-white teeth. Nor had it taken the seductive wattage out of his smile. His light blue eyes were almost opaque, as if you could take an eraser and with a few brushes wipe away the color. His mama said they looked alike. Caleb didn't want to believe that.

"Almost fifteen, aren't you?"

Caleb nodded.

"We don't have much time to talk, son. You're my last-wish department. I figured there were some things between us we needed to discuss."

His father kept rubbing his newly shaved head. He was nervous, acting much like an uncomfortable father faced with telling his son the facts of life. Or death.

"We all have regrets, son. We all do things we wish we hadn't. Sometimes that's all it seems like life is, one regret after another."

He tried to smile for Caleb again, but gave it up. "You can't always look back. It's not healthy. You have to look ahead. You understand what I'm getting at?"

Ever so slightly, Caleb nodded.

"I haven't been much of a father," he said. "I know you felt shortchanged."

Caleb didn't respond. Since his father's arrest he had learned to be guarded, to keep his expression blank and give little or nothing away. But that didn't mean he wasn't listening.

"Lots of things about my life I wish I could change. I have a list of regrets, but even at your young age I suspect you've done things you wish you hadn't."

They looked at each other, and his father found something to nod at once more.

"They say a leopard can't change his spots. I've always had lots of spots, Gray. I couldn't change them, though Lord knows I tried."

He knew his father wanted him to talk, but Caleb couldn't bring himself to say anything. He was still afraid.

"I wish I could leave you something besides regrets, son. I wish I could tell you everything's going to be all right, but I don't want to give you any false hopes. Someday you might have a son, and you might have better things to tell him than I've had to tell you. My daddy never told me much either. About the only thing he ever impressed upon me was that when I had a first-born boy it was my obligation to name him Gray.

"You're a son of the South, boy. That's how you got your name. That's how I got it. That's how your granddad got it, and your great-granddad. I told you about your great-great-granddad Caleb. That's where you got your middle name. Caleb hated Yankees through and through. He killed plenty in the War Between the States, but that was the kind of killing that makes a man a hero. They say ol' Caleb came home with half an arm and one leg, but that didn't stop him from having a passel of kids. He named his oldest boy Gray. We all did. The Gray and the Blue, you understand?

"Your name's the family legacy, son, such as it is."

The lights overhead started flickering again. "Old goddamn Sparky," his father whispered.

The large guard, the one called Sarge, looked at his watch and announced, "Time's up," but there was some leeway built into his pronouncement.

His father stopped noticing the lights. "There are so many things I wanted to tell you, Gray," he said, "so many things I wanted to explain. But we don't need to explain anything to one another. What happened previously is past, you understand? Water under the bridge. It doesn't do any good to get all caught up with things we should have done, and things we shouldn't have done. You taking any of this in?"

Caleb offered a nod.

"You're going to be the man in the family now," he said. "You're going to have to look after your mama."

His father shook his head and sighed. "I've been a bad father, but I was a worse husband. I wasn't home much, and when I was I always managed to set your mama to crying. But that's nothing you don't already know."

"Time's up, inmate," Sarge said.

Sarge's second pronouncement was made with a little more conviction, but his father never looked at him or acknowledged his words in any way. Instead, he stared off into the distance as if he could see through the prison walls. Sighing, he turned back to Caleb, then shook his head.

"It won't be easy for you," he said.

His father's sad tone struck Caleb much more than the words. Caleb already knew it wouldn't be easy.

"Crazy world, son. You look for answers, and sometimes there just aren't any. Don't beat yourself up trying to find them. There are enough others out there that'll be more than willing to do the beating on you, so there's no reason to do it to yourself. Choose your battles, boy. And make sure you're not fighting yourself. That's not a battle you can win."

His father looked embarrassed, as if he wasn't used to giving advice, or not worthy of offering it. But Caleb could see his need to talk was greater than his reluctance to counsel.

"When you wake up tomorrow, Gray, I want you to look at it like your life has just begun. Don't take my baggage with you. Can you do that?"

Caleb wasn't sure how to answer that. Finally, he just nodded.

"For your sake," his father whispered, "I wish it were as easy as all that."

"Time's up, inmate," Sarge announced. He put enough emphasis in his voice to show that he meant business this time.

His father motioned for just a little more time, his shackled hands held out like those of a supplicant. With his eyes he silently implored the guard, and in them Caleb saw a desperation he had never seen before.

"Another minute," Sarge said. His tone made it clear he would begrudge every one of those sixty seconds.

With the extra moments, Gray Parker Sr. tried to figure out what to say to his son for the last time.

"I'm sorry," he finally said. "You never disappointed me, son. Never."

His declaration surprised Caleb. Tears pooled in his eyes. He felt like a fish, with his mouth opening, and closing, then opening again.

"Shhh," his father told him. "There's no need."

"Time," Sarge said.

His father's last words to him were, "Be a good boy."

Caleb watched his father being taken away. Four hours later, on February 8, 1977, at 12:53 A.M., the State of Florida executed him.

9

Locking the door behind them, they heard a man shouting, "Pepper, come here, Pepper."

They could see him standing on the outskirts of the parking lot, leash in hand, whistling for his wayward dog.

Brandy and Joe said their good nights at the door. Joe's friends had a keg, and he was hoping they hadn't finished off all of the beer. He loped over to his van.

"Pepper. Come on, Pepper."

The parking lot was quiet, with only a few cars in the lot. Cardiff by the Sea was a quiet beach community that lived up to its tranquil name, closing down early on weeknights.

"Pe-Pe-Pepper." The man's tone was equal parts chastising and affectionate. Apparently he had spotted his wayward dog.

Brandy continued walking toward her car. Joe's van started up. He pulled away quickly, spurred on by the thought of suds.

"Come on out from under there, Pepper. Come on, boy."

The man was walking in the same direction as Brandy. He was hunched over, peering so as to be able to see under the car.

"Bad dog," he said. "Come here right now."

"He obeys about as well as my boyfriend," Brandy said, laughing.

"Is that your car?" the man asked.

"Yes," said Brandy.

"I'm afraid Pepper's taken refuge under it. I think he's eating some trash that he knows I wouldn't approve of. Give that dog a choice between a T-bone steak and two-day-old garbage, and he'll take the garbage every time."

He closed the distance between them.

"You're describing my boyfriend again," Brandy said, laughing some more.

The man yelled out, with some impatience, "Get out of there, Pepper."

Brandy bent down, tried to catch a glimpse of the dog. "I can't see him."

"He's hunkered down near your left front tire, chewing on something. Probably something I don't want to know. He's hard to make out, because he lives up to his name. Pepper. He's dark, very dark. I suppose you're going to tell me like your boyfriend."

Brandy laughed, but just a little. She tried to get a better glimpse of the man's face, but the way he kept bending over and moving, it was hard to see.

"Weren't you in tonight?" she asked.

"Where?"

Her head tilted back to the doughnut shop. "D.G.'s."

"Not me."

He turned his head toward her for a moment, before looking back to his dog. "You look familiar as well. I think I've seen you in class."

"You go to MiraCosta College?" she asked.

He didn't answer her question, instead seemed intent on getting his dog. He got down on his knees and stuck his head under her front bumper.

"Bad dog, Pepper," she heard him say, his voice muffled.

Brandy opened her car door, and listened as the man carried on a dialogue with his dog under her car.

"What have you got there, Pepper? Give me that. Give."

What did the dog have, she wondered?

"My God," the man said.

"What?"

"I'm going to be sick."

"What is it?" Brandy asked, hurrying to the front of her car.

The man eased his way from under her car. He was shaking his head and breathing hard.

"Should I call the police?" Brandy asked.

The man nodded.

"What should I tell them?"

"Tell them there's a dead woman under your car."

"What?"

As her face showed its horror, he threw the leash around her neck, twisted the loose ends in opposite directions, and pulled tight.

10

"Another Coke, Cal?" asked the taller of the two sheriff's homicide investigators, Detective Holt.

"Yes," Caleb said. "Please."

Sheriff's Homicide Detective Alvarez stood up. "I'll get it," he said, but before fetching the soft drink he made the observation, "Sweating a lot, aren't you, Cal?"

Alvarez didn't wait for an answer, and Caleb didn't offer one. Though the two detectives didn't look anything alike, Caleb thought they could have been brothers. Holt was fair complexioned, with light, thinning brown hair, while Alvarez was Hispanic with a bushy head of black, curly hair. They both had mustaches, but that wasn't what made them alike. It was their eyes. They looked at him with the same intensity, Holt with his blue eyes, and Alvarez with his brown.

"I'm beginning to think I should have a lawyer," Caleb said.

"That's certainly your right, Cal," said Holt, "but it seems to me when your writer friend talked with the sheriff she was adamant about our trying to keep this talk out of the news. The less people we bring in, the less will know what's going on. It'll be hard to maintain your anonymity, and keep your relationship with your father out of the news, if you bring in a bunch of outsiders."

The threat was veiled, but implicit. "You still okay with our talking, Cal?"

"I suppose."

"Is that a yes or a no, Caleb?"

"Yes."

But it wasn't. The interview hadn't been what he expected. At the best of times law enforcement frightened him. Now he was doubly scared. Caleb felt as if he had been ambushed. It was clear the Sheriff's Office had worked all morning and early afternoon finding out all that they could about him. They knew things, personal things. He hadn't expected that. Somehow he had thought he could just explain to them. He wished he'd taken Maryelizabeth's advice about bringing a lawyer.

The two detectives had taken turns asking him questions in the interview room. That had made Caleb feel trapped and claustrophobic. The interview room had a whiteboard that both of the detectives wrote on. Sometimes they'd take one of Caleb's words, or a phrase he used, and write it up on the board as if it had special significance. The walls of the interview room were lined with blue carpeting, which not only absorbed the noise, but gave the room the feel of a padded cell. Caleb suspected he was being filmed, though there was no camera visible.

Lita Jennings's name didn't surface until well into the third hour of questioning. Both the detectives had been upbeat and friendly the entire time, prefacing any tough questions with apologies, with phrases like, "Just to clarify matters," and, "I'm having a little trouble understanding."

Holt was the one who had said her name first. He was a nodder, always nodding at whatever Caleb had to say. "Do you watch the news, Cal? Or read the newspaper?"

He waited for Caleb to nod, then gave him a triple return on that investment.

"It's enough to make you sick. Did you hear about that college girl who died about a month ago? She had her whole life ahead of her. She was pretty, too. What was her name?"

Caleb didn't offer it. His silence lost him a nod.

"Lita something or other," said Holt, then pretended suddenly to remember. "Lita Jennings. It probably sounds like a stupid question, but you wouldn't happen to know her, would you, Cal?"

Caleb opened his mouth. His hands tried to orchestrate his words, but there was a lot more hand movements than there were words. "My wife's a nurse. . . ."

Holt was nodding nonstop, offering, "Uh-huh," with every one of Caleb's halting words.

"She knew her. The girl's father is a doctor." Caleb's hands kept trying to explain, trying to show the connection. "My wife's at Scripps, and that's the hospital her father works out of."

"Lita Jennings's father?"

"Yes."

"Do you know him?"

"Not really. I guess I've met him and his wife at a few parties."

"What about Lita?"

"It's possible I saw her a few times."

"Possible?"

"Probable. I just don't remember."

Lots more nodding and understanding. "But your wife knew her well?"

"I don't know if well is the right word."

"But she knows Dr. Jennings well?"

Caleb's hands stopped moving. "Yes."

Holt backed off, changed subjects, but both of them knew the subject was far from closed.

"We're trying to get a handle on a lot of things, Cal," said Alvarez.

Holt, ever affable, nodded at that assessment.

"And we were wondering if you could help us along with this whole matter."

"What do you mean?" Caleb asked.

"I think it'd make it easier on you and us both if you'd consent to a polygraph."

"You mean a lie detector?"

"It's no big thing," Holt said. "A guy asks you questions, just like we've been asking you."

Alvarez chimed in, "And this way you tell us, 'Hey, I was catching some z's with my wife when that happened,' or, 'I was at such and such a place at that time,' and this thing's able to corroborate what you say."

"Think of it as insurance for you," said Holt.

"Course it's all voluntary," Alvarez said.

"You mean do it now?" asked Caleb.

"Good a time as any," said Alvarez.

Holt nodded, his head willing Cal's to follow the same route.

"It won't take very long," said Alvarez. "Got a guy who's all set up to come in and do it right now."

"Everything goes right," Holt said, "and we'll all be home for dinner."

Maryelizabeth looked at her watch again. Seven o'clock. More than once she had thought about suggesting that Caleb's interview session be terminated for the night, but to do that might jeopardize her newfound position of trust at the Sheriff's Department. At the moment she was the golden girl. The inner circle credited her for bringing Caleb to them. They thought she was on their side, which meant they were much more receptive to sharing information with her. They assumed she was there for the same reason they were—to be in on the kill. Still, they didn't totally trust her. She had been asked to remain in a vacant office, had been kept away from the recording room where Caleb's interview was being monitored by other sheriff's homicide detectives.

Detective Alvarez decided to throw her a bone. His eyes were shining, reflecting an ebullience that had been noticeably lacking among the investigators. He didn't walk into her office so much as strut in. "We got him," he said.

Her eyes asked for more. Alvarez stopped his strutting long enough to give it to her: "Parker's been talking to the box. B.B.—Barry Brooks—is working him. We called Barry this morning and had him waiting here in the hope that Cal might consent to the box. During break time B.B. offered us some preliminary results. Apparently our Mr. Parker is a liar. But that's the least of his sins. According to the polygraph, he's also a murderer."

Alvarez pointed his index finger at her, smiled, and started to walk out of the room.

"Hey," said Maryelizabeth. "You're leaving me on that note?"

"Our bird's still wired and singing."

"Then how about giving me a few more notes?"

Alvarez hesitated, then finally decided to offer a little more. "It was textbook," he said. "B.B.'s going along all smooth, finessing him, and then out of the blue he asks, 'Have you ever murdered anyone,

Mr. Parker?' And our boy Cal sort of gulps, and then says, 'No.' According to B.B., at that moment the polygraph all but went *tilt.*"

Maryelizabeth did her best to match Alvarez's broad smile. It inspired him to talk a little more.

"Not only that," he said, "we've even got motive on one of the murders. We did some checking this morning. Apparently Cal's wife was involved with a certain Dr. Donald Jennings, father of Lita Jennings."

"Tell me—"

"Can't talk anymore. Got to get back."

"Are you going to book him tonight?"

Alvarez made a little face. "That's going to be Looey's call," he said. "My guess is we'll probably wait until tomorrow just to make sure everything is bundled up tight."

He again pointed his index finger at her, winked, then walked out of the room.

An hour later Caleb left the interview room. He was hoarse and terribly tired. Only when he had started slurring his words, and appeared ready to swoon, had the detectives reluctantly terminated the interview. Friendly to the end, they had advised him not to leave town until matters were "better clarified." They also asked him to come back for "a few more questions" the next day.

He had thought their questions would never end. Caleb had sweated through his shirt. He was surprised the polygraph hadn't shorted because of all his perspiration. Caleb shuddered a little. He didn't like being wired to anything.

They'd given him aspirin for his headache a few hours earlier but it hadn't helped. His head throbbed. All those questions. All those insinuations. And more than insinuations.

Do you love your wife, Cal?

Were you envious of your father's notoriety, Cal?

Did you want to be like your father, Caleb?

Did you know Teresa Sanders, Caleb?

They already knew so many dirty things. And the whole time that damn machine had kept reacting to what he had to say, always scratching, scratching.

Have you ever murdered anyone, Mr. Parker?

He pushed the door open, glad to be free of the building. The night air, and his soaked shirt, made him shiver.

"Caleb?"

Her voice came from the darkness and made him jump. Maryelizabeth rose from the stairs.

"God, you scared me," he said.

I'm the one who's scared, Maryelizabeth thought. And crazy for being here. The lie detector says you're a murderer. But she wasn't as certain. Her inner polygraph knew that Caleb had been less than forthcoming with her. He was hiding things. Which was why her hand was inside her purse, cradled around her gun. But taking precautions was different from pronouncing guilt.

Damn him, Maryelizabeth thought. His features were just like his father's. But she was standing there because he didn't feel like Gray.

"How'd it go?" she asked.

He shook his head.

There was a melancholy so deep in him that Maryelizabeth didn't know where it started and he ended. He averted his eyes when he talked with her. His father hadn't been like that. Gray had been much more confident.

"I have some things for you," she said, holding out a bag.

He took the bag without opening it, without asking any questions.

"My card's in there," she said. "I've written down all my numbers. There's also a number for my cell phone, but that's my emergency number."

Maryelizabeth used her phone to call out, but only very rarely took incoming calls. She didn't trust who might be listening in, and she also didn't like to be obligated to answer the phone unless she knew it was an emergency.

"I'd prefer you just paged me," she said, "and I'll get right back to you. There's also a toll-free number for my answering service and voice mail."

A number for every occasion, thought Caleb. Numbers he never intended to dial.

"I know you're probably exhausted now," said Maryelizabeth, "but I'd like to talk to you later tonight."

Caleb didn't commit himself with either word or gesture.

"There's also a book and an audiotape in the bag. They're my story of your father."

Caleb finally looked at her. She was shivering, he noticed. Is she trying to help me, he wondered, or is she just doing her best to get the inside track to my story?

"Why didn't you bring a lawyer with you?" she asked.

"Why didn't you tell me they suspected me of another murder?"

Neither answered. Neither had answers. Both just stood there looking at the other.

"I have to go," he said. "I have to talk to Anna. Prepare her."

But he didn't leave, not immediately. "You've been through this lots of times before," Caleb said. "You know the ropes. I don't know which way the authorities are planning to go on this. . . ."

Caleb paused, but Maryelizabeth didn't respond to the opening.

"But if they decide to take me in, I need someone to look out for Anna and the kids, someone to be a buffer. They don't know what kind of a zoo this can be."

"I'll help them," Maryelizabeth said.

His exhaustion lifted for a moment, replaced by a look of relief. "Thank you. You know how bad it gets. All the sharks come out to feed, and they don't care what they chew up in the process. Lots of innocent lives get ruined that way."

Caleb looked uncomfortable with having offered that autobiography. He shifted uneasily. "Well, good night," he said.

Maryelizabeth watched him walk away. He had respected her space, keeping his distance. She wondered if he had guessed about her gun.

She walked back to her car, aware of the night, of the sounds. Nothing appeared out of the ordinary. Over the years she'd learned to be vigilant, had been taught by the best, and learned lessons from the worst. She started her car, but didn't immediately pull away. Her father had worked in a car lot while she was growing up, and had trained his daughter to let the engines warm up before driving off. It was antiquated thinking, she knew. Newer cars didn't need that kind of coddling. But old habits were hard to break. Maryelizabeth's father had died ten years earlier, but the ritual of letting the engine run was her way of keeping kinship with him. While her car idled, she watched Caleb drive his gardening truck out of the parking lot. *Mister Tree,* his truck said.

No, she thought. *Mystery.*

Maryelizabeth was just putting her car into gear when Detectives Holt and Alvarez ran out to the lot. Their heads swiveled around in desperate search of something. Maryelizabeth drove over to them.

"You seen him?" Holt shouted. "You seen Parker?"

"He left a few minutes ago," she said.

"What was he driving?" Alvarez asked.

For some reason, she balked on the truth: "I—I didn't really notice."

"That fuck," Holt said. "That fuck."

"What happened?"

"A body was just discovered at the Presidio in Old Town," said Alvarez. "She's got Shame's handwriting on her—literally."

11

Caleb passed by the Interstate 5-805 merge. It was late enough that he didn't have to fight the usual bottleneck.

He wouldn't have minded traffic tonight, though. It would have delayed his having to confess to Anna. The night before he'd tried to figure out how to tell her all that had occurred, and had ended up sitting in his driveway half the night. He still didn't know how he'd break the news to her.

As the traffic lanes converged, Caleb looked to his right and left. In the darkness, he kept seeing a white envelope on the passenger seat. It wasn't empty, judging by a rectangular bulge. One of the kids must have dropped it there, he thought, but he didn't remember seeing it on the drive over to the Sheriff's Department. He had been so nervous, though, it was something he could have easily overlooked.

No, he thought. I would have noticed it.

His throat started to tighten. The envelope was out of place, just as the open door at the Sanderses' house had been. He reached for it, found it unsealed, and thumbed it open. There were some Polaroids inside. He turned on the map light, pulled the photos from the envelope, and took a look at them.

The pictures fell out of his hands. He grasped the steering wheel as if it were a life preserver, and he was in danger of drowning.

Another victim. Naked. *SHAME* scrawled across her privates. Seeing the photos was almost worse than when he'd been confronted with the body of Teresa Sanders. The Polaroids made him feel as naked as the victim, stripping away his illusions. Someone had targeted him. But as Caleb's breathing steadied, his defense mechanisms started kicking in. Maybe the Polaroids were old, or staged. Maybe the Sheriff's Office had planted them in his truck to put more psychological pressure on him.

He didn't want to look at the pictures again, but he reached for them anyway. He had to see. There was enough light to make out the woman's face. She looked familiar.

Everyone looks familiar, he tried to tell himself. More denial. But it didn't work.

"No," he said, but he remembered anyway.

The night before he had awakened from a grim memory to that sweet face. She was the smiling clerk from the doughnut shop. The girl—she was too young to be called a woman—had gently announced to him that it was closing time. He had been reliving his last meeting with his father. As far as he was concerned her interruption had been only too timely, a rope thrown to a drowning man.

Caleb didn't know her name, knew only that he was the cause of her death.

He paced the Solana Beach platform, waiting for the last train of the evening to downtown San Diego.

Caleb's truck was parked on a residential street a mile from the station, far enough away, he hoped, for the police not to immediately assume his intentions. Not that Caleb knew his intentions beyond boarding the train and trying to get a little time to figure who was setting him up. He hoped the authorities would assume he'd traveled north, to Los Angeles.

No one else was at the station. Caleb consulted the posted train schedule yet again. The *Coaster* was making its last southern run at 10:23. Five minutes from now, if it was on schedule. Time enough to address the question he'd put off: Did I kill them?

He found himself shaking. Caleb wanted to believe he wasn't capable of murder, but he knew that wasn't true.

The whistle of the approaching train grabbed his attention. It also awakened him to the possibilities of another form of escape.

Just put the bad penny on the tracks.

The platform began to vibrate. Caleb could see the train's light as it drew nearer. People who'd had near-death experiences often talked about the great white light they had seen. Caleb could almost imagine that was what he was looking at. All he had to do was focus on the light. It wouldn't even be necessary for him to step onto the tracks. He could just lean forward, his eyes on the light, and let himself drop.

But killing himself would be taken as an admission of guilt. And his children would be left with the same horrible legacy his father had passed on to him.

The train came to a stop. Caleb stepped up, entering a compartment with only two occupants, businessmen commuting back from a hard day of it in Orange County or Los Angeles. Each gave him the barest glance, then returned to their pursuits, one a newspaper, the other a portable computer. Before the train even picked up speed the conductor entered the compartment, offered the one-word conversation of "Ticket," then collected the ticket Caleb had bought from a machine at the station.

Caleb was traveling light, carrying only the bag that Maryelizabeth had given him. Passing lights illuminated his window in brief flashes. There was more darkness than not. He listened to the rails rattle, and tried not to associate the sounds with a death rattle. As a boy, he and Jimmy Doolittle had put coins down on the railroad tracks. He had proudly exhibited the results to his mother, but she hadn't been impressed with the flattened coins.

"Waste of money," she had said.

But he and Jimmy hadn't thought so. Caleb had kept the coins for years. He supposed they reminded him of better times. When he'd had friends. When he hadn't been the town's outcast.

"Cain't come out and play."

The words were offered behind the refuge of a screen door. The two boys looked at one another. Neither understood the necessity of the restriction. Three times in the last week Gray had sought out the company of his best friend, Jimmy Doolittle, and three times he had been rebuffed.

"Why not?"

"Mama says I cain't play with you no more."

Mamas were the law, but Gray knew the law was known to change. "When's she gonna let you play with me?"

A large body appeared behind Jimmy's. Mrs. Doolittle had her hands placed on top of her ample hips. She was scowling.

"You're not welcome around here, Gray Parker. Go on home."

Mrs. Doolittle had been nice to him up until the time his father had been arrested. Since then she had made it her business to keep him and Jimmy apart.

"And don't you come back," she said, shutting the door on him.

Gray turned around. "And don't you come back," he repeated. Her voice wasn't easy to mimic. He started down the walkway. "And don't you come back," he said again, but knew he still didn't have it quite right. Mrs. Doolittle always sounded as if she was winded, as if just getting the words out was stretching her air supply. That's 'cause she's fat, he thought.

"You're fat," Gray yelled in the direction of the house, but he didn't yell so's anybody could hear him.

Out on the street he started kicking a rock. Brad Forte was Gray's other best friend, but Brad had told him he couldn't play with him anymore either. Gray kicked the rock even harder.

His whole life he'd lived in Eden, Texas, but things had changed lately. Now people looked at him suspiciously, like he was some outsider they didn't know. They didn't wave anymore, just stopped what they were doing and silently waited for him to pass. It was like when a marsh hawk passed over the creek, Gray thought, and all the little birds and animals got quiet all of a sudden.

He kicked the rock again. Maybe he should go over to the creek. He liked listening to the birds and practicing their calls, was good at mimicking their whistles and chirps and songs and gobbles. Gray could copy any sound once he set his mind to it. He'd been born with that gift. He was working on a new one, the keen of a red-tailed hawk. Gray practiced the bird's shriek: "Keeeeeer." The sound broke through the humid air. Not bad, Gray thought. But next time he needed to make it a little harsher, and bring down the call as it went along. He decided to hold off practicing it, because he didn't want to scare all the animals into hiding. It wouldn't do to have the whole world going silent on him.

Gray reconsidered going to the creek. He'd been there the day before and met up with a group of older boys. They had tossed dirt clods at him, and then rocks. Gray had tried throwing back, but there were four of them and they had much stronger arms. They had yelled all sorts of things about his daddy as if they had known him real good. That was more than Gray could claim. His father had been away one place or another for most of his life.

Maybe he should go to the park. Usually there was a baseball game going on there. Or he could go to Wally's. After taking a few weeks off, Mama was back working there again. But lots of times she was too busy bringing food to tables to be able to talk with him. And he could tell Wally wasn't any too pleased to have him visiting there. It was almost as if Wally knew he was the one who'd put the Condemned by the Health Department sign on the front window. Even before all this business with his daddy, Wally had watched him close. He wasn't anybody you wanted to rile. Wally had big eyebrows that looked like fat, white caterpillars, and a chest that could have doubled for one of those German tanks, and he was always holding a cleaver or a spatula and looking like he'd turn and use it on you without much cause.

Wally looked like a killer, Gray thought. Acted like one, too. Maybe there'd been some mistake. His father sure didn't look like a killer. He was a handsome man. On that, everyone agreed. And he was smart, always was studying something or other.

The train slowed down as it approached downtown San Diego's Santa Fe depot. As Caleb nervously gathered his bag, he wondered which biography scared him more, his own or his father's.

12

The body had been found on holy ground, just outside the Presidio in Old Town. The killer had found his shrine. The mission's founder, Junípero Serra, was even being considered for sainthood by the Roman Catholic Church.

The victim still hadn't been identified. She was a young woman, believed to be no more than twenty, marked and posed like the others.

As if all that weren't bad enough for the Sheriff's Office, Caleb Parker still hadn't shown up at his home.

Promises to keep, thought Maryelizabeth, taking her leave of homicide headquarters.

"We got a situation here," said Detective Holt, calling from his car phone.

Lieutenant Borman wiped the sweat off his face. It had been his decision to let Parker walk. It was the right call. In a homicide investigation you had only one opportunity to do things right. If he had prematurely arrested Parker it would have jeopardized the whole case. No one had thought he was a risk to run. But now two hours had passed since Parker's departure. It should have taken him only half an hour to get home, which meant he was ninety minutes tardy. Parker still could be shopping, or at a bar, or talking with a friend, but Borman had a bad feeling that he'd skipped. A Pick Up Or Check directive had been sent out to all law enforcement, with a description of Gray Caleb Parker and the truck he was believed to be driving. The Sheriff's Office, SDPD, the feds, the Border Patrol, and the FBI all had that directive. That still hadn't produced Parker.

"What now?" Borman asked Holt.

"That writer just pulled up in her car. She's making for the front door right now. You want us to intercept her?"

"Shit," Borman said. Another decision. Something else for him to be second-guessed on. But his ass was covered on this one. The sheriff himself had given permission for that Line woman not only to circulate freely among them, but to be allowed access to their investigation. The boss probably wanted a chapter devoted to him in her next book, a really complimentary one.

"Don't try and stop her," Borman said.

Anna recognized the woman from the night before. She wished the house looked a little better, but with both her and Cal working, and two active children, it was a moral victory that it was as presentable as it was. For a moment, Anna wondered if Cal was having an affair with this woman. She was older than Anna, but still very attractive. Maybe that explained Caleb's behavior, and this woman's showing up at their house two nights in a row. She had announced herself at the door by saying she had a message from Caleb. Though not dressed for company, Anna had still invited her inside.

Self-consciously, Anna ran her hand along the collar of her bathrobe. "Can I get you something to drink?" she asked. "There's some coffee I brewed earlier."

"No, thank you," Maryelizabeth said.

They went to the living room, Anna using her hand to tidy her hair along the way. James and Janet were banned from going into the living room, which meant she didn't have to clear a path.

As they both took seats, Anna began their conversation: "You said that Cal gave you a message for us?"

"In a way," Maryelizabeth said. She didn't want to be enigmatic, but she wasn't sure how to approach what she needed to say. Maryelizabeth hadn't even been sure she would get this opportunity. She knew that at least two detectives were monitoring the house, and had half expected them to try to intercept her.

"Earlier this evening," she said, "I promised your husband that I would help you and your children."

"I don't understand."

"Do you know anything about your husband's family?" asked Maryelizabeth.

Anna registered surprise at the question, her thick eyebrows beetling together into one. "I know he doesn't have a family," she said. "His parents are dead, and he doesn't have any brothers or sisters."

"That's true," Maryelizabeth said. "But did he ever tell you anything about his parents?"

Anna shook her head. "Very little. I only know that his mother divorced his father when Caleb was a boy, and that she worked as a waitress to support him."

When Anna and Caleb had started going out, Anna had thought his orphan status had made him that much more irresistible. She had married him when he was twenty-five, and had been certain she could be his family, could be everything to him. Caleb's not having any living relations had been a positive thing as far as she was concerned. He had her. It had all seemed so very romantic.

"Did he tell you how his parents died?"

"His mother passed away when he was twenty or so. She had a bad liver . . ."

Cirrhosis of the liver, Maryelizabeth thought.

". . . and his father died after he was struck by lightning. But since Cal didn't even really know him, his death didn't affect him much."

Clever lies combined with wishful thinking, thought Maryelizabeth. Caleb had probably wanted to tell his wife a biography as close to the truth as possible, or as close to the truth as he dared make it.

"What Caleb told you was mostly true," Maryelizabeth said.

"Mostly?"

"His father didn't die by lightning, though that's a phrase that inmates often use. They call it *riding the lightning*. It's a euphemistic phrase for electrocution."

"What are you saying?"

"Twenty-one years ago Caleb's father, Gray Parker, died in the electric chair. He was known as Shame."

The color left Anna's face. "No."

Maryelizabeth forged ahead. She knew it was only the beginning of her bad news.

"Your husband spent most of today at the Sheriff's Department. He was being interviewed by homicide detectives. In the past month several women in the San Diego area have been murdered. The police think Caleb killed them. The women were strangled, and then the word *shame* was written across their thighs and pubic areas. It's the same way Caleb's father killed and marked his victims."

Anna kept shaking her head, each shake more adamant than the last. She was a nurse, used to dealing with crises, but this wasn't a situation she was trained to handle.

"No," she said.

"I am not making any judgments," Maryelizabeth said. "I am just telling you what information I have. I had conversations with your husband both last night and today, and in all of our talks he expressed his innocence."

"Where is he?"

"I don't know. We only talked briefly tonight after he was released from questioning. He told me he was on his way home, but he must have changed his mind, or something changed it for him. That doesn't matter; his not being here doesn't change my promise to him. I said that I would help you."

"Help me with what?"

"With all that's about to occur. Your husband knows the trauma you're about to face because he went through it. And he knows I'm familiar with what happens in this kind of a situation. I can be useful to you and your children."

"Who are you?"

"My name is Maryelizabeth Line. I'm a writer. Many years ago I wrote a book about your husband's father, and since that time I've written a number of other crime books."

Anna stopped shaking her head. The woman had looked familiar to her. Anna vaguely remembered having seen her interviewed on television.

"If time weren't of the essence," Maryelizabeth said, "I wouldn't have come barging in here uninvited. But in a matter of minutes detectives will be knocking at your door. They're going to have a search warrant, and they're going to have a lot of questions. And right behind them will be the media, who will make your life a living hell. They'll report dirt and innuendo and downright lies. What's worse is that people whom you consider friends will betray you. In hindsight, those former friends and neighbors will remember all sorts of terrible things about your husband, and you, and your family."

Anna's breath was short, her mouth dry. She managed to say, "You make it all sound so awful."

Maryelizabeth shook her head with regret. "I just gave you the best-case scenario."

13

The man entered the room, drew a deep breath, and looked around with the eyes of someone who had never been there before. There was a nervousness about him that caught Lola's eye. Married, Lola decided. Out on the town and looking for some forbidden fruit. But no, that wasn't quite it. Lola studied him from her seat at the lounge. He stayed in the back for a minute, giving her plenty of time to do her observing.

I know him, Lola thought, but then realized that was impossible. Still, the resemblance was uncanny. And so was her feeling that this was the person she had somehow been expecting for weeks.

The man sitting on her right had been trying to catch her eye ever since she had sat down. He finally decided to address her, even without the benefit of her full attention. "I just loved your Judy Garland," he said. "I closed my eyes and I swore it was Judy singing."

"Thank you," Lola said.

She was still watching the man who looked like Shame. He was making his way uncertainly toward the crowded bar. His face was pale, and he kept looking around. Afraid to be seen, thought Lola. Afraid he might be recognized by someone he knew. But she'd seen that kind of furtiveness enough times to know that wasn't quite it.

Her neighbor was still talking. "My name's Joe," he said. "You have a wonderful voice. I was in the theater myself, once upon a time. I—"

"Joe, I wonder if you would do me a huge favor," Lola said. "An old friend of mine just walked into the room. I hope it's not too presumptuous of me to ask for your seat."

Joe's mouth hung open in midsentence. He recovered enough to offer a martyr's nod. The diva had spoken. He reached for his drink and started to stand. Lola waved at the Shame look-alike, and patted the suddenly vacant seat next to her.

She's mistaken me for someone else, thought Caleb. He turned around, but there was no one behind him, and no one else around him. For some reason, the woman in the very colorful gown wanted to talk to him. Her eyes never left his. She had long eyelashes, and when she blinked, their folding and opening reminded Caleb of a butterfly's wings. What could she want?

Caleb was half convinced he should turn around, but he wasn't ready to face the streets again. The black-and-whites were out in force, and he had only just avoided coming face-to-face with a foot patrol by ducking into the club. He supposed he was in some kind of cabaret. In the back of the room was an elevated stage with seating beneath it. The lounge was in the front of the building. Between it and the seating was a control panel for the lights and music. The performance was apparently over, judging by the empty stage and the crowded bar.

He approached the tendered seat. "Thank you," he said.

She nodded. Her outfit glittered even in the dim bar, abounding with sequins and chiffon. The woman on her left was wearing an outfit even more iridescent. Performers, Caleb decided. That, or they were going to a midnight ball.

"The outfit's an original," she said. "So am I."

"So I see."

"Do you have a name?" Lola asked. She had a Southern accent, put honey on her words, but not cloyingly so.

So she didn't know him. Good. Caleb paused before answering, reluctant to give his real name. "Paul," he finally said.

"*Paul,*" Lola repeated, not hiding her skepticism.

He nodded.

"You didn't ask me my name, *Paul.*"

"What's your name?"

Her very red lips parted: "Lola."

There was almost a fluorescent glow to her lipstick. But she wasn't the only woman at the bar wearing a lot of makeup. In fact, she was wearing less than most. Stage makeup, Caleb decided. She was obviously part of the troupe. But that still didn't explain why she had called him over. He looked at her for an explanation, but all she gave back was a little smile. Lola had short dark hair that was combed up and back, with eyes the same dark color, but her skin was lighter, cocoa-colored. Instead of lifting her drink up, she leaned forward and brought her lips to her straw. Her appearance seemed to change with every shift of her head. She could have been Hispanic, Mediterranean, African, American Indian, or even Asian.

And she could have been a woman, a very pretty woman, but Caleb realized she wasn't.

He turned away, embarrassed, and found himself looking around the room at anything but Lola. With all that had happened to him that day, with his life literally on the line, Caleb knew it was absurd that he should be flustered by a drag queen. But he still couldn't bring himself to look her way. *His* way.

In a voice that only Caleb could hear, Lola said, "You really didn't know, did you?"

"No."

"The marquee says Female Impersonators in letters about as big as me."

More avoidance, more neck craning. "I missed it."

"I've been with lots of men who pretended they didn't know, but you're the first I ever believed."

"I was preoccupied."

"Must have been a hell of a preoccupation."

The room wasn't big enough for him to avoid her eyes indefinitely. He gave Lola a quick look and saw a small, knowing smile come over her face. *His* face, Caleb remembered.

The bartender picked that time to stop ignoring Caleb. "What can I get you?" he asked.

"Coffee. Black."

"Put it on my tab, Michael," Lola said.

"Oh, God," the bartender said, dramatically fluttering his eyelashes. "True love."

In a soft voice, Lola asked Caleb, "Sure you don't want decaf?"

"I'm sure." But a second later he asked, "Why?"

"Because you're as twitchy as a treed cat."

Hearing that made Caleb even more nervous. He found himself smoothing his hair first with one hand, and then the other. But instead of changing his order, he sat on his hands. Lola seemed to notice that, too.

The bartender filled a coffee mug, expertly tossed a napkin on the counter, and placed it in front of Caleb.

With not a little reluctance, Caleb turned to his benefactor, and offered a nod. "Thank you."

Caleb directed his attention to the coffee, becoming pointedly absorbed in it, but that didn't deter Lola from scrutinizing him. The staring made him uncomfortable. Caleb picked up a napkin and wiped some perspiration from his face.

"Are you hot, *Paul?*"

He didn't respond to the mocking tone, just nodded.

Lola moved a little closer to him. "Fact is, *Paul,* when you realized what a den of iniquity this is, I'm surprised you didn't run out of here like a bat out of hell."

"Maybe I was tired."

Lola's glowing lips edged near to his ears. "And maybe I know more than you imagine I do, Mr. Parker."

Caleb tried to hide his reaction, but didn't succeed. Lola moved away from him, forcing him to be the one to draw closer.

"How'd you know my name?"

"You couldn't be anything but your daddy's son. I used to study his picture for hours at a time. He intrigued me. I wondered how a man so pretty could be so evil. That's always been a fascination of mine, how people so pretty outside can be so ugly inside.

"My auntie used to say, 'Pride and grace dwell never in one place.' Was your father a prideful man?"

"I really didn't know my father."

"Pride makes us do all sorts of hateful things. When Auntie used to catch me looking in a mirror she'd say, 'Pride goes before, and shame follows after.' I wonder if your father knew that saying."

"I wouldn't know."

The movement of curtains at the entrance made Caleb start, but it wasn't the police, just another patron.

"What's troubling you?" Lola asked.

"Some people are convinced I'm suffering from a hereditary disease."

He kept glancing back nervously.

"There's a side exit," Lola said. "Maybe we'd better leave."

They walked two blocks without saying anything before Lola got tired of that. "If we're supposed to be looking like a couple," she said, "or even like friends, we're not doing a very good job of it. I'd suggest you walk next to me, not two steps behind."

Caleb closed the gap between them.

"You need a ride somewhere?" Lola asked.

"You don't know what you're getting into."

"I'd like to think that I'm rescuing you," Lola said, offering the smallest flounce of her skirt.

"I'm wanted by the police."

"Are you guilty?"

"No. But if I was, that's not something I'd be likely to confess."

"Are you trying to talk me out of helping you?"

"I'm just trying to figure out *why* you're helping me. You don't strike me as a professional do-gooder."

"Maybe you'd think differently if you saw me in my nun's habit. It's very modern, very chic, the kind of threads a nun on the fast track to being a mother superior might wear."

"You're a funny guy. . . ."

"Gal. Or lady. Or even bitch. Just make me something female. That's the etiquette."

"Miss Manners."

"Better."

"I was trying to tell you that you don't even know me."

"I know you."

"Just because I look—"

"That's how I noticed you, not how I know you. I took one look at you, sugar, and I saw more than the spitting image of your father. What I saw was someone with the weight of the world on his shoulders. Now if you have a problem accepting help from the likes of me then you better get over it, *Jack,* or *Paul,* or whatever you're calling yourself, 'cause my car is right over here."

There was no night attendant in the outdoor lot on Second Avenue, just signs posted everywhere. Half the signs said that management wasn't responsible for any valuables lost, while the other half warned that those who hadn't paid, or weren't displaying a current parking sticker, would have their cars towed away. Management seemed to have all bets covered.

Lola walked by herself over to a canary-yellow Mustang convertible. She didn't look back, just opened her door, sat down, closed the door behind her, then started the car. Caleb stood undecided for a long moment, then finally moved. He ran over to the Mustang's passenger door and tapped on the glass. The window lowered, but only slightly.

"My name's not Paul," he said. "It's Caleb."

Lola reached out with one of her long fingernails and deactivated the lock.

"Buckle up, Caleb," she said.

As they waited for the light to change on Broadway a siren sounded. Caleb visibly tensed, turning to the sound. Flashing red lights raced at them. Caleb only started breathing again when a fire truck roared by.

"You want to talk about it?" Lola asked.

Caleb didn't. But he had to. He let out a long sigh, and it was as if he let the air out of himself. His explanation came out flat, monotone: "There's a murderer out there who's copying my father. He's strangling women and writing the word *shame* on their bodies. He's managed to kill in such a way as to place me at every murder scene."

Lola didn't say anything. The silence built between them.

"If you want to let me out, I understand."

"Why haven't I heard about the murders?"

"You have, but just not the details of them."

"And the police think you're the killer?"

"Like father, like son."

"What's their evidence?"

"My lack of any alibis, and my heritage."

"That's it?"

A lifetime of being beaten down was voiced: "That's enough."

"With your hangdog attitude, it just might be. Right now you're wearing a Kick Me sign on your backside."

"All I've ever wanted was to be left alone."

"That your ambition in life?"

"Close enough."

"Doesn't sound like much of a life."

"Compare it to the one I'm leading now."

She could hear his teeth grind down on his own bitterness.

"I'm the son of Shame," he said. "Before last night that wasn't something I had admitted in more than twenty years."

"You never told anyone about your father?"

"No one. Not even my wife."

"Your big secret?"

He nodded.

"I've been there, sugar. I know what it's like to try and hide something from the world. The difference between you and me is I came out of the closet, and you were outed. You sure were outed. But the big question is: why?"

14

"Make yourself at home," Lola said.

Caleb reluctantly stepped inside. He wasn't there for a night's shelter, so much as for what came with it: a promised disguise. Lola was willing to change his hair color.

Her Hillcrest bungalow wasn't what Caleb expected. He had thought it would be as glitzy and showy as her dress, but instead he found it refined and homey. The decorations were eclectic, with needlework, paintings, Art Deco, and American Indian artifacts all somehow combining for a pleasant ambience. The Native American items, in particular, were displayed very respectfully, almost in the manner of a shrine. There was a wooden arrow with a pouch tied to it, mounted feathers of raptors, what looked to be a bear claw necklace, and a painting of a white buffalo.

"Are you an Indian?" Caleb asked.

"I'm Heinz Fifty-seven. But part of me is Indian."

"What tribe?"

"Lakota, better known as Sioux."

Caleb kept walking around the living room and looking at things. He was reluctant to sit down. Lola watched him pace. She was tempted to tell him that he was the one wanted for murder, and that she was the one who should be feeling ill at ease, but decided to hold her tongue. He was nervous enough already, but was trying to cover up by touring the room as if he were in a museum.

Caleb paused to study one of the paintings. It showed an Indian pausing in flight just long enough to taunt his pursuers. There were arrows in the ground around him that had fallen just short of their intended target.

"I have a friend who's an artist," Lola said. "He painted that for me. The French called that Indian Berdache, a Salteaux who was the best runner in his tribe. I call the painting *The Decoy.* That's what Berdache did. He set himself up as a decoy to a Lakota war party. He shot arrows at them, and taunted them to chase him, so that his people could escape."

Caleb took a closer look at the painting, and frowned. Lola smiled at his reaction.

"Yes, Berdache was a drag queen."

"For real?"

"For real. Among many Native American cultures there was a tradition that anthropologists refer to as *berdache.* It's a French word that means "slave boy," which is not at all an accurate picture of what berdaches were to their tribes. I, and many others, prefer the term Two-Spirited People, or Two Spirits, souls that embody both Mother Earth and Father Sky."

Caleb shook his head, still finding it hard to accept. "These Indians wore women's clothing?"

"In most cases. But I think you miss the point."

"What point is that?"

"What the berdaches wore didn't matter so much as what they were. The Lakota believe all objects have a spirit. They refer to their own berdaches as *winkte.* They believe that the spirit of both man and woman combine as one in a winkte. Winkte aren't deviant; they're special. Winkte can see with the vision of both genders, not just one. Their position gave them the freedom to move freely between men and women."

"Was that their role? Emissary?"

"In some tribes they acted as go-betweens for the sexes. In others they performed sacred duties. And in still others they took on many of the feminine roles."

Caleb moved away from the painting, but Lola wasn't ready to change the subject.

"There is a Cree word for berdache: *ayekkew.* The translation is 'neither man nor woman,' or 'man and woman.' I always thought that appropriate. Neither and both. That speaks to me."

"I'm glad you found some historical justification for what you are."

Lola ignored his condescending tone. "We're very alike, you know."

"In what way?" he asked.

"Like you, I was always the outcast, always different. I thought of myself as a freak. There were no role models for me. As a teenager, my father thought he could beat my anima out of me, and my classmates took up where he left off. I was kicked out of my own house and had to live on the streets until my aunt, my mother's sister, took me in."

Caleb didn't say anything, but she had his attention; he was even looking at her.

"But the beatings still didn't stop. I just administered them myself. And what was worse, I knew how to hurt myself more than anyone else could. I was a mess. I'm still not sure how I survived, but I remember the moment my life started to turn around. My aunt gave me this book on Native Americans and pointed out the section on the berdache tradition."

Lola's eyes teared up. "It was an epiphany." Her words came out hushed, choked. "It was like God tapped me on the shoulder and said, 'It's all right.'"

His entire life, Caleb thought, he had been waiting for that tap. He felt a twinge of jealousy.

"The more I studied, the more I learned there were berdache-like traditions in other cultures: the Mahu of Polynesia, the Hijra of India, the Xanith of Oman, the Chukchi in Siberia. And I came to realize that I have a place in this world. So do you."

"What's that supposed to mean?"

"The heyoka were thought of as Backward People. You might wonder why a culture would have a prized place for people who did everything differently. A heyoka might go naked in winter, and dress warmly in the summer. A heyoka might walk everywhere backward, and dry himself before bathing, and laugh at the tragic, and cry at the hilarious. By acting in such a way, the heyoka brought a sense of the absurd to the tribe. The heyoka made the

Lakota think and see things differently. In our lives, we have also been the bringers of reality change."

Caleb stifled the urge to say "Bullshit," but only just. "You make it sound as if we're on some kind of a holy mission," he said. "You wear women's clothing, and I'm the son of a serial murderer. There's nothing holy about either one of those things."

"Are you sure of that? Your presence reminds anyone who knows your history that life is short, and fragile, and something that shouldn't be taken for granted."

"My presence reminds people that there are sick and twisted individuals in this world. My presence reminds people to lock their windows and doors. I never wanted to be someone else's reality check. And I don't want to walk backward."

"Then why do you?"

"At least I don't do it in a dress."

A long moment passed, then Caleb said, "I'm sorry."

"I didn't take offense."

"I know you're trying to help. I'm sort of numb from everything that's happened. I still can't think clearly. I just feel like screaming, This is so goddamn unfair."

"I know the words to that scream if you need a chorus."

"If it was only me, that would be one thing, but it's not. My family's going to have to go through hell."

"You have children?"

A nod; a brief smile for a good memory. "A boy and a girl. Janet's ten, and James is eight."

"Do you have pictures?"

"Not on me."

The only pictures he was carrying were of a dead woman. Remembering that made him feel all the more helpless. Caleb started touring the room again, his way of avoiding personal questions. He paused in front of another painting. Center stage was a woman singing. She wore a translucent gossamer gown with a long train. Behind her was an elaborate stage with nymphs lolling by a stream, and fauns playing harps.

"Another man dressed as a woman?" Caleb asked.

"In a manner of speaking," Lola said. "He's a castrato."

Caleb didn't ask the question, but Lola answered anyway. "Becoming transgender—a transsexual, that is—has never been a goal or desire of mine."

"Why the painting?"

"It's pretty. And it's a reminder of the long history of gender-bender entertainment that even the Western world has accepted."

Caleb moved on to the last painting. It was centered over the fireplace, and was the focal point of the room. He examined the work closely. Two warring tribes were fighting. Caleb could see nothing in the hand-to-hand combat that suggested a man in woman's clothing. Pictured were braves, many of them fighting to the death. One brave in particular was leading the charge. Several enemies had fallen around him.

"His name is Osh-Tisch," said Lola, "which in Crow means Finds Them and Kills Them. The scene is drawn from the Battle of the Rosebud in eighteen seventy-six."

"Is there some significance that I'm missing?"

"Osh-Tisch was a Crow Two Spirit. On the day of the battle he took off his feminine garments and put on men's clothing. His bravery during the fight became renowned."

"Why do you think he changed clothes?" Caleb asked.

"Anthropologists would probably tell you that the berdache fulfilled a sacred role, and that by changing his clothes he was able to step out of that role."

"Is that what you think?"

"Yes. But I also think he didn't want to ruin a perfectly good outfit. Finding just the right women's clothing is such a chore."

15

"Last night you said you talked with the suspect at a doughnut shop, is that correct, Ms. Line?"

Detective Holt was being the hard-nosed cop. He had directed her to the Parkers' dining room table and had chosen to sit at its head, as if assuming the role of the patriarch. Detective Alvarez was interviewing Anna Parker in the living room. The murmurs of their conversation could just be heard.

"That's right," Maryelizabeth said.

"And what doughnut shop was that?"

"You know which doughnut shop. Why the question?"

"Do you remember anything unusual about last night?"

Maryelizabeth tried to hide her impatience. That would only prolong his questions. "Not really. I talked with Mr. Parker for about an hour. He appeared to be in a state of shock for much of our conversation."

"Can you clarify that?"

"He acted dazed. What seemed to bother him most was that the world was about to learn he was the son of Gray Parker."

"Did he say or do anything out of the ordinary?"

"Where is all of this going?"

"Please answer the question."

A short sigh. "He said that the man who identified himself as Mr. Sanders on the phone asked him, manipulated him even, to come over immediately and cut down an acacia tree. I'd be curious about when that call, or even if that call, was made from the Sanderses' house, because—"

The detective didn't let his interview get sidetracked: "Did Mr. Parker converse with anyone else at the doughnut shop? Pay particular attention to anyone there?"

"No."

"Did he buy anything? Doughnuts? Coffee?"

"No."

"What about you?"

"I had two doughnuts. One was an old-fashioned glazed. The other was a buttermilk bar. I thought both were excellent, but I'd give a slight edge to the buttermilk bar. Now, I'd like to know—"

"Who waited on you?"

Maryelizabeth took a decorative apple out of the fruit centerpiece on the table. The apple almost felt real. She was frustrated enough to want to bite into it and leave teeth marks. "A girl. A young woman. I don't know her name."

"Please describe her."

There. That was it. Maryelizabeth wanted to deny the feeling, the insight, but she knew with a certainty that this was what the detective had been leading up to. Even worse, she knew where his curiosity was taking him. Maryelizabeth looked at Holt's poker face, his death mask.

"Ms. Line?"

"She matches the body found at the Presidio. She's the one who was murdered."

Holt neither confirmed nor denied her surmise. "Could you describe this counter clerk, Ms. Line?"

Maryelizabeth remembered the girl's dimple, and her red cheeks, and her cheerful manner. But the detective wouldn't care about those. For his report he'd want race, height, and weight first, then hair color, eye color, and any distinguishing marks.

"White female," she said, speaking without inflection, "five foot five inches, a hundred and twenty-five pounds."

Friendly. Very human in the best sense of the word. And young. So very young.

In the same dead voice, Maryelizabeth continued: "She had

curly light brown hair. Her hairnet didn't hide how frizzy it was. Blue eyes, I think."

And that dimple. Only one. It had flashed on and off like a welcome sign.

"Anything else?"

Rosy cheeks, the kind that appeared on some women when they exerted themselves, even when they laughed. But in death you wouldn't see those cheeks. They'd be muted now, white.

"No."

"Did Mr. Parker interact with this woman at all?"

"What's her name?"

"I beg your pardon?"

"What's the woman's name? I don't want to call her the doughnut girl, or the clerk, or the victim. I'd like to know her name."

Holt didn't respond right away. He appeared to be deliberating on the right thing to do. Then, decided, he flipped his pad back several pages, looked, flipped over a few more, and found what he was looking for.

"Brandy Wein," he said.

"As far as I know, Mr. Parker never talked to, or even looked at, Brandy."

"What time did you leave the doughnut shop?"

"Ten-thirty."

"And where was Mr. Parker?"

"He was still seated when I left."

Had the son spared her like his father had? Maybe she just hadn't given him the opportunity to kill her. Brandy Wein hadn't known what Maryelizabeth knew, had no warning. Maryelizabeth fought off her nausea.

". . . many other people in there?"

She caught enough of the detective's question to be able to answer it. "We were the only people who took a table," she said, "but there was a steady stream of people coming in for doughnuts."

Maryelizabeth took out her own pad and started making notes. She did it to steady herself, for her sanity, but Holt was disturbed by her scratching.

"I'd like your full attention, Ms. Line."

Without looking up, she said, "You're not the only one working here, Detective. I need to make my own notes. But I'll try to answer your questions to the best of my ability. And perhaps you'll pay me the same courtesy."

"You mean like your courtesy in conveniently forgetting what kind of a truck Shame drove off in?"

She looked up, and for a moment saw Holt's mask slip, saw his anger and disdain. It was deserved, she thought. She couldn't explain to him, let alone herself, why she had lied to him earlier in the evening.

"I feel embarrassed at my lapse," she said.

She didn't specify whether her lapse was of memory or judgment, but her apology was enough for Holt to nod.

"Did you talk with him after his interrogation?" he asked.

Maryelizabeth nodded. "But just for a minute."

"What did he say?"

"He thought I'd betrayed him. He thought I should have warned him about the Lita Jennings murder. But mostly he was worried about what was going to happen to his family. That's why I came here. He asked me to look out for his wife and children."

"You agreed to do that?"

"I did."

"That didn't make you suspicious that he was about to run?"

"That wasn't my impression. I just assumed he was afraid of being arrested."

Alvarez entered the room, but stayed on the periphery, waiting for Holt to finish. The two men made eye contact, and Alvarez said, "Got something I think you'd like to see."

Holt stood up and walked over to him. Alvarez handed him some photographs. "I asked Mrs. Parker if she wouldn't mind getting me some recent pix of her husband, and told her to make sure they were all taken within the last year or so. I got 'em in order from most recent to least recent."

Holt flipped through the photos, then whistled a little. "Pictures are worth a thousand words," he said.

"What words?" Maryelizabeth asked.

The two detectives looked at each other. Alvarez shrugged.

Holt walked back to the table and tossed the pictures down in front of her. She thumbed through them. There were six photos. In most of the shots Caleb was posed with his children, pictures snapped during holidays and birthdays. That helped to determine the chronology, as did Caleb's appearance.

Some people don't change as much in a decade as Caleb had in an apparently very short time.

"The wife said he had a beard, and wore his hair long, from the time she went out with him," said Alvarez, "but six weeks ago he took everything off."

His beard had been full and long, Maryelizabeth observed, as if designed to hide his face. In the older photos Caleb's hair had been longer, and styled differently. If he had answered the door with his old look, she wouldn't have immediately thought he was the image of his father.

"Clear as a picture," Alvarez said. "He decided if he was going to kill like his father, he might as well look like his father."

16

Maryelizabeth was checking into the hotel very late. Or very early. The night auditor at the Amity Inn, a young man whose name tag read Henry, wasn't used to 6 A.M. arrivals. Henry could have played a vampire without any makeup. His skin was preternaturally pale, and the ingrained dark circles were dark enough to be mistaken for shiners.

"I'm really not sure whether I should charge you for last night's lodging," Henry said, "or just start with tonight's."

"I'm sure you'll decide on whatever's fair," said Maryelizabeth, "but right now I'd just like to get my family into its suite."

"I guess I'll ask the manager when he comes in. It's possible we'll only charge you a half-day rate for last night."

"Fine." She knew the clerk was just trying to be nice, but her body language said, *Give me a key.*

"You're planning on staying here a week?" asked Henry.

Give or take seven days, she thought. "That's right."

"I'll just need . . ."

Maryelizabeth extended a credit card to him. She knew the routine.

"Thank you, Mrs. Macauley."

That was the name she had checked in under, and the name on her credit card. If Maryelizabeth's purse was ever snatched, the thief would wonder at his take. She always carried half a dozen different driver's licenses, with credit cards matching the names on those licenses. Only one of those IDs had her real name on it, a name she rarely used whenever traveling.

"Will that be smoking or nonsmoking?"

"Non."

Her credit card, or at least Vera Macauley's, was processed. The banks had never questioned her fictitious names. They had only been zealous about raising the credit limit on her cards, and encouraging her to spend more.

Henry handed back her credit card. "Will you be needing any help with luggage?"

"No, thank you."

"One key or two?"

"Two, please."

Maryelizabeth had a room at another hotel under the name of Sue Price. She had considered switching hotels, but had decided against it. The Shame story was breaking, and as much as she didn't like it, Maryelizabeth was part of that story. Journalists would be trying to track her down because of her past association with Gray Parker. She didn't want to lead them inadvertently to the Parker family.

The night auditor handed her the keys, pointed out the direction she should go to park, and told her to enjoy her stay. Henry looked more asleep than not by the time she left the desk.

Maryelizabeth had parked her car out of sight of the front desk. She opened the door to a different make and model car than what she had written on the registration card, and for a moment wondered if there was a good reason for her having lied, or whether she just lied from habit.

Janet and James were asleep in the backseat, but Anna was only too awake. Her eyes were wide open, and she kept shaking her head as if to deny all that had happened.

Maryelizabeth handed her a key. "Room two-two-four," she said. "Better remember the number. All the rooms here look alike."

"Remember when hotel keys used to have the room numbers on them?" Anna said, looking at the key. "Lots more security these days but nobody feels more secure." Her head kept swiveling ever so slightly, saying: *No, no, no.*

"The name you're registered under is Vera Macauley. Say it aloud three times."

"What?"

"I always do that when I check into a hotel under an assumed name. It makes me remember who I am while I'm there."

"I'll remember."

"In the middle of the night? When the phone rings and a voice you don't know says, 'Mrs. Macauley?' It's easy to forget."

Anna reluctantly complied: "Vera Macauley, Vera Macauley, Vera Macauley."

"And now put a mental picture in your head of being near a tamale."

"Near a tamale?"

"Rhymes with Vera Macauley. It's easier to remember images than names."

"You always travel under an assumed name?"

"Yes."

The man from the radio show wasn't the first to tell her he wanted her dead. There had been others. Many others.

"Do you like living like that?"

Maryelizabeth didn't answer. It was a way of life, but in hindsight she wasn't sure it was the life she would have chosen. She remembered how Gray Parker had warned her of the consequences of "looking into the abyss." Too bad he hadn't offered her a warning about his own son.

"You're going to have to explain your new name to the children," Maryelizabeth said. "I suggest that you, and you alone, answer the phone."

"How long do you think we'll be hiding?"

"It's hard to say."

It actually wasn't. They would be the media's big game until her husband was captured, but Maryelizabeth didn't want to tell her that, at least not yet.

Anna sighed. "I now know why people confess to crimes they didn't commit. You get so beaten up by the questioning, you just want it to end."

The questioning wasn't over, just deferred, but Maryelizabeth didn't remind her. Anna had promised to keep Lieutenant Borman informed of all her movements. Not that he had taken her at her word. Detectives Holt and Alvarez had followed them in an unmarked car to the hotel.

"You and the children are going to have to keep a low profile while you're here," Maryelizabeth said. "If the media track you down, I'll find you another place to stay."

"Under yet another name?"

"Yes." Maryelizabeth noticed that Anna's head shaking had stopped, and considered that a good sign. She offered up a division of labor: "I'll bring up the bags," she said, "and you bring up the kids."

"Deal."

Maryelizabeth caught her head dropping forward. There was no time for sleep, she knew, but her body needed to be reminded of that. She forced her shoulders back and took a deep breath. Anna was in the next room, trying to coax her children to sleep for a few more hours. Janet and James had slept through all the excitement of the night before. It was just as well. They'd missed their father on the eleven o'clock news. The Sheriff's Office had identified him as a fugitive wanted for questioning in the murder of Teresa Sanders, but the whole story was yet to be told. Those revelations would come out at the sheriff's nine o'clock news conference. Instead of wearing his usual designer suit, Maryelizabeth thought, the sheriff should consider wearing asbestos.

She looked at her watch. Less than three hours to the news conference, and so much to do both before and after. There were interviews to arrange, sites to visit, and research begging to be done. Her finished books always surprised her the way they looked so neat and tidy on the bookshelves. They reminded her of processed meat, with the blood all but absent in the final packaging. That's how her words were marketed—the blood implied, but kept under wraps.

Maryelizabeth's head dropped again. She let her eyes close, not to sleep, but just to rest them. She could hear Anna's soothing voice far away, lulling her children back to sleep again. Once upon a time, she thought. Being around children always spoke to her own regrets, and her own once-upon-a-times.

* * *

"Doing anything right takes its toll. Are you sure you want to pay the toll?"

Gray Parker stared at her, assessed her.

"Yes."

"If you do this book right, you'll never look at the world in the same way again."

"You've already made me look at it differently."

"If you do this book right, you'll find yourself on a roller-coaster ride, and the ride won't stop with my death. You'll get into my head, but you might not get out of it."

"I'll take my chances."

"Yes, you will. And you'll keep taking them, like Russian roulette. If you keep doing your books right you'll have the same bug as the people you write about."

"Bug? Do you think of yourself as some kind of diseased person?"

"I'm the plague."

"And that makes me what, a potential carrier?"

"If you do this book right, you're going to be marked, sure as I marked those women."

Maryelizabeth felt sick, dirty.

"If you do this book right, you're going to get a glimpse of the face of God."

"How could you possibly," she said, her voice cracking with anger and disdain, "show me that?"

"No one can look directly at God's face without going insane. It's too complicated, too brilliant, too unfathomable. So what we do is use little funhouse mirrors, and we take our peeks, and we look at him from angles. We find roundabout ways to glimpse God, like how we look at the sun through our fingers, or the way we track an eclipse through reflection instead of direct observation."

"You might be able to show me the devil, but I doubt whether you can show me God."

"If you do this book right, you'll see both. Sometimes you never see God so clearly as through the devil."

"Is this some kind of jailhouse conversion you're going through?"

"If you do this book right, you'll know what I'm talking about."

"I have to go," Maryelizabeth said.

But she didn't leave before hearing his last assertion.

"If you do this book right," he told her, "you'll fall in love with me."

"No," she said, what she always said.

"Excuse me?"

It was Anna Parker in the flesh, not Gray Parker and his demons, standing in front of her.

"Nothing," Maryelizabeth said. "I was just talking to myself."

"I'm making coffee," Anna said. "Would you like some?"

"Please."

While the coffee was perking, James walked into the kitchen, rubbing his eyes. He was a handsome boy, had his mother's brown eyes and squarer features. There was little resemblance to his father. Or his grandfather.

"Mom, Janet's on the bed I want."

Anna was expert at officiating. "Let her have that bed today, James, and if you still want it tomorrow, it will be your turn."

"We're going to be here tomorrow, too?" he asked.

"Yes," said Anna, her tone saying, "I'm afraid so." But her son didn't share those sentiments.

"Oh, good," he said.

"Go to sleep now."

"Okay."

He walked out of the room, giving Maryelizabeth a small, shy glance as he passed.

"They think their dad's going to join us soon," Anna said. "I almost believe it myself."

She served the coffee, and both women sat and sipped quietly for a minute. They still weren't totally comfortable with each other.

"I hope you don't mind my asking you some questions this morning," said Maryelizabeth.

"No," Anna said. "At least I don't think so."

Maryelizabeth pulled a document out of her purse. Cops had their Miranda, and she had her release forms. "I'd like you to read this at your leisure. If you consent to what's on there, I'll need your signature. Boiling down all the legalese, what it translates to is your giving me permission to quote you."

"So you'll be writing about this?"

"I expect so. But I don't want you to think I'm coercing you into signing the release form. Even if you choose to not sign it, I still intend to help you. I made that promise to your husband, and I intend to keep it. I want you to be comfortable in my presence. I can't promise much, but I swear I won't stab you in the back. I may upset you, though, because I do write what I perceive to be the truth, and sometimes that is upsetting."

Anna touched the piece of paper, then drew her hand back. "I'll read it later," she said.

"Good."

"And I'd like to thank you for all you've done."

"I'm glad I could help."

Both women concentrated on their coffee for a minute. Finally Anna cleared her throat.

"I'm thinking of sending the children to stay with my mother," she said.

Maryelizabeth sighed inwardly, and wondered if she'd ever have any good news to offer Anna. "I'd advise against that. If your goal is to spare them from the media, that won't work. When the reporters don't find you, they'll take to dogging your friends and relatives. If they're not on your mother's doorstep today, they'll be there tomorrow. You also don't want your children to think you've abandoned them. What they need now more than anything else is a parent staying close to them, someone who can explain what's going on."

Anna's head started shaking again. "As if I really could explain what's going on."

Maryelizabeth nodded.

"It's so bizarre. And it's my fault."

"Your fault?"

She avoided answering the question directly, choosing to approach it in a roundabout way. "Those detectives are so wrong about Caleb."

"In what way?"

"In how they're thinking."

Anna's eyes strayed to the back room, then returned to Maryelizabeth. She lowered her voice. "Did you hear, did they tell you . . ."

"That you were involved with Dr. Jennings?"

Anna looked relieved that she didn't have to explain. "I guess

Donald and I deluded ourselves into thinking that no one knew," she said. "It seems that everyone did."

She bit her lip, again made sure her children couldn't possibly hear, and said, "They think Cal took revenge on Donald's daughter because he found out what was going on between us."

"I know."

"I asked them how that explained the other murders, and they said it was Cal's suppressed rage coming out, that his dam 'just broke,' and that he copied his father. But Cal would never, ever murder."

"How can you be so sure?"

"Cal doesn't get angry, or if he does, he doesn't show it. I think he's always been afraid of his emotions. When he can't deal with a situation, he just withdraws and gets quiet. In all our years together he's never raised his voice, or gotten physical. He was afraid of any kind of confrontation, afraid, I think, of being that involved with anyone.

"I suppose that's how . . . Donald and I . . . that's why we came together. I hungered for someone to talk to, someone open, and warm, and communicative. But I know Donald and I shouldn't have become involved. It was wrong. I'd never done anything like that before—"

Maryelizabeth interrupted to stop the woman's self-recrimination. "Anna, how did you and Caleb meet?"

The memory brought a fleeting smile to Anna's face. "We first saw each other in an emergency room. Caleb came in with a nasty gash on his arm. He was really stoic about it, said that it was his fault because he never should have trusted the branch that gave out under him in the first place.

"I remember thinking that he was the handsomest man I had ever seen. I expected him to be stuck up, but instead he was shy. I had trouble getting him to say much, but while I was dressing his wound I got him to tell me a little bit about his job. Working with trees sounded romantic to me. He probably could have told me he was a used-car salesman and I would have found something wonderful about that. I told him how much I loved the look and feel of sycamore leaves, and he did a lot of nodding like he felt the same. I got the impression he wanted to talk to me, but I also sensed this reluctance. When he left the ER without even saying good-bye, I figured he probably had a girlfriend, and that was that. Two days later, though, I received this huge manila envelope in the mail. Inside was a gigantic sycamore leaf. On it he'd written a thank-you note and his phone number."

Maryelizabeth didn't step on Anna's memory. She let her sit there and think about fonder days.

"I still have that leaf," Anna said.

"Were you shocked to learn who Caleb's father was?"

Anna shook her head. "It was almost as if I expected that, or something like that."

"What do you mean?"

"With Caleb there was always this . . . darkness. He had places in him that no light could penetrate. I don't know if I'm explaining myself very well, but there is this shadowy side, this sense of tragedy, that Cal always carries around with him. I wanted to help ease that burden, but he made it his alone. For most of our marriage I went to him. I'd massage his neck and shoulders, and then I'd sit on his lap and ask him what was wrong, and he'd tell me that nothing was wrong. I always knew he was lying. I knew there were secrets, things he wasn't sharing with me, but over time I began to accept his distance, and then I began to participate in it."

"You make him sound as if he was never happy."

"Happiness makes him feel guilty, as if he doesn't deserve it."

"Are you angry at him for not confiding in you?"

"Yes. But now I can understand how he thought he was doing the right thing."

"Did you have a whirlwind courtship?"

Anna shook her head. "No. We fell in love right away, but it was a year before Cal asked me to marry him. And when he finally did ask me, I could see how conflicted he was. At the time I thought it was just a guy thing. I only saw him that torn up two other times."

"What happened on those occasions?"

"When he learned I was pregnant with Janet, Cal wanted me to get an abortion. For a time he was adamant. 'It's a bad world,' he kept telling me. 'It's not a fit place to bring a child into.' But I told him, 'If a child is loved, the world isn't so terrible.' He kept coming back to me with his what-ifs, though. His favorite was, 'What if the baby's deformed? What if the baby isn't right?' He was terrified of that. I think he had the same fears with James, but by then he was head over heels in love with Janet, so he wasn't quite as terrified."

"What happened the other time he was upset?"

"Nothing really. It was so long ago. . . ."

"I'd still like to hear about it."

"I guess I remember it so vividly because it's the only time I ever saw Cal cry."

"What happened?"

"Cal was taking some junior college courses to please me. I had nagged him for what I thought was his own good. He was so smart I couldn't imagine him not excelling in, and enjoying, college.

"At first, everything seemed to be going fine, but one night I walked into the study and I found him sobbing. He tried to explain his tears away by saying he was just tired, but as I comforted him he opened up a little. He said he'd been reading something that bothered him. I didn't pry; I knew better than that. I just held him, rocking him in my arms, and that's when he opened up a little more. At the time it was hard making sense of what he said. He told me that his psychology class was studying nature-versus-nurture, and that he felt doomed either way. 'My whole life's been a Harlow experiment,' he said, and then he stopped talking, sealing himself up again. I kneaded his shoulders, and chest, but he wouldn't say anything else.

"I made him some cocoa, and told him he needed a good night's sleep. We went to bed, and we made love. I used to think I could take all of Cal's troubles, and make them explode between my legs. Eventually he slept, but I didn't. Maybe I always counted on him being Cal the stoic, and maybe I'm partly to blame for the way he's acted over the years. I don't know. I only remember feeling that my world was a less secure place.

"I went downstairs in the middle of the night, and I saw that he'd left his psychology textbook open. I sat and started reading about Dr. Harry Harlow and his awful experiments with rhesus monkeys."

"What kind of experiments?"

"He deprived young monkeys of their mothers, and set up all sorts of artificial mother substitutes, but Harlow's mothers weren't designed for love. They looked like something created in Dr. Frankenstein's laboratory. These were *mothers* who shot jets of compressed air at the baby monkeys that tried desperately to cling to them, air that almost separated their fur from their skin; these were *mothers* that rocked violently, bucking the babies to the floor; these were *mothers* designed to reject their babies, pushing them away with mechanical spikes until the little monkeys dropped to the concrete."

"What was the point of the experiments?"

"I think it was to create monsters, because that's what it did. The monkeys grew up to be very abnormal adults. They didn't know how to be social. They attacked other monkeys for no reason, and they abused themselves. And when they became mothers, usually as a consequence of Harlow's setting up a controlled rape, the results were tragic. Offspring were abused and killed."

Anna shook her head. "I'm a nurse. I've seen a lot of pain and suffering. But the pictures accompanying the text really got to me. Despite all the rejection, the young monkeys kept trying to go back to their artificial mothers. So great was their need for nurturing, they were willing to endure the source of their pain time and time again. I can still see their desperate faces. All they wanted was a little love."

"Did you ever talk about this with Caleb?"

"No. It was something else we swept under the rug. That week Caleb stopped going to classes. He said formal education didn't appeal to him."

"Did you believe him?"

"No."

Anna's expression showed how conflicted she was. She didn't want to be disloyal.

"But that doesn't make Cal a liar or anything. I'm certain he had nothing to do with those women's deaths. I know he's innocent."

The rising tone of her voice qualified her statement; a few moments later, so did Anna.

"I just wish he hadn't closed off so much of himself to me and the kids. I've lived with Cal for eleven years, and there have been times I wondered if I ever really knew him. He's this puzzle with all sorts of missing pieces."

A puzzle that saw himself as a Harlow experiment, thought Maryelizabeth. But an experiment at what stage? Had Caleb seen himself as the rejected waif, or the grown-up monster? By his own words Caleb had said he was doomed, but he had never specified whether his fate was as victim or victimizer. Maybe, at the time, he hadn't known.

Maybe he still didn't.

17

Sleep wouldn't come. The more Caleb pursued it, the more it eluded him. The room felt stuffy and cramped, and as time passed the bed and pillows went from being merely uncomfortable to instruments of torture. Caleb missed Anna and the kids. Their absence made his chest feel empty, almost as if there were a hole there.

It felt like everything was closing in on him. He tried to control his claustrophobia, but couldn't. The pressure kept increasing. Succumbing to the need for fresh air, he jumped off the bed, rushed over to the window, and pressed his head up against the screen, gulping in the night air. The thought of prison, of being shut in an even smaller room, made Caleb hyperventilate. He became lightheaded, and had to grab the window sill to avoid falling. But the walls still closed in. . . .

"Cal? Is that your name? I mean your real name?"

The pack tightened their circle, and cut off his escape. He looked around, desperate to find an opening. There wasn't one.

"I haven't heard an answer, Cal."

Eddie McGlynn had picked on Caleb from his first day at the high school. McGlynn put his face close to Caleb's, not more than two inches away, and waited for his answer with pretended interest.

"Cal or Caleb. Either one."

"Either one," said McGlynn. "Why, that's mighty generous of you, Cal."

He had never officially changed his name, had just dropped his first name of Gray and taken to using his middle name. Caleb had hoped the name change would put some distance between him and his father, and that people would forget, but that had proved a false hope. The people of Concho County had long memories. Since his father's conviction and execution, Caleb had always tried to be invisible, not to stand out, but few classmates allowed him to be anonymous. He was everyone's favorite target. The preferred rite of passage for most boys growing up in Concho County was to beat him up.

The circle of man-boys closed in on Caleb. Most of those who surrounded him were a year or two older than his sixteen years. He looked around for teachers, for help, saw Mr. Harriman, the math teacher, observe what was happening, but then saw him close his door and pretend not to notice what was going on.

"If your real name's Cal or Caleb," Eddie said, "how's come I've seen a different name on class lists and stuff?"

Caleb shook his head. "Don't know," he said.

"Now what's that name I saw?" Eddie scratched his head, then reached for suspenders that weren't there. His exaggerated mannerisms had his circle laughing. "Was some kind of color, I think. Pink maybe. Or Puce. Green, that's what it was. No, it was Gray. That's it. That's the name I saw."

Caleb shrugged his shoulders, and tried to get by again, but the pack wouldn't let him. They knew the fun was just beginning. "I got to get to lunch," he said.

"What's you going to eat?" Eddie asked. "Some pussy?"

Everyone in the circle snickered. The faces around Caleb took on a nightmarish quality. He was sport for hard eyes and mocking expressions and cruel mouths. There were pimples on most of the faces, as shiny and angry and eruptive as the boys themselves.

"Heard your daddy was a big one for playing with pussy. I mean he didn't beat around the bush, did he?"

There were yelps of laughter, and poking of elbows into ribs, and slaps on backs.

"Muff diving's one thing, but your old man, Jeezuss, I heard one time he took a bite out of a beaver. What'd he think, one gash wasn't enough?"

The crowd was growing. It wasn't just the pack now. Cal's

classmates were gathering on the outskirts, watching, laughing. There for the spectacle. That made it hurt all the more. Over the years Caleb had worked hard on not showing any pain in public. Every night he did his exercises: Mirror, mirror on the wall, who's the most miserable of all? *He called himself all manner of names, tried to harden anything that was soft in him, and face up to his own self-hate with a stoic face. But this time his conditioning failed. He could feel his throat tightening, could feel the onset of tears.*

"Your daddy was one sick puppy, wasn't he, Cal?*"*

"I want to get by."

Eddie pretended he hadn't heard. "But he was a proud, sick puppy, wasn't he, Cal? *Couldn't murder all those gals without leaving a signature, could he?"*

Caleb feinted a move in one direction, and then almost escaped through a space between two of the circle's sentries, but he was caught and thrown back. Eddie put his face close to Cal's once again.

"Your real first name's Gray, isn't it? Just like your daddy's real name."

Cal's tears started to fall.

"Anybody got a hanky for Cal, *here?" Eddie asked. His tone was anything but sympathetic. He was feeding on the other boy's pain. The audience moved in a little closer.*

"Ever see that movie about your old man on TV?" asked Eddie. "Not many people were shedding tears the night he fried. There was partying big time. There was a crowd down at the prison and lots of signs that said, Thank God It's Fryday. And there was one guy walking around handing out recipes for Shame Fried Fritters. Said if you ran a little short of your daddy's bodily parts, you could always substitute skunk."

Caleb punched him, put all his strength and anger into his right hand and sent it at McGlynn's face, but the bigger boy managed to move back and escape the brunt of the blow. It was the opportunity McGlynn had been waiting for, and used it to start pummeling Caleb. He wasn't alone. He never was. The other boys in the circle closed in, and took turns throwing punches. Caleb started gasping, the wind knocked out of him. There was no way out. . . .

* * *

Caleb pushed himself away from the window, away from the memory. Being weak embarrassed him. Pressing crowds still took away his breath, and whenever he felt boxed in he had to stifle the impulse to run. Like now. He decided he needed to eat or drink something, excuse enough to get him out of the room.

The hardwood floors didn't cooperate with his desire for silence. They announced his passage with creaks and groans. He felt his way forward in the darkness, moving down the hall and past the living room. The kitchen wasn't as dark as the rest of the house. The sink window was curtained, but the light from the full moon pressed through the colored fabric, painting the kitchen a translucent tawny rose.

Lola's refrigerator contained mostly juices and greens. In the back was a carton of nonfat milk. Caleb didn't examine the featured missing child on the carton, afraid, he hated to admit, of finding himself. He opened a few old cabinets, tried unsuccessfully to keep the ancient hinges from squeaking, and at last found a glass. He'd leave Lola some money, he decided. The last thing he wanted was to feel beholden to his hostess.

Caleb was in no rush to get back to the confines of his room. There was a cat clock in the kitchen that kept him company while he sipped the milk. The cat's large eyes moved in time with its pendulum tail. He tried to hypnotize himself by watching the moving clock. No matter how many times he told himself that he was getting sleepy, the clock just kept telling him it was getting later. He kept thinking about Anna and the kids, and the havoc his secret life was undoubtedly creating. Anna had always told everyone what a good father he was, but Caleb knew that good fathers didn't run out on their children. Maybe he wasn't much different from his own father. He shivered. Being like his father had always been his greatest fear.

The tightness in Caleb's chest returned. Changing rooms hadn't helped. The memories knew where to follow. Glass in hand, he started to retrace his steps back to his room. A voice emerged from the darkness of the living room. "Couldn't sleep?"

Caleb held on to the glass, but only barely. Lola was seated in the corner, her figure scarcely visible in the shadows. She leaned forward in the easy chair, half of her materializing. She was wearing a sheer nightgown with a low, clinging décolletage that showed off her curves. *His* curves, Caleb remembered. He wished Lola had just remained a voice; her revealed flesh bothered him.

"I didn't mean to startle you," she said. "I assumed you heard me come out of my room."

"I hope I didn't wake you," Caleb said. "It was just that I couldn't sleep, and I thought some milk might help. But I intend to pay you for it."

"You didn't wake me, and you're not going to pay me for the milk. My refrigerator, such as it is, is yours."

Caleb hesitated at the entrance of the living room, not sure whether he should continue down the hall, or take a seat.

"Would you like some light?"

"No," he said, "that's not necessary," then found himself sitting down on the sofa, albeit as far away from Lola as the room allowed.

"I've been meaning to go shopping. I doubt whether you found much of interest in the fridge."

She kept her voice low, little more than a whisper. It made the room feel smaller, more intimate. Her Southern accent was soft and beguiling, gentle and unaffected, and very feminine.

"I wasn't really hungry anyway," Caleb said. "I just thought I should put something in my stomach."

"When was the last time you ate?"

"Before this all began."

"Milk's a good start, then. And I suppose it's been a while since you slept?"

He shrugged, not sure if she could see the motion, but not willing to comment further.

"The secret is not putting pressure on yourself to sleep," Lola said. "If you find yourself getting tired, just tell yourself that you're going to take a little nap. That way you don't feel as if you have to perform to some standard, and it lessens the stress."

"Do you suffer from insomnia?"

"Suffer's not the right word. Sometimes I have trouble sleeping, but that's all right. My mind's just telling me it wants to do some thinking. Outlook is everything. It's a way of turning trials and tribulations into blessings."

Caleb wasn't in the mood for Norman Vincent Peale, and Lola read his skepticism in the silence.

"You've never been in therapy, have you?" she asked.

"No."

His eyes had gradually adjusted to the dark room. He could make out her figure, but not her face, and assumed he was similarly cloaked from her. The darkness comforted Caleb, offering anonymity.

"Did your sleeplessness bring you any answers?" Lola asked.

"No. Just questions."

"Such as?"

"Who's doing this to me, and why."

"Any theories?"

"No. If I believed in the supernatural, I'd say my father's come back to ruin my life again."

"That almost sounds like wishful thinking."

"I can assure you, it's not."

"I've known people who would be lost without their villains. Their villains are their reason to exist."

"That's not my case," Caleb said emphatically.

"Was your father abusive to you?"

Caleb didn't want to talk about him, but forced himself to. "He never hit me, if that's what you mean. But he wasn't around very much while I was growing up."

"So you felt abandoned?"

"I'm not keen on psychobabble. His going to jail wasn't what made my life a hell. It was how people responded to his crimes. In his absence, I became their target."

"Did your father love you?"

"That's a silly question."

"Why is it?"

"Psychopaths can't love. They can only mimic love."

"How do you know your daddy was a psychopath?"

"He murdered seventeen innocent women."

"That still doesn't rule out his loving you."

Caleb didn't try to hide his anger. "You make a mockery of the word," he said. "How could someone like him possibly love?"

"I know he was sick," Lola said, "but that doesn't mean all of him was rotten. I suppose it's easier, though, to picture him as a totally bad human being. If he did love you, that would only make everything hurt all the more, wouldn't it?"

He didn't answer.

"How old were you when he died?"

"Fourteen."

"I lost my father when I wasn't much older than that. But he didn't die like yours did. He just kicked me out of our house and told me never to come back again. He meant what he said."

"Are we supposed to be sitting here comparing sob stories?" Caleb asked.

"No. I guess I'm just saying in a roundabout way that you don't have a monopoly on pain. Lots of people can't walk out the door without being suspects for one reason or another: their skin color, their looks, their disability, their sexual orientation. Those people can't do anything about their situation. You can."

Rather than make a case for his own misery, Caleb returned to her biography. It was easier that way. "Where was your mother while your father was kicking you out?"

"Right behind him, subtly encouraging him to do it. Nothing too overt, you know. That wouldn't have been ladylike. But she was always ashamed of me. I was much darker than my mother. As an adult, I hear myself described as *exotic.* As a child, everyone just called me *ugly.* And when it was clear I was *different,* my father began to blame my mother for how I turned out. One of his favorite laments was that he never should have married a 'half-breed.' My mother never argued with him. She had fancied herself a very refined woman, and to her mind I was proof she had something to be ashamed of. And that was even before my femininity shamed her.

"Shame: that word was such a part of my early life. I think that's why your father's use of it had such a terrible appeal to me, and others as well. He made us confront our own shame."

"Serial murder therapy."

"That wasn't my inference."

"I know. I was trying to be clever. But I'm not good at being clever."

"I don't agree. Maybe you're too good at it, and that's what scares you. I think your whole life you've been thinking things, but not saying them. You didn't want people to know there was a growl in you, because you figured they might start looking for teeth.

Maybe the murderer was counting on that. Maybe you've already surprised him."

"How?"

"By not rolling over and playing dead. By not immediately becoming that perfect patsy."

"He's spun me like a top," Caleb said.

"But you're still spinning. You're not down."

"He watched me," Caleb said, unsuccessfully fighting the tremor in his voice. "He knows about me."

She heard his sense of violation, and anger. And something else. There was bedrock way down there.

"What are you going to do?" Lola asked.

"I'm going to become acquainted with my father," he said.

18

The sheriff's press conference was held in the Ridgehaven sheriff's main conference room. The only thing missing from the sheriff's opening announcement was a lit fuse. Even from the press, where showing any surprise is considered bad taste, his revelation was met with gasps. Around the room one word was repeated: "Shame."

Only two photographers had been dispatched to the press conference, but both felt the need to set off a year's worth of flashes. Reporters who had ventured to the sheriff's headquarters expecting to be underwhelmed by the so-called special announcement suddenly found their voices:

"Shame's son, Sheriff? Shame's biological son?"

And all the while one word continued to come out of disbelieving lips: *"Shame, Shame, Shame, Shame . . ."*

An awakened hive, all abuzz. It reminded Maryelizabeth of the time she had visited an ashram and heard a room of penitents chanting "Om." The power of their chorus had been astounding, with the sounds detonating around her, human voices raising thunder. She had been incredulous that such power could come from the repetition of a single word. Now another word was being invoked, if not as loudly, or by a chorus as organized. But still, it was producing a similar electricity.

In the front of the room, standing behind a lectern with a microphone, stood Sheriff Campbell. He was flanked by Sergeant

Hardy on one side, and Lieutenant Borman on the other. They all looked somber, funereal.

"A warrant has been issued for the arrest of Gray Caleb Parker," the sheriff said, "aka Caleb Parker, aka Cal Parker. He is wanted for questioning in the murders of Lita Jennings, Teresa Sanders, and Brandy Wein."

The shouting match started: "Sheriff . . ."

Campbell held up a hand. "I ask that each of you refrain from asking questions until we've all had a chance to finish our briefing."

Maryelizabeth looked around the room, tried to take down details like a courtroom sketch artist. *Flushed faces,* she wrote, *people unconsciously hugging themselves. Around me a shifting of bodies and heads. The reaction in here couldn't have been much more extreme had the sheriff announced that Jack the Ripper was alive and well and relocated in San Diego.*

It was the mythology of Shame at work, she thought. For whatever reasons, Gray Parker had found his way into the modern psyche. His bloodstains had been harder to scrub out than most.

Maryelizabeth was glad that helping Anna Parker hadn't made her persona non grata at the Sheriff's Department, even if she no longer had special privileges. Earlier that morning, press credentials had been issued to her, but her request to go behind the scenes had been politely refused. Now that the secret was out, she no longer had leverage.

She sat through the short briefing, and heard nothing new. The media were apparently going to get only the sketchiest of details. Maryelizabeth resisted an urge to leave, her curiosity piqued by the two shrouded easels sitting to the right of the lectern. A sheriff's deputy had been positioned in front of the easels, his presence prohibiting any peeking.

Maryelizabeth didn't have to wait long for the unveiling. Campbell did the honors, pulling back the coverings and revealing two blown-up black-and-white photos. Gray Parker's face still found its way into enough public forums to be recognizable. A stir passed through the room.

The sheriff patted one of the photos with his left hand. "Gray Parker Senior," he said, paused a moment, then patted the other photo with his right hand, "and Gray Parker Junior."

In her pad Maryelizabeth wrote: *The response by the Fourth Estate would have pleased a lynching mob. Did I condemn as easily? The sheriff's presentation feels like a magic act. Only it isn't a woman being sawed in half and put on display, but Caleb Parker.*

"Questions?" asked the sheriff.

"Is apprehension imminent?" a reporter asked.

"We are confident of an early capture," the sheriff said.

"Was the word *shame* written on all the San Diego victims?"

"We will not be commenting on the crime scene or answering any inquiries addressing the demise of the victims."

The magic act was over, she thought, though the sheriff tried to give the impression that there *was* still something up his sleeve. As the questions heated up, the sheriff quickly proved to be generous about handing off inquiries, especially the sticky ones, to his subordinates.

Maryelizabeth found her attention divided between what was going on in front of the room, and what was going on in the back. Flip phones had been pulled out, and stations and papers were being called.

"That's what I said, Shame's son . . ."

"Big story? No shit, Sherlock . . ."

"Serial murders, three linked so far . . ."

"Parker, spelled P-A-R . . ."

An Asian-American woman finished her call and dropped her phone into her handbag. She wore a lot of makeup, the better for the television camera. She was young, but tried to appear older, had a face too serious for her years. The woman looked at Maryelizabeth, dismissed her, and then after a long moment came back to her again. Her expression asked, Where do I know you from? Maryelizabeth looked away, pretending interest in the press conference. The woman approached anyway.

"Excuse me."

Maryelizabeth was forced to look up. Their eyes met.

"Lisa Wong, KGSI-TV. I wonder if we might talk."

The reporter spoke very quietly, but her expression said, Gotcha. It was apparent she didn't want to announce Maryelizabeth's name in front of anyone else for fear of others' recognizing her find.

"Later, perhaps," Maryelizabeth said, pantomiming interest in the news conference.

The tactic didn't work. Lisa took a seat next to her.

"I still don't understand," asked a reporter, "how the suspect was in custody, and then released."

"As I've already stated," said the sheriff, "the suspect came in voluntarily while we were still in the process of gathering evidence. As for particulars, Lieutenant Borman might better answer those. . . ."

"Can we set a time?" Lisa whispered. "And I'd like to make this an exclusive interview."

Shoe on the other foot, thought Maryelizabeth. Now she was the one who wanted to duck the spotlight. "Let's talk outside for a minute," she said.

Lisa signaled to her cameraman that she'd be back, then walked out of the room with Maryelizabeth. With no one around to overhear, she asked, "You *are* Maryelizabeth Line, aren't you?"

"Yes."

"What are you doing here?"

"The same thing you are."

Lisa didn't buy it. "But you're not from around here, are you?"

"No, I'm not."

"Then you had to have some foreknowledge of the story. You knew something was going on."

"Like you," said Maryelizabeth, "I don't know nearly as much as I would like to."

"Are you working with the Sheriff's Department?"

Not anymore. "Only to the degree that you are."

"Are you writing another book?"

"There's always that possibility."

"How long have you been in town?"

"Not long."

"Which means what?"

"Which means that what's going on in the press conference is the story. I'm not."

"But you knew his father better than anyone."

"This story isn't about his father."

"Of course it is. That's why you're here, isn't it? And that's the beauty of this piece. It's almost like a plot for a horror novel, with the evil passing on from one generation to another."

"Try as I might," Maryelizabeth said, "I don't see that beauty. If you'll excuse me."

"I didn't mean it like that," said Lisa, talking quickly. "But you can't pretend the father-son twist isn't going to make for good play. That's why I need to talk with you on camera. It will just take a minute of your time. I only need a few of your impressions. A déjà vu thing."

"I have to go," said Maryelizabeth, walking away from the meeting room, and the reporter.

"Can I have your number at least? I'd like to give you a call later."

Maryelizabeth kept walking. The reporter called out one last question: "What are you hiding?"

She'd learn, Maryelizabeth thought. Ambush journalism worked only when a camera was running. Instead of alienating Maryelizabeth, the reporter should have followed after her and pressed a business card with her home number into her hand. That's how Maryelizabeth did it. And it worked. People often called her later just to talk.

But while it might be true that Lisa Wong had a lot to learn as a news journalist, there was nothing wrong with her instincts. Her last question trailed Maryelizabeth back to her hotel. *What are you hiding?* Maryelizabeth wasn't sure that was something she was ready to answer, even to herself.

If they ever resurrected the show *This Is Your Life,* Maryelizabeth thought, her segment would be played out in a hotel room. The dimensions changed, along with the interior design, but mostly there was a sameness to all such rooms. She'd spent the better part of her adult life in anonymous rooms like this one, a prison of her own making. Take away the turndown mint, and add some bars, and her sentence would be complete.

Six large boxes filled Maryelizabeth's cell, boxes her assistant had retrieved from storage and overnighted to her hotel. Facing them, Maryelizabeth remembered that she had still another promise to keep. Caleb Parker had asked her to look through her old Shame files, had asked her to flag anything that stood out and could possibly have a connection with the present-day murders, but just hours after making his request Brandy Wein had been murdered and he had disappeared.

There were fewer boxes than she remembered. While working on *Shame* Maryelizabeth had been naive enough to think that no book had ever been so thoroughly researched. The boxes showed the passage of time, the cardboard blanched and slightly brittle. In some places the masking tape had frayed. The past wanted to spill out.

This is what a book is, she thought, lots of pieces and threads and gathered memories. There was nothing neat and tidy about the process at all, especially with a true-crime book. The pain was all there, just waiting. Pandora's boxes. Unbidden, she heard the echo of Gray Parker's words: "If you do this book right, you'll fall in love with me."

I didn't do the book right, Maryelizabeth thought, as if to satisfy a point of honor. The book had made her reputation, and a lot of money, but she had never been satisfied with it. There had been too many unanswered questions.

Maryelizabeth took a knife and sliced through some masking tape. She had packed everything up the day after Gray Parker's execution, had symbolically tied up all the loose ends. Her manuscript had been all but completed, and her publisher was waiting to rush it into print. Only the ending, those last few pages, needed to be written. Her editor had flown into town to baby-sit her through them. At the time, Maryelizabeth had no idea how extraordinary that treatment was.

She tentatively reached inside the box, felt around without looking, then pulled out a picture of Virginia Clayton. Virginia had been one of the later victims. Number fourteen, Maryelizabeth thought. No, fifteen. An only child. She remembered Virginia's parents, a mother that never seemed to stop crying, and a father who had responded to the news of his daughter's death by setting his face in stone and never offering another expression to the world.

I'm looking for a needle in a haystack, she thought, a needle that probably doesn't even exist. So why was she so afraid of getting pricked?

Maryelizabeth removed a pile of notebooks, and then opened

one. Over the years the highlighting had faded. She still used the same method, jotting down impressions, and musing, and afterward highlighting what might be potentially useful. Reading her old notes embarrassed her. The thinking seemed so sophomoric, right out of Psychology 101. Even the highlighted parts. Especially those.

SHAME. Think of all the expressions employing the word: For shame; I thought I'd die of shame; shame on you; I blushed for shame; it's a shame; sense of shame; overwhelmed by shame.

It's a word with its roots in guilt, and false pride, and embarrassment. It's the opposite of doing what's right. Shame makes us avert our eyes. Shame makes us shrink. When we feel shame we've usually violated some rule or standard or more, or fallen short somehow.

The Book of Genesis, the springboard of the Bible, is imbued in shame. Exposure before God, the metaphor of Adam and Eve ashamed of their nakedness. Our Judeo-Christian culture starts on that note of guilt. Maybe I should play up Original Sin and Gray Parker.

Maryelizabeth had talked with a number of mental health professionals, had asked them about the emotion of shame, and why Gray Parker might have written that word on all of his victims. They hadn't run short on theories.

Men often respond aggressively to shame, Dr. Levy says. Rather than confront their shame, they're more likely to lash out against it. He theorizes the murders could have been a response to that anger, and the writing Gray's contrition after the act. Shame is an emotion that often lingers, he said. One of the most common symptoms of shame is depression, often severe. Shame can debilitate, causing mental and physical breakdowns. Patients will often do anything to avoid confronting their shame, Dr. Levy said. They'd rather live with the consequences than focus on the shame itself. For them, that's the easier way "out."

Maryelizabeth reread the last three sentences. A sense of unease came over her. She couldn't help but wonder about her own easier ways out.

Dr. Levy says I should offer myself as Gray's confessor. He explained that when shame is confessed, people feel better. Sometimes they even feel redeemed.

Confessor. Maryelizabeth almost laughed. She had been more Gray's toy than savior.

Maryelizabeth continued flipping through the notebook. The name of Sheila Vickers kept appearing, another psychologist she had consulted.

Sheila says I should make a study of whatever Gray says he doesn't remember. She says that therein I might find the roots of his shame. Sheila also suggested that I be aware of any patterns of avoidance.

Maryelizabeth had tried that for a time, had taken copious notes about everything, until Gray had complained.

"You make me feel like a laboratory animal," he had told her. "All you do is scratch, scratch, scratch on that pad. Ever stop to think with all that scratching we're not doing much real talking?"

Maybe it was her own avoidance she should have been taking note of. She'd always felt uneasy about the book, as if by writing it she had made a deal with the devil, or come as close to that as humanly possible. But Gray hadn't been the only one doing the using and manipulating. A Johnson needs his Boswell.

Maryelizabeth had known that liking him wasn't right. It was stupid and irresponsible and wrong. It betrayed the memory of her friends, and double-crossed all those intimacies afforded her by the families of the victims. She had always had nothing but scorn for those women who had married prisoners. *Outmates,* she called them, women who'd become outcasts by marrying inmates. Fools. She saw them lined up on visiting days, even got to know their stories, and their grand illusions. In many cases they'd thrown away everything for misguided love: money, family, self-respect.

Idiots.

But was she raging at them, or herself? Maybe she'd never really been very different from them. Maybe she was an *outmate.*

Let it out, Maryelizabeth told herself. Tell your anger.

"Damn you, Gray Parker," she whispered. "You died with secrets.

You held out this carrot in front of my nose and you led me in circles, and I don't know whether I knew you any better in the end than I did in the beginning."

Her voice grew incrementally louder. "Damn you, Gray Parker, for bringing your namesake into this world, and for all but willing that boy to follow in your footsteps."

More, she thought. There was so much more. "Damn you, Gray Parker, for causing pain and misery and heartbreak wherever you went. You could have been anything, but you chose to be worse than evil.

"Damn you, Gray Parker, for murdering innocent women, and murdering innocence, and ultimately murdering yourself. If you were in such a hurry to die, why didn't you just kill yourself?"

A quick, deep breath, but she wasn't done, not even close to being done: "Damn you, Gray Parker, for doing everything you could to win me over. I suppose I was one last game for you. One last person to hurt.

"Damn you, Gray Parker, for always being so nice and thoughtful to me, for showing me only your best, most considerate side, and leaving me to wonder if all the kindnesses you offered me were only manipulation."

Her voice became more shrill: "Damn you, Gray Parker, for your last words. Leave it to you to cloud my mind even at the end. You had no right to tell me that you loved me, no right at all."

He'd made his offer of love in the face of death. They'd been his parting words to her. He had known that the next time she saw him he'd be strapped into the electric chair.

Maryelizabeth found herself shaking uncontrollably. Unwanted tears fell. There were so many things twisted up in the Gray Parker story, so many elements that should never have merged in the same breath: murder and love; gentleness and brutality; intelligence and sickness.

"Damn you, Gray Parker," she said, her last curse the most vehement, "for even suggesting that I could fall in love with you. I wasn't willing to love you then, and I'm not willing to love you now."

Maryelizabeth took a few deep breaths, and wiped away her tears. Then she started digging through the boxes again, on the hunt for answers past and present.

19

The woman was out taking an early morning walk by herself. A power walk. Her strides were purposeful and measured, her body and mind intent on getting the proper workout. She carried hand weights, and pumped her arms back and forth. Every so often she consulted her watch to make sure her heart and pulse rates were at their desired levels. She never stopped to smell the flowers—indeed, took little notice of anything but her regimen.

That made it easy for the predator to move in on her unnoticed.

Caleb matched her pace, but his legs were longer. Almost imperceptibly, he closed the distance between them. The woman wore her brown hair short, and that accentuated her long neck. He focused on that. She wore form-fitting workout clothes that hugged her shapely figure like a second skin.

He narrowed the gap from twenty yards, to fifteen, to ten. There was no need for him to muffle his footsteps. Like him, the woman was wearing a headset that tuned out the world. But she wasn't listening to the same tape he was. If she had been, he was sure, the woman would have been more aware of her surroundings. In Caleb's ears, a voice buzzed, and in his mind's eye he watched another woman being stalked. He was a witness to his father's moving in for the kill. . . .

Gasping for breath, Caleb pulled up. Ahead of him, the woman kept walking. He yanked Lola's Walkman from his head, then turned around. He felt dirty, felt as if he desperately needed a shower, even though he hadn't yet broken into a sweat.

Caleb started trembling. What the hell had happened there? One moment he'd been walking, and the next he'd been playing some twisted mental game. At least he hoped it was a game and not his father's sickness coming to the fore. The deeper he got into his father's biography, the more he felt touched by his darkness. He had always wondered, and been afraid to find out, what part of him was his father. That answer seemed to be closing in on him.

Even with the headphones removed, Maryelizabeth Line's voice kept circulating through his head. She had narrated her own book. Every grisly detail. Her voice hadn't changed over the years, was still slightly breathless, with a touch of the Midwest, and just a hint of a gravel floor. Hearing her had bothered Caleb. She had brought an added intimacy to the work. In her telling, it was almost as if she was in his father's head, as well as his own.

He hurried back to Lola's bungalow, had to force himself not to sprint. After all these years, he thought, and I'm still running away. But he'd never found a way to lose his shadow.

Caleb opened the front door quietly, mindful of not waking Lola, but his precautions weren't necessary. He heard footsteps, then saw her come rushing out of the guest room. She looked as if she had been caught doing something wrong.

"I—I wondered where you were," she said, backing up toward her room so as to not expose her back. Her face was to him, but she refused to meet his eyes.

"I went for a walk."

"Oh."

"What's wrong?" he asked.

She continued to back up. "Nothing."

Lola's answer was too quick, and her tone too falsetto. The pictures, Caleb remembered. He'd left them in an envelope on the nightstand.

She was at her door, opening it.

"Those pictures made me run as well," Caleb said.

Lola edged through the door sideways, then swung it closed behind her. Caleb listened as locks were turned. He didn't come any closer, but spoke loudly enough to be heard.

"I found those photos in my truck yesterday," he said. "Someone either followed me to the Sheriff's Office, or knew I was going to be there, and planted them. I noticed the envelope when I was driving home.

"You ever see that painting *The Scream?* That's what I felt like when I pulled those pictures out of the envelope. Inside and out I didn't feel human. All of me was just this scream that was desperate to come out.

"I didn't know what the hell to do. I thought about killing myself. But then I realized I couldn't do that even if it was the only way to end the pain. I couldn't kill myself, because my kids would have been condemned to growing up like I had. I couldn't be that selfish."

From behind the door, she broke her silence. Her voice was small, still frightened: "Why didn't you just contact the police?"

"I was afraid to go back. I'm claustrophobic, and I knew that if I gave them the photos, this time they wouldn't let me go."

"Did you know the girl?"

"No—that is, I don't know her name, but I know who she was. She worked behind the counter at the doughnut shop where I met Maryelizabeth Line the night before last. After Maryelizabeth left I just zoned out sitting there, trying to make sense of things. This girl had to tap me on the shoulder to wake me up. She kept apologizing for disturbing me, and said that she wouldn't be bothering me except that the shop was closing."

"She was the girl in the photos?"

"Yes."

"You said that when you first saw those pictures you wanted to scream. Did you?"

"No."

"Why not?"

"I was afraid if I started, I'd never stop." After a minute of silence, Caleb finally spoke again.

"If you want," he said, "I'll leave."

He waited for an answer. Just when he decided one wasn't forthcoming, he heard the locks turning. Lola walked through the door with a towel in hand.

"Go shower," Lola said, "but don't dry your hair."

* * *

Lola set him up at the kitchen table, positioned him with his back to her. It was almost like facing up to major surgery, thought Caleb, looking at the bottles, tubes, and ointments lined up along the table. In a box, but at the ready, were curling irons, setting pins, lotions, sprays, and metal implements that looked like instruments of torture but probably had something to do with hairdressing. Worst of all was the chemical smell. Caleb breathed through his mouth.

She draped a plastic poncho over him, and gave him a hand mirror. At first, they were about as comfortable together as two sixth-graders matched up on a dance floor. Caleb was rigid, had to force himself not to shy away from her touch, while Lola was tentative, still not sure if she was doing the right thing.

She worked the hair coloring in with gloved hands. There was a stilted politeness to their conversation, their speech usually initiated by some stubborn tangle of hair, Lola offering high-pitched apologies while working at the clump, and Caleb assuring her it was fine. Gradually, both of them loosened up.

Half an hour passed before Caleb was emboldened to look at himself with the mirror. He cringed at what he saw. "I thought I was going to be a blond," he said. "I look more like a redhead."

"As one of the songs in my act goes, 'We've only just begun.' It's going to take a few more applications."

"How did you happen to have blond dye?"

"Could have made you red, white, or even blue. I used to change my hair color about as often as I did my underwear. No more. Change my hair color, that is. I do change my underwear."

Caleb didn't smile, or respond, in any way.

"You always been this black hole?" Lola asked.

"What do you mean?"

"It's like your mood sucks all the light out of the room."

"Under the circumstances, I don't feel like Mr. Happy."

"Were you ever Mr. Happy?"

"I was happier. . . ."

"That's no answer."

"You're right."

"When in doubt, be the sphinx, that it? I suppose you think you were being noble by not telling your wife about your past."

"Noble's not the word. I just didn't see any reason to burden her with it."

"You did, anyway."

"That's not true."

"Course it is. And don't think you didn't put the *mojo* on your children, either. You don't think your family knew something was wrong? You don't think they sensed your secrets? They knew the family curse, even if you never gave it form."

"It's sure enough got form now," Caleb said.

Too much form. Thinking about his family made Caleb ache. He became restive in the chair, felt the need to act, to do something. The tick-tocking from the damn cat clock was driving him crazy.

"How much longer?" he asked.

"An hour or so."

He sighed, started fiddling with the hand mirror for want of anything else to do. He held the mirror up, pretended to look at his hair, but really sneaked a few glances at Lola.

"Maybe I should have just gotten a wig."

"Wigs are obvious. When I'm through here, you'll look like a natural blond, especially with your baby blues. All you'll need is a surfboard rack and everyone will think you're a native."

"Better not make me look like a native," he said. "They're the real minority around here."

"Ain't that the truth. I've been here a year, and just about everyone I've met is from somewhere else."

The transient nature of southern California was what had made it easy for Caleb to settle in San Diego. He'd never had to work at being anonymous.

"How long you lived here?" Lola asked.

"Almost twenty years. I left Texas when I was eighteen and kept going west until the ocean stopped me."

"You don't have a Texas accent."

"I got rid of it."

"Wasn't that hard?"

"Not for me. I've always been good at taking on other voices, so I just picked one I liked and copied it. I lost lots of things when I came to California."

"Such as?"

"Lost my first name for good. Lost my accent, lost my history, lost my face, and I tried to lose my demons."

"How'd you lose your face?"

"Covered it with a beard."

Lola frowned, removed one of her gloves, and then ran a long-nailed finger down his smooth cheek.

To Caleb, the tingle didn't run so much down his face as down his spine. He suppressed a shiver. "I shaved a month or two ago," he said, "and got rid of a beard I'd had for around twenty years."

"Why?"

He thought about not answering, but with a shrug of his shoulders did. "I wanted Anna to take notice of me. She'd never seen me without a beard."

"An attention-getting device?"

"I suppose."

"Did it work?"

"Not really."

Lola stopped working at his hair, waited for an explanation. Caleb wasn't sure what had prompted his confession: his need to talk, or his desire for her to finish with his hair.

"She was seeing another man, a doctor."

"I'm sorry."

"I followed her to find out for sure. Can you believe that? I stalked my own wife."

"Did you confront her?"

"No. That's the most pathetic thing of all. What kind of a man allows his wife to go off with another man, and does nothing about it? I saw them going into a hotel room together. And while I was watching them someone must have been watching me. I'm sure I looked like the weak, simpering fool. Of course the detectives have me figured for a different role. They think I am a murderer, not a fool."

"And who do they think you killed?"

"The doctor's daughter. They think that was my way of getting revenge."

The way he offered the explanation, Lola thought, almost sounded like a confession. She watched as he held his hands parallel to each other, clenching and unclenching them. The movements made Lola uncomfortable. Was it just nervousness, she wondered, or a reenactment?

His hands balled into fists. "He's got me so tied up," Caleb said, his voice small.

"You start with the small knots then. You loosen them."

"I still don't have a plan. I keep looking for one. I started reading my father's biography. I figured that maybe somebody hated him enough to want to get revenge through me. But I don't think that's going to get me anywhere."

"Why not?"

"There's no shortage of people who hated my father. But killing innocent people seems a roundabout way of getting revenge. Why not just kill me?"

"Maybe he wanted to make you suffer all the more."

Caleb shrugged. Unconvinced, he said, "Maybe."

"That would explain why he left you those pictures."

"No," said Caleb. "He left those to show me his disdain."

"Disdain?"

"Last year our neighbors' house was burgled. What upset them most wasn't what the burglar took, but what he left behind. He soiled their Berber carpeting. Taking their valuables wasn't enough. The burglar had to add insult to injury. A deputy told the Howards that crime scenes were often *marked* in that way. I think that's what those pictures were. The murderer took everything from me, but that wasn't enough. He left me something much worse than a piece of shit, left me something I'll never be able to get out of my mind."

Once again, Caleb's hands started to clench and unclench.

"I'm a private person. Knowing I was watched makes me feel powerless and dirty."

Caleb's uneasiness was contagious. Lola turned her head to the kitchen window, half expecting someone to be looking in.

"Don't worry," Caleb said. "I made sure we weren't followed. No one's ever going to catch me unawares again." He lifted the mirror and looked at himself critically. His hair was lighter than before, at the sandy-blond stage. "Just a few more applications," said Lola, "and we'll get it so that you won't even know yourself."

The notion didn't displease Caleb. "I don't think I've thanked you for all you've done."

"Now you have."

"You always in the habit of rescuing strays?"

"Sometimes. But usually I'm more of a sucker for the four-legged sorts. The two-legged have taught me to be wary. But I had this feeling that something was going to happen, and I was ready to be receptive to it."

"You took me in on a feeling?"

"Not exactly. Don't be angry when I tell you that your father has been in my thoughts on and off for the last few weeks. I don't know why. I hadn't thought about him in years. But his image kept coming to me. That's why I wasn't really surprised when I saw you. It was almost as if I expected you, or at least someone like you."

"Or like him."

"Yes."

"You're a psychic?"

"I wouldn't call myself that. But at times I've had glimpses of the future. It's not as if I've known everything that was going to happen, but I have been clued into some events that would. Among certain tribes Two Spirits were known for their ability to foretell things."

"Feminine intuition?"

"It goes beyond that. I wanted to leave San Diego, but I stayed, trusting to my feelings that something significant was about to happen."

"Why'd you want to leave town?"

"What else? Love gone wrong."

With his mirror, Caleb caught her vying expressions: a shaking head, a wistful smile, and a few sighs.

"A sailor boy," she explained. "He swore to me his love undying. We met in New Orleans, where I was the headliner in a show. He was on leave. My sailor boy wooed me here by sending a steady stream of roses and love letters. He said we could make it work."

"What happened?"

"He fell in love with someone else."

"I'm sorry."

"So am I. She'll never love him like I did."

"She?"

"You sound surprised."

"I am. I just assumed it was another man."

"As a rule, my lovers haven't been gay."

"But you're still—male—aren't you?"

"I'm not transsexual, if that's what you mean. And yes, my male parts are intact."

"Doesn't that make you and your lover homosexual?"

"Not to my thinking. I don't consider myself a male. And my lovers, almost to a man, have been heterosexual. I know it's a bit of a gender-bender, but it's all perception. How do you see me now, as female or male?"

"Both. What's that word . . . ?"

"Androgynous. On the street we're known as 'chicks with dicks.'"

"Do you want the operation?"

"No. I am a berdache, a winkte with two spirits, male and female, combined into one. I don't need an operation. I already am what I should be."

"Then why did you enhance your breasts?"

"What you see is a result of estrogen and hormones. I never had an operation."

"What about your facial hair?"

With a laugh, Lola said, "'My, what big teeth you have,' said Little Red Riding Hood." She shook her head. "My face is much as it always was. My beard was almost nonexistent, so very little depilation was needed. Most of my changes were internal, not external. The way I see it, gender is found between your ears, not your legs."

"Do you think of yourself as a woman?"

"I think of myself as a Two Spirit, neither man nor woman, but something feminine, something in between."

"You've taken a woman's name."

"Yes. Taking another name is nothing unusual. Lakota winkte used to do naming ceremonies, offering boys sacred names. Sitting Bull and Crazy Horse were given winkte names as boys. As men, it is said, they even took winkte wives. I gave myself the name of Lola. Most people think it comes from The Kinks' song about a transvestite named Lola, but it doesn't. I took the name from Lola Falana. I wanted to be a stage performer just like her."

"So you stayed in San Diego just because of this feeling?"

"Yes. And I suppose there was a little part of me that kept hoping, without any real hope, that my sailor boy would come back to me. There was another Lakota winkte who fell in love with a military man and lived with him for almost twenty years as his wife. The couple even adopted two children. No one ever suspected the winkte was biologically a male."

"Didn't that winkte live a lie?"

"The world didn't, and doesn't, understand."

"That sounds hypocritical. You lectured me that keeping my secrets was all wrong, and yet you sound proud that this winkte fooled the world. Is that what you would have done with your sailor, tried to pass for a woman?"

"I don't know. I only know there's a difference between making choices out of love, and choices out of fear."

"That's a convenient distinction."

"No, it's not. I came to terms with what I am. I was willing to go through that pain to come out on the other side. You still haven't done that."

20

From her hotel room Maryelizabeth had called her service. What she had imagined would be no more than five minutes of messages had turned into an hour's worth and counting. She was the media's flavor of the day. Everyone wanted her comments on the new Shame murders, or if not everyone, at least forty-six of her first forty-nine callers. She wrote down yet another name and number on a page filled with people to call back, and imagined her publicist probably had a list twice as long.

". . . Jeremy Levett. You might remember we had you on our show, *Good Morning, Omaha,* when you were promoting your last book. . . ."

The unspoken message was, "We scratched your back, now it's time for you to scratch ours." They had publicized her books in the past, and would in the future, but for that they expected their piece of her now.

". . . so we'd like to do an on-air spot tomorrow. Call me at my home number, would you? Look forward to talking. . . ."

She wasn't listening closely. Virtually all the messages were the same. She probably should have been working and listening at the same time, but she hadn't wanted to delve any further into her old Gray Parker files. Sifting through one box had roiled her insides enough. The other five unopened boxes could wait. Her avoidance wasn't helping, though. Gray Parker's ghost kept materializing in her mind.

* * *

"You want children?"

Gray was leaning against the bars, thumbs in his orange prison jumpsuit. Somehow, even in handcuffs and wearing orange, he still managed to look sexy.

"Yes."

"The way you're going you won't have any."

"Why do you say that?"

"Because being on the go has already become a way of life for you, and it'll only get worse. You're not the kind to marry out of convenience, or have a baby by accident. And the appeal of a white picket fence and all things domestic won't seem exciting enough for you until it's too late."

"Is that what happened to you?"

He didn't answer directly; he rarely did. "I arrived in the town of Eden with a crick in my neck from looking back at San Antonio and wondering if a few of my minor peccadilloes were following me."

"Were they?"

"Nope. You know my record. For the longest time it was clean as the driven snow."

"What did you do in San Antonio?"

"Practiced a few of my future dance steps. Stopped short, though."

"So you ended up in Eden."

"It seemed as good a place as any to get lost for a spell."

"And that's where you met and married Clara Wallace."

" 'I'm in the family way.' That's what she told me. Couldn't even say she was pregnant. Ever read Nietzsche? You should. Clara was what he'd call a pale criminal. She could do the deed, but not face up to the consequences afterward."

"Yet you married her."

"She couldn't stand the shame of her baby not having his daddy's name. I tried to tell her that neither she nor the baby would want my name. I said she'd regret it more than anything, but she insisted, so I went through with the charade."

"You never divorced her."

"That's right."

"And she still loves you."

"More's the pity."

"Over the years there were times when you visited her."

"Usually when John Law was on my tail."

"Usually, but not always."

He shrugged. "Short stops on my merry-go-round. Round and round, you know, or you will know, lessen you get off it now. There's no law that says you have to do that next book."

"What next book?"

"The one your publisher's waving in front of your nose. I'm all but dead, they're telling you, even if they're not saying it that way. Time to commit to your next book, they're saying. Strike while the old iron's hot."

She hadn't said a word of this to him, and felt defensive. "Nothing's been formalized. . . ."

"And after that there will be the next book, and the next book. Face it, lady, you're going to be like me."

"How so?"

"You're going to choose death over life."

The memory was so vivid that at first she didn't take notice of the new caller. He was speaking in a hoarse whisper, making it difficult for her to hear, but when he identified himself she suddenly became alert.

". . . people are nearby, so it's hard to talk. This is Caleb. We need to meet. I've got information that can prove I'm innocent, but I need your help."

He had made the call from an outdoor pay phone. Maryelizabeth could hear the sounds of passing traffic, both four-wheeled and two-legged. Caleb stopped whispering at the loud approach of what sounded like some adolescent males; either he didn't want to compete with them, or he was afraid of being overheard. After they passed he continued, his whisper that much more staccato and desperate.

"We have to meet. According to the paper, the *Constellation* is coming into port today at one o'clock. It'll be docking at the NAS North Island in Coronado. I want you to be there waiting for it, and me."

He stopped talking, interrupted by the long blast of a car horn.

"Get there early if you can. Park at the lot nearest the ship on

Colorado Street and Quay. If I don't see you there, let's meet at the front gate at the stern of the ship. If something prevents my showing up, like too many police or shore patrol, I'll make other arrangements for us to meet later."

Caleb stopped talking, but she could still hear the background noise and his heavy breathing. He was apparently loath to hang up. "I know everything looks bad," he whispered, "but don't give up on me. You're my only hope."

It felt like a New Year's countdown, thought Maryelizabeth. The only things missing were the champagne and party favors, though the Navy League was handing out complimentary coffee and doughnuts. The navy band added to the festivities. John Philip Sousa was big on their play list.

Before coming on base, Maryelizabeth had made a call to NAS North Island's Public Relations Office. She had made up a story about using the homecoming as "flavor" in a forthcoming book, and the PR people had offered to roll out the red carpet.

Thousands of San Diegans were on hand to greet the aircraft carrier. Maybe Caleb had been to a homecoming before and had known what kind of a zoo the naval base would be today, thought Maryelizabeth. But if Caleb had wanted anonymity, why hadn't he picked a public spot like the zoo or Sea World? She thought it strange that a wanted man would place himself in potential jeopardy. That is, if he was here. She looked around again. Still no sign of him.

An officious master chief had met her outside the base. She had followed his car through the huge complex and he had seen to it that she got a VIP parking spot. The chief had introduced her to several officers with lots of gold braid, and probably would have stayed at her side had Maryelizabeth not requested some "quiet time to take in impressions." She had last seen the chief hovering around the camera crews from the local television stations.

Though she had a media pass, Maryelizabeth stayed among the crowds at the mobbed landing area. She expected that Caleb would be in the waiting crowd if he was here, but still, he would have to single her out among so many. Several tugs were bringing the *Constellation* into the pier, making the crowd grow ever more vocal. The aircraft carrier dwarfed the much smaller vessels. Something that large, Maryelizabeth thought, shouldn't be able to float. She had vacationed on islands that were smaller. She scanned the PR packet that had been given to her, and found the dimensions of the ship. The *Constellation* was 1,046 by 265 by 37 feet. More than three football fields long. So large that 5,500 personnel called it home for months at a time. From a distance she could see the sailors and officers stretched along the ship's railing and deck, long lines of white.

The docking was a laborious process, the proper positioning of the leviathan no quick matter. Maryelizabeth spent some of her wait sketching the outlying area in her pad. San Diego Bay was calm, although a few sailboats were finding enough of a breeze to push them along. To the right, she could see the expanse of Coronado Bridge. The *Constellation* was blocking her view of San Diego's downtown, but she'd had peeks of it across the water. This was her first visit to San Diego, and so far the weather was as good as everyone had always said it was. It had been seventy degrees when she arrived, was seventy degrees today, and the weather forecast was for seventy degrees tomorrow. For three hundred days of San Diego's year, that's where the mercury hovered, give or take two degrees. The natives took the weather for granted. Maryelizabeth had seen T-shirts with the writing, Another Boring Day in Paradise.

Murder in Short Sleeves, thought Maryelizabeth, thinking of a potential title for her book. She took in the physical sights around her not so much for her own pleasure as for how they would play out as a scene. More and more often, that was how she looked at the world, and less and less often did she recognize or regret it.

Another announcement came over the PA. Mothers with new babies that the fathers had never seen were directed to go to the VIP tent. Another announcement came after that. All pregnant women to go to a different VIP tent. There were plenty of those. The *Constellation* had been deployed at sea for more than six months. A long line of pregnant young women stepped forward, all about seven months into term.

Gray had said she probably wouldn't have any children. Bastard. Too many of his predictions had come true. Like him, she'd spent most of her adult life going from place to place. For all practical purposes, her home was a P.O. box. A friend had once given her an embroidered sampler that read, Home Is Where Your Portable Computer

Is. She'd yet to settle in one place long enough to hang the sampler.

Nearby, a balloon popped. The sound was getting all too common. That, and the crying of little children whose balloons had escaped their hands.

Mooring lines had now secured the *Constellation.* For want of anything else to do, Maryelizabeth counted the lines. There were twenty-four of them. The crowd was getting more restive, reacting with more enthusiasm to everything. When the *Constellation*'s foghorn sounded, everyone burst into wild cheers. Blue and white pavilions were set up everywhere, providing information and refreshments and a sense of community. The thousands waiting, of all colors and nationalities, seemed to be part of an extended family.

The favorite game for those waiting was Find Your Sailor. There was so much ship-to-shore waving and whistling and shouting that her ears hurt. Excited conversations were going on all around Maryelizabeth, though many weren't in English. She heard Spanish and what she assumed was Tagalog, as well as several languages unknown to her. Those waiting were holding flowers, and balloons, and posters. It was a military exercise, but also an exercise in "I Love You." That's what most of the messages said, although one teenage boy had a unique way of advertising it. His poster read: Dad, I Love You. How About a Raise in My Allowance?

That's what I should have done, Maryelizabeth thought. Advertised my appearance to Caleb.

The long docking process was finally completed, and those waiting were allowed to go forward along the pier. Maryelizabeth was swept along with the crowd. She could almost believe that she was waiting for her man to disembark. Amid the jostling and movement she turned her head, looking for Caleb. He still wasn't to be seen.

A piercing whistle drew her out of her reverie. The whistle captured the attention not only of Maryelizabeth but of most of those on the dock. The whistler, waving from on deck the aircraft carrier, was no slouch in the shouting department either.

"Corinne," a sailor yelled. "Hey, Corinne!"

Standing near Maryelizabeth was the apparent object of the sailor's attentions, a young woman waving so vigorously that she was shaking from her fingers to her toes. "Right here, sweet stuff!" she said, somehow matching his volume.

"You're looking GOOD, Corinne!"

The crowd laughed at the sailor's exuberance. Corinne preened for him, tilting her head back and running her hand through her braided black hair.

"You're looking FINE, Corinne."

Corinne threw out her arms wide as if to embrace her man and span the distance between them. "I've been WAITING, Willie."

And not willing to wait a minute longer, by the sound of it. From ship to shore, everyone seemed to be laughing. In the vocal department, Willie and Corinne were the perfect match, their calls heard over the sea of other voices.

"You put that MATTRESS in the bed of the truck like I told you, Corinne?"

"Couldn't wait that LONG, Willie. I tied it to my BACK!"

Over all the raucous laughter, Willie was heard to say, "That's my woman!"

Maryelizabeth remembered the classic picture of the sailor kissing a woman on the street during the VE celebration in New York City, two strangers caught up in a moment of exuberance. There was the flavor of that all around her. She didn't know any of these people, but she was still caught up in their excitement.

The gangway was being lowered, with the exodus about to begin. Winners of the First Kiss Contest were being lined up to kiss their sailors. The band was playing "The Star-Spangled Banner." There was no war on, but the crew was still getting a heroes' welcome. Much of Maryelizabeth's adult life had been spent around scenes of intense anticipation, but this was very different from awaiting the verdict at a death penalty trial, or being part of the countdown to an execution. The electricity was just as strong, but it wasn't generated by storms.

Sailors walked down the gangplank. They appeared to be under orders not to run, but were hard pressed to obey. Sea legs that in other circumstances might have been unsteady held up just fine for their long-awaited reunions. All at once, everyone seemed to be kissing and hugging and holding. Babies were lifted high, some being held and seen by proud fathers for the first time.

The giddy emotions were contagious. Even those sailors who had no waiting loved ones disembarked with wide smiles. Liberty was liberty, and San Diego awaited them. The men in white didn't need to ask directions for a good time.

Maryelizabeth watched a half hour's worth of reunions. It was the show that kept her there more than any expectation that Caleb was going to appear. There was at least an hour more of reunions waiting to happen, judging by all the sailors still lined up to come off the *Constellation.* But Maryelizabeth's reunion was looking ever more doubtful. She finally joined the exodus walking away from the pier. From behind her, Maryelizabeth heard the sound of hurried footsteps. Four sailors were running up behind her. She stepped aside to let them pass, but two of the sailors slowed as they ran by, twisting their heads back to give her the once-over. It *must* have been a long voyage, Maryelizabeth thought. She offered no encouragement to their neck craning, and they continued forward. They had survived the voyage, only to arrive at the greater dangers of port.

She wasn't in any great hurry to get to her car. Maryelizabeth could never understand why people rushed to their cars after the conclusion of some public event. The same traffic jam awaited them all. As she approached her car, Maryelizabeth saw what looked to be a ticket on her windshield.

So much for VIP parking, she thought. But it wasn't a ticket. The writing on the paper, in block letters, read: *Couldn't chance talking with you. When you exit from base park on 6th and H, I'll be looking for you.* It was signed *C.*

She jumped into her car and became one of those jockeying drivers she usually reviled for being foolish. The drive out wasn't as bad as she expected; nothing was impeding the general exodus from camp. According to the Thomas Guide map she had bought, 6th and H was just a few blocks from the base. Once she exited NAS North Island, it wouldn't be more than two or three minutes away.

Her pager went off. She checked the display. There was no message other than an unfamiliar telephone number. Maryelizabeth took a second look at the readout. Something bothered her, something about the call. It was apparently a local number. She hadn't given out her pager number to very many locals; several people at the Sheriff's Office, Anna, and, of course, Caleb. She didn't call back immediately, not feeling comfortable talking and driving at the best of times, and especially not in an area with which she wasn't familiar. After parking, she would return the call.

Everyone exiting the base was headed for the Coronado Bridge. Maryelizabeth turned right on H Street, and immediately found relief from the traffic. The surrounding area around NAS North Island was residential and pricy. At one time Coronado had been a popular place for high-ranking officers to retire. Now very few in the military could afford the real estate tariffs.

Maryelizabeth parked on the street. Around her were large, whitewashed houses with green lawns. The street was wide and pleasant with tamarisk, palm, and pepper trees providing a pleasant canopy of green. There were other cars parked on the street, but no drivers behind their wheels. She swiveled her head around. Again, no Caleb. She waited for a minute, and when he still didn't show up she studied her pager again. There was something nagging at her, but still, she couldn't put her finger on it. Maybe when she called the number her unease would pass.

Then her subconscious finally kicked in, and she made the connection that had been bothering her: Caleb had her pager number, so why had he left a message on her service?

His leaving a VoiceMail message with her service didn't make any sense. He couldn't have known she would get his message in time, or even whether she would agree to meet with him. He should have paged her, or even called her emergency number.

There was a thump overhead on the ceiling of the car, and then a tennis ball bounced off the hood. The diversion had her head moving as the glass shattered behind her. For a moment she didn't know what was happening, and that was the moment he needed.

He closed the back door behind him and had the rope around her neck even before she could open her mouth. He pulled hard, slamming her head against the seat. The garrote tightened. She tried to scream, but the rope stifled any sounds.

Maryelizabeth grabbed at the rope with her hands, but she couldn't pull it away from her neck, or get her fingers underneath it. Her instincts only made matters worse. She strained forward to try to pull free, and that tightened the noose all the more.

"Did you know," the man said, not straining, speaking for all the world as if he were just having a conversation, "that John C. Woods said he always slept like a baby?"

She saw stars, recognized she was blacking out, and suddenly reversed tactics. She pushed her head and body back against the seat, loosening the choke hold for just an instant. As she gasped for breath her hands reached for the steering wheel. She felt around desperately with her fingers, searching for the horn.

God, so many buttons and knobs. One of them had to work. . . .

There. The horn was sounding. Or was that just the pressure building in her ears? The choking was shutting down her senses. She felt as if she were on a plummeting jet. She couldn't hear. And though her eyes were open, it was almost like a curtain had been dropped in front of them. Or a shroud.

Her own thoughts became whispers. What was she saying? What was so important?

All those scene-of-the-scream photos she'd had to examine. Her life flashed before her, and she saw all those tragic faces. She couldn't, wouldn't, become one of those.

The pressure suddenly eased. Her first breath was ragged and labored. The pain in her neck was awful.

Behind her the car door opened, and then closed.

She turned her neck, the motion adding to her agony, and saw him crossing the street. But she never saw his face, dammit. And he was wearing a sailor's outfit.

An older man with a dog on a leash came running over. Doors to houses began to open. Maryelizabeth wanted to yell instructions, but she didn't have the breath, and they wouldn't have heard her over the horn.

Part of her was aware that the horn was still blaring, and that she should disengage her hands from it, but her fingers wouldn't, couldn't, release their hold. A woman came through the back door, and talked to her. Gradually, she was able to regain control of her fingers and pull back from the wheel. The horn was silenced.

People kept asking her if she was all right, and that made her feel weepy, and stupid. When she gulped it hurt, and when she cried it hurt even more.

The police had been called. She could hear sirens. But before they arrived her pager went off again. Same number calling.

She dialed with her cell phone. Caleb answered on the first ring.

21

The uniformed officer put a blanket over Maryelizabeth's shoulder and helped her over to his patrol car. Officer Lowery was young, but had a calming way about him. He spoke slowly and sincerely, and reminded Maryelizabeth of a youthful Jimmy Stewart with a Kevlar vest.

Before taking a seat, Maryelizabeth carefully turned around in a full circle. It was an awkward way of surveying what was going on around her, but it spared her from having to move her neck. A handful of police were already on the scene. Some were taking statements, while others were cordoning off her car with crime scene tape. Maryelizabeth resisted Officer Lowery's guiding hand. She stood her ground, trying to remember something, doing her best to be unmindful of the whispers and stares of the bystanders.

"The ball," rasped Maryelizabeth. She spoke through clenched teeth. It hurt less to talk that way, but it still hurt.

"What ball, ma'am?" asked Officer Lowery.

Maryelizabeth swallowed some saliva. She'd had strep throat before, where every swallow was painful, but this was much worse.

"Tennis ball," she said. "Should be over there." She pointed in the direction. "He tossed it on top of the car to divert my attention." Another swallow, enough for her to finish the sentence. "Maybe you'll find some trace evidence."

"I'll tell that to the detectives, Ms. Line. They should be here any minute now."

He motioned for her to sit down, and only then did Maryelizabeth allow herself to be seated in the squad car. She felt better for having remembered, for having at least tried to contribute something. It embarrassed her that she hadn't been able to offer more.

"Try to get comfortable, Ms. Line," he said. "An ambulance will be here shortly."

"No . . . need," she rasped.

"How about we let them determine that? Now I know you're in pain, but I wonder if you can give me a description of your assailant. All we have so far is that he's dressed as a sailor, and there's certainly no shortage of those around here."

Maryelizabeth nodded. She coughed slightly, and reached up to her throat, as if trying to ward off the pain.

"You want some crushed ice?" the officer asked.

She shook her head. Even doing that hurt. In the distance, Maryelizabeth could hear a siren. The ambulance.

The officer pulled out a pad. "Did you get a look at who attacked you?"

"I did," she said.

Then she took a big gulp, but this time not for the pain. "I can even tell you who did it."

Caleb froze at the door, hearing voices inside, then realized it was only the television. He'd borrowed Lola's Mustang to go call Maryelizabeth. Now he followed the sounds to the living room, and found Lola sitting on the sofa. Even though she had to have heard him enter the house, she stiffened slightly upon seeing him, and her greeting sounded strained.

"You've been on the TV," she said, nervously running her fingers up and down the buttons of her red silk blouse. "Lots."

Caleb said nothing, just sat down on the sofa and frowned at the television.

"They've been doing all sorts of live new spots. From sheriff's headquarters, from your house . . ."

"Anna and the kids weren't there, were they?"

She shook her head. "They're in hiding, or at least that's what one report said."

"Good." Maybe Maryelizabeth had actually followed through, he thought, and helped them.

"I thought I'd be better about all this," Lola said. "But I'm feeling awfully uncomfortable. I guess I'm not as brave as I wanted to believe."

"Few of us are."

She kept biting her lower lip, wanting to say more, but resisting the impulse.

Caleb sensed the unsaid: Lola wanted him out. "I'm not the man they're talking about on the television," he said. "I'm not my father."

"I know that."

"I wish I had your intuition."

"It doesn't mean I don't have my doubts. I do. But they're as much about me as you. There are times when I want to do what's safe, as opposed to doing what's right."

Welcome to my world, thought Caleb.

"Is that writer going to help you?" Lola asked.

"I don't know."

The television volume went up, not for a commercial, but another news break. "Here we go again," said Lola.

A news anchor sat at his desk in a studio. He offered an extra-somber face to the camera, his expression so serious as to allow a few wrinkles to emerge through his thick pancake makeup. "This is Donald Jones with KGSI News," he said. "We have a breaking story on Caleb Parker, son of serial murderer Gray Parker, who is a suspect in three recent murders in San Diego County. Our own Lisa Wong is on the scene in Coronado. Lisa?"

The shot changed to the reporter on the street. "Thank you, Donald. I'm standing on H Street in Coronado where just minutes ago it is believed that Caleb Parker, son of infamous serial murderer Gray *Shame* Parker, attacked and attempted to strangle true-crime writer Maryelizabeth Line in her own vehicle."

"What?" Caleb's outburst was shrill. "That's impossible," he said, then turned to Lola. "You know that's impossible."

He stopped talking so that they could hear more.

". . . where Ms. Line escaped serious injury by sounding her horn and attracting attention. According to witnesses, the assailant was dressed in a sailor's outfit. Unfortunately, that's the dress of choice for many thousands of San Diegans today, as the aircraft carrier *Constellation* just pulled into port this afternoon. Despite that, police are continuing their search for Parker throughout the downtown area."

"What the hell is going on?" said Caleb. He slapped the arm of his chair, and then smacked his own forehead. Lola pretended not to notice; her eyes never wavered from the television.

"Maryelizabeth Line is probably best known for writing the book *Shame,* a biography of Parker's father. Whether Line is acquainted with Caleb Parker is not yet known, but she *has been* in the San Diego area for at least the last two days. I had the opportunity to interview her this morning at the sheriff's press conference, where she proved very reluctant to talk about her involvement in this case."

"Who says I attacked her?" asked Caleb. "Who the hell says that?"

The camera shot changed from the street to the studio. With somber and stentorian voice, the anchor asked: "Lisa, have the police confirmed that Parker was the assailant?"

The anchor believed in practicing journalism the way trial lawyers practiced jurisprudence: always know the answer before asking the question. The screen split, allowing viewers to see both the anchor and the reporter.

"Police on the scene won't say anything for the camera," said Lisa, "but I just got off the phone with SDPD spokesperson Karen Coben, and she told me that Maryelizabeth Line herself identified her attacker as Caleb Parker."

"No," said Caleb. His mouth was open and his head was shaking. "No."

Lola sat very still, frozen like an animal trying to escape being noticed.

"Maybe that's why she couldn't talk to me," Caleb said. "I noticed her voice sounded funny, but I didn't really think about it. She was breathing heavily when she called, and her voice sounded raspy and strained."

Lola didn't say anything, still wouldn't look at him.

Caleb's voice rose in anger: "She told me to page her tonight. That's what she told me."

Lola managed to offer a mollifying nod without meeting his eyes.

"You don't believe me," Caleb said.

"That's not it," she said quietly. "Like you, I'm trying to figure out what could have occurred."

"I'm not insane, and I don't have rabies."

"I never suggested . . ."

"Your tone did. You don't need to be scared of me. I haven't murdered any women. And I didn't attack Maryelizabeth Line. I just wish I'd stayed here so that you could be sure of that."

Caleb tried to think of something, anything, to make her believe. But he'd already exhausted his resources in gaining her tenuous trust. There wasn't anything he could say or do. It was a wonder she wasn't already screaming.

In desperation, Caleb said, "Tie me up."

"What?"

"You're ready to call the police, and I don't blame you. So tie me up for a few hours. That way you'll know I can't be a threat to you or anyone else."

Now she was looking at him. "Tie you?"

"Or lock me up, or cage me, or do whatever it takes to give you peace of mind. I don't know why, or even if, Maryelizabeth identified me as her attacker. I only know I didn't do it, and she can tell you that same thing."

He put his hands together and held them out, not to beseech, but to be tied.

"That's not necessary," Lola said.

But both of them knew that it was.

Caleb sat trussed up on the sofa. Lola had used duct tape to secure his hands and feet. While she was binding him, they didn't speak, but Caleb had trembled uncontrollably. Lola had put a comforter over him, but it hadn't helped. Caleb's claustrophobia made being bound a torture.

Together they watched the local news, and Caleb saw his greatest fears being played out in front of him. His nightmare worsened when he saw the trailer on national news. If he hadn't been tied up, Caleb would have run out of the room, out of the house. The anchor said, "Like father, like son, the Shame murders past and present," and then Caleb saw a face from the past: "Why's everyone so surprised he's a killer? Over twenty years ago he tried to kill me, and I told everyone it was just a matter of time before he started murdering people just like his daddy."

"I know her," Caleb said. Even through her overly generous use of makeup, and the passage of years, he recognized Earlene Crosby.

"Who is she?"

"A girl from high school."

Not just any girl. Earlene's folks had owned one of the biggest ranches in the county. And she'd been pretty, Texas pretty. Along with her looks, Earlene had been the class sprite, the provocateur; the boys had all wanted to please her, had ached to do her bidding. In many ways it had been easier for Caleb to face up to his male classmates. With the boys it was mostly a physical thing. They were happy with beating him up. But the girls were more dangerous. To them he'd been a curiosity, a regular novelty, and Earlene Crosby had been the most curious of all. Caleb had been afraid of her interest, and at the same time desperate for it. Earlene had a car, a Ford Maverick, and when they were both seventeen she had coaxed Caleb into going with her on a private ("Just our secret, Cal") picnic out to O. C. Fisher Lake.

"When Mr. Toad said that the warriors in that religion used to drink bull's wee-wee," Earlene said, "I just about lost it."

Mr. Toad was the name for Mr. Joad, Caleb and Earlene's world history teacher. The previous week they'd been studying religions of the world.

"Now what religion was that?" Earlene asked.

"Zoroastrianism," he said.

"Zor-ro? I can't even say it. How are you supposed to practice a religion you can't even pronounce?"

"It's not widely practiced anymore. People found something else to worship."

"Well, I shouldn't wonder, what with their men having to drink that you know what."

"Makes Sunday communion look wonderful in comparison, doesn't it?"

She started laughing. "Stop it, Cal, 'fore I split a gut."

Caleb couldn't believe he was making Earlene laugh, couldn't believe that she was there with him. Girls like Earlene were in another class, like that other religion they had studied, Hinduism. She was a Brahmin. And he was an Untouchable. Definitely an Untouchable. Lower than low. That she had arranged for their being together was a miracle. Cal had been suspicious about that. He had figured she was somehow setting him up. But to be with Earlene, he had been willing to take that chance.

And maybe, just maybe, it wasn't some trick. Earlene was daring enough. She had a reputation around school of being fearless, like the time she'd ridden Tommy Lee Baker's motorcycle, done a wheelie as she drove past the Riva Cinema Theatre, even though she'd never been on a bike before. It was the kind of thing only a movie star, or Earlene, would have done.

Caleb dared another quick look at Earlene. Her complexion was very white; she had a few moles scattered around her body that showed just how white she was. She had straight brown hair, and her bangs went almost to her eyebrows. Earlene was small, not much more than five feet, but most of that was curves. She wore tight blouses and tighter pants.

"How do you say that religion again?" she asked.

"Zoroastrianism." A religion, remembered Cal, that believed there was a universal struggle going on between the forces of light and darkness.

"Zor-ro-ass . . . Forget it. You're smart, Cal. But you're always so quiet. Course they say it's the quiet ones you got to watch out for."

He basked in her praise. The farther they had gotten from Eden, the more human Caleb had felt. Earlene made it easy for him. She was a great talker. He could almost forget who he was, what he was. Little by little he had become more comfortable. He knew other kids did things like this. Caleb saw them going places together after school, and heard about their parties. But he had always been the outsider.

Caleb had always imagined how nice it would be to just have a friend. That was about as far as his fantasies had taken him. Caleb thought about the opposite sex, dreamed about them, but he was grounded in the reality that he was Shame's son, which meant he was dirty and defiled and something to be feared. Untouchable.

The lake was out of the way, far enough from Eden for them not to have to worry about seeing anyone they knew. That made it spe-

cial, like they were the only two people in the world. Earlene had outdone herself with the picnic basket. Though Cal had offered to take her out to lunch in San Angelo, she had told him a picnic would be more fun, and had forbidden him to provide anything. "It will be my pleasure," she had told him. Earlene had made three kinds of sandwiches, potato salad, some ambrosia, and even a pecan pie.

"This is great," said Caleb, holding up a sandwich.

"Oh, come on."

"This is great," Caleb said, digging into the ambrosia.

But the truth of the matter was that he couldn't taste anything. He was overwhelmed at being with her. That was what was great.

Afterward, they fed the ducks and then walked around the lake. A few times Earlene's body brushed up against his, and on each occasion it took his breath away. He had never felt so right with the world in all his life.

As the sun was setting, Earlene gave him a long look and said, "I want to take you where you've never been before."

"Where's that?"

"Oh, you'll see," she said. "Oh, yes, you will."

The way she said it, the way she promised so much with just her tone, made his stomach feel funny, and his heart race. He was afraid, but not in the way he was usually afraid.

She drove to an overlook just outside the city of Wall, a spot that was deserted and quiet—a good place, Earlene said, for them to "talk."

Caleb had no expectations for what might happen there. Just being with Earlene made him as happy as he could ever remember, but that wasn't what she wanted. She took Caleb by the hand, led him to the backseat of her car, and took a seat on his lap. His hands were sweaty. They didn't even feel like his hands. He was all fingers as he tried to unlatch and unbutton her clothing, and was more a hindrance than a help in removing it.

A full moon revealed her white skin, her nakedness. She looked like one of those classical statues. Cal had never seen anything so beautiful, or so intimidating.

"Come closer," she said.

At first Caleb was afraid to touch her. He didn't trust his hands to do the right things, and was sure no boy had ever been so stupid, but she drew him to her, and demonstrated that he was more than ready for the dance, even if he wasn't sure of the steps.

"That's right," she told him, "that's right."

Because of who he was, Caleb had been sure he'd always be alone. He couldn't believe he was actually holding a girl, couldn't believe he was touching her skin. She felt so soft, so wonderful. He cupped her breasts, felt her nipples harden.

She reached for him, guided him into her, helped him get started. Caleb found her rhythm, and for once, he forgot everything. He didn't know who he was, didn't remember his name and his roots, was just totally taken by the moment. His climax released him from gravity, from everything. He felt alive, felt as if his lifelong sentence had been commuted. The weight that was always with him, that forever seemed to be crushing his chest, was lifted.

I love you, Caleb thought. And he would have told her that, but Earlene spoke first.

"I used to see your daddy on the TV," she said, "and in the magazines and papers. All the other girls had crushes on the Bee Gees, and Barry Manilow, but your daddy was my first love."

Caleb thought he was going to be sick, but Earlene just kept talking. He wished he could just run away. Caleb felt violated. Used. Earlene kept referring to Shame as his "daddy," as if that were the most natural reference in the world. Caleb had never called him that. Never.

"I used to dream about him. They were wild dreams. I was the only one who could tame the beast in him. That's how I pictured us, beauty and the beautiful beast. But not the fairy-tale version."

Caleb reached for his pants. He wanted to cover himself, but Earlene collected his hands into hers.

"You look like him, Cal."

"Do not."

"Oh, you surely do. You have his same hair, and teeth, and you're already growing into his build."

"We're nothing alike."

Earlene scrutinized him, pinned him like a prize butterfly to some matting, and was satisfied with what she saw. "Only thing that's different is your eyes. He had cat eyes. Wild."

"We better get back."

"Not yet." She moved her hips in a soft roll, and closed her eyes. "I want you," she said.

It's not me you want. Caleb knew that. He wanted to just put on his pants, but Earlene reached for him, and brought him atop her. He could have pulled away, but he didn't. Caleb felt himself responding. He wanted that amnesia again, and was willing to pay the price. All his father had ever brought him was pain. He deserved a few moments of pleasure, even if they weren't real.

Earlene started moaning. She kept saying, "Gray, Gray." It was the name Caleb had been born with, but it was no longer his name. It was his father's name. She was calling out to him.

Their pushing into each other became more frenzied. The passion brought out her calls. Between gasps, Earlene kept saying, "Squeeze my neck."

Her words became rhythmic and demanding, exclamations offered between her moaning and thrashing.

"Squeeze it! Squeeze it! Squeeze it!"

Her command was ever more frantic.

His hands rose. They traveled up her body, but stopped at her shoulders. Earlene was bucking, crying.

"My neck," she said. "Squeeze it," she said, and between her pants she rhythmically repeated her command: "Squeeze it. Squeeze it."

And he did squeeze, but her shoulders. He gripped them with a fury, pressing his fingers into her flesh, letting his anger come out in his hands while he spent himself inside of her.

Caleb found himself straining against his bonds. Squeezing his hands. The present intersected with the past. Earlene was on the television. She was heavier, but the extra weight added to her voluptuousness. Her eyes had lost none of their magic. Even through a camera's lens, they beguiled.

"I made the mistake of going on a date with Cal when I was in high school," she said, "and I almost didn't live to tell about it. I came home with black and blue marks all over my shoulders and neck."

Squeeze it. For years Earlene's cries had haunted him, had made Caleb even more afraid of himself. She had initiated him into the mysteries of sex, but had tainted that experience by bringing his father into their lovemaking.

By bringing his father back from the dead.

That's what had scared him most. That she had summoned Shame like some spirit, and that he had been there with them.

All the following week Earlene wore sleeveless blouses to school, blouses that showed her black-and-blue shoulders to maximum effect. They were her badges of honor, of her brush with death.

Rumors of how she got the bruises were whispered around school. Earlene dropped a few details to friends, told them how she had fought off the son of Shame's animal advances, how his fingers had come perilously close to her neck.

Caleb was used to being the pariah. Earlene's revelations made him that much more of an outcast, but that was something he could live with.

What was harder to live with was the memory of Earlene's words. "Squeeze it," she had kept saying.

And he had wanted to. God help him, but he had.

22

Caleb tried to find a comfortable position, but there wasn't one. He hated being tied up. Not being in control was almost more than he could stand. He had designed his life to have that control, but now he had to rely on someone else. Worse, he was at her mercy.

Lola noticed his contortions. "Can I get you a pillow?" she asked.

"I'm fine," he said. "Are you all set to make that call?"

"I ought to be. We've been over it three times."

"Remember, don't give her your name. Don't even give her your sex."

"That explanation would probably take too long anyway."

"Make everything short and sweet. Just say you're my friend. You can identify yourself as an intermediary."

"I think I prefer the word *in-between.*"

Her pun made Caleb frown.

"Don't worry, I'll go by the script," Lola said. "I'll ask her why she identified you as her attacker."

"It had to have been a publicity ploy," Caleb said, as if trying to convince himself of that.

"And then I'll ask her if she has had any luck in finding anything from your father's past that could tie in with what's occurred."

"Tell her I'm carefully reviewing her book. But what I need are the stories that aren't in the book."

"And last, you want me to ask about your wife and children, find out if she's helped them, and how they are."

"Maybe you should take a checklist with you."

Lola shook her head emphatically. "Santa Claus might need to make a list, and check it twice," said Lola, "but I don't. I'm a performer. I'll remember my lines."

Caleb shrugged. Tied up as he was, that was about all he could do.

"But I guess I've got Santa's job, don't I?" Lola said, suddenly serious. "I'm the one who's going to have to determine who's been naughty or nice."

Their eyes met, took in one another beyond their usual furtive glances. She wasn't what he expected. The only drag queens he'd ever seen had been on television, and all they had wanted to do was make spectacles of themselves. Lola wasn't that way.

He looked away first. It wasn't only the duct tape that made him uncomfortable. Lola did. She was wearing a tight black dress with sheer sleeves.

"Do you always wear women's clothing?"

"Always. Except on Halloween. Sometimes I dress like a man."

"But you are a man."

"My soul, my anima, is feminine, while my parts are masculine. I have no problem with that union, even if others do. It unsettles some people, offering them possibilities that scare them. To be different is to be suspect."

"No argument here," said Caleb, opening a small autobiographical window.

"I watch faces as I perform," said Lola. "I see lots of civil wars going on out there, men both attracted and repulsed by me. Oh, how those faces talk."

"Have you always been a performer?"

"Uh-huh. I don't think I'm qualified to do anything else except maybe sell cosmetics, and I don't think too many department stores would want me working behind the counter."

"Do you like your work?"

"Ever hear of a diva that didn't? Most of the impersonator revues are just lip-synching, but I get to do some of my own singing, and my own editorializing."

With *a cappella* ease, Lola did her best Smokey Robinson snippet, singing the words "tears of a clown." Her voice was clear and vibrant, and the four words seemed to mean a lot to her.

"Drag queen national anthem," she said, "usually sung as our makeup's being removed."

Caleb raised his tied hands. "You'll have to imagine my applause," he said.

Lola reached her hand out, stopped just short of touching his bonds, and his hands. "I don't feel good about leaving you like this. What if there's a fire?"

"What if you untie me, and there's another murder?"

Lola didn't answer. There hadn't been time enough for either of them to come up with an alternative to tying him.

"I can stand it for a few more hours," Caleb said.

"Imagine your father having to put up with it for his entire childhood."

"I don't know much about that," Caleb said.

"It's in the book."

"I skipped over his childhood. I didn't see how it could be relevant to my situation."

"You don't know your Alice."

"Alice?"

"In Wonderland. When the Duchess says: 'Everything's got a moral if only you can find it.'"

"I'm more interested in finding a clue than a moral."

"Maybe they go hand in hand," Lola said. She looked at her watch, made a frightened little noise. "I got to go."

"Break a leg."

"You sure you don't need anything else?"

"I think you've thought of everything."

The table in front of him was stocked with food ready to be grazed, opened drinks with straws, and a portable phone. Lola had set up a boom box for him to listen to his *Shame* audiotapes. Even with his restricted mobility, Caleb could press buttons. And at his feet was a chamber pot. He hoped he wouldn't have to use it.

"Maybe I should have thought about tying up my sailor boy," Lola said. "He always told me he'd be here waiting, but he never was."

She sighed, announced she'd be back by one, then walked out of the room. Caleb listened as the door opened and closed. With Lola out of the house, he examined his bonds, flexing against them. She had made the mistake of tying his hands in front of him, or maybe it was just her way of trusting him, at least up to a point. But duct tape had made a professional out of a non-Boy Scout. There was little, if any, play in the binding. Still, he could move his arms, could even get up and hop around if he wanted. Lola had to have known that.

He reached over to the boom box, pushed the Play button. Maryelizabeth Line started narrating.

Why'd you lie? Caleb wondered. Why did you tell the world I attacked you? It didn't make sense. She didn't need to sell any more books, and her false accusations rankled.

He rewound the tape, and decided that he should listen to his father's childhood, at least for a little while.

Winona Parker was always worried about the evil out there.

Her "out there" was a nebulous but all-encompassing place. She worried for herself, but mostly she worried for her boy Gray.

Gray was the baby she had prayed for, her change-of-life miracle born to her when she was forty-seven. Winona believed herself to be a modern Sarah, and her husband Abraham. Gray was her blessing, or at least her mixed blessing. Winona had always dreamed of having a little girl. She liked to describe her son as "both a miracle and my cross to bear."

Winona's husband, Gray Sr., didn't see anything miraculous about the birth. In fact, becoming a father seemed to be a remarkably uneventful occurrence in his life. He worked as a field representative for a carpet company, and was on the road when his son was born, but even when he was home Parker never appeared interested in his boy, treating him more as a curiosity than his own flesh and blood. All child-rearing duties were his wife's domain, a situation that delighted Winona.

Gray was Winona's doll—her girl doll. She dressed the baby in pink, and continued dressing him in girls' clothing until he was five. Winona grew his hair long. Those who didn't know his sex often commented on "what a beautiful girl" Gray was. And they were right. With his light blue eyes, long, dark locks, and perfect features, he was beautiful. Winona dressed him in lace and frills, and adorned his tresses with ribbons. Gray was given dolls and encouraged to play "house" and have tea parties. Winona kept a close watch over her child. She did her best to keep him away from "bad influences," which included all little boys. But despite her best efforts, "evil" found Gray.

From his window, Gray watched troops of boys pass by his house. They wore boys' clothing and did boys' things. He wanted to join them, but was ashamed to go out dressed like a girl. Besides, his mother wouldn't let him. So Gray became an observer, watching the world from his window, but he found ways to rebel, including the acting out of his anger on the dolls his mother kept bringing him. Some he beat the stuffing out of; others he disfigured; most he dismembered.

When Gray was five, his father finally objected to Winona's trying to make the boy a "sissy." He bought Gray boys' clothing, and forbade Winona to dress his son up like a girl. It was the only time Gray remembered his father ever intervening in his behalf. Three years later, when Gray was only eight, his father died of an aneurysm in his brain.

Winona became more unbalanced after her husband's death. Family and friends and neighbors had long been aware of her eccentricities, but chose not to intervene, even when it became more pronounced. Winona began to see evil everywhere, except where it was truly rooted: in herself.

To protect Gray, Winona took to tying him up. Gray raged against the treatment, but was helpless against the bonds. On several occasions Winona had to revive her unconscious boy, her constraints all but strangling him. Occasionally Gray slipped out of the ropes and chains, and reveled in his short time of freedom, but he always paid the price when his mother caught up with him. She was sure that the evil had tainted him, and did her best to beat it out of him.

Caleb suddenly realized his eyes were tearing. With his bound hands he wiped harshly at his cheeks, then punched at the boom box, pushing the Forward button to move his father's life along. He stopped and started the tape, wanted to begin with the fourth homicide, but ended up listening as his father left behind Heidi Ehrlich, his third victim, in Chimayo.

While driving away from the Santuario de Chimayo, Parker said, a change came over him. He decided that he would no longer try to fight his impulses. He said that a part of him recognized that he had degenerated into a monster, but a larger part of him only wondered why it had taken him so long to become that thing.

His father's epiphany chilled Caleb, touching his every insecurity. He replayed the passage over and over, each time getting more upset. For most of his life he'd been afraid that one day he would give in, just as his father had.

Caleb took a few deep breaths and tried to clear his mind. He needed to concentrate on the murder of Linda Harper, his father's fourth victim, needed to be dispassionate while listening to his father kill. As her story unfolded, he tried to break the narrative down to its essentials: she was a freshman at the University of Texas, a pastor's daughter experiencing her first taste of rebellion. A short-lived taste. Linda had attended a Theta Pi beer bash. A few of her friends had noticed her talking with a man, but their memories were hazy. Everyone had been drinking.

Her body had been left in the brush near the fraternity house. She had been stripped and marked like the other victims, but Linda's death signaled a new phase in his father's predations: his murders became more hurried and opportunistic, and less ritualistic.

The monster had emerged.

Caleb looked for parallels in the attack on Maryelizabeth, but couldn't find any. Physically Linda was nothing at all like Maryelizabeth. She was short and on the heavy side, with brown hair. It was possible, Caleb supposed, that the copycat had felt there was no need to imitate his father beyond the third murder. But it was also clear the attack on Maryelizabeth wasn't some random act. There had to be some explanation or reason to attach to it.

He rewound the tape. Something was nagging at him. No, it was doing more than that. He felt sick, had this feeling of impending doom that weighed on his chest and made his breathing labored. He listened to the details of Linda Harper's life and death again, but nothing came to him, and that only added to his frustration. He knew there was something he should be seeing, some connection he should be making, and was certain it was important. In his mind's eye Caleb charted the details, mentally marking the words in red.

Preacher's daughter.

Too much drink.

The stranger, his father.

The fraternity.

Pledge week.

University of Texas.

Her body left in the bushes near another fraternity house.

Shame.

Shame.

Shame.

Try as he might, the answer wouldn't come. In frustration, Caleb strained against his bonds, pushing at them until his arms and legs shook with the effort. He wished he were wearing chains. At least he could have rattled those. He couldn't think tied up. A sound escaped him, guttural, angry, very much like a gorilla's bark. He sank his teeth into the duct tape, and tried to shred the fabric, but when he pulled his mouth away he could barely see the indentations of where he had bitten. His failure to wreak any damage frustrated him all the more, made him feel weak and helpless. For so long he'd tried to do everything right, to be above reproach. Growing up he'd tried to be perfect, thinking that would keep him from being like his father. His secret formula. But the only thing it had kept him from was being himself. Maybe Lola was right. Maybe he didn't know who the hell he was.

As his rage diminished, the writing in his mind began to fade, the emblazoned red words cooling, disappearing. He closed his eyes. Only a few words remained.

Fraternity.

Pledge week.

Shame.

His father had always been attracted to university settings. During his reign of terror he'd kept more lights on in dorms and sororities than anything short of a calculus final. . . .

The connection, or at least part of it, came when he wasn't expecting it. For a moment, Caleb's world stopped. Maryelizabeth Line's sorority sisters had been murdered over a quarter century earlier. That's what had been grabbing at him. His father had lured his fourth victim away from a Greek Week party.

The attack on Maryelizabeth suddenly made sense. She was the Kappa Omega who had gotten away, and the new Shame had wanted to rectify that.

Caleb was certain of it. More than that, he had picture proof.

He jumped up, forgot that his legs were tied, and crashed into the table, knocking everything onto the hardwood floor. Pushing himself to his feet, he hopped to the guest room. Brandy Wein's pictures were in his coat pocket.

He'd looked at them only that one time in his truck, had never wanted to see them again. Most of the Polaroids were close shots, but there were also two full body shots, one with Brandy posed on a lawn with her legs spread, the other with her in a car, her head propped against the glass as if she were staring at something outside.

That was the picture he wanted. He held it between the fingertips of his tied hands. Visible in the background, illuminated by a spotlight, was a sign that started with the letter *K.* He could just make out the second letter: an *A.* The rest of the lettering was obscured by Brandy's face. The letters were ornamental and large, archaic-looking. Greek.

Kappa.

Caleb held the picture closer, trying to see better. The photo had been taken at night. Brandy Wein's lifeless eyes seemed to be offering up a warning to the living. Caleb tried to imagine the mindset of a killer driving around with a corpse in his backseat, a killer who had posed Brandy to stare out at a sorority house, the dead looking out at the quick. The killer had taken her with him to scout out future victims.

Caleb understood his message. And maybe his sickness. The killer had given him a portent of what was to be. And with it a time frame. Maryelizabeth was the first Kappa Omega he had wanted to kill, but not the last.

The sorority had to be warned without delay.

Caleb hopped back to the living room and saw the mess he had left behind. Food and drink littered the hardwood floors. He reached for the portable phone. It was sticky, had apparently been bathed in a combination of Schweppes ginger ale and Diet Pepsi. Caleb pressed the Talk button, heard some odd clicking noises, then smelled burning circuitry.

The phone was dead, victim of the soda bath, the fall, or both.

Caleb dropped it. Maybe there was a second phone in Lola's bedroom. He hopped over there, scanned the room, saw nothing.

Phone book, Caleb thought. Get the address and phone number of the Kappa Omega sorority house. And then find a way out of his bonds.

He located the white pages on a kitchen shelf. With his bound hands, Caleb had trouble turning the thin pages. Breathing hard and cursing harder, he finally managed to get the page he needed. The sorority was located on Montezuma, a street adjacent to the San Diego State University campus.

Caleb memorized the telephone number and the street address, then looked around desperately for a knife. There were none sheathed in a wood block on the counter, and none were hanging. He flung kitchen drawers open until he found a butcher's knife. Getting a grip on the knife was difficult, trying to cut the tape was impossible. Some sort of vise was needed. He opened the kitchen window, and closed it on the knife to try to secure it. With his chin he pushed down on the windowsill, but was unable to supply enough resistance to keep the knife from moving.

He opened a kitchen drawer, positioned the knife's handle, then closed the drawer on it. The blade pointed skyward, with the sharp side facing away from him. But to get the knife to stay in place Caleb had to lean hard into the drawer, his belly and rib cage pressing into the blade. Awkwardly, laboriously, he pushed and pulled, moving his taped hands in an up-and-down sawing motion against the blade.

Sweat began to pour off him. He tried to work through the pain shooting through his arms, tried to resist the temptation to stop, but the cutting motion kept bringing on cramping. As he fought through a charley horse he was distracted for a moment, long enough for the knife to start slipping from its hold. Caleb overreacted, pushing forward too hard against the drawer.

The blade cut into him just under his sternum. At first, with so many places on his body hurting, he thought he had just scraped himself, but then he saw the redness spreading throughout his shirt and he felt the throbbing pain. Shit. Just what he didn't need. But he couldn't slow down. He went back to trying to free himself. His sawing was as ragged as his breath. Blood and sweat dripped on the blade, lubricating it.

He tried to hold the tape taut, tried to offer resistance to the cutting edge of the knife, but the tape was slow to give. Caleb kept at it until there wasn't any part of his arms and shoulders not in agony. When the last fiber finally separated, Caleb's arms fell to his sides, and then he dropped to the floor. For a short time he didn't have motor control over his hands. They flopped up and down like fish out of water. It seemed like minutes before they yielded to his directions. He pulled the tape off his hands and arms, then lifted off his bloodied shirt. He grabbed a dish towel and wiped the blood from his wound. For what looked like a relatively small cut there seemed to be an awful lot of blood.

Caleb applied pressure to the wound with his left hand, and with his right hand he reached for the knife and began cutting at the tape around his ankles and calves. It took him less than two minutes to free himself. He pushed himself halfway up, then slipped on the blood that had pooled on the floor. He reached out for a counter, and righted himself. His bloody handprints were all over the linoleum and the counter.

He tried to stanch the flow of blood before running down the hallway to Lola's room. In her bathroom medicine cabinet he found gauze pads and bandage strips. He tried to doctor his wound, but did a poor job of it. His hands were too slick, and the gauze pads filled with blood too quickly. Impatient, not wanting to waste time, he applied enough tape at least to slow the seepage of blood. He wasn't used to dressing his own wounds. Anna always tended to his cuts. He thought of her sure hands, his memory taking him back to when they'd first met. She was a healer, and he had been in need of her healing. How much, she'd never known.

Caleb left his bloody shirt in the sink. He went to Lola's walk-in closet and flipped through the hangers, desperate to find anything he could wear. The closet was overflowing with outfits, but there was nothing he could use. He continued his search, rummaging through a wardrobe, then a dresser, then a second dresser. In the bottom drawer of the second dresser he found a sweat suit. The top was oversized, would have been stylishly baggy on Lola. As it was, it was a size too small for Caleb. He put it on anyway.

As he ran for the door, Caleb caught a glimpse of the cat clock. Small whiskers on the eleven, large whiskers on the five. Caleb seemed to remember that his father had attacked Maryelizabeth Line's sorority sisters at a little after midnight.

The cat's eyes moved from side to side, and its pendulum tail flicked back and forth. It was a clock, Caleb knew, but it was still a black cat.

He ran out of the house.

23

"Sh, sh, sh, sh."

Dana Roberts awoke to the shushing sounds coming from right above her.

She thought she was dreaming, until a hand slapped tape across her mouth and a body fell on her, pinioning her arms. She tried to scream, but the tape swallowed the sounds. The only sounds that filled the room were his.

"Sh, sh, sh, sh."

Dana tried bucking him off, but he was too heavy. She lifted her head and attempted to butt him, but he slammed her forehead with the flat of his palm, a blow that snapped her head back and left her dazed.

And the whole time she heard: "Sh, sh, sh, sh."

Dana tried to take in her situation and think through her panic. As her thrashing ceased, the intruder's tone changed, becoming more lulling than demanding.

"Shhhhhhhhhhhhhhhhhhhhhhhhhhhhhhhhhhhhhhhhhh."

The sound gradually became softer until there was only silence in the room.

"I won't harm you," he said.

Dana exhaled pent-up breath through her nose. She had wanted to hear those words more than any others.

"I need money for a fix," he said. "I want your jewelry and CD player, and CDs."

Her head moved forward, a frightened nod, but glad.

"I need your cooperation."

Another nod.

"Give me your hands."

In the darkness she could see him holding plastic ties. Dana tensed. He could feel her body tightening up.

"Shhhhhhhhhhhhhhhhhhhhhhhhhhhhhhhhhhh."

He massaged her panic, put it in check again. In his calm voice, he explained: "All I want is your valuables. After this room, I'm going to try a few others and I don't want you raising an alarm. Give me your hands."

He eased his weight off of her. From under the covers, Dana felt her arms rising, as if they'd been summoned by a hypnotist.

Plastic loops were slipped around her wrists, and then the ties were tightened.

"And now your feet."

He reached for the blanket, lifted it. Dana was glad she was wearing her pajamas. She didn't want him reaching under the covers, so she offered him her ankles.

"Good," he said, applying the ties.

He got off the bed, moved a few steps away from her. The room was too dark for Dana to make out his features.

"Ah, university life," he said. "Nothing like it, is there? Young, active minds in search of knowledge. Do you like poetry?"

He didn't sound like a junkie, Dana thought. She shook her head.

"Pity, that. I was going to quote you some Whitman, a short poem, his 'Your Felons on Trial in Courts.' But I'll respect your wishes. In truth, I don't much like poetry myself. But I do like universities. John W. Deering had the right idea when he willed his body to the University of Utah. Just before he was shot by a firing squad, Deering said, 'At least I'll get some high-class education.'"

He definitely didn't sound like a junkie.

"I've always been attracted to gallows humor," he said. "To be insouciant in the face of death is a way of cheating it, don't you think? When George Appel was being strapped into the electric chair he looked around at the somber faces of all those who were assembled and said, 'Well, folks, pretty soon you're going to see a baked Appel.'"

Dana tried to loosen the tape around her mouth, tried to scream, but the sounds were muted.

"Sh, sh, sh, sh." More summons for quiet, but behind them she heard his amusement.

Dana kicked off her covers. She could at least hop if nothing else.

"Sh, sh, sh, sh."

He was insane, Dana was sure, but she still couldn't be sure he meant her any harm.

As if hearing her doubts, he said, "I told you that I wasn't going to hurt you."

His declaration stopped her from doing anything rash. She huddled at the head of her bed, trembling. Dana listened as he rummaged through her belongings. The sounds reassured her. Then he made his way toward her door. Every step away from her brought that much more relief.

He was painstakingly slow about opening the door to the hallway. He stood very still for several moments, looking and listening to make sure that all was clear. Then he turned back to her.

"Don't try and raise an alarm," he whispered. "Don't do anything more than breathe for the next five minutes."

As he slid out the door, she heard him say ever so softly, "I told you I wouldn't harm you."

The door closed behind him.

For Dana, there was a long moment of blessed relief. She offered up a prayer of thanks, but it was interrupted. The door flew open.

"I lied," he said.

24

Caleb all but sprinted the four blocks over to University Avenue. This time he could do something other than just run away.

The open service station was just what Caleb was looking for. He ran up to the cashier's booth. Sitting in the cinder block fort was an older black man who was smoking his cigarette behind thick, yellowed Plexiglas. The cashier studied Caleb's hurried approach with a resigned expression that said he had seen it all, and wasn't keen on the reruns.

"Do you sell gas cans?" Caleb asked.

The cashier took a long drag of his cigarette, did a little mental cataloging, then exhaled his answer. "Eight ninety-nine," he said, his words coming out of a tinny microphone. "Plus tax."

Caleb reached for his wallet, pulled out a twenty, and put it in the slot. The money disappeared.

"You gonna want a gallon of gas?"

"Yes," said Caleb, offering the expected answer without any hesitation, though until that moment he hadn't even thought about getting gas. The can was to be his prop for getting a ride, his explanation for walking the streets at night.

"You want unleaded or premium?"

"Unleaded."

"Pump three." The cashier rang up the transactions, put the change in the plastic slot drawer, and pushed the drawer toward Caleb. "Can will be outside the door."

Caleb grabbed his change, and then ran around to the back of the booth and picked up the gas can. He quickly pumped the gas, then took up a spot under a streetlight on University. Thumb cocked, he waited on a ride. It had been over twenty years since he'd last hitchhiked. When the first few cars passed him by, Caleb started worrying. He looked at his watch, and then considered calling a cab. It was almost eleven-thirty. The sorority was about ten miles away, and he needed to get there by midnight.

The killer won't make his move before then, Caleb told himself, convinced himself.

Another car drove by. Caleb found himself unable to just stand around waiting for a ride. He began to pace, but that made him feel like a caged animal in a too-small enclosure. He started walking east, and then, between lulls in passing cars, began jogging. The killer wasn't going to beat him to the sorority. If necessary, he'd run the whole ten miles there.

The traffic on University was Saturday-night steady. A few drivers slowed, looked Caleb over, but then continued on their way. What are they seeing? Caleb wondered. Maybe they sensed something wasn't quite right. He tried to give the appearance of being a harmless, out-of-luck motorist, but his act made him self-conscious. So did the reflection he kept glimpsing in storefronts. He didn't know the stranger with the blond hair.

Turn, thumb, and then run. Caleb's routine took him at least a mile along University. He had this sense of being on a Cinderella schedule, and that at midnight his whole world could change. At the sound of another approaching car he turned, and stuck out his thumb. Again, no luck. But he didn't start running right away. Another car was coming, but as soon as he got a better look at it, he didn't solicit the driver with his thumb.

The police officer might or might not have seen him hitchhiking. Caleb turned his back on the patrol car and started walking. *Don't stop,* he thought. *No need to be curious or helpful.* His head filled with mental messages, all aimed at the police officer: *I'm fine, I'm fine, I'm fine.* He walked with measured steps and a posture that tried to exude confidence that said everything was under control and his car was nearby. He could feel eyes on his back, the cop eyeballing him with X-ray vision.

The cruiser slowed up as it came alongside him. The officer made eye contact, inquired as to how Caleb was doing with a backward nod of his head. Caleb nodded in return to show that all was well. The cop drove on.

The short encounter almost brought Caleb to his knees. He stood for a minute, getting control of his weakened legs, then stuck out a trembling thumb to a passing car. If he was so afraid of a cop, how was he going to face up to a killer?

A red Trans Am interrupted his self-doubts, pulling over to the side of the road. Caleb ran up to the car. As he reached for the door handle the Trans Am patched out on the pavement, leaving behind a skid mark, fumes, and taunting laughter that hung in the air even longer than the exhaust.

Caleb shook his fist at the retreating car. "Fuck you!" he screamed. "Fuck you!"

He offered his curse to the world. He was tired of being its punching bag, but the world didn't seem to notice his challenge. Around him all was dark and quiet. He looked at his watch. Almost eleven forty-five. He couldn't let his opportunity slip away, couldn't let his time—and maybe the sorority's—run out.

Caleb wished he were more clever. Someone more clever wouldn't be in his position. He would have found a way to get free without almost committing hara-kiri, and figured out a better plan than hitchhiking in the middle of the night. He would have hotwired a car, or cajoled a ride out of someone. His father had managed more escapes than Houdini, had never lost his cool even when the police were closing in on all sides. His father would have done something audacious.

Like step out and stop traffic, and then use his silver tongue to get a ride.

Caleb took a tentative step out into the street, but then stepped back. He didn't have to be like his father. There were other ways of doing things.

Another car approached. Caleb's expression all but willed the car to stop. Whether it was his look, or just luck, the Ford Escort pulled over to the curb. Caleb ran to it, opened the door, and jumped inside.

"Thanks."

The driver was Latino, around twenty-five, with a goatee. He was wearing black, baggy clothing. Over the blare of the radio, he asked, "Run out of gas, man?"

"My girlfriend did," shouted Caleb. "She took my car and forgot to look at the gas gauge, and now she expects me to bail her out."

The lie came easily to him, emerged without any thought.

"Sounds like my girlfriend, man. Anything goes wrong with her car and it's like, 'You're the guy. You take care of it.'"

Caleb nodded. He didn't try to compete over the loud Latin pop on the radio.

"So, where's your car, man?"

"Out near State."

The driver weighed the location, and opted for continuing along his straight line. "I better drop you off on College, then."

"Thanks," said Caleb, then tried to remember his East County geography. The drop-off spot would be a mile or two from the sorority. He looked at his watch again.

"Want to make five bucks?" Caleb shouted.

"Doing what?"

"Driving me to Montezuma. My girlfriend was sort of spooked about having to wait outside for me."

The driver shrugged his shoulders a little, then his head started bobbing in agreement. "Spooky times, man. No problem. You just hired yourself Antonio's Taxi Service."

Caleb wished Antonio had the lead foot of most cabbies, but the driver was content to go the speed limit. As loud as the music was, the station breaks were even louder. The disk jockey's staccato and voluble Spanish made it sound as if he were having an apoplectic seizure. Caleb looked out his window. The ethnic mix that lived in the neighborhoods surrounding University was revealed in its restaurants. Polyglot signs advertised everything from taquerías to dim sum to Ethiopian take-out. Somehow immigrants kept fitting in. That's all I ever wanted to do, Caleb thought, just fit in.

As they drew closer to San Diego State, Caleb found his heart racing. Pounding. Sweat dripped off him, soaking Lola's sweatshirt. His wound stung, the perspiration finding its way into the cut. Caleb patted the sweatshirt, feeling to make sure the gauze strips were still in place. They were, but his hand still came away sticky and red. He looked down and saw a dark patch in the front of the sweatshirt. He was lucky the sweatshirt was navy blue. It masked the blood, especially at night. To the casual eye it looked like sweat.

"Make a right here," Caleb shouted, "and then drop me off anywhere."

He pulled out his wallet, and then wiped his hand on his pants. It wouldn't do to hand Antonio a bloodied five-dollar bill.

Antonio didn't immediately pull over. He turned his head right and left, trying to catch sight of a woman waiting by a car.

"Where's your lady, man?"

Caleb didn't say anything, just craned his head as if he expected to see his waiting girlfriend. Montezuma was a mixture of apartment buildings, residences, and sorority and fraternity houses. Cars lined the streets. Caleb pointed out a VW Jetta that was parked farther away from the curb than the other cars.

"That's my car," he said.

"So where's your *chica?*" asked Antonio.

Caleb motioned with his chin. "She's got a friend who lives over at that apartment," he said.

He handed Antonio the money and hopped out of the car. Caleb offered a wave and started walking toward the apartment he had pointed out. Behind him, he heard the Escort make a U-turn, and then drive off.

Caleb reversed his steps and started walking up Montezuma. He knew by the street numbers that the Kappa Omega sorority was several blocks away, apparently at the end of fraternity and sorority row. As he covered the distance, Caleb tried to think like the killer. Around him, the complexion of the neighborhood changed. Shrubs became hiding places; opened windows were invitations for him to visit. The role of killer, he found, was all too easy to assume.

He took up his first position from half a block away, hid behind a eucalyptus tree while scouting the area. The sorority house wasn't as large as he expected, was just a converted two-story town house that had undergone several additions. The house was situated in the middle of an oversized lot. On one side of it was an apartment house, and on the other a home that by all signs was rented out for student housing.

Caleb left the shelter of the tree, and made his way forward along a pathway of trodden iceplant. As he neared the house, he noticed the street was darker than it should have been. Looking up, he saw that the street lamp wasn't working.

And neither were the two spotlights used to illuminate the Kappa Omega sign.

He's already here, Caleb thought. Maybe I'm too late.

But part of his mind was still thinking like the killer's. The lights would have been sabotaged the day before, or earlier in the week. That's how my father would have done it, Caleb thought. And that's how I would have done it.

Bending low on his haunches, Caleb surveyed the area around him. He scanned the cars parked on the street. None was fogged up, and he could see nothing that made him believe any were currently occupied. Maybe his enemy had yet to make his appearance.

Caleb studied the front of the sorority house. The setting looked very familiar to him, and then he realized that Brandy Wein must have been photographed very near to where he was standing. Dead and cooling and naked, she'd been used as a prop by the killer.

He heard a scream and jumped up, but then realized it was only a burst of loud laughter coming from inside the sorority.

The unexpected laughter offered him hope. He could do something to help himself, and help others, this time.

From where he was standing, Caleb could see four bedroom windows. There were lights on in two of them. But Caleb was sure the killer wouldn't try to gain entry through the front of the house. Even with the diminished lighting, the street was too well traveled, and the front too visible. He'd try to gain access through the back.

Caleb crossed the street and walked across the white, decorative rocks that took up most of the front landscaping of the sorority. Though he tried to walk quietly, the stones crunched under his feet. As he passed the side of the house a motion detector tripped on. He ran to the back, out of the light's range, and waited to see if an alarm was raised. None was.

He knelt behind some lawn furniture. There wasn't much to the backyard: a barbecue area, redwood decking, a struggling vegetable garden, and some haphazard shrubbery. There was no foliage near the house, no way anyone could lurk without being easily seen. Above the patio's sliding glass doors was another motion detector. Stickers were affixed to windows warning intruders of the house's alarm system. Caleb wondered whether all the strategies and devices had succeeded in keeping out the uninvited.

The backyard allowed him a better vantage point to observe what was going on inside. Two rooms offered the glow of television sets; in another he could hear a stereo; one woman was sitting at her desk reading.

With the two additions, there were nine or ten bedrooms to the house. Caleb studied the layout, and tried to figure out how an intruder could get inside. With so many occupants, it was likely that security was often compromised by opened windows or propped doors, but he hadn't seen any of those, and this wasn't an opportunistic killer. This was someone who planned his murders.

Caleb scanned for skylights. None. And no attic window either.

There was nothing to indicate the house had been compromised. And there was no sign the killer was anywhere nearby.

But then what usually marked his presence was a body.

Caleb made his way around to the east side of the house. He maintained his distance from it, kept at bay by yet another motion detector, but there didn't appear to be a need for him to approach any closer. This side offered only two darkened rooms and what appeared to be a secure door.

Hunched over, he circled his way back to the lawn furniture. It seemed as good a place to wait as any. Over the next half hour, the night claimed its victims. First a light went off, and then a television went dark, but from what Caleb could see and sense, only the Sandman was responsible for the outages.

The night grew quieter, and little sounds grew louder, but that's all they were, little sounds. Caleb's vigil seemed fruitless, until he saw the stealthy movements in the recreation room.

There were no lights on, but through the partially opened vertical blinds he could make out someone moving around. No, two people. There was an exaggerated furtiveness to their maneuvering about. They paused at the door, played with what looked to be the alarm panel, then the vertical blinds separated and the sliding glass door opened.

Caleb flattened himself on the lawn. Giggling, the women, a blonde and a brunette, walked outside. Their movements activated the motion detector, which caused them to laugh a little more. They were apparently familiar with the sensor's range, and proceeded beyond it, taking up their spots near the barbecue. Only ten feet separated them from Caleb, but they didn't notice him. After a minute the motion detector's light kicked off, and he started breathing again.

He wasn't the only one who welcomed the darkness. The two women seemed to relax, their whispers becoming more conversational. The purpose of their stealth became clear when a lighter flashed, and the women leaned over the flame, one lighting up a cigarette, the other a joint. Caleb suspected the tobacco was being used to hide the smell of pot, though in California it was possible it was the other way around.

The blonde was the first to exhale. "Did you see how Brunhilda acted? Right away she came to me and asked, 'Were you smoking, Vicki?' That cow thought I was the one that set off the alarm."

"Sh," said her friend. "Don't wake her up."

"Nothing's going to wake her up. Did you hear the way she was snoring? We could sneak in the football team tonight and she wouldn't know it."

"I wish."

They both giggled. The more they tried to suppress their laughter, the more they failed.

"I'd rather have the track team," said Vicki. "I met a high-jumper at the Zetas' party last week. He could jump me any time."

Both of them laughed again, then exchanged their smoking sticks. They kept looking around, probably wary of being found out by the house mother.

"It's so boring tonight," said the dark-haired one.

"I know. I thought I'd get all this work done, but I didn't even finish my report."

"It was that dumb alarm."

"No, it was Brunhilda. She should join the army. I mean, like we all knew it was a false alarm, but first she has to take roll, and then she has to make sure there isn't a fire or anything before resetting that stupid alarm. Like we all weren't telling her, 'Turn off the alarm.' It was like she wanted our eardrums to pop."

"Maybe she just wanted to show off her nightgown. Did you see that thing? God. Industrial-strength flannel."

"In prison-guard green."

They laughed a little more, finished up their toking exchanges, then carefully disposed of the evidence, shredding the remains and depositing them among the charcoal. As they walked toward the house they tripped the sensor light again. Under the spotlight, Vicki did a little dance. Her shadow jumped all over Caleb, and pushed him that much further into the ground.

The women disappeared back inside, and the sensor light deactivated. Caleb raised his head, and tried to think. He was bothered by what he had heard. The false alarm could have been an accident, or a malfunction, but he couldn't take that chance. In the chaos of everyone running outside, the killer could have gotten inside.

Was inside.

He had to act. Gas can in hand, he ran over to the west side of the property. There was a thicket of pampas grass that separated the sorority from the neighboring house. On occasion, Caleb's job required him to clear brush by setting controlled fires, and he knew that pampas grass was extremely combustible. He poured the gas around the brush, then tossed the can in the middle of the pampas grass.

The pampas grass hadn't been trimmed back in years, if ever. The interior, with all its old and dead leaves, was a fire waiting to happen. He applied his lighter, saw the fire catch, and then watched as the flames quickly torched upward. As he ran up to a side window, he could see the reflection of the fire behind him. The orange flames seemed to be catching up to him. In a matter of moments, the pane was awash with the fiery glow. Caleb picked up one of the ornamental rocks, and rapped it hard against the glass. The pane didn't break, and neither did the alarm go off. He hit it again, and this time the glass cracked and the clanging started.

Caleb ran across the street, looking for a vantage point from which he could see, and yet not be conspicuous. There wasn't any good spot. Maybe he should have set a second fire. Maybe he should have done lots of things.

He hid behind the line of cars. The fire would draw plenty of spectators, and in a minute or two he'd be able to circulate among the gawkers without drawing any attention. Already he could hear voices, people shouting. He looked over the hood of the car. Figures were spilling out of the sorority. A woman with an imposing figure and a loud voice took charge. Her green nightgown identified her: Brunhilda.

Under the house mother's directions, the Kappa Omegas pulled the front hose over to the side and started spraying the pampas grass. At the same time, their neighbors on the west side were pulling their own hose into play. But the garden hoses didn't seem to have any immediate effect on the torching pampas grass.

Sirens approached. Two cars, with lights flashing, came to dramatic stops. Campus police. In the distance other sirens could be heard. But Caleb was more interested in Brunhilda. She was doing a head count, making sure all of her charges were present.

"Where's Dana?" she called. "Has anyone seen Dana?"

The house mother didn't get an answer she liked. She ran inside the door. Even over the alarms her voice could be heard yelling, "Dana."

Caleb almost didn't notice it. With all the confusion it would have been only too easy to overlook the motion detector going off on the east side of the house. People had flocked to the sorority, but they were all moving toward the fire, not away from it. Someone or something had set off the detector on the side of the house opposite the fire.

He ran across the street, had to sidestep a group of young males who were bemoaning the fact that they hadn't brought marshmallows and beer, then ran from right to left along the front of the sorority house, making sure no one was emerging from the back. The east side had just gone dark again when he reached it. His appearance reactivated the motion detector. Caleb scanned the area but didn't see anything.

"Dana?"

Brunhilda's voice was near. Overhead a light went on in one of the upstairs rooms, followed by a scream: "Dana!"

Caleb started running. He ran to catch the killer, and ran to get away from the scream. I didn't know, he told himself. I couldn't have known. But he had. To save himself he'd been willing to gamble with the lives of others.

He ran blind, headed south without consciously thinking about it. The way felt right, though. Caleb was sure that the killer hadn't parked his car near the sorority. He would have parked a street or two away from it, and he would have scouted the terrain to plan his escape. That's how his father would have done it. Caleb fought his way through fifty yards of brush, the remnants of a small, urban canyon, and came out at a fenced-in apartment complex.

Another choice. He could go right, or left, or scale the chain-link fence. Caleb chose left.

His stomach felt as if it were on fire. The cut had opened, and the wetness was spreading along his belly. His breathing was ragged, but he never slowed. He couldn't. The killer had at least a minute's head start on him, and the knowledge of where he was going. But as Caleb broke free to the street, he heard the sound of a car door closing.

Caleb looked for the appearance of headlights or brake lights, but saw neither. He tried to quiet his breathing. In the distance he could hear the sorority's alarm, and the sound of still more sirens. He started walking forward.

An ignition turned over, and an engine revved. Still no lights, but Caleb could see the car. It was almost hidden by the darkness, and the shadows of a tree, and its own color: it was black, a sedan. He ran toward it.

The car pulled away from the curb, but didn't attempt to avoid Caleb's rush. It wanted to meet him more than halfway. Accelerating, the vehicle headed for him.

Caleb tensed, then made the conscious decision to leap for the windshield, to throw his body at the glass. He cared more about shattering the glass than shattering his bones. It would be his chance, maybe his only one, to reach for the killer's throat.

The car came at him. He tensed to jump, but self-preservation took over. Instead of launching himself at the car, Caleb threw himself to the right, belly-flopping on the pavement. The car braked and swerved, narrowly avoided running into the curb, then came to a stop a hundred feet away.

Caleb raised himself from the asphalt. His chin and face were numb. He'd left a layer of skin behind on the street. He struggled to rise, but his legs kept betraying him. The car was sideways to

Caleb. He couldn't see the driver, was denied getting a good look by the dark night, and the lack of lights, and the car's privacy glass. But he could see the driver staring at him.

The car's engine revved. Taunting him. This time Caleb would be helpless to avoid it.

The car revved again.

Son of a bitch. Caleb started staggering toward the sedan. He couldn't walk a straight line. But he went two steps forward, three steps to the side, and then he started forward again.

The black car's engine sounded, but it didn't run him down. Instead it reversed, and pulled away.

Caleb suddenly found himself immersed in lights, but at first he couldn't understand why.

"Get out of the road, you idiot!"

The shouting was coming from behind him. Caleb turned around unsteadily, and was blinded by the headlights of a pickup truck. He could vaguely make out a man's head outside the driver's window.

"Move it, would you? You're in the middle of the fuckin' road."

It took him a moment to make sense of the words. Caleb tottered over a few steps, enough for the truck to pass him by. Good advice, he thought. Get out of the road. It made sense. The black car could be coming back for him. By trial and error, Caleb made his way to the sidewalk.

His coordination was coming back, as was his awareness. So many parts of him hurt that he found it hard to think, but he knew he needed to think like never before.

Head back toward College, he thought. The commercial district was only about half a mile away. He could find a pay phone there. But who could he call? There wasn't anyone. He'd call a cab, he decided, but then reconsidered. There was no safe place to go.

Another siren. It sounded close. His appearance alone would be a magnet for the police to question him.

Childhood fears overwhelmed him. The pack had always been after him. He'd learned to be stealthy, had spent countless hours figuring out how to avoid capture, how to escape being seen. He had to act before the bullies saw him.

It was dark, but he could still see well enough to make out all the trees around him by their silhouettes. Caleb rejected the cypress, palms, eucs, and pines. A Pacific dogwood was too thin, and a box elder wasn't leafy enough. There had to be a good tree. Enemies were coming.

He decided on a California laurel, a tree that stood about fifty feet high. It wasn't perfect, but it would do. Adrenaline straightened out Caleb's senses long enough for him to trot over to the laurel and begin climbing the tree. Its bark was scaly enough to get a good hold, and he could reach almost all the way around its trunk. Most of the laurel's branches weren't thick, but they were close enough together for him to spread his weight over two or more limbs at a time. Two thirds up the tree, he decided, was high enough. He settled behind a particularly dense thicket of leaves, but knew the camouflage was probably unnecessary. It was the rare person that looked up. People had their heads in the sand, not the clouds.

Caleb tried to get comfortable. He wished he had his harness. That was one of the perks of his job. He'd hang from a limb, secure in his harness, and it was better than a hammock. Sometimes, staring up at a canopy of green, he'd lose track of time and self. Usually he felt more at home in trees than he did anywhere else. But not this time. Now he had to face the enormity of his failure. He had been given a chance, and didn't know if he would get another. Dana certainly wouldn't. Another innocent murdered. And this time he couldn't say it wasn't his fault.

He assessed his wounds and scrapes, decided he'd live, but wished he were more excited at the prospect. His lips were chapped and his mouth was dry. Dehydrated already, and the siege was just begun.

Sirens sounded nearby. They were coming closer. He felt like a bear treed by hounds. Death kept baying. Caleb remembered another tree, another time.

Up in the big pecan tree, up higher than he'd even been before.

His mama said the tree was over a hundred feet high. It had been there all his life, sitting out in their backyard. When he was little he'd thought the tree stretched up as high as Mr. Moon. As a boy, he'd looked up and been sure the moon rested on the tree's branches.

The big pecan was the first tree he'd ever climbed. He had been six. In the five years since, Gray had gotten more daring, but he'd never been anywhere near this high before.

It was windy. A storm was coming. Even though it was night he could still see the storm clouds gathering. They were darker than sin. Maybe a twister was going to come down on them.

Gray didn't care. Far as he was concerned, the wind could blow their house to hell. That would serve his mama right. She hadn't paid him no mind all day. That's how it always was when Gray Senior came home. He became invisible. He even lost his name. Mama called him Cal so's not to confuse the two of them.

Not that it really mattered. The man would be gone soon anyway. He never stayed long, even though Mama always begged him to. She even tried to get him to join in. "Tell your father how much you missed him, Cal." But he never said a word. That seemed to amuse the man. He'd smile, show his big white teeth, and then wink at him.

Not that he wanted him to wink. No sirree.

He wasn't his father, not like the kind of father his friends had. The man didn't even know his birthday. Mama had reminded him that he had a birthday coming the next week. "That so?" he said, then asked, "How old you going to be, boy?"

Gray could hear their noises coming from the big bedroom. He knew what they were doing. Their sounds made him angry. He started climbing even higher. The branches kept getting thinner, but he didn't stop. He could still hear his mama. She sounded like a train. And the man kept talking. "You missed that, didn't you? You like that, don't you? Show me how much you like it. Show me."

The wind was really beginning to blow. Gray held on to a swaying branch. He was sure that if he let go, the wind would carry him away like a bird. His clothes billowed and snapped.

Lightning lit the sky and Gray started counting, "One Mississippi, two Mississippi, three Mississippi . . ." Thunder stopped his counting, thunder that seemed to shake the tree and set all the leaves to trembling. He was reminded of what Mama always said when she heard thunder, "That's God talking, and He's angry."

But this time Mama wasn't making her usual solemn pronouncement. He could hear her cries: "Oh, God, oh, God, oh, God, oh, Gawwwwwwd."

More lightning, and closer. "One Mississippi, two Missis . . ."

The thunder exploded in his ears. But still no rain. Gray knew he shouldn't be in a tree when there was lightning around, but he didn't care. He was as angry as God's thunder.

The wind blew. He was just one of the leaves. He lost track of time, finally awoke to the man's angry voice.

"Bitch."

Their voices carried up to him. There wasn't enough thunder to drown them out.

"Gray, I don't wanna fight. . . ."

"Then why'd you ask me your damn fool question?"

"I love you, Gray."

First they went at it like cats, then they went at it like cats and dogs. That's how it always was.

"You love me putting it to you. That's all you love."

"Don't talk that way. Don't make our love dirty. You know I'll do anything for you. I send you money whenever you ask. And I wait here while you go off to who knows where to do who knows what."

"What do you mean?" His voice was mean, and sounded like a whip.

And then the lightning came, and the thunder was right on top of it, and he couldn't hear their voices for half a minute or so, and when he did, his mama was crying.

". . . article about this Shame fellow, and the picture they had, it looked like you, but I know it wasn't you, but these women been dying in the same cities I've been sending you money, and I'm afraid someone's going to mistake you for Shame, and all I want you to do is stay here with me and Callie."

The words came between sobs, with no start or stop to them.

"You think I'm the killer?"

"Oh, no, Gray, I know you're not. I know how smart you are, and that you're going to school, but maybe you can stay a while this time. Gray Junior's growing up, you know, and it would be nice . . ."

"Truth never meant much to you, did it?"

"Don't you start saying nasty things again, Gray."

"You spread your legs for me, and you think that's love. Ever stop to think I only come to this godforsaken place because it's convenient for me? That's what it was in the beginning, and that's what it is now."

"Don't!"

"Don't tell the truth? That's what you mean, don't you?"

He could hear his mama's sobs, could hear his father saying things to her that made her cry all the more, but the winds had shifted. He couldn't make out all their words. But he made out enough.

Then the rain finally came. It poured with a vengeance, the water striking him, almost flaying his skin.

God wasn't only angry. He was crying.

25

Maryelizabeth adjusted the scarf around her neck before stepping out of the car. It was not her usual accessory piece, but it did cover the discoloration and bruises extending over her neck. She had brought a second scarf along, but not for herself.

She put her hand in her purse and cradled it atop her Smith & Wesson. Before getting out of the car she looked all around. With all the law enforcement in the area it seemed like a silly precaution, but after having been attacked in the middle of the day just outside a military complex she wasn't about to assume she was safe anywhere.

There weren't as many onlookers at the Kappa Omega sorority house as she expected, no camera crews or press to be seen. It was evident the media weren't yet aware of the Shame tie-in. The area had been secured with crime scene tape that stretched beyond the house itself. Memories started coming back. Maryelizabeth's throat tightened and her eyes burned. Ancient history, she tried to tell herself. Something that had happened almost two thousand miles from here. But she couldn't deny her feelings. She thought of Tracy and Paula, her sorority sisters and friends.

Maryelizabeth slipped a lozenge into her mouth and stepped out of the car. She sniffed the air, and smelled the remains of a fire. Lieutenant Borman had said something about that. He had told her that SDPD had control of the crime scene, but that a friend of his on the force had alerted him to the incident. His call to her had been brief, and she'd been in her new rental car within two minutes of the time they had talked.

Their alliance, initially uneasy, was solidifying. Hours earlier Borman had agreed to participate with Maryelizabeth's ploy to blame Caleb Parker for the assault on her. The lieutenant wasn't ready to concede that Caleb might be innocent, or that there might be another murder suspect in the Shame killings, but neither had he wanted to drive Maryelizabeth's assailant into hiding.

A uniformed SDPD officer intercepted her approach. "I'm sorry, ma'am. Only authorized personnel . . ."

"My name is Maryelizabeth Line," she said. "Lieutenant Borman of the Sheriff's Department is here, and he's expecting me."

The officer wasn't ready to take her at her word. He motioned for her to wait while he went and consulted with a higher-up. Maryelizabeth tried to clear her throat. Her voice was still raspy. For dinner she'd had tea and honey and mushy crackers. She fingered her scarf, and felt she was deceiving no one, felt like a chemo patient covering up her baldness.

She looked at the darkened Kappa Omega sign. Maryelizabeth assumed the sorority sisters still identified themselves as Kayos, KO being the boxing abbreviation for "knockout." She and her sorority sisters had liked the idea of being knockouts, but always got a quick reality check when the frat boys called them "knocked-ups." Times had changed, she supposed. *Knocked up* was a phrase she hadn't heard in years.

Maryelizabeth hadn't pledged Kappa Omega until she was a sophomore. And she'd never even finished out her junior year. After the attack, she never went back to the sorority. Her belongings had been packed for her. This would be her first time back inside a Kappa Omega house, or any sorority for that matter, since the night she'd first met Gray Parker.

"Ms. Line?" The officer was holding up the crime scene tape for her.

She ducked her head, felt the stab of pain in her neck, then followed the policeman into the house.

"The lieutenant is upstairs, ma'am," he said, motioning her to go first.

Maryelizabeth paused for a moment on the stairwell to take in the scene. Evidence techs were working both outside and inside, and uniforms were patrolling the grounds with flashlights. Interviews were going on in several rooms. There was lots of nervous laughter, lots of tugging of robes and nightgowns. In a short while the girls would be able to convince themselves that nothing really bad had happened, that no one had really been hurt, and that their lives could continue as normal. Maryelizabeth didn't stop to introduce herself as a Kayo who knew differently.

Lieutenant Borman greeted her at the top of the stairs. The lieutenant's dark circles were deeper than her own. She wondered when he had last slept. With SDPD controlling the crime scene, Borman looked like a fire dog confined to the station.

"I was able to get you cleared for a brief talk with the victim," he said. "Her name's Dana Roberts. According to the paramedics, she's more upset than she is hurt. They're just about finished with her now.

"They haven't started the formal interview yet, but they have asked her some general questions. She doesn't think she can identify her assailant. The room was too dark. The thing that saved her was the second alarm.

"The first alarm went off at around ten-thirty. That's when they think he got in. At the time everyone just assumed it was a false alarm and not some diversion. The second alarm went off at around twelve-thirty. It was accompanied by a deliberately set fire. A gas can was left at the scene of the fire. SDPD has some good latents on the can. There are also some blood droplets on the scene. Someone wanted that alarm to go off. A glass pane was broken. It's possible the blood resulted from the breaking glass."

"Any recent history of arson in the area?"

"From what I understand, no. Maybe a vandal just had great timing. Or it could have been a divinely inspired frat prank."

"Can I talk with her now?"

"Let me go see."

While Maryelizabeth waited, the door at the end of the hall opened, and two paramedics, a man and a woman, emerged.

"How about pizza?" the man said.

"How about Mexican?" she said.

"We had Mexican yesterday."

"We did not."

"Did too."

Their argument continued as they went down the stairs. They sounded more like an old married couple than an emergency medical team.

Borman signaled to her, and Maryelizabeth walked over to the room the paramedics had just vacated.

"Two minutes," Borman said.

She motioned for the lieutenant to precede her inside. Her own blocker. As they entered the room four sets of eyes turned to them. Maryelizabeth briefly acknowledged the two SDPD detectives and the house mother, then focused her attention on Dana. She was sitting on the edge of her bed, her arms hugging herself. Around Dana's neck were ice packs held in place by a neck brace. Just hours earlier Maryelizabeth's neck had been similarly adorned. Sitting next to Dana, with an arm draped over her shoulders, was a large, protective-looking woman who appeared to be in her early thirties. Maryelizabeth thought of Mrs. Jackson, her onetime house mother. The woman looked nothing like Mrs. Jackson, but like her, she was obviously concerned about "her girl." Maryelizabeth remembered how Mrs. Jackson had visited her in the hospital, and how she had ended up being the one doing most of the comforting. Mrs. Jackson was never the same after two of her girls were murdered.

The room was small, was barely designed to accommodate one person, let alone six. The shelves were crowded with personal effects, teddy bears and stuffed cows predominating. Hanging on the walls were an Aztecs pennant, a Monet print, and a Victorian garden scene with a mother and daughter wearing long pink dresses and carrying matching parasols. A small desk housed a computer and a CD player, and a CD tower extended from the floor almost to the ceiling.

After the lieutenant made introductions to the detectives, Maryelizabeth went forward and took up a spot in a chair next to the two women sitting on the bed.

"Hilda Conners," the larger woman said, "I'm the house mother. And this is Dana Roberts."

Dana limply accepted Maryelizabeth's hand, but didn't look at her.

"Ms. Line wants to ask you a few brief questions that might aid in the investigation," the lieutenant said. "Is that all right with you, Dana?"

The girl offered an almost imperceptible nod. Her face was still very pale, and looked all the more so because of her dark hair and eyebrows. She was thin, and the way she was huddled made her look brittle.

Maryelizabeth sat in the chair, her knees all but touching Dana's. She didn't say anything for several moments, just stared at Dana until the girl finally responded enough to raise her head and direct her red-rimmed and puffy eyes back at Maryelizabeth.

"I'm sorry you were attacked tonight, Dana. I know how upsetting all of this is for you. I know, because this afternoon someone tried to strangle me."

Maryelizabeth leaned closer to her, and lifted her scarf. Each woman became the other's audience, the onlookers forgotten. Maryelizabeth's gesture was as intimate as it was revealing. She held her veil up for several seconds. Tears welled in both their eyes. They knew the horror.

"I brought you a little present," Maryelizabeth said, holding out a scarf for Dana.

The girl stopped clutching herself. With her right hand she reached for the scarf, and then she extended both of her hands to Maryelizabeth.

"We're a member of a club neither one of us wanted to join," said Maryelizabeth, "a club we should make sure gets no more members. I want to know if the same man attacked us, and want to know if you'll talk with me about what happened to you."

"Yes," said Dana.

They shared a similar hoarseness as well.

"Was this man familiar to you in any way?"

She shook her head very carefully.

"Did he use your name, or seem to know anything about you?"

Another shake of the head.

"Did he talk to you?"

A half nod: "He said he only wanted my valuables, and that's when I let him tie my wrists and ankles."

Maryelizabeth felt her hands tighten on hers. Dana was angry that she had allowed herself to be trussed up without a fight. Good. She'd need her anger.

"He told me he needed his drug fix, but the way he talked made me suspicious."

"Why is that?"

"He talked like some professor."

"Professor?"

Dana took a second to find the right answer. "It was the way he spoke, like he was lecturing or something, and the things he said. It didn't sound like he was just there to steal."

"What was he lecturing about?"

"About men that had been executed."

"Do you remember any of their names?"

Dana started to shake her head, but then stopped. "One of them was named Appel," she said.

"Good. How did you remember that?"

"Because of the story he told me. He said that before he was electrocuted Appel told everyone that when they finished with him he'd be a baked apple."

"Do you remember any other names?"

She shook her head, albeit gingerly and with a little wince. "But I remember him saying something about this other criminal who arranged to have his body donated to some college because that way he said he'd get a good education."

More capital punishment references. Maryelizabeth had been offered a name as well. While gasping for air, as her life was slipping away, he had told her that John C. Woods always slept like a baby. She had whispered that name to the detectives, and later they had come back and told her that Woods had been the busiest hangman in American history, having hanged 347 men.

The translation, Maryelizabeth thought, was that her death wouldn't bother him in the least.

"Did he say anything else? Ask you any questions?"

Dana tentatively shook her head. "No. He mostly kept trying to calm me, kept shushing me."

She shuddered. The motion seemed to jar her memory. "He asked me whether I liked poetry," she said, suddenly remembering.

Maryelizabeth opened her mouth to ask a question, but her throat tightened, and her stomach did flip-flops, and the words wouldn't come out.

"He said something about Whitman. I don't really remember what."

"Try." The word sounded like a croak.

"He was going to recite some poem to me."

"Which?"

Dana felt Maryelizabeth's imploring in her hands, heard it in the word.

"I don't . . . I was just so frightened." A moment's pause, and then: "He told me the title. It was something about felons."

Your Felons on Trial in Court, she thought. Gray had once told her it explained his epiphany, and his evil.

"Why?" she asked.

He looked at her, showed his large white teeth. "Fellow I know said there was this philosophy professor who once asked that question on a final exam. Three-hour final it was, and all the students were scribbling furiously, taking up all that time to answer that question, all except one fellow who wrote: "Why not?"

"Why?" Maryelizabeth asked again.

"People are going to tell you it was my childhood and my mother. But I don't believe that."

"Do you feel things?"

"Finish your sentence, Mar-E-eh-Liz-a-Beth."

His exaggerated way of saying her name always made her smile. It succeeded again. "What do you mean?"

"Do you feel things," you asked. "But the unsaid part was, 'like a normal human being?' And my answer to you is that I feel things even more than a so-called normal human being."

"Then why?"

"Because hell's tides continually run through me. Whitman. If I weren't so set on being cremated, I'd probably ask for the last few lines of his poem to be chiseled into my tombstone."

"I'd like to hear them."

"Is it that you want to hear the words, or that you want to be able

to write, 'On Tuesday the eighth Gray recited another one of Whitman's poems to me'? People seem to be all excited about the fact that I read books and enjoy poetry."

"Most murderers don't like poetry. Most murderers don't have an IQ of one eighty-three."

"You didn't answer my question. You're not going to try and make me into something other than what I am, are you? I'm no tragic figure, and I'm not anything special. Your book's going to be a failure if it paints me as anything other than what I am."

"And what are you?"

"I'm the exact opposite of a tree."

"What do you mean?"

"I never set roots, I never gave the world shade, I never warmed a room, I never filled a table with fruit or nuts, and I never stretched for the sky. Instead of nurturing nests, I destroyed them."

"So the exact opposite of a tree is death?"

"No. The exact opposite of a tree is worse than death."

"Do you like being an enigma?"

"What I don't like is being given a nobility I don't have. I knew someone who knew someone who served with that Birdman of Alcatraz. Burt Lancaster made him seem all noble in that movie, but the truth of the matter is that he was a horrible human being who just happened to like birds. And just because he cared for his birds people wanted to believe there was some deeper humanity in him. It's like you trying to make something out of this poetry thing."

"What are the words that will never be on your tombstone?"

The air came out of his nose, an amused exhale. He shook his head, but Maryelizabeth knew it was show. She waited on his words. He acted as if he had all the time in the world, and yet he was due to die in less than a week. As he started reciting, his voice became softer, almost wistful.

"Inside these breast-bones I lie smutch'd and choked,
Beneath this face that appears so impassive hell's tides continually run,
Lusts and wickedness are acceptable to me,
I walk with delinquents with passionate love,
I feel I am of them—I belong to those convicts and prostitutes myself,
And henceforth I will not deny them—for how can I deny myself?"

She awoke to the past and the present both clinging to her. It took her a moment to realize the vibration was coming from her pager.

"Excuse me," Maryelizabeth said, letting go of Dana's hands and reaching for her pager.

She looked at the number, then said, "I have to leave."

The exact same words, Maryelizabeth remembered, that she'd said to Gray Parker after he had finished reciting that poem to her.

26

Half the tables at Jimmy Sun's Red Dragon were occupied, something Maryelizabeth didn't expect at two in the morning, but with the bars just closed she suspected the restaurant had acquired unofficial after-hours club status. Voices were loud, the volume fueled by the offerings of the recent last call. The crowd was mostly young. Judging by all the tantalizing smells coming from the kitchen, they were also hungry.

There were no singles sitting in the restaurant, no sign of Sue.

"Just one?"

The accented voice made Maryelizabeth jump. Her close call with death had her on edge. An older Chinese woman with thick glasses hustled out from behind the maître d' stand.

"No. Someone will be joining me."

The woman impatiently motioned for Maryelizabeth to follow her. At the first vacant table she dropped the two menus. "Enjoy your meal," she said, her parting words sounding more like a command than a pleasantry. The table was too exposed for Maryelizabeth's liking, and too near an exuberant party. She moved herself over to a booth.

A busboy brought a pot of tea over to her. Maryelizabeth poured herself a cup. Blowing on the steaming tea, she took a few grateful sips. She cradled her hands around the cup, glad for its warmth. On the wall nearest her were pictures of celebrities who had apparently dined at the Red Dragon. Maryelizabeth tried to put names to the familiar faces, but found she could match very few of them. Something had to be wrong with her life, she decided. She was more familiar with the FBI's Top Ten list than she was with Hollywood's.

A face came between Maryelizabeth and one of the pictures, a pretty face, dark and sensuous. "Ms. Line?"

"Sue?"

They shook hands, and the woman took a seat. She looked flustered. "Confession's supposed to be good for the soul, isn't it?" she asked.

Maryelizabeth barely had time to nod before the woman continued: "My name's not Sue, Ms. Line. I gave you a fake name. Caleb didn't want me to give my real name. I figured that since I'm part Sioux Indian, it would be clever of me to call myself Sue, though I'm not feeling very clever right now."

"Maybe we should reintroduce ourselves. I'm Maryelizabeth Line."

"Lola Guidry."

They shook again. "I don't exactly know how to start this conversation," Lola said, "but I suppose we should begin at our impasse. Earlier tonight you wouldn't tell me whether or not Caleb attacked you. You said you had reservations."

"I still do. I don't know you."

"I'm Caleb's voice while he's in hiding."

"So you say."

"I know things he would have only told a confidante. I know that the two of you talked on several occasions. I know that the murdered girl left at the Presidio was the same girl that worked at the counter of the doughnut shop where the two of you talked. I know that you gave Caleb one of your *Shame* books and audiotapes. I know you were supposed to be looking through your files to try and figure out who from the past might be committing the murders. And I also know you made a promise to help Caleb's wife and children. But what I don't know is whether he was the one who tried to kill you."

"Your knowing all these things," Maryelizabeth said cautiously, "still begs the question of why Caleb isn't the one talking with me."

"I'll be glad to tell you why, but first you're going to have to meet me halfway."

Maryelizabeth thought about her options for a moment, then relented. "He didn't attack me."

Lola sighed in relief. "But why . . . ?"

"I didn't want to drive my attacker into hiding. I thought it possible that he was *the* murderer. After what happened tonight, I'm all but convinced of it."

"What happened tonight?"

"What happened to give and take?"

Lola raised her hands, signaling for patience with her long, artistic fingers. "When we first talked," she said, "you asked me why Caleb wasn't the one questioning you, and I told you that he was afraid to go out in public."

Maryelizabeth remembered. That had contributed to her own reluctance to be forthcoming. "Sue's" answer had rung as true as the name she had given.

"The truth is that Caleb was tied up—literally. When I heard those reports that he had attacked you, I didn't know what to do. So he volunteered to be tied up until I talked with you."

"Is he still tied up?"

Lola shook her head. "I came home and found him gone. It looked like a tornado had gone through my place. It seemed like everywhere there was blood, and I lost it when I saw the bloody knife. I screamed. Luckily, my neighbors weren't home. Because it suddenly occurred to me that the whole mess wasn't the the sign of some struggle, but just Caleb's trying to get free."

"You think the blood was all his?"

"I'm sure of it. He had to cut through duct tape, and I guess his pound of flesh as well. I discovered more blood in my bathroom. It was all over my medicine cabinet, and all over the bloodied bandage wrappers he left behind. There were also bloodstains on my walk-in closet doors."

"How long was he left alone?"

"I was out of my house from half past eight until one."

Maryelizabeth nodded, pursing her lips in thought.

"The way everything was strewn about makes me think he was in some big rush."

The Asian woman who had seated Maryelizabeth suddenly appeared in front of them. Without wasting time for pleasantries she asked, "What you want?"

Lola didn't need to look at the menu. "Cashew chicken," she said.

Maryelizabeth opened the menu, looked for something that could be swallowed easily, and decided on lo mein. The server grabbed the menus and ran off.

"What happened tonight?" asked Lola.

"There was another attack."

"Did he kill again?"

"No, thank God." Maryelizabeth fingered her scarf. "He was interrupted for a second time today. But I'm afraid he's not the kind that gets easily discouraged."

"Did anyone see him?"

"Not well enough to make an identification. He got into a sorority house, but it was too dark for the woman he attacked to get a good look at him."

Lola started to fill her teacup. "What sorority?"

"Kappa Omega."

Lola stopped in mid-pour. "What is it?" Maryelizabeth asked.

"There was a telephone book in my kitchen. Caleb had to have left it on the table. It was opened to the *K*'s."

Both of them played with their teacups, neither one looking at the other. "No," Maryelizabeth said, breaking their uneasy silence. "This was a planned attack. The killer wouldn't have been looking up the sorority's address at the last minute."

"You said the attack was interrupted. How?"

"Someone deliberately set a fire and then set off the sorority's alarm."

Lola offered a word, a hope: "Caleb."

"How would he have known?"

"He's intuitive. He wouldn't agree, of course, but he is. He probably saw or heard something that prompted some association. I know he's been listening to your tape. I also know how bothered he was by it. He played some parts over and over again."

"What parts?"

"I don't know. This morning he was wearing my Walkman and

had on the headset. All I know is that when he took it off he had the fidgets. He could hardly sit still while I was dyeing his hair."

"You dyed his hair?"

"He looks like a natural blond now."

"You must be a good friend."

Lola smiled, as if enjoying a joke. "I must be."

"How long have you known one another?"

"A little over a day."

Maryelizabeth shook her head. "You barely know this man, and yet you sheltered him, disguised him, bound him, and claim to know the workings of his psyche?"

"I forgot to tell you about our Las Vegas wedding."

Maryelizabeth tried not to laugh, but she couldn't help herself.

"Not that it was love at first sight," said Lola. "The first thing I had to do was get over how much he looks like his daddy. I knew Shame's face from studying his pictures in your book. I read your book over and over when I was growing up. It was like a rite of passage for me. It taught me how I couldn't let shame rule my life."

"I'm glad."

"Course knowing Gray Parker from pictures isn't the same thing as knowing him in the flesh and blood. Maybe to you, he and Caleb don't look all that much alike."

"No. They do."

"Did you have a problem with that?"

Maryelizabeth nodded. "It brought up a lot of old feelings. I even found myself not looking at Caleb because every time I did it was like I was experiencing vertigo."

"I think I had the opposite problem. I couldn't keep my eyes off of him. And it wasn't his good looks that kept me looking, but this sadness I sensed in him. I know my helping him must seem crazy, but I didn't have it in me to turn my back on him. From the moment he walked into my club, it was like I knew we were meant to connect."

"What club?"

"Randy Randi's. It's where I perform."

"What do you do?"

"I like to call it cabaret, but the public seems to prefer the term *female impersonation.*"

Maryelizabeth did a double take. The sudden appearance of their entrées allowed her a chance to pick up her chin from the table.

"Who got chicken?"

"Here," Lola said.

Their server hurriedly placed their entrées in front of them, put down a pot of steamed rice, and then left the bill on a plate beneath two fortune cookies. Lola breathed in appreciatively, then looked up and smiled. Maryelizabeth averted her glance. She hoped she wasn't blushing, but knew she was. With her fair skin and red hair it always showed. She could never tell a lie without her body giving her away. Pinocchio syndrome, she called it. Being honest hadn't been an option in life, but a necessity.

Her tone terse, Maryelizabeth said, "I thought you were a woman."

"It's a mistake I often make myself."

"I don't know who I'm angrier at, you or me. You should have told me."

"I'm sorry that I didn't, but if we get to know each other better, and I hope we will, you'll see that this wasn't some guest appearance by my feminine anima. What you see is who I am."

Maryelizabeth said nothing.

"I can understand your being angry with me," said Lola. "But why be mad at yourself?"

"For not noticing. I pride myself on my powers of observation."

"Sometimes pride gets in the way of seeing. You think you already know the answers. Maybe you needed to encounter a heyoka."

"A what?"

"It's a Lakota word and sensibility. In my culture, the heyoka was someone who often did things backward, or the opposite of what was expected. A heyoka makes people think."

"Is that why you dress like a woman?"

"No. I do it because it's right for me. In the immortal words of Popeye, 'I yam what I yam.' "

"I didn't expect it," said Maryelizabeth. There was less frost in her voice.

"Without the unexpected, we wouldn't have nearly as many insights. At my home I have this map of the world. Everything is reversed in it, or at least the opposite as we're used to seeing it. South America is on top of the world, North America on the bottom, and so forth. It's all geographically accurate, but the map bothers some people. They don't like their world changed."

"That's understandable. Most people don't like being told that down is up."

"But that's not what the map represents. It only shows a picture of the world in another way."

"It's not as simple as that. I once interviewed a concentration camp survivor. She told me she was haunted by one particular war picture. In my mind's eye I expected the photo to be some horrible scene of carnage, but it wasn't that at all: the picture was of Hitler happily playing with his dogs. As far as this woman was concerned, Hitler was the devil, and playing with dogs wasn't something the devil did. She had a hard time reconciling the happy, smiling face in the picture with all the atrocities Hitler perpetrated."

Gray Parker's picture often bothered Maryelizabeth in the same way, but she never admitted that. Maybe she was attracted to contradictions. Most of her books had centered on such: the Eagle Scout driven to murder; the beauty queen becoming as ugly inside as she was pretty outside. Milton had shown the way: fallen angels always made for a compelling read.

They both turned to their food. Maryelizabeth painstakingly cut up her noodles into very small pieces, mashed those with her fork, then chewed carefully. Though swallowing still hurt, the pleasure of eating was worth the pain.

Lola noticed the exacting way she was eating. "Did you think you were going to die?" she asked.

Maryelizabeth touched her scarf. Lola wasn't the only one in disguise. "Yes."

"And did your life pass before your eyes?"

"Yes and no. I remember some fleeting images, and I remember feeling some regrets, but mostly what I felt was anger and terror. I wasn't as brave as I would have liked to have been. But I was stubborn. I just didn't want to die like that."

"How do you want to die?"

"Not prematurely."

"Maybe you picked the wrong line of work."

"I've considered that."

"What are we going to do?"

"Regarding what?"

"Caleb. We have to find a way to help him."

"At this point I hope he'll help himself by surrendering to the police."

"He's not going to do that. He doesn't trust the police. And he doesn't expect anything better than a lynch-mob mentality out of the public."

"If he contacts me, I can't encourage him to continue being a fugitive. He's deluding himself if he thinks he can get to the bottom of all this by himself."

"He managed to save a girl's life tonight."

"We don't know that."

"I think we do."

"Let's assume you're right. What are we supposed to do? Unless he contacts us we can't do anything. He has all my numbers."

Maryelizabeth suddenly frowned.

"What is it?"

"Someone else has one of my numbers. I was duped today by a message left on my service. The caller spoke in a whisper and identified himself as Caleb. I wanted to hear from Caleb so much that I believed him."

"He knew your weakness."

"Weakness?"

"The caller. The killer. He knew how to push your buttons. It's possible he knows you."

"Why do you say that?"

"The way he manipulated you. And his having your telephone number."

Getting the number for her service wouldn't have been that difficult, thought Maryelizabeth. But what else did he know about her?

"I keep thinking there was something familiar about him," said Maryelizabeth, "something in his voice, I think. Maybe Caleb's right. Maybe the answer is in my old Shame files, in the past."

"But whose past?"

"What do you mean?"

"Remember my map. It's all in the way you look at things. Caleb might not be the only target here."

"You're not very reassuring."

"Don't blame the messenger."

They both put down their forks, hungry no more.

"Let's go look for Caleb tonight," said Lola.

"Look for him where?"

"He doesn't have a car. He has to be hiding somewhere near that sorority."

"I hope he has a good hiding place then, because half the police department is out there. Patrol cars are everywhere. And short of using a bullhorn, I don't know how we'd signal him."

Lola reluctantly nodded. "I better go home then. Maybe he's trying to call me right now. I'm going to borrow a friend's phone, and I'm going to go sit by it. But if tomorrow comes, and I haven't heard from him, then bright and early I'm going out on a manhunt."

27

Junior had surprised him. For the moment, Feral couldn't lay any more stones on him. But just for the moment. The pressing would continue.

In America's history, only one man had ever been pressed to death. That was a pity. Feral couldn't understand why pressing had never grown more popular in the States. On the Continent, it had commonly been used to torture and kill. What Feral liked was its simplicity. Pressing was easy. You just piled stones on a person's chest, one atop another. As the weight of stones grew heavier, breathing became more difficult. It was the rare person who didn't break down, who didn't capitulate with whatever the presser wanted.

Junior had shown surprising mettle. Feral had thought him an unworthy son before. Weak. Afraid of his own shadow. A simpering cuckold. But the way Junior had managed to avoid capture, and the way he had even figured out one of Feral's schemes, showed he was at least a resourceful coward. In a moment of weakness, Feral had even been tempted to end his life on that road, but that wouldn't have served his plans. There was still a stone or two he needed to lay on Junior's chest. Heavy stones. Headstones.

Feral was sure Junior wouldn't prove to be any Giles Cory. He wished he could have been present at Cory's pressing in 1692. Who said that the Pilgrims didn't have any fun? Cory was the only colonist ever pressed to death. He had refused to plead either guilty or innocent to the charges brought against him. There was a reason for his silence. Because he refused to plea, his possessions couldn't be confiscated by the state. Though the stones had piled up on his breast, they hadn't broken Cory's spirit. Feral suspected that was the presser's fault. He was confident he had just the right straw for the camel's back.

Pressing. The thought invigorated him.

Feral thought of other stones, and found himself getting excited.

As she had been getting out of her car, he had sneaked up behind her and said, "Do you know what Charles de la Roi said to the warden the day before he was sentenced to die in the gas chamber?"

She had jumped, and then she had seen who it was standing there, and her expression had become disdainful. She had said his name, had announced it as if it were some pitiful thing, but she never came up with an answer.

"He said, 'Warden, I'd like a little bicarbonate, because I'm afraid I'm going to have gas tomorrow.'"

She was used to his morbid histories, but she wasn't ready for what followed. He had laughed, and she had seen something in him, and heard something in his laugh. She became aware of Feral for the first time. Then she had spotted the large rock in his hand, and knew that the wilding was about to take place.

"No," she had said. "Don't."

Her last words were not at all original, not at all.

It was a happy memory. Pity today didn't go as well, thought Feral. To use a tiresome cliché, he'd been so close, yet so far. It annoyed him to have done so much planning for such an unsatisfactory climax. He had been twice denied. But that's what contingency plans were for.

Patience, he told himself, patience. His inner sermonizing reminded him of one of his favorite cartoons. The picture showed one very annoyed vulture telling another vulture: "Patience, my ass. I'm going to kill someone."

Feral understood that kind of killing hunger. Like the vulture, he was tired of waiting. But he wasn't a carrion feeder. He was a hunter grown impatient.

"Patience, my ass," Feral said aloud. "I'm going to kill someone."

And soon.

It was time to get back to work. He referred to his notebook, picked up a pen, and dialed a number.

"Yes, can you please connect me with Ann Dickens's room?"

Feral had methodically entered the name and telephone number of every San Diego area hotel and motel into his notebook. The private dick had documented that Queenie invariably registered under any one of six names. The detective was good. He had worked for Feral on several occasions until he'd had his untimely accident.

"Ann's not there?" Feral did his best to sound surprised. "She was supposed to be traveling with Angel Lake. Can you check and see if she's registered there? Yes, the last name is Lake."

The night auditor sounded none too happy being bothered in the middle of the night. Feral hoped the cretin was being methodical.

"She's not there either? Hmmm. Well, thank you."

He wrote down the names, and the time of his call. It wouldn't do to call back the same hotel for several hours.

Another name, another hotel.

"Yes, could you please connect me with Vera Macauley's room?"

Feral checked the other name he would be asking for. Jean Keys. Where did Queenie come up with her names? Maybe he would ask her that the next time his hands were around her neck.

Suddenly, the line started ringing. He had been connected to Vera Macauley's room. Feral listened for a moment, made sure there wasn't some mistake, and then hung up.

Time to check in, he thought.

Aloud, he announced, "Patience, my ass, I'm going to kill someone."

28

Too much cold, too much pain.

As Caleb shifted, the branches creaked, but not as much as his bones. He hurt everywhere, and was so thirsty he'd taken to licking the leaves for their moisture. Lapping up the dew made him feel like a dog. He was afraid that at any moment he might start baying at the moon.

Maybe he already had. His mind kept drifting. In a way that was a blessing, for time passed that he wasn't even aware of, but it was also scary. Only minutes earlier he had awakened to the sound of other voices, or at least thought he had until he'd recognized those voices were his own.

He had gone through several spells of trembling, each worse than the last. Caleb wished he had brought along a coat, and water, but of course he hadn't planned to be up a tree. Now, with all the patrol cars going by, leaving his perch wasn't an option.

There was little to do but stare up into the sky and think. It was a cloudless night, and the stars were tantalizingly near. Caleb wished he could name the constellations. Another regret. He wondered if you could wish upon stars whose names you didn't know, or whether that voided the whole process. He made his wish anyway. "Wish I may," he whispered, "wish I might, wish my family's well tonight."

If I survive this, he vowed, I'll take my family on a special vacation. And this time I won't take along the same baggage I've carried for so long. It had weighed everyone down on their last trip. They had traveled up the coast to San Francisco, their first vacation in over a year. Caleb had known his marriage was in trouble, and he had thought a getaway might help it. They had gone on an outing to Fisherman's Wharf, and there the children had been seduced by the flashing lights of the Ripley's Believe It Or Not! wax museum.

"Let's go to the wax museum! Let's go to the wax museum!"

Janet started the chant, and then James joined in. Their exhortations grew louder.

Laughing, Anna surrendered to their demands. Though they entered the museum as a family, the kids quickly ran ahead. "I better stay with them," Anna said.

"I'll do it."

"No, let me. Take your time."

Both he and Anna were reading from the same overly polite "you first" page. What Caleb should have said was, "Let's all stay together." But that thought came too late. Anna had already gone ahead.

He could have run after her, but he didn't. Alone, he made his way through the exhibits. There was a mazelike feel to the museum, the twists and turns opening up to the displays of the bizarre and strange and morbid. The exhibits were realistic, making for a sideshow feel, but no carnival barker was needed. Many of the wax figures were triggered by motion detectors, voicing their incredible stories to all passersby.

At times Caleb closed in on his family, could hear his children's excited laughter two or three displays ahead. Their reactions offered him previews of what he was going to see. But he wasn't forewarned, at least not enough.

When Caleb walked into the Hall of Shame, it lived up to its name—literally. They were all there, gathered together like fraternity brothers: Bluebeard, Attila, Bundy, Speck, Gacy, Hitler, Dahmer, Manson, and Amin.

And Shame.

His father was standing center stage and smiling. In his hands was a book of poems, an anthology of Whitman. His father was by far the handsomest man in the group. He also looked the most self-assured.

Caleb's presence set off his recording: "Seventeen women, a dozen of them college students, died by my hands," he announced. "I strangled them, and left my signature on the naked body of each.

Not Gray Parker, the name I was born with, but the name I came to be associated with: Shame.

"My killing spree lasted for three years. I left behind bodies in five states. I was described as having the looks of an angel, and the heart of the devil.

"Before being executed for my crimes in the state of Florida, I was asked if I had any last words. And I told the world, 'Shame on you. Shame on you.'"

The laughter started, and went on for ten seconds before it abruptly cut off. Caleb stepped back. He didn't want to start the recording again.

That's not his voice, Caleb told himself. Some actor had spoken those lines, someone with a dramatic voice and laugh. It wasn't even close to his father's voice. Even after all those years, Caleb remembered exactly what that sounded like. Of late, he'd been hearing it all too often in his head.

All the old feelings returned: his embarrassment, his fears. For so long he had tried to bury those emotions, but now they overwhelmed him. It was as if every good thing in his life had been stripped away and the only thing that was real was his past.

Caleb hurried out of the Hall of Shame, but before leaving the room he threw a quick glance back. What he saw made him all the more afraid. His father's eyes were following him, not like the Mona Lisa's, but like those of the devil himself. Even when he was outside the hall, Caleb had the distinct feeling that his father was still watching him, and that no matter where he went, and no matter how fast he ran, he wouldn't be able to escape those eyes.

The encounter had ruined Caleb's, and his family's, vacation. He had pretended that all was well, but the more he'd made believe that everything was fine, the more tension he'd created. Even after returning home Caleb wasn't able to shake the pall of the Hall of Shame. His everyday life had felt futile, as if he knew the tide was eventually going to go out and pull him with it. That's why his encountering Teresa Sanders's body hadn't really surprised him. It was just the other foot dropping on him.

God, he was hot. Caleb felt his forehead. He was burning. Some people were talking nearby. Didn't they know how late it was?

* * *

I'm so tired of all this.

A hero is someone who somehow hangs on just a little longer.

Is that what you think you are, some kind of hero?

No.

Then why are you hanging on? Everyone knows about your father now. Your dirty secret's out. Even if you convince some people that you didn't kill anyone, they'll still never look at you the same way again.

I'm not my father.

When are you going to learn that doesn't matter? Remember when you were younger and you tried so hard to be perfect? You brought home perfect report cards, and you put on your mask that you called a brave face, and you let the townsfolk spit on you, and the boys beat you up, and you never retaliated. But no matter how good you were, it never helped your situation. No one forgave you for being Shame's son. And that's what you are again. That's what you are always going to be.

I can be more than that.

Or less than that. You're a victim of the proverb "What you're afraid of overtakes you." It has. It did. And the person you might have been, we'll never know.

No.

Oh, yes.

The conversation gave way to chattering teeth. Only moments before Caleb had been so hot, and now he was freezing. He was aware enough to know he was out of control, but not aware enough to do anything about it. It felt as if he were on a roller coaster, and it was all he could do to hang on.

Her legs opened. She wanted him. He saw Earlene reaching for him. And then she was offering up her neck, and telling him to squeeze it.

Earlene's head changed, became raptorlike, a harpy's, then her sharp beak was driving into him, savaging his chest and pulling out his heart.

And his father was laughing, but it wasn't his father's laugh. It was the mechanical laugh from the museum.

"Go away," said Maryelizabeth Line, but she wasn't saying it to him, she was waving off the harpy, and trying to stuff his heart back into his chest.

"Mine was taken in almost the same way," she told him, and then she shook her head in great sadness.

"I know," Caleb said.

Maryelizabeth's face changed, became Lola's. She stared at him. He could see her compassion. For the first time he noticed how pretty she was. She looked like a woman, a beautiful woman, and he reached out to touch her hair, but as he did her hair changed into a headdress of feathers, and he pricked his finger. Lola had changed. She was still Lola, but she was a brave now.

"My name is Osh-Tisch," she said.

"You're different."

"No. I just had to dress for battle."

"You gave up your makeup for war paint."

"Yes."

Caleb wanted to reach out and touch the designs, but he remembered his bloody index finger.

His bloody index finger. That was real. It throbbed. He must have cut it on the tree. He focused on the finger. It was something tangible. He used it as a reality check, a way out of the kaleidoscope. An awareness filtered through: he could see his finger. There was now enough light for him to examine it. Daylight had finally arrived.

Caleb lifted his head, fought off the dizziness. Nearby he heard voices. Hallucinating again, he thought. He clenched his teeth together, but unless Caleb was a ventriloquist he wasn't responsible for the verbalizing. The loud voice was familiar to him. It projected, as if playing to an audience, and came across as equal parts playful, saucy, and enticing.

"I'm looking for my pussy. You haven't seen her, have you? I have a description of her right here. She answers to the name of Precious. She's a real purr-box, black and soft and gentle."

Lola.

Impossible, of course. His mind had to be playing tricks. But he could even see her on the street. She was only about fifty yards away, as the hallucination flies. She was wearing a form-fitting red bathrobe that had little underneath it, and walking around in slippers.

But this delusion was different from the others, wasn't so dreamlike and frenzied. And the fantasy didn't shift or disappear. Lola kept talking about her missing cat. Strange hallucination, Caleb thought. He knew that Lola didn't have a cat.

"You sure you haven't seen her? Can't keep that pussy at home. No, sir."

The young man appeared very sympathetic. Phantasmagoria, Caleb thought, pulling the word from somewhere in his head. But that certain knowledge didn't vanquish the images. He could still hear them, and see them.

"Well, thank you anyway," said Lola. "Keep your eyes open for me."

The student looked more than happy to accommodate her request. In fact, she needn't even have asked. His eyes were all over her, but it wasn't the young man's fault. Lola was acting the coquette.

You're not even a real woman, Caleb almost yelled. But he didn't, because he was suddenly certain she was real.

Lola finished with the student. When he got into his car, there was a big smile on his face. The smile was still there as he drove past Caleb's tree.

"Lola." His voice was weak. Even Caleb could barely hear it. "Lola." Louder this time, but hardly a shout.

It stopped her, though. She looked around.

"Up here."

She scrutinized the tree until she picked him out. "There you are, sugar," she said, as if she had expected to find him there. "You just stay put while I get the car."

She turned around, made a left at the corner, and was lost from sight. In her absence, Caleb began to doubt what he'd seen. He was so lightheaded that focusing was difficult. His lips were dry and cracked, and his throat ached from being so parched. His clearest thoughts revolved around water.

"Come on down."

Her voice again. Below, he could see her motioning for him to climb down. Caleb loosened his hold on the branches, but getting down wasn't easy. Everything hurt. Moving just reopened wounds. He felt as if he were being killed by inches. He thought of letting go and dropping to the ground, but he still had enough awareness to not want to break any bones. Lola talked him down.

"That's it, honey. You're almost there. Just a little more. I can see it hurts, but relief's only a few feet away. That's it."

She reached up to ease his descent, and he ended up in her arms. Together, with Caleb leaning heavily on her, they made their way over to the Mustang.

"You're hot," she said, then felt his forehead with the back of her hand. "Oh, Jesus. You're burning up. I got some Evian in my workout bag. Now don't you go collapsing on me. I can't carry you. Come on, just a little farther."

Once in the car, Caleb sat unmoving, his eyes closed, but he revived at the sound of a water bottle being uncapped. His eyes remained closed even as he upended the bottle and started drinking. Lola thought he looked like a newborn animal in the zoo nursery. Sometimes she went there just to see them, little ones too young to open their eyes, but old enough to hold on to their bottles for dear life.

"I'm taking you to the hospital," Lola said.

He shook his head, and the empty bottle with it, before removing it from his mouth. His eyes remained closed.

"I need some more time to think," Caleb said. "I almost caught him."

"Is that how you got so scraped up?"

A nod. "Look for a car with my skin on it."

As Caleb spoke, his voice grew softer, and his breathing became more regular. He slept the rest of the way, and awakened to Lola trying to help him out of the car. She walked next to him up the path and into the bungalow, and then tried to guide him into bed, but he resisted, insisting on the sofa instead.

"I need your tape player," he said, "and the *Shame* tape."

"What you need is some doctoring. That tape can wait."

"Can't. There might be some clue."

"You're in no condition to be a hero again."

"What?"

"What part don't you understand?"

"The hero."

"Your setting off that alarm saved the girl in the sorority."

"She's alive?"

"Yes."

Caleb fought off unfamiliar tears. It had been so long since he had heard any good news.

"Of course no one in law enforcement's ready to pin a medal on you," Lola said. "They think you probably have some partner in crime. That explains how you were able to call Maryelizabeth right after she was attacked."

Caleb shifted on the sofa, and then wished he hadn't. Lola noticed his flinch. "Sweatshirt's going to have to come off," she said, "and so's the shirt. They're looking like some petri dish experiment."

Caleb struggled to get the garments off. He tried not to groan aloud, but the sounds kept escaping him.

"Let me help you," Lola said.

He was in no position to resist her efforts, and besides, it was so much easier, and she was so gentle about it. When she removed his garments Lola stared at his exposed chest and drew in her breath.

"That cut looks ugly. It looks like you tried to carve yourself another belly button."

She took a closer look at the cut, then shook her head. "I'm no Florence Nightingale, but I think it's infected."

"There's disinfectant in your medicine cabinet."

"That's not an answer."

"When you put it on, you can wear your white nurse's outfit."

"Only if you're in the market for an enema as well."

She left the room. On the end table nearest to him Caleb noticed a newspaper. He reached for it, took a look at the front page, then wished he hadn't. The picture was yellowed with age. He had hated it then, and hated it just as much now.

He'd been surprised when the photographer had jumped out and snapped the photo, and that showed in the picture, but to the casual viewer, he knew, he just looked defiant. The snarl caught on his face gave him a wild look that was further accentuated by the particular baseball cap he was wearing. The headline read: Picture Proves Prophetic. Caleb threw the paper down in disgust. He didn't need to read the story.

Lola walked into the room with a bottle of disinfectant and some washcloths. She saw the newspaper being tossed, and saw Caleb's expression. She never commented, just walked out to the kitchen and returned with some aspirin and a gallon of water. Most of that gallon disappeared within minutes. When his thirst was slaked, she took a washcloth, wet it with water, and placed it on his forehead.

She wasn't as certain about what to do with the other washcloth. She poured some disinfectant on it, said, "This will probably hurt," then tentatively started in on the minor scrapes. As Lola dabbed, it was her face that showed the pain.

"When I was young," she said, "my mother believed the only good kind of disinfectant was one that hurt. So when I'd get a cut, she would pour Merthiolate on it and I'd scream out in pain. No one else I knew had to endure that. Their mothers used stingless ointments."

Lola took on her first major abrasion, tried to gently clean out the dirt. "You can talk, you know," she said.

"I know."

"I'm nervous," she said. "I don't know how those people in the ER do it. I'd hate to have someone's life depend on my every move. I couldn't take that kind of responsibility."

Caleb shrugged.

"You probably don't talk or laugh during sex either, do you? Out of necessity, you learned to swallow your pain. Problem is, your joy got swallowed up as well."

She started to work on his very raw jaw. "What was that newspaper picture all about?"

He chose his answer carefully. "No lie like an old lie."

"It wasn't you?"

"No. It was."

Caleb sighed, shook his head, then started talking. "That picture was shot a few weeks after my father was arrested. By then I'd already learned to be wary of reporters, but apparently not wary enough. Mama had told me they lied better than politicians, and she was right about that.

"Two of them were waiting for me outside my school. I remember the reporter had a big mouth, and in that mouth was enough gum to make it look like a chaw. The photographer was a short, fat guy with three or four cameras around his neck.

"'Hey, Gray,' the gum chewer called to me, all friendly like. I didn't trust him. I walked away from him, and when he started following me, I ran. I took the back route home. But they knew where I lived.

"Mama was at work, so I was by myself watching TV when I heard our doorbell ring. I pulled back the curtain a little and saw the same two men. The curtains to our house were drawn. That's how we coped with the outside world. From the day my father was arrested, to the day I left Eden for good, we never opened those drapes, never let any sunshine in."

Caleb took a deep breath. Had he ever opened those drapes, he wondered? But he only allowed himself a moment of self-pity.

"The men kept knocking, and Mr. Chaw kept calling out my name. 'Just want to talk to you for a minute, Gray,' he kept saying. 'I'll make it worth your while. Give you fifty bucks if you just have a few words with me.' I didn't say a word, though. Mama had taught me that if I said anything, even the word 'No,' it just encouraged them.

"What I remember, though, is how tempted I was just to talk. Not so much for the money, but because nobody at school was speaking to me other than to call me names. The town mothers had figured I was contagious or something, and had told their kids to stay away from me. But I didn't talk with those reporters, didn't say a word, because Mama had been as serious as death about me not having anything to do with them.

"The gum chewer tried calling me out every which way, but finally he seemed to give up. He must have known I was watching him, though, 'cause he called out, 'All right, Gray, I'm sorry you don't want the money, but tell you what, I'm going to leave you some presents in this here bag. Going to leave you my card, too. You can watch me leave the bag on the path right here.'"

Caleb realized his voice unconsciously took on the tones of the gum-chewing reporter. He still remembered his voice.

"The man dropped the bag down on the dirt path that led up to our house. Then he walked over to this shiny van parked on the street, started it up, and drove away.

"I kept looking at that bag. Watched it for maybe five minutes. Finally, I opened the door and looked around. No one was in sight. I walked down the path, but I didn't pick up the bag right away, just worried it with my foot a little. Nothing happened, so I opened it up. Inside was a baseball cap and some gum and some chocolate. I dumped the bag out, pocketed the goodies, and then I tried on the baseball cap. It fit just right. I didn't bother to check out the writing on it, or the patch. That was my mistake.

"The patch showed two hands reaching for a throat, and beneath it was the word *shame.* I heard some clicking going on, and I turned toward the sounds. The fat guy was hiding behind one of our pecan trees, shooting pictures of me as fast as he could. I ran back into the house, but it was too late. A week later I saw myself on the cover of one of those tabloid newspapers. The banner headline said: 'I Want to Be Just Like My Daddy!' Says Son of Shame.

"Everyone in town seemed to have a copy of that paper, and everyone seemed to believe what they read. That made-up article justified their every prejudice towards me."

Lola said nothing. She started working around the knife wound. It had to be tender. It had to hurt like hell. But the physical pain seemed to bother Caleb far less than the mental. He didn't even appear to notice her ministrations.

"There was another story in the paper," said Lola, "one you didn't read. Two of your employees vouched for you. They said they had worked for you for years, and that there's no way you could be a killer. They told about the time you tried to talk a man out of cutting down a tree because there was a bird's nest in it, and that when the man insisted it be cut you took the nest and the birdies home and hand-raised them."

"The whole family helped." Caleb had never been so happy as when those birds fledged. It had been an around-the-clock project.

His character references, and the bird story, had to have been supplied by his two longtime employees, Roberto Zúñiga and Tyrone Hayward. His workers, whom he called the Cisco Kid and Sheriff Bart, had thought he was a little crazy to take the birds home. He'd nicknamed his employees after screen cowboys, the one brown and the other black. On tree jobs there was a lot of use of ropes, and both men handled them like cowboys, lassoing branches and passing equipment up and down rope trams. With Sheriff Bart and the Cisco Kid on the job, sometimes work even sounded like a roundup.

"That's the story you ought to read," said Lola. "Not the other."

"It's the other that people will remember."

She started putting Band-Aids on his smaller cuts, then worked up to bandages for his chin and stomach. Her hands were cool against his hot skin, gentle. He didn't flinch at her touch.

"You're still awfully hot," Lola said.

"I'll take a few more aspirin."

"You've already taken four."

"Really? I don't remember."

Caleb could feel his mind drifting. He tried to rein it in. "Can you get me that audiotape? I need to listen to it."

"You need your rest even more," Lola said, but her tone already conceded him his wish.

She left the room again, returned with her tape deck, and set everything up on the side table next to him. Caleb was watching her. His eyes were glassy.

"Thanks," he said. "For everything."

"You're welcome."

He looked around the room. "This is all real, isn't it?"

"What do you mean?"

"I was having these dreams. I even dreamed about you. It was like I noticed you for the first time. I could never see that you were pretty before. I couldn't get beyond what you were. But in this dream I finally saw you. And it didn't seem wrong that you were pretty. And you weren't a spectacle. You were just you."

Lola knew it was his fever speaking, and that without it he would never talk like this, but she still said, "Thank you."

He didn't hear it. Caleb's mind was already somewhere else. "After the Second World War German youths didn't want to admit they were German," he said. "They said they were Swiss or Austrian. They didn't want to be guilty by association. But it was more than that. I know it was more than that. They were afraid that the beast lurked inside of them as well."

"The beast?"

"I don't think young Germans worry about that anymore. They say the Holocaust happened a long time ago. Do you think my children could also be free of the guilt?"

"Yes."

Caleb shook his head as if trying to remember something, and then did. He turned to Lola, suddenly focused. "Where's the tape?" he asked.

"Right next to you."

Caleb reached for it, hit the Play button, listened expectantly for a moment, then appeared satisfied that the tape was in the right spot.

Look through the classified ads of the New Orleans Times Picayune [Maryelizabeth Line's voice said], *and you'll likely see more ads to Saint Jude, the patron saint of lost causes, than in any other daily in the country. The volume of ads is that much more impressive when you consider that New Orleans the myth is larger than New Orleans the city, with its reputation far exceeding its numbers.*

The daily supplications to Saint Jude extend to a number of areas. Some ads thank Jude for his generosity, for having listened to and answered their prayers, but most are cries of desperation, people trying to raise their heads above water for a third and last time.

Parker was almost that desperate when he fled into Louisiana. No longer was he this nebulous figure, this Bogeyman of the night who signed SHAME on all his victims. The law now had a good description of him, and his likeness was being circulated throughout Texas and beyond. The police were getting ever closer to him.

Perhaps because of that, Parker's killings had become ever more hurried and less well thought out. His MO never changed, though; he continued to kill with his hands, his murders "personal." He didn't want the distance or dispassion that a gun allowed, or even a knife, the almost "third person" of me, you, and the weapon. When he strangled another human being there was no third part of the equation, no tool doing the killing. Parker described his actions as the "sacrament of murder." He spoke of his murders reverentially, relating how there was a sacred moment when the victim's "life force" gave out, and how this energy entered back into him, strengthening him. In his own mind, Parker was convinced that all the deaths were necessary.

Apparently, even his own.

Caleb reached over and hit the Stop button. He didn't acknowledge Lola's being in the room, just started mumbling to himself. At first Lola couldn't make out his words, only noticed that his voice was higher-pitched than usual. And then she started making sense out of what he was saying. Caleb was repeating some of the phrases he had just heard.

"'No longer was he this nebulous figure,'" he said. "'MO never changed. No tool doing the killing. All deaths were necessary.'"

Caleb shook his head. "'All deaths were necessary,'" he said once again.

The voice sounded like a woman's, Lola thought.

"'All deaths were necessary,'" he said for a third time, "'apparently even his own.'"

Not just any woman, Lola realized, but Maryelizabeth Line.

"'Apparently even his own.'"

Caleb's mimicking ability was so uncanny that Lola felt uneasy. It was as if someone else were inside him. She was glad when he reached over and pressed the Play button.

It was in New Orleans that Parker first experimented with a victim. Jenny Lucas was found with the usual Shame MO, but he didn't leave her body with only his signature. Her breasts were found ravaged with tooth marks; her right nipple was almost completely severed. There were also bite marks all around Jenny's labia.

Parker didn't use lipstick to do the lettering on Jenny. Lab results confirmed what the police on the scene had guessed: that Parker had applied his signature with Louisiana hot sauce. Hot sauce was also found inside her vagina.

Caleb turned off the recording. He appeared agitated at what he'd heard. He kept smoothing his hair. His cheeks were flushed red, but the rest of his face was drawn and pale.

Lola went over to check his fever. She took away the washcloth. Steam all but rose from it. She put the back of her hand on his forehead.

"Oh, God," she said. "You're so hot."

"Louisiana hot sauce," he said, but in Maryelizabeth's voice.

Lola wished a priest were at her side. She thought Caleb was possessed and in need of an exorcism. It was all she could do not to run screaming from the room.

"Some Louisiana hot sauce," he said, "that's what I need."

This time he didn't speak in Maryelizabeth's voice. But it wasn't Caleb's either. Lola felt chilled. She was sure it was Gray Parker voicing the request.

29

"Can't escape me," Feral said. "You know that, don't you?"

Feral thought of Robert O. Pierce, and how he had tried to escape his appointed destiny with death. On the night Pierce was due to be executed he managed to get a piece of glass and cut his own throat. The wound had been too deep for the prison doctor to treat him successfully, but instead of taking Pierce to the hospital, the guards had carried him to the gas chamber. And there he had lived just long enough to die by gas.

It still bothered Feral that he'd had his hands around Queenie's neck and she had gotten away. But like Pierce, she was about to go from the frying pan into the fire.

Feral started up his car and pulled away from the curb. He was taking his time scouting the exterior of the Amity Inn. He had already driven around the parking lot, but hadn't seen Queenie's car. She probably had a new rental. Queenie had been suspicious enough to begin with, and after yesterday's tête-à-tête, she would be even more so.

Didn't matter, he thought. She and Robert O. Pierce could compare notes in hell.

Feral parked in the white zone in the front of the lodge. The Amity Inn wasn't the kind of establishment that had bellmen waiting at the curb. It was designed for the long-term business traveler. Perfect for Queenie's anonymity, and his own as well. At a hotel there would have been more employees and guests milling about, more potential witnesses.

From where he was sitting, Feral could see the lobby. He was tempted just to walk in and ask the clerk which room Vera Macauley was in, but he didn't want to expose himself. The staff might be on alert to anyone asking for her, and even if they weren't, most clerks were trained not to give out a guest's room number. It was a suspicious world. Shame on it.

No, Queenie was going to make this as hard as possible. Feral whispered from an Andrew Marvell poem: "'Had we but world enough, and time, / This coyness, lady, were no crime.'"

He would have liked to recite the words to Queenie herself. She was smart enough that she might even appreciate them. His former girlfriend had never liked his recounting couplets or ditties. She had thought him a pedant. That was one of her excuses for breaking up with him. Of course she hadn't used the word *pedant,* not with her limited vocabulary. What she had said was, "You always talk about weird stuff, and creepy stuff." He had accepted her rejection in a very understanding manner, but that had been easy for him to do. For rejecting him, Feral had known, she had to die.

No woman was ever going to reject him again.

Feral remembered a line from W. C. Fields: "'Twas a woman who drove me to drink, and I never even had the decency to thank her." Feral felt much the same way. He had his girlfriend to thank for all the murders, but he hadn't even had the decency to thank her. Instead, he had murdered her. And then he had emulated the Cave Man killings a second time. He'd killed again to allay potential suspicion. The second victim had been his insurance policy. Feral had known the Cave Man's troglodyte luck would soon run out. But Feral thought it possible that after his capture the Cave Man might take credit for his murders, and if not, the murders could always be attributed to one of those pesky copycats.

Funny how in such cases no one said imitation was the sincerest form of flattery.

As it had turned out, the Cave Man *had* initially claimed the kills as his own, but later recanted. The police were looking into his change of heart, and so was Queenie. Feral had been thrilled when he first heard she was coming to Denver to write a book on the

Cave Man murders. Her timing had been impeccable. She had saved him from having to seek her out. And how ironic it was that she asked him for an interview. How positively delicious. She had no idea of their ties to one another. To her, he was just another grief-stricken loved one of a victim.

Kismet had brought them together. When they had talked at his place of business, Feral had been tempted to drop hints of what he knew about her, and make some allusions to their mutual past, but of course he hadn't. He probably knew more about Queenie than anyone, for the detective who had researched his own history had also delved into hers.

The PI's snooping hadn't stopped there. The dick had proved quite adept at surreptitiously tracking down half a dozen other individuals. All had a common denominator: each and every one of them had been sired by some notorious serial murderer. Feral had explained to the PI that he was writing a book called *Cain's Children.* Not that the detective had really cared about anything except getting paid. But the detective's competence was offset by his attitude. He had presumed an annoying familiarity with Feral.

Feral still remembered the way the man had walked into his office and acted as if he owned it. The detective had finished all his background work, and took pleasure in tossing his report down onto Feral's desk. "Demon spawn," he announced, showing him a cocky grin. "Everything you wanted to know about the children of serial murderers, but were afraid to ask."

His report, though, was professional. The man might not have had any couth, but he was always thorough. How unfortunate that the detective had recently been killed by a hit-and-run driver. But as it was best expressed in Ecclesiasticus, "He that toucheth pitch shall be defiled therewith." The detective had apparently touched too much pitch. And hadn't he said it?

Demon spawn.

30

The more Maryelizabeth tried to discount Lola's words, the more they came back to haunt her.

The killer had manipulated her. He had known her weaknesses. And he had targeted her.

Other nagging doubts surfaced. Her sorority sisters had been Parker's ninth and tenth victims. So why had the copycat attacked her out of sequence? He'd tried to make her his fourth San Diego victim. And if he wasn't a copycat . . .

Maybe she was the target, and had been all along. By doing her job well, Maryelizabeth knew, she had made her fair share of enemies, but there had been no overt death threats recently, unless you could count Ken's poetry on talk radio.

Poetry. The connection with her past made Maryelizabeth wonder if Ken might have been an invention, yet another ploy by the killer, another false trail for the police to follow in the event of her death.

Caleb was right, she decided. The answers were in the past. She was the one who had been dragging her feet, afraid to look back.

Now, unflinching, she needed to do just that.

Lola applied another cold compress to Caleb's forehead. He wasn't as delirious now, though his temperature was still over 103.

"Take another sip of this," Lola insisted.

Caleb dutifully took a sip. But he was only giving lip service, literally, to being there. Between the fever and listening to the audiotape, he had been drifting in and out of consciousness.

At least he wasn't doing those voices anymore, Lola thought. They had all but driven her from the house.

"How about another sip for your Aunt Lola?"

Caleb sipped again. And the tape, and Maryelizabeth's voice, played on.

Because Gray Parker was tried for murder in the State of Florida, he had a bifurcated trial. The first part of the trial was the criminal hearing; the second part the penalty phase. With the overwhelming evidence against him, and because Parker had already admitted his guilt and was an advocate for his own death, there was little in the way of courtroom suspense, but the courtroom still proved to be anything but a dull place.

George Bernard Shaw wrote that "murderers get sheaves of offers of marriage." Parker, with his Hollywood looks and lively mind, was one of the first serial murderers to gain celebrity status. Despite the heinousness of his crimes, he was inundated with suggestive mail from women. His cell smelled like a perfumery from all the letters sealed with perfumed kisses, and his cell's "wallpaper" consisted of hundreds of revealing photos that women had sent him. The prison turned away as much as it delivered, returning items it deemed "obscene" along with a warning notice to the senders not to send such material again.

Even seemingly respectable women lost their sense of reason when it came to Parker. Many felt they could "save" him with their love, and were willing to forgive his horrid past. All of the attention amused Parker. He was even moved to write a poem about one woman's proposition to him:

Got another offer of marriage in the mail today,
Woman said she wanted my hand,
Said wasn't no big thing where my hands had been before,
Said she could understand my strangling some no-good whore.

This woman sent along a photo of her in the raw,
Said it was worth a thousand words,
She had a body that would drop any jaw,
And said when I was sprung she'd let me eat my words.
All thousand of them.

But many women were not content to be only pen pals with Parker. They became regulars at his trials, spectators who swooned at his every glance, laughed too long at his every witticism, and cried too loudly at his reflections.

These trial groupies, what the press labeled as "Shame's Dames," or "Shame's Gang," evidenced no respect for the victims, or the families of victims. Their fawning over Parker mortified most observers. They appeared oblivious to reality. On those occasions when the prosecution took pains to detail the terrible things that Parker had done, their eyes remained dry and fixed on him, even as the rest of the courtroom wept.

"It was as if they were all hypnotized," said Lonnie Green, the bailiff for most of the court proceedings. "They were kind of like that Manson Family, except instead of blindly committing murders, they blindly forgave them."

To my mind the Shame gang were, and always will be, the "Tell Gray" women. Because they knew I had access to Parker, virtually all of these women tried to enlist me as a go-between. "Tell Gray," they would always say to me. "Tell Gray." And though I reiterated time and again that I would pass on no messages, they never stopped asking me.

Leslie Van Doren was the most forward of the Shame groupies. Van Doren's fixation on Parker was such that she had moved from her home state of Colorado to live in Florida for both of his trials.

Van Doren worked nights as a cocktail waitress, but by day she was a courtroom observer. Like so many other women in Shame's Gang, she was quite attractive, a five-and-a-half-foot curvaceous blonde. During the first trial her courtroom garb was very provocative. She liked wearing leather skirts and favored clinging, low-cut blouses. Van Doren rarely wore a bra. Usually she could be found leaning forward, showing off as much skin as possible, desperate to catch Parker's eye.

Her shameless antics sometimes worked. When Parker would flash her a smile, or wink at her, Van Doren would act as if she had received a boon from the gods. Notes were sometimes smuggled back and forth between the two of them. They acted like naughty schoolchildren who couldn't wait for recess. But with no school playground available to them, there was only one alternative.

Van Doren became a frequent Death Row visitor at the peniten-

tiary. At Raiford, the visitors' room is hardly what you would call a romantic spot. There are no sofas, no easy chairs, and no dark corners. The room is institutional, with harsh fluorescent lighting. Tables and stools, the only furniture, are bolted to the floor. The room smells of desperation, with an unpleasant mingling of cigarette smoke and body odors and disinfectant.

The visitors' room bathroom is even less appealing. The room is all concrete and cold. There is no door at the entrance, and no windows inside. The stalls have no dividers and offer no privacy, and the toilet seat covers are made of metal. There are no mirrors, no place to primp. The bathroom is a step up from a hole in the ground, but not a big one. It is a place for bodily wastes.

And the place where Leslie Van Doren carried out her seduction of Gray Parker.

The Florida penitentiary system allows no conjugal visits, but the visitors' room bathroom at the Union Correctional Institution was known by Death Row inmates as "the honeymoon hotel." For a fifty-dollar bribe the correctional officers would turn their heads and allow the visitor and prisoner a joint five-minute "bathroom break."

It is hard to imagine a less romantic spot to engage in intimacy, but that is where Parker and Van Doren met for their silent and hurried assignations. Parker described their time together as "Wham, Bam, Thank you, Ma'am," but it wasn't remembered that way by Van Doren, who, by description at least, managed to make a silk purse out of a shit hole.

Their passion, she said, was one for the ages. One for the wages might be more accurate. It was Van Doren who paid for their time together. She funneled the money to Parker, who in turn distributed most of it back to the guards. As for their weekly rendezvous, Van Doren painted a picture of their passion that even the most flowery romance writer would be loath to put a name to. But their intrigue did provide a number of diversions, not the least of which was Van Doren's becoming pregnant.

Her pregnancy was showcased during the penalty phase of Parker's trial. There, Van Doren tried to change her image from that of vamp to that of mother and apple pie. Gone were her racy outfits, all replaced by maternity clothes. With each passing day, her burgeoning belly drew that much more notice, a notoriety that Van Doren clearly relished and sought out. She made no secret of who the father was, proudly revealing her lover, and the circumstances of the conception. It was difficult to tell who was more chagrined: Florida's Department of Corrections or Parker's wife, Clara. As a result of her pregnancy, a No Contact visiting area was established, with inmates and visitors separated by Plexiglas. But the deed, quite apparently, was already done.

As Van Doren's pregnancy came closer to term, the tension in the courtroom increased. Parker's long-suffering wife tried to ignore Van Doren, but she was a difficult woman to overlook. Every day she sat center stage in the gallery knitting blue booties, the modern-day and even more horrific version of Madame Defarge.

"A half brother," Caleb said. "I have a brother."

His voice sounded so different, and so hopeful, that at first Lola thought he was still delirious.

"No," she tried to tell him, but he wasn't listening.

"When I was growing up I always dreamed of having a brother or sister. I thought if I only had someone to talk to, someone to share the pain . . ."

"You have no brother."

In the background Maryelizabeth's voice continued to narrate.

"I don't understand."

Lola reached over and turned off the tape. "That woman did have a baby boy, but he wasn't any brother of yours, even though she tried to pass him off as one."

The momentary hope left Caleb's face. His features became hard. "Whose baby was it?"

"Whose baby wasn't it? I don't think they ever determined who the real father was. Miss Van Doren wasn't the most discriminating of women."

"That speaks well of my father, doesn't it?"

"Maybe it does."

"How so?"

"Listen to the tape. It explains things. In his own way your father tried to be responsible. I think he was trying to spare you and your mother."

"That's bullshit. The man never thought about anybody but himself."

"Maybe. Maybe not. You ever hear that old Johnny Cash song, 'A Boy Named Sue'?"

Caleb shook his head.

"It's about a father who only stayed around long enough to name his boy Sue before leaving home forever. Because of his name, the boy had a terrible time growing up. With a name like that, you can be sure, other boys put him to the test. He had to constantly struggle and fight and stay strong. As an adult, Sue finally met up with his father. He'd waited for that moment his whole life. He wanted to hurt the man who had made his life so miserable. But the father said that he had named him Sue because he knew he wouldn't be around to help the boy grow up. Your father knew that as well."

"What's your point?"

"That maybe your father gave you some things you're not even aware of, or that you are not willing to accept."

Caleb's face reddened, and not because of his fever. "Listen. You are a man who wears dresses and because of that you've seen a lot of headshrinkers, but that doesn't mean you know what the hell you are talking about. Serial murderers have no empathy for other people. None. They don't feel the pain of their victims. And that's what I was, just another victim."

"But isn't it possible sometimes your father saw beyond himself, saw beyond his madness?"

"That's wishful thinking. My father saw nothing. He was a mimic. He mimicked the emotions of other people like I can mimic a noise or a voice, or the way you mimic being a woman."

"I don't think of myself as a mimic."

"Oh, that's right. You're a *berdache*." Caleb's voice hardened: "Tell me, do you squat when you pee?"

"I'm sorry you're hurting," Lola said. "But lashing out at me won't help you."

She stood up, but before leaving the room she felt his forehead. "You're still very hot. You need to rest."

"Not before the grand finale."

Lola looked at him quizzically.

"My father's death," he explained. "It's coming up."

Caleb reached for the tape deck, turned it back on.

* * *

. . . when Judge Irwin announced Parker's death sentence, the nine months pregnant Van Doren fainted in court. Three days later she delivered a boy, whom she called Gray Junior (not taking into account, or perhaps not caring, that Parker already had a son with that name). She did her best to make the birth of her son a media event, and was shameless in using the baby to get center stage. At a press conference held just two days after giving birth, Van Doren held the newborn up as if he were a trophy, and said, "The governor should show clemency to Gray Parker, the father of my baby."

I was out in the audience, part of the media. I probably should have kept my mouth shut, but her crocodile tears prompted me to shout, "Isn't that a bit like the story of the boy who shot his parents, and then threw himself on the mercy of the court because he was an orphan?"

Ms. Van Doren didn't like the ensuing laughter. But the laughter didn't stop there. I had come to the press conference prepared.

"Can you tell me your blood type, Miss Van Doren?" I asked.

"My what?"

"Your blood type."

"I don't know what you're talking about," she said.

"Apparently not. For your information, your blood type is A positive. And your baby's blood type is O positive."

Standing at her microphone, she looked very confused. "So what?"

"So who's the real father of your child? It can't be Gray Parker, because his blood type is B positive."

The press conference exploded with questions, some for me, and some for Leslie Van Doren. I told the reporters that Gray Parker had suspected the child wasn't his, and had asked me to investigate. At the time, I told them little else.

As for Van Doren, she very loudly declared, "Either Gray is the father," she declared, "or it was Immaculate Conception."

In subsequent days, reporters proved conclusively it wasn't the latter. According to several published accounts, Van Doren had done as much hooking as she had cocktailing.

As for Parker's suspicion that the child wasn't his, he never told me much more than "I tried to not give her my seed."

Though I asked him several times, he never elaborated on why he had practiced this birth control. Perhaps Parker was distrustful of

Van Doren's self-aggrandizing, and knew that she would use a baby in just such a way. Or it might have been that he didn't want another child of his born into the world. By his own account, he hadn't been a very good father, and with his imminent death, it was clear he wouldn't be able to improve upon that track record.

Maryelizabeth sat in the middle of her hotel room, overwhelmed by the emptied boxes. She'd have to put the Do Not Disturb tag on the door. There was no way the maid would be able to clean the room.

She wondered if she had some Walter Mitty complex about being a superdetective. That wasn't what crime writers did. They didn't solve crimes, just documented the circumstances surrounding them. So what the hell was she doing?

Maybe I'm trying to be like that actress who played me in that movie-of-the-week version of *Shame,* she thought. She had been embarrassed at how they had portrayed her as a busy little sleuth. No, Maryelizabeth decided, I'm not playing that actress. I haven't had my breasts augmented yet.

Maryelizabeth picked up a stack of pictures of Gray Parker. As a child he hadn't yet learned to hide his feelings. In almost all the pictures he was frowning, not afraid to show how unhappy he was. But his mother had taught him to put on a cheery face in public, and that anything else was unacceptable. As Parker matured he learned he could get by more easily by pretending to be who he wasn't. In almost every picture she had of Parker the man, he was flashing a broad smile.

Maryelizabeth continued to sort through the pile. She found one of her old speeches. It had been typed, and whited out, and had several pasted inserts that were now threatening to come apart. Public speaking hadn't been as easy for her back then. As a crutch, she had always typed out a prepared speech. Now she was more confident. Her notes were usually written on an index card.

She read the last page of her old speech.

Parker was, and always will be, an enigma. The easy thing to do would be to paint him as rotten to the core, but he confounds such a broad brush. His behavior was sometimes good, even noble, and that's bothersome. It is disturbing to see a so-called cold-hearted killer demonstrate a capacity for caring. From both a personal and a societal standpoint, it's easier to think of a serial killer as a total monster than as someone with any vestiges of humanity. It complicates matters, it jars the psyche, to see images of a murderer not in keeping with the headlines, or the mind's eye.

I think the most terrible thing of all to accept is that for the most part Gray Parker was only too human. He is someone we can't easily dismiss, and if we look carefully in our own mirrors, there are times when his reflection stares back.

At the bottom of the page were the names. Maryelizabeth felt she knew these women better than anyone else. It had been her tradition always to read the names of Parker's seventeen victims at the end of her talk. Maryelizabeth thought that by remembering their names she honored their memories.

It had been a long time since she had finished her speech with that memorial. To herself, she read the names aloud.

31

Feral knew the transformation would come soon. He loved watching old horror films, especially those with transformations, like Lon Chaney turning into the Wolfman. That's how his legal name was. It amused him that all he had to do was switch a few letters, and he became what he was: wild. A savage and untamed beast.

He started on his second walk around the inn. He had already checked the temperature of the spa, dipped his finger into the pool, made stops at the sundry machines, lingered over his selections of a candy bar and then a soda, and had stopped several times to smell the flowers, but he still hadn't seen any sign of Queenie.

He considered how else he might learn which room she was in. Later, he could visit the night clerk and do a Gary Gilmore on him, get the information while making the clerk's death look like a robbery, but that would mean waiting until after midnight. And it would entail additional risk. Gilmore was said to have had a death wish. Feral most certainly didn't.

What Feral liked most about Gilmore was his sense of humor, something he never lost. Gilmore had told one of his lawyers, who was bald, that he could have his hair after the Utah marksmen shot him dead. Volunteer marksmen. Who said citizens shirked their civic responsibilities? There had been no shortage of volunteers for that job. But the shooters had never known if there was a bullet or a blank in their chambers. None of them could have the certain satisfaction of the kill.

Though death by firing squad seemed like an easy way for a state to kill, it wasn't a popular form of capital punishment, Utah being one of the last states to practice that art. But then the Beehive State had long exhibited a different kind of sensibility about executing its criminals. In 1857 it had even hanged a horse.

Warren Drake, a member of the Mormon militia, had been convicted of committing bestiality with a mare. He and his horse were sentenced to be executed, but Drake ended up being excommunicated from the Mormon Church and exiled from the territory.

The horse wasn't so fortunate.

How typical, thought Feral, to punish the innocent. That's what had happened to him.

He had never known his mother, but his hired detective had submitted an extremely edifying report. And he was well acquainted with what Queenie had written about her. Neither Queenie nor the detective had offered a very complimentary picture of Mother. If he had been Shame's son, things might have been very different, but when Mother's little lie became public knowledge his fate was sealed. Mother had loved Shame, and not him. She had shown her true colors by washing her hands of him, by saying good riddance to her little bastard.

It was too bad Mother had died before he was old enough to reintroduce himself to her. But there were others deserving of his justice. At the top of the list was Queenie, who had exulted in exposing Mother, who had taunted her in person and castigated her in print. It was Queenie who had graphically described Mother's willingness to rut in the filth. Queenie's message was that Mother was worse than a fallen woman; she was a slattern who had paid to be fucked and humiliated and deserved no better treatment than she received.

Of course she'd had a partner in crime: Gray Parker. Shame and Queenie had conspired to make a laughingstock out of Mother. Shame had been too good to deposit his seed into dear Mother. He was willing to poke, but not plant, was happy to humiliate, and debase, and degrade Mother, but not willing to give her his precious seed. Like Onan, he'd preferred to spill it on the floor.

"I coulda been a contender," whispered Feral.

He could have, should have, been the son of Shame. For a few short days he had been the *other* Gray Junior. And then he'd been nothing, nothing at all.

His hired detective had concluded it was highly unlikely that Feral would ever know who his real father was. He had been fifteen before his adoptive parents had told him he wasn't their biological child. Deep down he hadn't really been surprised, for it was hard for him to imagine that those two fossils could have been his parents, but he still felt angry and betrayed. He had been deceived, lied to for years.

Reason enough, and then some, for him to act as he had when he came of age. He had been Mater and Pater's sole heir. Their deaths had been *so* tragic, but they'd left behind a considerable amount of money, as well as a small manufacturing company. Not that Feral dirtied his hands at work. That's what good managers were for. But it pleased him that he was still the boss.

"How to succeed in business without really trying," Feral whispered.

He put his right shoe up on a railing, and took his time tying it. Feral never bothered looking at the shoelace. His attention was on the block of rooms overlooking the pool.

There were three maid carts in sight, but no maids. They had to be cleaning the rooms. A door opened, and a man emerged. His briefcase gave him away as a businessman. The man looked at his watch and apparently didn't like what he saw.

It had been a long shot thinking he could just run into Queenie. She was probably holed up in her room. Feral wondered how he could flush her out. She'd be suspicious of any call. Once burned, twice learned. But maybe he didn't even need to talk with her. He could get a cell phone and then call the hotel and ask for Vera Macauley's room. If she wasn't in he might be able to pinpoint where her room was by the ringing of her telephone.

But if she was in he might make her even more wary than she already was. No, he didn't want to take that chance.

Another door opened, and two kids came running out. For a moment Feral didn't recognize them. But then he saw Anna Parker. She was wearing a hat and dark glasses, but to Feral that only made her stand out all the more.

"After you get the sodas, come right back," she yelled.

The children weren't listening to her. They acted as if they had been cooped up for days. And getting a little taste of freedom, Feral thought, was like letting the genie out of the bottle. Getting it, and the children, back in would be difficult.

Feral finished tying his shoe. He made a point of not looking at Anna or her children. Mama Bear was clearly on alert, and Feral wanted to appear to be just another anonymous guest.

He walked toward the parking lot, intent on his thoughts. Queenie must have used one of her aliases to get the room. Feral thought it unlikely that Queenie was staying with the Parker family. While working, she was always the lone wolf. He was betting she was at another hotel.

Feral weighed the possibilities. This could all work out well, very well.

32

Maryelizabeth was almost done sifting through her Parker boxes. She'd winnowed the past, had decided what needed to be studied, and what could be put away forever. Intent on her organizing, she had resisted the temptation to do too much looking back, but seeing the framed calligraphy made her pause. It had been Gray's parting gift to her.

The lettering was ornate and beautiful. He had learned calligraphy while in prison, had seemed to get immense satisfaction out of transforming his crabbed handwriting into a thing of beauty.

His gift had surprised her. He had used parchment paper, and had obviously taken great pains over the work. The dark ink, and the gold filigree, had faded very little over the years. He had given her a work of art, but she had hidden it away. Elaborately inscribed were three passages from Whitman's "The Sleepers":

The blind sleep, and the deaf and dumb sleep,
The prisoner sleeps well in the prison . . . the runaway son sleeps,
The murderer that is to be hung next day . . .
how does he sleep?

The earth recedes from me into the night,
I saw that it was beautiful . . . and I see that what is not the earth is
beautiful.

I too pass from the night;
I stay awhile away O night, but I return to you again and love you;

Why should I be afraid to trust myself to you?

I am not afraid . . . I have been well brought forward by you.

It had given her more pleasure to study the flourishes than the words. Gray had picked Whitman's poetry to express his mortality, his regrets, his hopes, his gratitude. And perhaps his love. Maybe he'd been unable to say those things himself and had needed another's proxy words, or perhaps the inked poem was his last, and greatest, manipulation. They had never quite trusted each other—how could they?—but each had offered the other important pieces of themselves.

"I have been well brought forward by you." And so he had been, she thought. The self-proclaimed "exact opposite of a tree," stunted, twisted, and blighted as he was, had somehow flowered at the end. Most would say she was deluding herself to think that. They would point to his calligraphy and the poem and say they were but Shame's way of controlling her even in death.

The vibration of her pager made her shiver. It almost seemed as if Gray were calling her.

And maybe he was, or the closest thing to him. The pager displayed Lola's phone number, but she had already talked with Lola at length that morning. Maryelizabeth was sure that Caleb was paging her.

Maryelizabeth used her calling card to dial out. He answered on the first ring.

"I would have called earlier to see how you were doing," she said, "but I was hoping you were sleeping."

"I don't think I've slept. Maybe a little. My mind's been sort of funny, the fever, you know." His voice sounded weak and distant. "I just finished listening to the tape."

"Oh." Lola had told Maryelizabeth how intent Caleb had been on listening to the tape, how even his illness and delirium hadn't kept him from it.

"I think—given the subject matter—you did a good job."

It sounded as if it hurt him to admit that. "Thank you."

She heard him draw in a deep breath. "I learned a lot of things from your book, but not the kind of things that can help me in my situation. I'm not exactly sure what I should do next."

"I think you should turn yourself in."

"A normal person could do that. I can't."

"Why not?"

"My father. The law wants to bring us both in. Did you see all those articles in the newspaper today? My favorite was the Associated Press article with the headline Bad Seed. Did you read it?"

"No."

"You should. It talked about different fathers and sons that had been executed for their crimes, and made it sound like murder was a game the whole family, no, generations of the same family, could play. It gave a rundown of some bloodlines that had produced killer after killer. There was even a side story on Gerald Gallego. Gerald's apparently a chip off the old block. His father was executed by the state of Mississippi, and now Gerald is on Death Row in Nevada. One geneticist all but said, 'The apple doesn't fall too far from the tree.' He was using me as his reference."

"Newspapers are in the business of selling papers."

"Are you saying you don't have your own doubts about me?"

A momentary pause: "I believe in you."

"Should I pretend I didn't hear you hesitate?"

"It's just that I have a few questions."

"Ask them."

"Now's not the appropriate—"

"Ask them."

"A little over a month ago your appearance changed drastically. You cut your hair and lost your beard right before the first murder. With your clean-cut look, you became the picture of your father."

"I wasn't trying to look like my father. If anything, I was trying to look like Dr. Jennings. I knew Anna was having an affair with him, and I thought if I looked more like him she'd notice me more. That, and I was tired of hiding my face."

"There's also the matter of the polygraph. You failed it."

"Yes."

"When you were asked whether you had murdered anyone, the galvanic response was very significant."

"I don't know what to tell you. I was nervous, I know that. I was sweating terribly."

He sounded nervous now, thought Maryelizabeth. She wondered whether he was again sweating.

"And how did you know to go to the sorority?"

Caleb explained, or tried to. His voice started cracking when telling her about the Brandy Wein photos, and that made him angry.

"If I have to convince you," he said, "what chance do I have of making the police believe me?"

"Even they'll have to concede that you couldn't have been in two places at one time," said Maryelizabeth. "It would have been impossible for you to simultaneously attack me and call me, just as you couldn't have been setting the fire, and setting off the alarm, at the same time you were supposedly inside the sorority."

He considered her argument for several moments, long enough for Maryelizabeth to think he'd hung up, but his sigh told her that he was still there.

"I'm tired," he said. "And I'm still sort of fuzzy. What I'd like to do is talk to Anna about all of this."

"I'll arrange that."

"Why don't you just tell me where she is and I'll call her?"

"Because I don't know if the Sheriff's Department is monitoring her phone. If they are, they'll be breaking down your front door a few minutes from now, and nothing looks worse than being led off in handcuffs. If you're going to be taken in, I would much rather you surrendered to them."

"Is it possible that you still don't trust me?"

"Your family is staying at the Amity Inn in the Golden Triangle. Your wife is registered under the name of Vera Macauley. Are you satisfied, or do I have to prove I believe in you in some other way?"

"I'm sorry. Not enough sleep, I guess."

"That's two of us," she said. "Look, after we finish talking I'm going to visit your family. I'll have Anna call you from some safe phone within the hour. Okay?"

"Thank you."

"In the meantime, try to rest. You've been through a lot."

"So have you. Is your neck . . . are you . . . ?"

"I'm fine."

"I feel like I'm the plague." Caleb stopped to cough. It sounds as if he has the plague, thought Maryelizabeth. "People around me keep dying."

"You're not alone in this. And you're not responsible. I don't think you're the only target. I'm beginning to believe all of this was done as much for my sake as for yours."

"What makes you think that?"

"The way he's cast his web and drawn us both in. But seeking revenge has made him vulnerable."

"Have you found something?"

"No. But I'm looking. I think you're right about finding answers in the past, but I don't want to overlook the present either. I think there must have been some recent trigger, but I have no idea what."

"Whoever he is, his hate has to be enormous."

"Yes. And that much hate is hard to hide."

They both contemplated that. And then Caleb remembered something about her book that had bothered him, a section he'd found cryptic, different from the rest.

"It's probably not my place to ask, but . . ."

"Yes?"

"I was curious about my father's death. Your book was personal in so many ways, and yet when it came to describing his execution your writing was very . . ."

Maryelizabeth found the word for him: "Mechanical."

"Yes."

She had her pat answers; that the book was about the living Gray Parker; that death speaks for itself; that she hadn't wanted to be a ghoul; but those were lies.

"I have to make an admission: I had a great deal of trouble writing about your father's death. That's something no one knows except my editor."

Maryelizabeth continued haltingly: "Your father all but asked the world to do away with him. He was the one who called up the police and said, 'Here I am.' And he was the one who streamlined the legal process to expedite his death, doing his best to handcuff his own defense lawyers. At the same time, though, he had what I would have to call a love of life. Ironic, isn't it, that he could kill so callously and yet love life. And so I kept trying to dig for answers. In the end, it was hard digging."

"I see."

Maryelizabeth shook her head, frustrated with herself, and her answer. I'm lying again, she thought. She expected Caleb to be honest with her, and yet she wasn't willing to reciprocate. Shame syndrome. They were both expert at avoiding their pasts.

"That's not really it, though," she said. "I tried writing about his death as I experienced it, but it tore at me too much. I tried and tried and tried. And what I finally did write, my editor didn't like. She said it wouldn't play in Peoria."

"What wouldn't?"

"My thoughts on his death. She said they were too sympathetic. She reminded me over and over that this was a man virtually everyone wanted to see dead. Final justice was what the country wanted, both in person and in print. She told me my observations were *disjointed and emotional.* I remember how harsh those words seemed. She said my objectivity was lacking. But what she objected to most was the elephant."

"The elephant?"

"The elephant that kept trumpeting in my head. Not an angel of death, but an elephant. I wrote how in your father's final hours on this earth I kept imagining this elephant's agonized cries as I watched everyone getting ready to kill him. My editor thought it read like Sylvia Plath meets James Joyce, when what it should have been was Truman Capote meets Norman Mailer."

Maryelizabeth shivered, and was glad Caleb wasn't there to see that. "Your father invited me to watch him die. That's not the kind of invitation you get every day. I was ambivalent about going, but my publisher insisted.

"I arrived early, and spent that time walking outside the prison, nerving myself up before going inside. Around me it felt as if a pep rally were going on, not a death watch. I made my way through the crowd. Most who were there were young, and loud, and drunk. There were vendors selling buttons, and T-shirts, and Shame voodoo dolls. There was even a disc jockey broadcasting live. Every hour on the hour he threw eggs and bacon on a hot pan, and then played the sizzling sounds over loudspeakers. That was always good for deafening cheers. The countdown to death was like waiting for the ball to drop on New Year's Eve. But the music, the crowds, even the cheers were just background noise to me. What I kept hearing was that elephant trumpeting.

"I know the reason for it. There's a logical explanation. There always is. While researching capital punishment I discovered that Thomas Edison was one of those who had worked on building a better fatal mousetrap."

"Edison?"

"It surprised me, too. I always thought of Edison as this dedicated scientist who tirelessly worked for the sake of scientific inquiry. I remember in school I had this teacher who always used to quote Edison to motivate us. I can still hear her now: 'Genius is ninety-nine percent perspiration, and one percent inspiration.' But I learned about Edison's strange sideline show. He paid the children around his Menlo Park neighborhood a quarter each for every stray dog and cat they could round up. Thirty pieces would have been more appropriate. Those were animals earmarked for death. They were paraded about in much-publicized shows. Then Edison's assistants forced them out onto a sheet of tin where they met their deaths from the high voltage of an alternating generator.

"Of course, Edison had a reason for those spectacles. He and George Westinghouse were vying to get acceptance of their electrical currents. Edison wanted to show everyone that Westinghouse's AC current was much more dangerous than his DC current, so he went around electrocuting animals with AC current. Edison also said he wanted to provide a more humane way for people to die. But isn't it strange how ostensibly noble motives can bring about such ignoble results?

"Edison's experiments weren't done quietly. On film, he proposed a unique experiment to the nation—the electrocution of an elephant. The three-ton challenge, right? I got to see an old movie clip, the same clip that filmgoers throughout the nation saw. It demonstrated the result of Edison's so-called experiment. A full-grown African elephant was led out to an iron grid, and the killing switch was flipped.

"In death, the elephant screamed. Its feet smoked and its trunk writhed and twisted. When the animal toppled over, its flesh stuck to the iron grid."

Caleb could hear her unsteady breathing over the line. It was his turn to be the calming voice. "Where was the one percent inspiration in that?" he quietly asked.

"Yes," Maryelizabeth said. "Where was it?"

"You don't need to tell me any more. . . ."

"Yes, I do," she said. "I know it sounds crazy. I suppose the elephant was just some kind of defense mechanism my mind came up with, something to divert me from all the horror at hand. I had all these conflicting emotions. I saw Mr. and Mrs. Krulak, Tracy's parents, for the first time since her funeral. I remembered how Mrs. Krulak had always sent Tracy 'care' packages at Tulane, packages meant to be shared with us. I felt guilty seeing them, felt the guilt that survivors feel, and wondered why I had been spared and Tracy hadn't. And I saw others I had interviewed for the book. There were thirty of us altogether, twelve official witnesses, twelve from the news media, and six staff members. We were crowded together in the witness area. It was such a strange gathering, all of us there to watch a man die.

"Your father was brought into the room wearing a black rubber mask. I remember being grateful for that. I didn't want to see his expression as he died. And yet, even with that mask he wasn't anonymous. He sought me out among those in the gallery. He nodded at me, and I nodded back. I think there was some hissing among the gallery at our signaling—there wasn't much sympathy for your father in that room—but I can't be sure. The elephant was trumpeting nonstop then. It made it hard for me to hear, hard for me to focus on things in a linear fashion.

"I remember how time slowed down for me in his last moments. In my mind, everything is so defined. Even with the din in my head I remember the expressions on the faces around me. Even now, I can still picture everything and everyone. But the sounds come back whenever I think about it. Everything intermixes. Death and trumpets.

"The electrodes were attached to your father's head and leg. All that remained was for him to ride the lightning. I stopped watching your father immediately after the first two thousand volts were administered. I listened, mostly. Around me I heard gasps and prayers and sounds that weren't words. A few of the men cursed your father as if dying weren't enough. And for just a little while the elephant kept trumpeting, and trumpeting.

"And then I heard nothing, nothing at all, and that was the worst sound of all."

There was an unwilling tremor in Maryelizabeth's voice as she finished. This time she was the one who was angry at showing a side of herself she always kept revealed.

"I wish your editor had let you write that chapter just the way you described it," Caleb said.

"Even if she had, I wouldn't have been satisfied. I've always had this feeling that the last chapter was yet to be written. Something always nagged at me, always told me that there was more there, but I never found it."

33

Maryelizabeth took the stairs up to the second floor of the Amity Inn. I need the exercise, she told herself, but even more than that, she didn't want to have to worry about sharing the closed space of an elevator with a stranger. Since the attack, her unease had grown, not lessened. Even walking up the stairwell made her apprehensive. It wasn't an open stairway, but an enclosed tower. She hurried up the steps.

Being attacked, and knowing she was a target, had forced her to rethink her standard precautions. Though she was working under an assumed name, it wasn't a new one. She had kept her current half dozen aliases for at least three years. It was time to get some new IDs, time to switch her routines around.

Maryelizabeth exited the stairwell on the second floor. The inn was midday quiet. Even the pool was deserted. She started forward along the walkway, her footsteps loud and hurried. Maybe I should get a bodyguard, Maryelizabeth thought, at least for a few days. The idea didn't sit very well with her. She didn't like being dependent on anyone.

Just ahead of her a door opened, and a man backed out carrying two large suitcases. Heavy suitcases, judging by the way he was straining to lift them. She couldn't understand people who didn't have wheels on the bottom of their luggage. Maybe it was a male thing. Maybe it was also a male thing to try to carry too much luggage in one trip, as he was doing. He put down his bags and reached for two hanging bags that were hanging along the railing. With all the luggage in her way, Maryelizabeth couldn't pass.

"Excuse me," she said.

The man suddenly straightened, apparently surprised by her voice. As he turned toward her the thought struck Maryelizabeth: it's late to be checking out. Her realization came an instant too late.

His blow caught her on the side of the head. As she was falling he grabbed her by the hair, then pulled her head toward him. He covered her mouth and nose with a wet rag that reeked of some chemical. Maryelizabeth stopped breathing. She shook her head violently, trying to pull her face clear of the rag.

His grip tightened, and he started to drag her into his room. With her mouth covered she couldn't scream, but she bucked and kicked. It was broad daylight. Someone had to see what was going on. But he had picked the perfect spot to ambush her, had used the stairwell tower, his shoulder bags, and the right angle of the walkway effectively to block his assault from anyone's view.

With a vicious yank, she landed in his room. He kicked the door closed behind them. Maryelizabeth again tried to shake her head clear of his hand, but he pressed it all the tighter against her face.

Don't breathe.

With his mouth next to her head, he spoke, his breath hot on her face. "Before being led to the gas chamber, Robert H. White was asked if he had any last wishes, and you know what he said? 'Yes. A gas mask.'"

Maryelizabeth tried to butt him with her head, but succeeded only in bumping his chest. She was already lightheaded, and began to see stars.

Don't breathe.

Maryelizabeth tried falling forward, but he held on. Her lungs were burning.

Don't breathe.

She tried to flail, to make some kind of noise, tried pounding the flooring with her feet, but the carpeting was too damn thick.

"Still with us?" he asked. "This one's my favorite. Tommy Grasso wasn't happy with his last meal. While being led off to his death he said, 'I did not get my Spaghetti-O's. I got spaghetti. I want the press to know this.'"

He started laughing, and Maryelizabeth tried to buck him off of her, but even she knew the attempt was feeble. Without oxygen, her limbs couldn't respond. She couldn't bite, couldn't knee, couldn't scratch. All she could do was pray, and even that took air.

Don't . . .

She took a breath. Still, her lungs burned for more oxygen. Everything started growing fuzzy. In her mind's eye, Maryelizabeth saw her own picture. She had become part of that terrible collage, part of the scene of the scream.

Maryelizabeth took another breath, and blessedly lost consciousness.

Feral lay on a chaise longue at the side of the pool. Predators, he knew, liked to wait in ambush around some watering hole.

The last light of day was giving way to darkness. His time. Feral stretched. He could feel the anticipation. He raised himself from the chaise and put aside the magazine he'd been pretending to read.

Four people were in the spa. Boiling away. Fools. Feral didn't like making a lobster of himself. There was only one other adult in the vicinity, a man in the pool, a Type A assiduously doing his laps.

And there were the two children.

"Marco," yelled James.

"Polo," yelled Janet.

James lunged, swimming furiously in the direction of her voice, but just as quickly Janet was swimming away, evading him.

Feral stretched, then dove into the pool.

"Marco," yelled James.

"Polo," said Janet.

"Polo," said Feral.

For a moment James hesitated. The man's voice was very near to him. And he'd been "it" for a long time.

"Marco," screamed James.

In unison, Feral and Janet said, "Polo."

James dove and tagged Feral.

"I guess you got me," Feral said.

"How many times have you paged her?" asked Lola.

"Four," said Caleb.

"Maybe her pager's not working."

He shook his head. "More than two hours ago she said she was going to talk with Anna, and then she was going to have Anna call me. Something's wrong."

"Let's call her up," she said.

They had the number for her cell phone, the one they were supposed to call only in an emergency. Lola took her card from her purse and dialed the number, then handed the phone to Caleb. One ring, two rings . . .

"Marco," yelled Feral.

"Polo."

The boy was to his left and drifting back. The girl was off to his right, probably near the edge of the pool, ready to make a break for it. Both were close.

Feral faked left, then broke right. He swam with strong strokes, reaching, reaching . . .

Got her.

She was laughing, but it was a frightened laugh, the kind that bordered between being excited and being frightened. And then Feral heard something else.

"Excuse me," he said. "Somebody's calling."

He pulled himself out of the pool, and walked over to the ringing cell phone.

Three rings, four rings. And then the ringing stopped. But the line wasn't dead. Caleb could hear breathing.

"Maryelizabeth?"

"I'm afraid she's unable to come to the phone right now."

Caleb knew that voice. Remembered its every inflection. It was the voice that had drawn him to the Sanderses' house. Hate rose up in him. Pent-up emotions choked Caleb. He wanted to kill. "You . . ."

"Yes."

"Where's Maryelizabeth?"

"She's safe. She's sleeping now. Poor girl was exhausted."

"What do you want?"

"What I've always wanted. A face-to-face with you. A chance for us to communicate. Kindred spirits should talk."

"Kindred spirits?"

"Yes. We have much in common."

Lola moved her head close to Caleb's, trying to hear what was being said.

"We don't have anything in common."

"Methinks thou doth protest too much. Oh, I've studied you, Gray Junior. I know you like no one else knows you. I might have done the killings, but you were there with me in spirit. Kill one for the Gipper, eh?"

"You're insane."

"Don't kill the messenger, Gray Junior. Hard as you might find this to believe, I've never meant you any harm. I even think of myself as your friend."

"Friend?"

"I'm prepared to prove that. I have certain—mementos—that will allow you to have your life back, if that's what you truly desire. These items will prove your innocence—such as it is."

"I don't believe you."

"I could have killed you last night, but I didn't. Besides, it's not as if you have a choice in the matter."

Feral held the phone out, keying on the two voices coming from the pool.

"Marco."

"Polo."

Caleb covered his mouth with a suddenly trembling hand, then moved his shaky hand over the receiver. "He's with my kids."

"Do you have access to a car?" Feral asked.

"Marco," his daughter shouted.

"Well?" Feral said.

Caleb forced himself to speak. "I can get one."

"Then do so, and drive to La Jolla."

"Polo," said his son.

"There's a restaurant in downtown La Jolla called the Top Hat. Be at the maître d' stand in forty five minutes. Don't be late. And don't bother to order any food, because you won't be staying to dine."

In the background, Caleb could hear the cries of Janet and James. Their voices paralyzed him: "Marco," "Polo," "Marco," "Polo" . . .

"But first, Gray Junior, the ground rules. Obey them, and your children will live. No tricks. No police. Just the two of us. Is that understood?"

"Yes."

Feral lifted the cell phone up again, held it so that Caleb could hear his children's voices.

"It's one thing for some strangers to die," he said. "Family is different, though. . . ."

"If you touch my children, I'll kill you. I swear to God I will."

Feral didn't hang up right away. Caleb heard his daughter yell, "Marco."

And then, before the line went dead, he heard the killer's answer: "Polo."

"Give me the keys to your car," Caleb said.

He got up from the sofa, staggering for a moment on unsteady legs.

"Look at you," said Lola. "You're ill."

"Give me the keys *now.*"

"You're too sick to do this alone."

He took a threatening step toward her.

"Let me go with you." She moved back, trying to keep her purse away from him.

Caleb grabbed her by the arm. His hands were merciless. She squealed with pain as he wrenched the purse from her hands. He didn't acknowledge her hurt. Seeing his face, Lola backed away from him. He had always muzzled his emotions before. Now he wasn't trying to hide his rage, and it frightened her.

But it's only fear for his family that's showing, Lola told herself. "I can hide in the backseat of the car," she said. "I can help you."

He turned the purse over and started emptying its contents.

"You need me," she said. "Not two hours ago you were out of your mind with fever. You're still not thinking clearly. You couldn't be. Or else you wouldn't just be walking into his trap."

He found the keys.

"You'd be thinking how to stop him once and for all. That's how you can make your family safe. Not by sacrificing yourself."

He started to walk toward the door, but Lola stepped in his

path. She spoke quickly, before he could throw her out of the way. "We can talk things out in the car. Together we can come up with some kind of plan."

Caleb didn't push her aside. He looked at Lola, and she at him. His eyes frightened her. They looked into her, and made her reconsider what she was trying to do. I'm not brave, Lola thought, and I'm not *a* brave. I am a Two Spirit. And I'm very afraid.

All I need to do is look away, she thought. That would say everything without her saying anything. As he passed by she could tell him Godspeed and God bless. And then, to make herself feel better, she could call the police. She could promise herself that somehow she'd get the goddamn cavalry out to help him.

But that would be a lie, and she wasn't good at lying to herself. Not now, not anymore. Oh, she'd tried telling herself lies for the longest time, but she had always known what was true and what wasn't. Like now. She was afraid, and there was reason to be scared, but to deny Caleb would be like denying herself.

"Let's go," Lola said.

And she steadied him, and he steadied her, as they walked out to her car. When they reached the car she said, "I have to go get something."

He sat there for a minute, wondering if he should turn the ignition, wondering if she just wanted him to drive away, and just when he'd decided that she did, Lola returned with a bag and an Indian blanket in hand. She opened the passenger door, put the seat forward, then went to the backseat and lay down.

Caleb started the car. When he looked back in the rearview mirror she had all but disappeared under the blanket, but he could still hear her rustling through the bag.

"What did you bring?"

"My medicine bag. A Bible. Some clothes. Oh—and a gun."

34

Let me out. Lola practiced mouthing the words under her blanket. Lip-synching almost made them a reality. Lola knew that she only needed to say those three words and she'd be safe. But they were fifteen minutes into the drive and she still hadn't said them.

She heard a cough from the front seat that sounded as if it was covering a sob. Though he was physically sick and mentally tortured, Caleb was still trying to maintain a brave front. She knew without his saying anything that all he could think about was his children.

"Maybe we should discuss a plan," Lola said. Her words seemed to echo back at her, smothered by the blanket covering her.

His hard tone overcompensated for his pain: "How's this? Loan me your gun and I'll kill him."

"The gun's yours. I've always doubted I could pull the trigger anyway."

"That won't be a problem for me."

"Are you sure?"

"I'm sure."

"He's not going to just let you shoot him," Lola said. "He'll be watching you, manipulating you."

And making sure no one's helping you. She could tell him that, make Caleb think her presence was jeopardizing his children, and he'd be the one to insist she leave the car. That way he would be making the decision. She could live with that, couldn't she?

But instead she said, "He might fix it so he knows you don't have a weapon on you."

"I'll use my hands, then."

Caleb's voice was measured, even anticipatory. She shivered a little.

"Don't let revenge cloud your thinking," she said. "I could call the police, and tell them Maryelizabeth has disappeared, and where we're headed."

"No. I don't want to send him into hiding. I want it to end tonight."

"So does he. And he knows a hell of a lot more about you than you do about him. He's controlling how the two of you will meet, and he's prepared his playing field."

"I'm used to uneven playing fields."

"Maybe it doesn't have to be so uneven. Maybe we can do something to distract him."

"Like what?"

"I don't know. Maybe we can scare him somehow."

"Maybe you could do one of your stage numbers. That ought to really distract him." A moment later, Caleb said, "Sorry."

"Don't be. I know just the one I'd like to do. *Staying Alive.* At the club we always bring out the bubble machine for that one. And I wave a lot of big feathers. Bee Gees music always needs lots of feathers. And my six-inch platform shoes, of course. Sometimes I segue into Nancy Sinatra's 'These Boots Were Made for Walking.'"

She sang the chorus from the song, but then found her voice wavering. She had this premonition that the boots were walking over a grave.

"My stomach hasn't felt like this in a long, long time," Lola admitted. "It feels like we're going to war. Not the kind of war with uniforms, and marching, but a more personal kind of war, like when I used to go to high school and I'd know I was going to get beat up, even though I could never be sure when and where the attack was coming."

Caleb didn't say anything, but Lola knew he had similar memories.

"Back then I used to drink Pepto-Bismol for breakfast," she said.

"I tried to wear the right clothes, men's clothes, but that didn't help. The clothes couldn't hide how different I was. I wasn't the bad boys' only target, though. There were other kids who didn't fit in. I remember praying that today would be their turn, and not mine.

"I'd like to think I have changed since then, that I got stronger when I started putting on dresses, but I don't know if that's true. I'm still afraid that all it would take is someone looking at me wrong and there I'd be, begging those bullies to go pick on someone else instead of me. I wonder if we ever really change."

"We do change," Caleb said. "We have to." He fervently wanted to believe what he was saying.

"Or is it that as we get older we just try to find ways to avoid conflict, ways that allow us to pretend that we've grown stronger? I remember the first time I went out in public in women's clothing. I was sure everyone was looking at me. And I was sure they were all thinking, 'There goes the freak.' And gradually it dawned on me that few, if any, people were taking notice of me. Mostly it's still that way. When I go out I don't know whether I'm being bold, or whether I'm passing for a woman, or whether the world's unobservant, or whether people just don't care."

"It may be a little bit of each," Caleb said.

"I've never been brave, you know. Sometimes I do a very un-Frank Sinatra version of 'My Way.' But I didn't really do it my way at all. Wearing women's clothing really wasn't a choice for me. It was as necessary as breathing."

"If you weren't courageous, you wouldn't be helping me now."

"Don't pin a badge on me," Lola said. "Truth is, the only reason I haven't jumped out of the car is because I'm afraid of how much analysis it would take to make me feel right about myself again."

"Fear," Caleb said. "Everyone's great motivator."

Lola heard the echo in his pronouncement. His own fears talking. She could tell he was thinking about his family again.

"Your kids were playing in a pool," she said. "He wouldn't have had the opportunity to snatch them in front of other people."

"He knows where they are. That's all that matters now."

"If something—happens—I'll call the Sheriff's Department. Maryelizabeth said they were keeping tabs on your family. They'll be able to protect them."

"Thanks." His gratitude sounded raw and exposed and desperate.

"I always wanted kids myself," said Lola. "I had this fantasy that I would meet a man with little children, a widower, and that I'd be their mother. Silly, huh? I'm one of those fools for love, and what's even dumber is that I keep setting myself up for failure. The kind of man I want is the kind of man who invariably runs away from the likes of me."

"Love happens when you don't expect it," Caleb said. "I didn't think I'd ever fall in love, or that anyone could fall in love with me. But when it happened, I treated it more like a curse than a miracle. I resisted love's blessings so much that it was almost like I was embracing Anna and pushing her away at the same time. I guess I was afraid—no, I was sure—that she couldn't possibly love the real me."

"Oh, I can name that tune, sugar. All of us with our shame. All of us built up like porcupines. Reminds me of that question: How do porcupines make love?"

"I don't know."

"Very, very carefully."

Caleb didn't laugh, but she didn't expect him to. "The only creatures that got to be more careful than porcupines," Lola said, "are us two-legged kind."

She was right, Caleb thought, right about lots of things. It did feel as if they were going into war. That explained their talking like this. No one wanted to die alone. And neither one of them wanted to die that night.

"There's this part in the Bible," said Caleb, "where Jesus says, 'And if thine right eye offends thee, pluck it out.' I always wished I could do that, just pluck out all my bad parts. But then I wasn't sure if I'd be left with any good parts."

The car slowed down. "I'm turning on Prospect," Caleb announced. "Parking's always tough around here."

Getting closer to the war, Lola thought. He was evidently thinking the same thing.

"Can you give me that gun?" Caleb asked.

He listened to her rummage through her bag, then saw her arm come out from under her blanket with the gun.

"It's loaded?"

"Yes."

He stuck the weapon in his coat pocket, and they drove in silence until Caleb found a place to park the car.

"Showtime," he said.

The crowds were out in downtown La Jolla, lots of beautiful people wearing expensive clothing, out to see and be seen.

It felt surreal walking the streets, Caleb thought. No one else knew about his war. They were too busy window-shopping and laughing to notice him. He knew how Lola had felt going out in drag for the first time, was sure he was experiencing the same feelings of exposure and uncertainty. He was the Bogeyman, had been on the front pages of all the newspapers, and beaming out at these people from their television sets, but he was passing among them like a ghost.

Caleb tried straightening his coat before walking into the Top Hat. He wasn't dressed for the restaurant. Lola had done the best she could with his shirt, had mended it and tried to wash out the bloodstains, but they were still visible if you looked closely. His chin was bandaged and his face scraped from his run-in with the asphalt, and he needed a shave. Caleb could see his dark stubble in the reflection of the glass front door. His five o'clock shadow contrasted starkly with his newly blond hair.

The interior of the restaurant had a lot of burnished wood and stained glass, but people weren't there for the atmosphere so much as the panorama below. Top Hat diners had prime viewing spots of La Jolla Cove and the Pacific Ocean, and the patrons were taking advantage of their aerie, gazing at the ocean while sipping their drinks and nibbling on their shrimp cocktails. No one appeared to notice him, save for the hostess.

Caleb cut off her pleasantries, merely told her, "I'm waiting for someone," then took a seat.

"Perhaps you'd like to wait in our lounge, sir . . ."

"No." Caleb turned his back on her, not giving her another glance. He didn't take in her name tag, or the color of her hair, or anything about her. For her sake he ignored her. He remembered his brief encounter with Brandy Wein, and how that had been enough to condemn her.

It was twenty-five after six. Caleb had arrived five minutes early. Time passed, each second making him more jumpy. He tried not to be a clock watcher, tried to resist looking at his watch, but found he couldn't hold out for long. Every time the phone rang it gave him a start. He was looking at his watch when the phone rang again.

The way the hostess was talking, Caleb knew it wasn't another reservation call. "Why, yes," she said. "I think he's sitting here. Mr. Gray?"

Caleb acknowledged the name. He took the phone from her, put it to his ear.

"Sorry to have kept you waiting," Feral said, "but you know how time passes when you're having fun."

"No," Caleb said, "I don't."

"I stopped to chat with Maryelizabeth. I wish I could have stayed a little longer with her. I told her I'd be borrowing her cell phone for a few more hours. She didn't *voice any objections.*"

His emphasis was supposed to be cluing Caleb to her condition. He was telling him that she was unconscious, or gagged, or dead.

"I want you to take a walk," said Feral, "a little stroll down to La Jolla Cove. There's a gazebo at the park there. It's right across from the lawn."

"Walking's hard for me," Caleb said. "I had an accident last night."

"I think the exercise will do you good. You know what they say about people who don't exercise—they're at risk—and by extension, so are their loved ones."

Caleb didn't respond to the threat.

"You'll find further instructions at the gazebo. I'd hurry if I were you."

The line went dead.

Caleb cut through the La Valencia Hotel, taking its courtyard pathway down to the cove. He tried to be on alert, aware of everything going on around him. As he crossed Coast Boulevard, he sensed that he was passing over a demarcation line, an upstairs-downstairs division that had the rich above, and the hoi polloi below.

The cove wasn't crowded, but the air was pungent with smoke from fires and barbecues. Caleb took the roundabout way, following the pathway along the rocks. He stopped to tie his shoe, and glanced back to see if anyone was following him. No one. But he was still sure he was under surveillance. The only people near him were two tidepoolers probing with a flashlight to see what the retreating tide had left behind. As Caleb rounded the bend he encountered Frisbee players tossing their disks under the lights. Their boom boxes were positioned around the park and techno vied with disco as he passed through. Dogs barked, or they might have been sea lions. Caleb knew the sea mammals liked to gather on the rocks around the cove. The end of daylight had brought the surfers in, but hadn't closed the door on all ocean sports. Several night dives were taking place. The scuba divers themselves were mere shadows, their outlines only hinted at by the glow of their underwater green lights.

Caleb felt like one of those divers. He was having to work his way through darkness, and his illness made it seem as if he was doing everything in slow motion. A mist was hanging along the coast, light but building. The shroud seemed to cling to Caleb, hanging on to him. He tried to fight off the illusion, but wished he had one of those green diver's lights. They reminded him of a wizard's scepter. That's what he could use, a magical wand. . . .

I should have taken more aspirin, Caleb thought. His forehead was beginning to burn again. He couldn't lose it, not now.

Someone was in the gazebo. Caleb reached for the gun. There, he thought, touching the metal. The gun would serve him better than any wizard's scepter. He didn't pull it out, but kept his fingers gripped around it. He crept closer to the gazebo, willing himself to be invisible, imagining himself as part of the fog.

Fever talking, he thought.

Inside the gazebo the shadow was moving, twisting. It was like some huge goddamn snake. Caleb took out his gun, and stepped inside the structure.

A couple looked up. Young, no more than fourteen. They stopped their kissing, interrupted by a man with a gun. They were terrified, mouths open, eyes wide and panicked.

Caleb put his gun away. He didn't know what to say. Further instructions were supposed to be in the gazebo, but what kind of instructions?

"Was something left here for me?" he asked. "Some kind of package?"

Drugs. He could tell that's what they immediately assumed. And with his sweaty face and dazed manner Caleb knew he probably looked like the most demented of dope fiends.

"There wasn't any package," the boy managed to say.

Caleb searched the darkened structure anyway, the boy and girl silently huddling together in the corner. Then he went outside, and began examining the exterior of the gazebo. If he hadn't been looking for the envelope, he wouldn't have seen it, tucked as it was under one of the side eaves. As he reached for it, Caleb remembered the other envelope, the one with the pictures of Brandy Wein in it. His heart started racing. He pulled the envelope down, and was glad to feel its lightness. That meant no new pictures. The envelope was addressed to Gray Junior. Inside it was a slip of paper on which was written, "Mount Soledad Cross. Fifteen minutes. Seek, and ye shall find."

He heard noises behind him, and whirled around. The boy and girl were fleeing the gazebo. His sudden turn made the girl scream.

"It's all right," Caleb yelled. "I'm one of the good guys." He wasn't sure if that was true, but they didn't stop to listen anyway.

The fog was rolling in. It looked as if the waves were carrying it ashore. Not twenty feet below him the ocean was pounding the shore. Caleb had an impulse to jump down and bathe his hot head and aching body in its water, but he knew he had to keep moving.

As he started back, Caleb looked for the night divers, but couldn't see them. Their green, guiding lights had gone out.

"I wondered if you were ever coming back," said Lola.

"Sh," Caleb said. "He might be watching."

He started the car, and drove off, maintaining the silence until he was sure they weren't under surveillance.

"We're on our way to Mount Soledad," he said.

"To do what?" Lola asked. "Pray?"

The large white cross that stood on the mount's summit had been a point of controversy for years. Various groups had been lobbying for its removal, saying its presence was a violation of the doctrine of separation of church and state, and that it had originally been erected to warn off non-Christians from the area. Proponents said it was a war memorial, and that it had graced the mount for too long to be removed. Everyone agreed it was a symbol, though no one could agree what kind of symbol.

"He called me at the restaurant," Caleb said, "and sent me on a wild-goose chase down to La Jolla Cove. That's where he left instructions for me to go to Mount Soledad. I'm sure he was watching me."

Caleb opened the window, let the wind whip his wet face. The mist wasn't only along the coast. It was working its way up the hill.

"Are you hot?" Lola asked.

"Yes."

She was cold. Freezing.

"You want me to close the window?"

"No."

"We're approaching the cross. We'll have to stop talking now. He might be watching."

The cross was on an island in the middle of a turnaround. Several cars were parked along the perimeter of the lot, with people taking in the view, or making out, or doing both. Caleb drove around the cross once, slowly, before parking the car.

He sat and waited. No one approached him. The note, Caleb remembered, had read, "Seek, and ye shall find." He opened the car door, and walked toward the cross, again afraid of what he might find. The image of Teresa Sanders flashed across his mind. She had been left for him. He tried to not think about her.

Caleb had been atop Mount Soledad one time before, but that had been during the day. He remembered he had been able to see south all the way to Mexico. Now, with the fog, the viewing was severely limited, but that didn't make it any less spectacular. The mist softened the world below him, bringing clouds to the earth. It was as if he were looking upon something not quite tangible, like looking at the world through a good dream.

The cross, immense and whitewashed, was bathed in lights. There was a wrought-iron fence around it. On one of the metal points, pierced, he found another envelope. Caleb started breathing easier. No body this time, and no pictures. He pulled the envelope down off the spike. It was addressed to Junior. There were enough lights illuminating the cross for him to read. The note contained only two words: "Call me." It was signed *M.*

"But how can we call Maryelizabeth?" Lola asked.

"We can't. When he called me at the restaurant he told me he was using Maryelizabeth's cellular phone. I didn't think anything about it at the time. I thought he was just taunting me, but that was his way of telling me he was carrying her phone because he knew he was going to make me call her number a little later."

"No," said Lola. "It's more than that." How much more, she wasn't sure, or was afraid to see. She had this feeling, this premonition, and it frightened her, but at the same time she felt it necessary that she help.

"He's creating a trail through her phone records," Lola said. "He's purposely making calls from her phone, and having you call him back. That makes me believe that Maryelizabeth's still alive. And it makes me suspect that he wants her time of death to be the same as yours."

Lola took the blanket off her head. She needed to breathe. She didn't want to think anymore, didn't want to feel what was *out there.* Her second sight had never scared her so.

Caleb reached for her car phone.

"No," Lola said.

It wasn't an answer he expected. Refusing him surprised Lola as well. She had answered out of instinct, but after a moment's reflection she knew her unwillingness to let him use her cell phone made sense.

"Why not?" asked Caleb.

"We don't want him to know we have a car phone."

An idea began to form in her head, the beginnings of a plan. "Slow down," she said. "We need to think."

Caleb called from a convenience-store pay phone. He was answered on the first ring.

"Where are you calling from?" Feral asked.

"A pay phone down in La Jolla Shores."

"Close. Or, as your children might say, 'Marco.'"

Caleb bit his lip. He didn't want the other man to know his agony. But apparently he already did.

"You seem to be sweating an awful lot tonight, Gray. Are you sick?"

Again, no answer.

"Because you look sick. Maybe tonight's not a good night for our getting together. I don't want to get the flu or anything."

"I'll try not to kiss you."

Feral hid his annoyance. He was the only one who should be making jokes. But Junior wouldn't be laughing for long.

"Next stop, Torrey Pines Gliderport. Do you know where that is?"

"No."

"As the crow flies, it's directly north of you, not much more than a mile up the coast. But you can't go that way unless you can fly. It's a bit of a circuitous path to get to the nosebleed seats, the cliffs. You'll need to go where eagles dare not perch, where the hang gliders like to step off onto a shelf of air.

"And you'll need to follow all of my instructions very carefully. . . ."

35

From the fringe, Feral watched the approach of the yellow Mustang. There was only one entrance to the Torrey Pines Gliderport, a single gate that was latched with a master lock every night at eight o'clock. Feral had cut that lock, allowing for passage along the dirt road. The thick fog and the dirt clouds the car was kicking up made it difficult for Feral to get a good look at the approaching car. He needed to make sure that Junior, and Junior alone, was coming in for a landing.

Damn fog. It made his surveillance more difficult, but Feral had already walked the area and made sure it was clear of people. Feral sat there listening, alert to all the sounds of the night. There were no footsteps, nothing unexplained.

The Mustang crunched along the dirt road, pausing at the knoll. It was a popular area during the day, the spot where hang gliders and paragliders readied their craft, and spectators congregated at the Gliderport Café to watch the pilots leap off the cliffs.

Go right, thought Feral. He had instructed Junior to park off the main road on the far north side of the knoll. The car started moving again. Yes, it was headed just where Feral had directed it to go.

The car finally came to a stop and the gliderport became that much more still. With the patience of a hunter, Feral maintained his position and listened. Everything was still. In the distance he could just make out a yellow glow. The car's headlights.

He waited for three minutes, no more, no less. Time for him to come in from the fringe. *Fringe.* The word gave Feral pleasure. He liked being on the edge. With cat steps, Feral made his way forward. He paused several times to listen, but all was quiet save for the sounds of the ocean. These were moments to be savored. The slate was finally about to be wiped clean. Old debts were going to be paid.

The fog made him feel like the invisible man. Under its cover he closed in on where Junior had parked his car. And there, standing like a good soldier, was Junior. He was near land's end, illuminated by the car's headlights.

Feral had imagined it just this way, except for the fog. The car's headlights were getting swallowed up by the mist, and he couldn't see Junior as clearly as he would have liked. The man could be a ghost. He wished he hadn't told Junior to leave the high beams on. Normal lighting would have been more effective. But the fog, Feral decided, was a mixed blessing. It was so thick he couldn't even make out the distant Salk and UC San Diego buildings. He and Junior were now a world unto themselves.

He crept a little closer. Junior was wearing a Padres cap, but was still squinting from having to stare into the headlights. That was the beauty of the setup. Junior couldn't see his approach. Feral had hunted deer that way. All you had to do was get a lantern in their eyes and it confused the stupid creatures. Blinded them into immobility. It was like shooting fish in a barrel. Feral liked it that way.

Junior kept moving his head from side to side. Did he sense his presence? Or was he just anxious for him to appear? The anticipation seemed to be a bit much for Junior. He was trembling violently. Junior acted as if he were in Antarctica instead of San Diego. His hands were in his pockets, and his shoulders were hunched.

Weak, Feral thought. It was sixty degrees or more and not cold so much as blustery. The wind was blowing even more than normal. It would have been too gusty, thought Feral, for even those fool hang gliders. He had enjoyed watching them while scouting the territory. Some of the daredevils had a ritual he liked; they yelled as they ran toward the edge of the cliffs, a victory call that climaxed as they threw themselves off. It was a long drop down, hundreds of feet, but they had their faith, believing in the wind, counting on updrafts and thermals to send them aloft, or at least in their finding enough of an air cushion for them to float down to the beach far, far below.

Feral had told Junior to wait for him beneath the knoll, not too far away from that jump-off spot. He was about a hundred feet away from the edge of the cliffs, but with the wind blowing so hard he was probably afraid to get too near to the abyss. The story of Junior's life, Feral thought. He was too timid ever to know the thrill of being on the edge, of dancing along the precipice of life. Feral had observed enough of his monotonous existence to be disdainful of it. Junior's father had done what he pleased with women, but the son couldn't even control his own wife. He'd watched another man take her and done nothing. Cuckold. Wimp.

The fog was getting thicker. Feral thought that the wind might have blown the haze away, but it was sticking like wet snow. Junior kept fading in and out of his view. Not that it mattered. Feral knew Junior would stay where he had been instructed. He had promised Junior answers, and more important, the evidence that would show him to be innocent of all the murders.

"Maybe you will be able to understand my motivations then," Feral had said. "Maybe we can be friends."

Not that Junior had believed a word he had said, but Feral enjoyed planting little seeds of hope. He had done the same thing with most of the women he had killed, had told them that he wasn't going to hurt them, and just as they were relaxing, just as they were exhaling away some of their anxiety, he had always made his move.

Sometimes he took them with just his hands, and other times he subdued them with one of his little tricks. The sleeper hold was a wonderful thing. "Pleasant dreams," he always told his victims.

Feral crept up to Junior's car. He reached for the driver's door handle, and felt around for it. The fog was so thick he could hardly see his hand in front of him. Feral silently pulled on the door handle. Damn. It was locked. He had wanted to turn the headlights off for a moment and throw Junior into a panic. But there were other ways.

He moved to his left, backtracking along the knoll before heading west to the cliffs. He'd approach Junior from his south side. With the lights shining in his eyes, Junior wouldn't be able to see anything anyway. He approached closer, and still closer. He wanted to get near enough to smell Junior's fear. When he wasn't more than ten feet away, Feral stopped. Junior looked like a wraith, seemed to have been absorbed by the fog. The last few days had made him even more of a shadow. He looked smaller, and thinner, and more insignificant than ever.

"Marco," Feral yelled.

Junior jumped. Oh, yes, he did. His head swiveled around wildly, trying to get a bead on the voice. But Feral had already moved.

"Take your clothes off."

He wished he could see Junior's look of surprise.

"What?"

"Take your clothes off. Now."

"Why?"

Feral said nothing. He wasn't going to speak and give away his location. Or his motives. Nakedness was innocence and guilt. A baby coming into the world. An adult using her nakedness to get what *she* wanted. Bitch. Not that Mother hadn't been pushed into her life's decisions, though. Feral decided to punctuate his command with an exclamation point. Another announcement to get attention. Feral raised his gun, and shot at the ground near Junior's feet.

Another leap in the air, but this jump even higher. Feral had expected a louder bang, but the gunshot was muted by the open space. All the better. Feral doubted the sound could be heard much beyond a hundred yards. But it must have sounded a hell of a lot louder than that to Junior. At the moment he wasn't jumping for joy. He was cowering on the ground.

"Get up, and take off your fucking clothes. Now."

Junior didn't answer, but he did stand up. Feral moved quietly behind him. Keep him guessing. But now the lights were in Feral's eyes as well. And he was casting a shadow. If Junior turned, he'd be able to see it and him. But Junior looked as if he was too scared to move. He was just standing there like a statue. Or maybe he was just being stubborn and thought that making like stone would spare him from stripping. Feral raised his gun again, and fired it.

He moved out of the glare of the lights back into the darkness. Now Junior's arms were in the air. He was surrendering. As if he hadn't already.

"No more warning shots," Feral said. "Take off your clothes. Now."

Junior reached down to his shoes and started untying them. He kicked one off, and then the other.

"That's it," said Feral, his voice coming from yet another spot. "I want you to prove to me there's nothing up your sleeve. You'll do that by stripping down to nothing."

Junior took off his coat.

"Toss it away from you," Feral said. "Do that with all your clothes."

He did as instructed. It took him a few tries, but he finally loosened his belt, and his pants fell. He kicked his trousers away, then just stood there.

"Everything comes off," Feral said. "Everything."

Junior was apparently modest. That didn't surprise Feral. He watched him reach for his briefs, hesitate, then reluctantly drop his underwear to the ground.

"Finding it a bit cold, are you?" said Feral, laughing.

Junior started unbuttoning his shirt, or tried to. His hands were shaking so much that he was having a hard time with the buttons. He turned away from the wind, offering his back to the lights, and Feral. The wind didn't let up. It gusted, blowing hard at the shirt, pushing it up, exposing his back. Feral was reminded of Marilyn Monroe's stepping on a subway grate and the breeze blowing up her dress in much the same way. Hollywood had used the scene to showcase her legs. But something was bothering Feral. He wished he could see better. The fog was playing tricks on his eyes. He thought he had glimpsed . . .

The telephone started ringing.

Feral's arms shot up. Reflex thing. It was just lucky he hadn't pulled the trigger of his gun. Goddammit. The ringing was unexpected and ill timed. It was like an alarm had gone off in his ear. Goddamn Queenie's phone. Who the hell was calling?

Maybe it was a wrong number.

Maybe it signaled trouble.

The phone was ringing for a second time when he saw a movement. From the corner of his eyes he could see Junior making a break for it. Feral didn't hesitate. He fired his gun, stopping Junior three steps into his escape attempt.

"Son of a bitch!" Feral screamed. "Move another inch and you're fucking dead."

The phone rang a third time.

"Get on your fucking knees. Down, I said. Now crawl back to where you were."

The phone rang a fourth time, then stopped ringing. Feral looked at it suspiciously, as if not trusting the silence, then turned his full attention to the sprawled captive.

"You better keep yourself fucking planted there," he said. "I'm not going to miss next time. And take off the rest of your fucking clothes now."

The phone started ringing again.

Not a wrong number, no. Feral looked at the phone, as if by staring at it he could discern who was calling.

Second ring.

He shook the phone, treated it as if it were a wrapped present. Feral wanted to divine what was inside, or in this case, who was inside. His detective had documented Queenie's methodology. The cellular phone was her emergency number. So what was the emergency?

Third ring.

Feral glanced quickly at Junior. He was still on his knees. He was looking away from the lights, had his backside facing Feral. The pose reminded Feral of the way subordinate primates presented themselves.

"Turn around," Feral barked.

Junior started to do that, inch by trembling inch. The only clothing he still had on was a baseball cap. He hadn't been wearing a cap earlier in the night, Feral remembered. But the musing didn't hold his attention. Feral needed to make a decision on the ringing phone.

Fourth ring.

Feral flipped the phone open, but said nothing. He could hear the breathing of the caller on the line, and then there was the voice, but not just any voice.

"You son of a bitch," she said.

Queenie's voice. Feral felt as if he had been struck. How the hell had she gotten free? This was bad, impossibly bad.

Feral threw a quick glance Junior's way. No threat there. He was naked, in shock, sitting on his backside and hugging his chest.

"Before the police arrest you," Queenie said, "and they will, momentarily, I'd like to take advantage of this wonderful interview opportunity."

"How did you get out?" Feral asked.

"I'm the one asking the questions," she said.

He'd drugged Queenie, and tied her up. Even if she had somehow gotten free she wouldn't be, couldn't be, talking like this. She would be in a stupor. What the hell was going on?

He heard the patter of bare feet, and reacted to it. Junior had been faking his helplessness. Now he was trying to make his break, trying to escape into the fog. Feral fired three shots, heard a scream, and then watched as Junior started to fall. For a moment the mist cleared, and Feral's vision was unobstructed. Everything was unclouded, but everything looked wrong.

Tits, Feral thought. That's what he'd glimpsed earlier when the wind had been pulling at Junior's shirt. And that's what he saw now. A bleeding man with tits. How could that be?

"Polo."

It wasn't Maryelizabeth's voice coming from the phone. It was Junior's. What the hell was going on?

The car engine started. The headlights turned on him. Feral couldn't see the driver, but he suddenly knew who was sitting there. The car started toward him.

Feral raised his gun, got off two quick shots at the car, but it didn't stop. He started running, but the car was gaining on him. Without breaking stride, Feral pulled the trigger in rapid succession. The car was on top of him. It was so near Feral knew he couldn't miss. And he didn't. Glass shattered and the car braked to a sudden, violent stop.

Got 'em, Feral thought.

It was his moment of pride before the fall. The edge had caught up with him.

As Feral went over the cliff he started screaming. His screams pierced the fog, and the night. He'd courted death assiduously, but never looked it in the eye.

The screams suddenly stopped.

He who was so fond of last words never offered any of his own.

36

The memorial service was more of a wake than a somber occasion. The color of the day wasn't black. Most of those in attendance were wearing vibrant tropical outfits. The individuals were as flamboyant as their garb, and fully half the people there were drag queens.

A minister led the service. He was equal parts cheerleader and spiritual leader, and had a talent for getting others to do the talking. And remembering Lola took a lot of talking. A life was discussed, was laughed over and cried over.

"Lola never liked to miss a good party," said Michelle Connelly. Michelle had very broad shoulders. Some of her older friends called her "Mike," evidently the name she had been born with. "I keep expecting music to start up, and Lola to begin singing.

"She's here, though, center stage, people. I feel her. All we have to do is listen to our hearts and we can hear her last, and best, performance. And Saint Peter, you better watch out, baby, 'cause Lola's going to come up and rock that house."

Amid all the cheers and whistles, Caleb found himself reaching out for the microphone, accepting the hand-off from Michelle. He hadn't wanted to speak, had hoped others would say all that needed to be said, but he realized he owed Lola this last tribute, and much more. He took a deep breath, and waited for the noise to stop, and his heart to settle. Caleb hated that all eyes were upon him, and that he had to speak, but he confronted his fears. No more running. The media, under orders not to be intrusive during the memorial, suddenly came alive. Caleb tried to ignore all the cameras pointed at him.

He cleared his throat, and looked out upon a very different Torrey Pines Gliderport than the one he had experienced only three nights before. The day was bright and sunny, and the ocean blue and inviting. Caleb swallowed hard. Lola had a lot of friends.

"The local newspaper called Lola *an unusual hero,*" he said. "Any hero is an unusual person, an extraordinary person. And that's how I'll remember Lola—as a hero, and an extraordinary individual."

Caleb blinked away his tears. Not far from where he was standing Lola had died in his arms. He found himself looking at the spot. Everyone followed his gaze. There were piles of flowers there, solemn reminders that brought a quiet and stillness to the crowd, but a hang glider broke the spell. He ran past the spot where Lola had fallen, and let out an exuberant yell, then soared straight out toward the blue expanse of the Pacific Ocean. The hang glider caught a thermal, and started to rise higher and higher.

Very different, thought Caleb, from the last man he had seen go over the cliffs.

Everything had happened so quickly that night. Caleb remembered braking hard, stopping the Mustang just short of the cliff's edge. The screams of the killer were still in his ear when he jumped out of the car and went in search of Lola.

It was too dark and foggy to see her, so he yelled, and kept yelling, until he heard a weak "Here."

"Where?" he shouted.

"Here," she said.

They repeated their calls. Caleb knew he was getting closer, just as he knew her voice was getting progressively weaker. Another, even more desperate game of Marco Polo, he thought.

"Here."

The whisper in the darkness that was so close. He waved his arms in the mist, trying to push it away, trying to swim through it. And there she was.

So much blood. The mist couldn't hide that. He hovered around helplessly for a moment, then dropped to his knees. He didn't know what to do, but at the same time he knew there was nothing he could do. So he held her.

"Most of you have read the story of what happened that night," Caleb said, "or at least versions purporting to be the story. I'd be dead now if it weren't for Lola. She was the ultimate Good Samaritan. She took me in, and believed in me, and in the end she saved my life."

It was her plan, all of it. Rehearsed and practiced on the drive up to the gliderport.

"When you were sick," she said, "when you were delirious, you spoke in Maryelizabeth's voice. Can you do that now?"

"Yes." Caleb didn't have to think about it. He'd talked to her in person, and listened to her tape for hours on end. Her voice was in his head.

"Show me."

"We're both Doubting Thomases," he said. No. Maryelizabeth said it.

"Pull over," Lola said. "Find a place we can park."

He'd turned at the light, and pulled into a parking lot on the UC San Diego campus.

"Take off your clothes," said Lola.

"What?"

"Osh-Tisch," she said.

The memory hurt, and the pain of it made Caleb remember his audience. "Many of you might not know that Lola was part Indian. I think that heritage was very important to her. As she lay dying, she told me that she was going to *Wakan Tanka*, the Great Mystery. I don't know much about the Lakota religion. I only know that a great spirit has joined her ancestors."

No, he thought. Two great spirits wrapped in one.

"Hush."

He tried to stop sobbing, tried to respect Lola's wishes. Her voice in the night kept telling him there was no need to cry, kept offering him absolution for all of his guilt.

"Hush," she said again, but the word was offered to comfort him.

Holding her in his arms, Caleb said, "You beat the bully." And then he started crying again.

"Hush," she said for the third and last time, making the word sound like a gentle blessing.

"Don't let them bury me in these clothes," she said. "And nothing black either. Make it like this mist. White lace."

"You're not going—"

"It's all right," she said. "I go to Wakan Tanka."

She struggled for another breath, then managed to say, "I'm only a quarter Lakota. I'm not even a real Indian. . . ."

It was Caleb's turn to say, "Hush." But he offered the sound in the spirit she had, a blessing to dispel all doubts.

"You're all brave," he said, "a warrior like Osh-Tisch."

"No," she said, gently chiding him, "I'm a Two Spirit," and they both had a little laugh, and then she whispered, "Hanta yo," and was gone.

She went to meet Wakan Tanka with a smile.

Later, Caleb learned "hanta yo" was a Lakota war chant that translated to, "the spirit goes ahead of us." Both spirits, thought Caleb. He found strength in her last words and accompanying smile, and passed on her smile to those who were gathered.

"I only knew Lola for a short time, and yet there are so many things I feel I should say. Lola looked at the world differently than most, and I thank God for that. One of her eyes was feminine, and the other was masculine, and that gave her a unique perspective. She wasn't judgmental, because she had been judged so harshly herself, and because of that, she didn't automatically burden me with the sins of my father. I wish I could have been as nonjudgmental of her. I wish I could have done a lot of things differently. But if Lola taught me anything, it's that we need to live in the present, instead of letting the shame from the past rule us."

Caleb sighed, shook his head, but then remembered her smile. She hadn't been afraid of the Great Mystery.

"I'll miss her," he said, and nodded several times. "I'll miss her."

He put down the microphone. No one else took it up. The minister didn't have to announce that the memorial service was over. Everyone knew.

There was a lot of spontaneous hugging. An impromptu line formed, people waiting to commiserate with Caleb. Lola's father was dead, and her mother had chosen not to attend the funeral. With no relatives there, Caleb had become Lola's family. Maybe that was the secret, he thought. If you're born into the wrong family, form a new one.

Michelle Connelly gave Caleb a bear hug. She had the arms to do that. "Lola wouldn't have wanted anyone to be down," Michelle whispered.

"I know."

"We're going to get together at Randi's tonight, going to have the kind of party that Lola would have wanted. It's going to be an after-hours thing, starting at one."

"I'll be there."

The line started moving through, with just about everyone offering a word to Caleb. He didn't know why he was the object of their sympathy, but he was glad for it.

Anna joined him at his side. "Are you all right?" she asked. The question came with a hug.

"I've gotten more hugs today than I have in my entire life," Caleb said. "Suddenly I'm a huggable sort."

"You always were," said Anna.

Maybe he could believe that now. He returned Anna's hug. They'd been talking almost nonstop for the last three days. There was still a lot more talking for them to do, but now they both knew there was time. And there were still so many things he wanted to say to her.

"I was thinking of taking the kids home," Anna said, "before James decides to hitch a ride on one of those hang gliders."

"Good idea."

Another hug, and then a kiss for each of his children. Caleb and Anna had driven in separate cars, both knowing he would need to stay longer.

Reporters started calling questions out to Caleb. For days they had been dogging him, and he'd been polite, but mostly monosyllabic. The full story, he had told them, was being given to Maryelizabeth Line, and she would be releasing the information as she saw fit.

Like father, like son, Caleb thought. He had picked the same confidante. She came forward to shield him now, to be the diplomat, but a woman stepped in front of her, another mourner who wanted to give Caleb a hug. Caleb wasn't sure whether he was hugging a biological woman or not, but it no longer mattered to him.

A hug was a hug.

37

"Will you be going back to work soon?" Maryelizabeth asked.

"I'm not sure," Caleb said.

The two of them had taken an outdoor table at the Pannikin, La Jolla's answer to good coffee, and they were sitting in the very back corner to get the privacy they wanted and needed.

"For the past couple of days," he said, "it seems as if everyone in San Diego's been calling to have their trees trimmed."

"Everyone loves a winner."

"Or a sideshow act. There's no shortage of people who want a piece of me. The media. Movie types. Publishers. They're waving lots of money."

"It's time you talked to one of those business managers I recommended."

"Maybe. Or maybe I'll just tell everyone to go away. What do they really want from me anyway?"

"The same thing they want from me: a firsthand account of the devil. They're curious about John Farrell. They want to hear about the new Shame versus the old Shame. They want our impressions, our feelings."

"For me," said Caleb, "Farrell will always be a figure shrouded in fog."

"I need to see him more clearly than that. I've devoted the last few days to learning all I can about him. There's a lot there. He's going to keep me busy studying him for a long time. The ironic thing is that I interviewed Farrell a few months ago. His girlfriend was originally thought to be one of the Cave Man's victims. Now it's evident that Farrell was the one who killed her.

"The Cave Man—Ron McNeill—was charged with the murders of eight Colorado women. He originally confessed to all the killings, but when I talked to him he partially recanted, saying he was responsible for only six of the deaths. McNeill liked the notoriety of having killed more women than he really had, but the fifth and sixth victims were both blondes, a hair color he isn't partial to. McNeill decided he couldn't take credit for those two victims because they weren't good enough to be in his 'trophy collection.' His words.

"In addition to murdering his girlfriend, I think Farrell also killed a second young woman who looked like her. Her death, I suspect, was to divert suspicion from himself for his girlfriend's murder. When I interviewed Farrell he knew I believed McNeill's revised story, but in retrospect I think he was more amused than threatened."

"Why would he have been amused?"

"Because he was already planning to kill me—to kill us—when I showed up in Colorado."

"How do you know that?"

"I've been in regular contact with the Denver Police Department. Among Farrell's effects were copies of reports submitted to him by a Vincent Coleman, a private detective who worked for Farrell on and off for several years. Judging by the detective's reports, Farrell's been interested in us for at least two years. If you'd like to read all about yourself, and maybe learn things you don't even know, I can get you a copy."

Caleb sighed. Having been spied on still rankled. "I'll pass."

"I was hoping Coleman would be able to answer a number of my questions," she said, "but he's dead, and I don't think his death was a coincidence. He was struck by an automobile a month ago, just days after he finished a two-week surveillance of you. The Denver PD is in the process of examining Farrell's vehicles to see if they can find any evidence that either his truck or his car was involved in the hit-and-run.

"I suspect that killing was a way of life for Farrell for some time.

When he was twenty-one both his parents died in an automobile accident. Their car went off the side of a mountain pass. As a result, Farrell inherited a substantial amount of money, as well as a business. That happened six years ago."

"Was it a suspicious accident?"

"Authorities didn't think so at the time. Now they do."

"Wonderful thing, hindsight."

"I'm guilty of it myself. When I interviewed Farrell, I never suspected him of having murdered his girlfriend. I remember him as being well spoken, even overly solicitous about my comfort. The two questionable homicides had me believing that some kind of Cave Man copycat was involved."

Maryelizabeth waved a notepad. "I had my Farrell interview notes overnighted out of Denver. Mostly I just took down his quotes, but I did make a few observations about him."

She turned to one of the paper-clipped pages. "'*Very bright,*' I wrote, '*but a bit grandiose.*'" She flipped some more pages until she came to the next paper clip: "And here I jotted down, '*John is enamored with his own voice, even a bit stuck-up, but perhaps he's overcompensating.*' So much for my picking up on the fact that he hated me."

"That wasn't something he wanted to advertise."

"True. He did a great Prince Charming imitation."

She shut her notebook more firmly than was necessary.

"I doubt whether I'd want to read your early observations of me," said Caleb. "I am not even sure if I'd want to see your most recent ones."

Maryelizabeth picked up a pen and started scratching furiously on a napkin. Caleb leaned over and looked at her scribbling. "Worse than I thought," he said.

She put her pen down. As their smiles faded, a lull in the conversation followed. Both pretended interest in their coffee.

"So what do you do now?" asked Caleb.

"Look for Rosebud."

Caleb gave her a quizzical look.

"*Citizen Kane* reference," she said. "I love that movie. I think Welles would have been a hell of a crime writer. He loved scratching beneath the surface. That's what I try to do. If I look hard enough I'm convinced I can find Rosebud, or at least a few petals. That, more than anything else, motivates me to write my books."

"You probably like doing puzzles."

"No. They're too limiting. The human puzzle is much more interesting. There are no boundaries, and the colors change, and you have to connect pieces that to the eye just don't fit. I like it when I make my readers say, 'Aha!' I like doing my Paul Harvey thing. There's nothing quite so satisfying as revealing 'the rest of the story.'"

And maybe nothing so frightening, Caleb thought. For so long he'd wanted to tell the rest of the story, but he had never dared.

"I like being surprised myself," Maryelizabeth said. "The day before yesterday I found out that Farrell was adopted. And then yesterday I started learning about the rest of the story. His biological mother was Leslie Van Doren. You remember that name?"

Caleb's mouth opened. He remembered.

"That's right," Maryelizabeth said. "Farrell was Van Doren's grown-up baby, the one she tried to pass off as your father's son, the one whose original birth certificate listed him as Gray Parker Jr.

"After your father's execution, Van Doren left Florida and returned to Colorado. She kept the boy, whom she continued to call Gray, until he was twenty-one months old. By all accounts she wasn't a good mother. Her drug and alcohol use escalated, and her baby's needs became secondary to her own.

"The state intervened, and declared her an unfit mother. They took away the boy and determined that he should be put up for adoption. Van Doren didn't attend any of the proceedings, and never contested losing her child.

"The boy was adopted by an older, wealthy couple, Thomas and Dorothy Farrell. They never discussed the adoption with John. He grew up thinking they were his biological parents. Apparently he didn't learn differently until he was fifteen."

"He must have been incredibly angry," Caleb said.

"Yes."

"Did they tell him about his mother?" asked Caleb.

"I doubt the Farrells were even aware of her history," Maryelizabeth said. "That's something I'm researching, but so far there's been nothing to indicate they knew anything about her past, and it's unlikely they were informed of her death. Van Doren died at the age of thirty-three of a drug overdose that might very well have been a suicide."

"What kind of a child was he?"

Maryelizabeth shrugged. "I'm still finding out. Now that he's notorious, lots of people are saying that Farrell was always bent."

"That's what they lined up to say about me."

"I know that. That's why I'll need to apply my hindsight filter. That's my euphemism for a bullshit detector. But one thing people seem to agree on was that Farrell was undeniably bright."

"Why did he hate us so much?" asked Caleb.

"I don't know," said Maryelizabeth. "Right now I only have a few half-baked theories. That's all I might ever have."

Caleb knew that before Maryelizabeth was through she'd have more than that, but he was also only too aware that sometimes even Maryelizabeth Line didn't unearth all the secrets.

"I think you were a target because he was insanely jealous of you," Maryelizabeth said. "He hated you because you were the chosen child."

"Chosen? That's a laugh."

"You got your father's name, Caleb."

"It wasn't something I wanted."

"That doesn't matter."

"But Farrell wasn't even my biological brother."

"He could have been. He was brought into the world with the name of Gray, but even that was taken away from him. Perhaps your choosing to lose the name Gray added insult to his injury. He didn't have that choice."

"I never did anything to him."

"That doesn't matter. This certainly wasn't the first time you were targeted for the sins of your father."

"Sins? For once my father did the right thing. He didn't have a child by this woman. He wasn't the father."

"Try a logic jump," said Maryelizabeth, "albeit a convoluted logic jump. By withholding his seed from Van Doren, your father also denied Farrell. He never gave him a chance to be his son."

"That's crazy."

"It's a theory. But I'm sure there were any number of factors that entered into Farrell's equation of hate. By his thinking, your father probably betrayed the love of Van Doren. He humiliated her, and made it clear that she wasn't worthy of carrying his child. Maybe Farrell decided your father drove her into the arms of other men, and made her what she was. And because Gray contrived with me to reveal Van Doren's deception to the world, because he helped make her a laughingstock, Farrell might have decided he had to take up that gauntlet and avenge the death that he perceived we drove her to."

"Why? It wasn't as if Van Doren was the Mother of the Year. She abandoned him."

"As you know only too well, you don't get to choose your family. And for all her shortcomings, Van Doren was still his mother."

"It still seems crazy."

"I'm not ruling that out either. Farrell was fascinated with the criminal mind. He studied capital punishment at length, and was attracted to notorious felons, especially those who exhibited a certain bravado. In many ways his curiosity was self-fulfilling. He was looking at his own pathology.

"Farrell was methodical if nothing else. He studied you very closely because he wanted to learn what would hurt you the most. He knew you were gentle, and kind, and good, and he knew he was none of those things, and he probably hated you all the more for that."

Gentle and kind and good. The words echoed around Caleb's red ears. He felt embarrassed, unworthy.

"He was interested in how you had run away from your past, and he knew the biggest hell of all would be for the sins of your father to catch up with you.

"As for me," Maryelizabeth said, "I was the messenger, and he didn't like my message. I'm the one who told the world about his mother."

Caleb could hear regret in her voice.

"Maybe this will turn out to be another book where I'm short of the answers to the biggest questions. Maybe your take on Farrell, that figure in the fog, will ultimately prove to be the most accurate of all. But I'm going to do my best to remove that shroud."

Caleb reached for his coffee cup, but didn't drink from it. He only looked at it. Murky. Like his insides. Over the past few days he had been learning how to be honest. The process was a scary one. He considered the implications of what he might do, of what he could and should do, and was terrified. His heart was pounding so much that it hurt him. He knew that he didn't have to say anything, and that his life would be easier if he didn't, but he felt compelled to at least broach the subject.

"I'm not comfortable with how you've been portraying me," he said.

Maryelizabeth sipped her coffee before answering. "How have I made you uncomfortable?"

"You're making me out to be a hero."

"Was it easier being a villain?"

"No," he said, but then he thought about it for a moment and reconsidered. "Maybe it was. I know it felt more right. But I guess the truth of the matter is that I can do without being either."

"In my mind," she said, "you are a hero. I'd be dead if it weren't for you and Lola. And you saved that girl in the sorority."

"I was trying to save myself."

"I don't believe that's all there was to it."

"You're right. I wanted to kill Farrell."

"You've taken so many slings in your time. Is it so hard for you to take a few bouquets?"

"Don't make me noble," he said, his voice stretched tight. "Don't make me out to be more than I am."

"Your father said much the same thing to me."

"Maybe we're the same."

Caleb opened his mouth to say more, then closed it. He shook his head, and moved his arms and hands. His body was doing a lot of speaking, but he still couldn't find the words.

"You've been telling me this whole time," said Maryelizabeth, "that you are not your father's son."

"Wishful thinking."

She heard the desperation in his voice. "What do you mean?"

Here it was, Caleb knew. It was so ugly he didn't want to look at it. It was in him, like a terminal tumor, or a bomb. And he was going to explode it. He really was.

"The rest of the story," he said.

"Go on."

"My polygraph . . ."

"Yes."

". . . was accurate."

"I don't understand."

"You said it yourself: writing about my father's life was the hardest thing you ever did. And you said you felt there were so many unanswered questions."

"There always are." Maryelizabeth's response gave Caleb an out, a chance to escape. But he didn't take it.

"I murdered my father."

"What are you saying?"

"You heard me."

"How could that be possible?"

"Little Mister Mimic. That's what my mother used to call me. I wonder if Lola suspected. She came up with the idea to save you. 'Use Maryelizabeth's voice,' she said. She heard me talking when I was delirious, heard me using your voice. And I don't think that's all she heard. I think she discovered my deception. She heard me use my father's voice. I suspect I relived the event. Lord knows, I've thought about it enough. I was good at mimicking dear old dad. Since he wasn't around much, it was my way of keeping him near. I could bring him out when I wanted to, conjure him up. I hated him, but I loved him."

"You were the one . . . ?"

"You said how it always bothered you. How you knew he died with secrets. I was his big secret. I was the one who called up the Concho County Sheriff's Office and identified myself as Gray Parker. I even knew to make myself sound a little liquored up. I was a precocious little bastard.

"There was a storm that night, a bad storm. I rode it out sitting in a huge pecan tree in our backyard. The wind blew at me, and the rain poured down on me, but I stayed up in that tree. No one knew I was there. I heard so much up there; my parents making love, and then their arguing, and then their fighting. I heard him strike my mother. I heard her cry out in pain, and I hated him almost as much as when I had heard her cry out in pleasure.

"But for once, I could get back at him. I'd heard something up in my tree, something I knew was big. Small pitchers have wide ears. I knew who Shame was. Everyone did. He was the Bogeyman of my school. Mother never came out directly and announced that my father was Shame, but I knew from what she said that night. His guilt didn't matter to her. She loved him, and tried to talk with him, tried to get him to stay in Eden, but he wouldn't think of it. He all but admitted who he was, and he taunted her with that knowledge, and told her that he didn't love her, that she was only convenient. He killed her in a thousand little ways.

"Later that night, when both of them were asleep, I came down from the pecan tree. The two of them hadn't even noticed my absence, had never checked on me. I'd had time to do a lot of thinking up in my tree. And practicing. I talked back to the storm, but I didn't use my own voice. I knew exactly what I wanted to do. I called the Sheriff's Office, and I made my confession in my grown-up voice, my father's voice. 'Come and get me,' I told them. 'I'll be sleeping off a little booze.'

"I was the only one awake when the authorities surrounded the house. I could hear their footsteps. I knew they were taking up their positions. And then all of a sudden everything happened. Doors got thrown open, and windows were broken, and people were shouting, and three men were grabbing my father, and I was watching the whole thing.

"No one took any notice of me—except my father.

"As they were throwing the handcuffs on him, amid all the craziness of the moment, he looked at me. Our eyes met, and it was like we were the only people in the room. In that moment, so much passed between us.

"I heard the officers asking him about it. 'Why'd you confess, Shame? Why'd you call us up?' And he answered while looking at me. 'Because it was time to give it up.'"

Maryelizabeth reached out a hand, touched his wet cheek.

"Bastard," said Caleb. "Bastard."

She wasn't sure if he was talking about his father, or himself.

"No one ever suspected," Caleb said. "Not even my mother. That night I probably would have told the officers what I'd done, except for that moment that had passed between us, and the understanding that had come with it. His eyes had warned me, had told me I could never tell. Being the son of Shame, he knew, would be bad enough. But it would be even worse to be known as the boy who engineered his father's death. Who betrayed him. He spared me that stigma. The son of a bitch protected me. And what was worse, he never held it against me that I betrayed him. The last time we talked, he even told me he was proud of me."

Caleb reached for his coffee cup, tried raising it up, but couldn't. He covered his eyes with his shaking hands. Between hiccups, he said, "How—could—a—fuck—ing—ser—i—al—mur—der—er—act—so—no—ble?"

So that's it, thought Maryelizabeth. And now she was crying as well. For so long it hadn't made sense. Gray had been protecting his son. He had been given a role to play, the killer who wanted to die, and he had never deviated from it.

No more ghosts, Gray, she thought. No more ghosts.

"You didn't kill him," said Maryelizabeth, "you saved him. You offered him his only chance for redemption. Before you made that call his life was already over. And it was wasted, so wasted. He knew what a terrible person and a terrible father he'd been, but you gave him an opportunity to do the right thing. It was his way of showing you that he cared. I know it's hard for you to see it, Caleb, but what you did was the best possible thing for him. It saved him from killing again, and it was a chance for him to do right by you, his only chance."

"I killed him."

"He killed himself."

"I don't think you understand, Maryelizabeth. Maybe you better get your tape recorder out, or bring out your pen so you can take some good notes."

"Why?"

"For the rest of the story. The kind of twist your readers are going to eat up."

"I think you should go home to your family, Caleb." Again, she offered him an out.

"Are you telling me you'd walk away now? You, the Queen of True Crime?"

"You're distraught."

"That doesn't make what I'm saying any less true. All this time

I've been telling you that I was nothing like my father. Well, that's not true. The biggest sin of all wasn't my calling up the Sheriff's Office and posing as my father. No, that's not even close. My sin was that I enjoyed the whole thing. I got a thrill out of knowing I was responsible for his death. Even as a boy, I sensed how addictive that power could be. I knew how I could get pleasure from taking another life. So when it comes right down to it, Maryelizabeth, I'm not much different from my father."

He expected her to react with horror, but instead she reached for his hands.

"Oh, Caleb," she said. "You look like your father, but you're nothing like him. Just because you wanted to see your father dead doesn't make you some depraved criminal. What child at some time doesn't feel that way? You're not an evil person, Caleb. You were glad when your father was removed from your life, but that became your secret shame. You took some pleasure in his death, and that became your shame as well, because you learned that your father cared about you. But that doesn't make you a killer, Caleb. It only makes you human."

"You don't know some of my thoughts. . . ."

"And you don't know some of mine."

"I've wondered how it would be to kill."

"So have I."

"But I'm sure not like . . ." He stopped, confused. "When I listened to your tape, there were times I was attracted to the violence."

"It might have seemed seductive to you, Caleb, but I know the reality wouldn't have been."

"But there have been times in my life when I've been so angry, and so afraid of what I might do."

"People get angry, Caleb. Everybody does. But you're not Dr. Jekyll and Mr. Hyde."

"I'm still afraid of what I might be."

"Helen Keller said, 'Life is a daring adventure, or it's nothing.' I think your life, your adventure, is about to begin."

"Whether I'm ready or not." Then he surprised himself with a good memory, and a little smile. "Lola said that the murderer 'really outed' me. She was right."

"How does it feel now?"

"I don't know. In some way my secrets were my life. They dictated how I acted. I guess I'm still getting used to my freedom."

"You were a prisoner for too long, and you started thinking like one. You forgot that the bars were holding you in, not holding you up."

Caleb nodded. He still wasn't sure whether he believed her. Maybe he would always feel tainted, one of Harry Harlow's monkeys. Or maybe, just maybe, having experienced the bad in life he could now appreciate the good.

Their coffee was cold, and the sun was setting, but neither made a move to leave. Caleb sat with a calm he could not remember ever having felt before. He felt so light.

Maryelizabeth didn't share his relief. She was fiddling with her spoon and napkin. She wanted to get up and leave, but was afraid Caleb would take it personally. But staying, she knew, was dangerous. She knew about playing with fire and getting burned. This whole Shame thing was risky for her. She felt off balance, but most of all, she felt ashamed. She knew she had tried to dissuade Caleb from telling his story, had given him all sorts of chances to keep his secrets buried, but she hadn't done it for him. She had been afraid to hear what he had to say, afraid of what it might do to her. Honesty brings out its own madness.

"There's evidence that Farrell was writing a book," she said. She tried to sound casual, but her voice was much higher pitched than usual. "His title for it was *Cain's Children.* It was going to be about the children of serial murderers. His private detective—Coleman—had done anonymous background checks on some children of serial murderers.

"It's an interesting premise for a book. Maybe it's a topic I might write about someday. But some books are better in concept than they are in print. I once tried to write a book called *The Club.* It was about smart women who made dumb decisions because they fell in love. These were women who involved themselves in terrible schemes that violated their own ethics and morals. In some cases these women ended up murdering family and friends, all in the name of love. Afterward, they wondered how they could have done such things. Some of them did their wondering in prison. Others in prisons of their own making. They looked at their emptied bank accounts, and emptied lives. 'It wasn't me,' they all wanted to say. 'It couldn't have been me.'"

Just because Caleb had gone and made his confession to her, Maryelizabeth told herself, didn't mean she had to feel obliged to do the same thing. This didn't have to be quid pro quo. But her mouth kept moving and the words kept coming out.

"I set out to write that book," said Maryelizabeth, "because I felt I was a Club member in good standing. Some parts of the book were going to be autobiographical."

One part. One large part. The book was supposed to be her big catharsis. She had felt this need to tell, but when confronted with what she had done, she couldn't do it. Maryelizabeth had thought there would be safety in numbers, and that she could hide behind the shield of being blinded by love, but it had proved to be too personal. The telling was never done, and the book never written. She had tried to mitigate, and forget, and worst of all, she had tried to lie to herself.

Caleb's feeling of lightness met her gravity. He focused on her, and saw her distress.

"Maryelizabeth?"

"The shame immobilized me for so long," she said. "I'd read about rape and incest victims, and I'd empathize with them, but I knew that wasn't fair because what happened to them wasn't voluntary. With me it was. But our sense of shame wasn't that dissimilar. Like many of those victims, I felt I couldn't tell anyone.

"Farrell had a right to be angry with me. Not to kill me, no, but he had a legitimate grievance. I didn't just expose the story of Leslie Van Doren. I made it my vendetta. I wanted her to look unsavory and ridiculous. I wanted to lord my power and position over her. I didn't want her to be only dirt, I wanted to grind her in that dirt.

"You see, I was jealous of her, but I couldn't admit that to myself. I made Van Doren and her ilk out to be the scum of the earth. I was oh, so supercilious about those women carrying on relationships with prisoners. *Outmates* I called them. The nuns of the iron bars.

"I don't know when I fell in love with your father. I think I only realized it a few weeks before he died. Even then, I knew it made no sense. I knew it was worse than wrong. This was a man who had murdered two of my sorority sisters, girls I was so close to. Because of what he did, because of his horrible, horrible acts, thousands of tears were cried on my shoulders, and I was forced to become intimate with the pain he'd caused to so many. I knew all about his dark side; no one had studied it as closely as I. And I knew how manipulative he could be. But none of that stopped me from falling in love with him.

"If I look for excuses I suppose I can find them. Our close proximity; his imminent death; his reciprocal, or so I want to believe, feelings. But nothing excuses what I did.

"In my heart, I think he changed. I know there are those who say that men like him can't change. I've read the psychological studies. They'd explain our relationship by saying I was this challenge for him, his full-time job while he was in prison, and that he used all his free time to figure out how he could inveigle his way into my affections. But it wasn't like that, or at least I don't think so.

"We were in the lawyers' room, with a guard outside, when there was this disturbance in the cell block. I don't know the details—I never learned them—but the guard felt compelled to leave his post. He'd seen me in there hundreds of times with Gray, and he knew that Gray wasn't a threat to me.

"Sometimes I think I dreamed up what happened next. It seems unreal, implausible, and my memories are blurry. I might have gone to Gray, or he might have come to me, but I think we met in the middle. We started kissing, and the madness, and desperation, took both of us. I'd like to blame the fever of the moment. But I can't. Our hunger was mutual. Everything happened so quickly I can almost pretend that nothing occurred, almost convince myself of that. Our physical union was so rushed it hardly qualifies as lovemaking. I can count off the seconds and say, 'There. That was nothing.' But it was something.

"As the clock ticks, we probably weren't left alone for more than three minutes. When the guard returned we were seated. No one ever suspected. But because I'm the only one who knows what happened, does that make it any less real?

"I don't believe anyone can ever really say, 'I wasn't myself.' I've tried those words on for myself, but they don't fit. I know that what

I did was the antithesis of professionalism. I know our being together was an unconscionable act. I was fully aware that this was a man who had murdered time and again, and he deserved no comfort, but I still wanted that intimacy between us.

"We never talked about it. It was another secret your father took with him. I think it was a defining moment for me. Maybe what I learned was even worth all the shame I've had to carry.

"I came to understand that lives can change in a single moment, and that under certain situations people can do things that they would normally believe unimaginable. And I learned that everyone carries around secrets. Everyone. And these secrets, no matter if they're great or small, shame us. I came to understand that all of us know things about ourselves that we don't like to admit. Because of my own hidden shame, I became more attuned to ferreting it out in others.

"Of course, it took time to learn those things. Now I wish I could go back and rewrite my first book. I wasn't fair to Leslie Van Doren. I tried to make her pay for my sins. She was more honest about her love than I was. But I wanted to have my cake—wanted to be known as the noble poet survivor—and eat it too. So I lied to myself. I tried to convince myself that I didn't love him, and that nothing ever happened, and that just made everything worse.

"Maybe now, though, both of us will be able to put our shame, and our Shame, aside."

Their hands came together, her left, his right, and their fingers intertwined like hands put together in prayer. They both shivered.

"It's cold," said Maryelizabeth.

Caleb shook his head. "We've just been clothed in our secrets for too long."

38

Some rise by sin, and some by virtue fall.

—William Shakespeare,
Measure for Measure

One of my favorite characters in literature is the little boy who says of the emperor, "He's not wearing any clothes." When people ask me about my work I recount that story and I say my job is often writing about the emperor's new clothes.

It was necessary for me to be that Hans Christian Andersen character throughout this book. I constantly asked myself what was real, and what was false. I needed to be certain that my perceptions were based on truth, but in so doing, I learned a hard lesson: sometimes we don't know the naked truth even when we are looking at it. Certain revelations in this book were difficult for me, for I found that in the past I had contributed to the emperor's new clothes, and though my fabric might have been invisible, my lies of omission were not.

This is a story where things were never as they seemed. Take, for example, the names of the three central characters. As adults, none had the name they were born with. Lyle Guidry not only changed his name to Lola Guidry, but also changed his identity from male to female. Caleb Parker was born Gray Parker Jr. He lost not only his first name, but for the longest time the paternity of being a "junior" to an infamous serial murderer. And then there was John Farrell. He was born Gray Parker Van Doren, but he lost that name when he was adopted as an infant.

There are two other characters in the book. I am one of them. In this book I am both narrator and participant. You will be the judge as to whether I told my part true, or whether I again wove some fabric out of thin air.

The other character, who was over two decades dead when this story begins, still managed to cast his long shadow throughout these pages. I have told Gray Parker's story before, and I never imagined I would have to tell it again.

But then our sins, and our shame, have a way of following us.

—From the introduction to Maryelizabeth Line's *Shame Will Follow After*